The Road to Thule

by

David R. Lee

First Edition.
Published by *attractor,* Full Moon June 4th 2012, Common Era

ISBN-13: 978-1492274780
ISBN-10: 149227478X

The Road to Thule online at:
www.chaotopia.co.uk/TheRoadToThule

Thanks to everyone who gave me ideas, who encouraged me in the writing and who had the courage to criticize me after it was written.

In particular I must single out the Sheffield SF and Fantasy Writers' Group, as fine a bunch of constantly-improving writers as you could hope to meet.

(Details of meetings can be found at http://uk.groups.yahoo.com/group/sheffieldwriters/)

September 2169, Common Era

Chapter 1: The Chilterns

Fitful red light surged over bare walls. Thania came half-awake; in her dozing mind an image-track played, of a school-years video-feed from the day of the Burning City, the screen overloading with the brutal light of the nuclear flash. Then the scene jumped – she was in her lab at University, her skin frying in the heat of vonnie overload. She jerked awake, the dream-pain resolving into the shock of the raider-alarm shrilling under her skin, then she and the other three women were jumping out of bed, throwing on their land-and-water gear and scrambling for the amphibious craft.

They sprinted out of the low bunker across the cracked old asphalt, Thania twisting her strong shoulders through the unfamiliar straps of her pack. The night bloomed into rolling orange and black as the second fuel tank went up. The troops piled into the craft, which lurched out into a landscape of black mud lit by laceworks of fire.

Thania joined the backup team on the big land-and-water craft, their mobile base. It was a clear night ahead, away from the blaze. The two lightweight craft she'd learned to call Ducks sped north up the Thames Channel, picking up a radar trace of the retreating raider. As scout, her brother Duncan would be on the front Duck.

Thania looked round. Everyone was bent to some task. She turned to the stocky woman who'd just finished handing out ammunition. 'Freya, tell me what's going on.'

Corporal Ward looked up at Thania and smiled tightly, facial muscles flexing in the blaze of some stimulant. 'Pure Light Duck with six, maybe seven in it stripped a farm at Blewbury then took out the Wantage fuel depot.'

Thania nodded. 'What are we going to do?'

'At some point, they land, to hide from us. We catch up with them and use our last few rockets.'

'And then?'

Ward shrugged. 'We shoot at them.' She slapped at a mosquito on her neck and turned back to her work.

Thania stayed standing, wide awake now. Eighteen hours ago, she'd been undergoing her induction training and swallowing a gloopy sol of von Neumann seeds, fast ones that would grow under her skin into a transceiver of networked nanotubules. Three days before that, she'd received her MD from Bristol University and, against her brother's express advice, but thrilled and inspired by Duncan's tales of service as a scout, she'd joined up as a medic in the same unit as him, Prince Siward's Wessex Specials.

They'd given her very basic instruction in driving their main assault vehicle. 'This is called a Duck,' said the instructor, 'either in honour of its twentieth-century ancestor, the DUKW, of which this is basically a lighter, more efficient descendant, or through a lack of inspiration in the naming of military vehicles designed for a world of mud.' He turned and looked at each of them, the battered steel of his prosthetic hand gleaming as it flexed. 'You will learn to drive one. Wessex Specials are a multi-skilled elite.'

Half an hour later they cut their engines. A half-moon was rising, and Thania saw their two Ducks up ahead and a dark hump of land forming a horizon in the cold light. Something flashed up there, and the distant crack of a weapon sounded, some small projectile that never reached its target. Her keen eyes picked out something moving over the horizon line, and she felt a rush of gratitude in a soft, sudden ache in her knees.

The three craft headed for the muddy beach and crunched up the slope, the old engines screaming. It was moon-bright now, and as they moved cautiously up the hill Thania could see down to their left the remains of a town shattered by war, ghostly stumps of buildings on a lip of land above the black water. She supposed it was Princes Risborough, and swallowed nervously; her unit regarded the Chiltern archipelago to the north of there as Pure Light territory.

Pursuit was easy. The Duck they were following gouged up the soft turf, leaving massive muddy tracks on hard ground, and their infra-red picked out its heat-plume in the swathes of cloud-shadow. As they crossed the rise of the land and began their descent they could see the enemy craft clearly. It was obvious they were following a crippled vehicle. Ward passed Thania her binoculars and she saw it veering about from a damaged track-wheel. She swung the glasses round. Down there was Great Missenden, presumably where the raiders would have to hole up.

At the bottom of the hill, the two Ducks in the front started a cautious approach through the darkened main street of the little town. Everyone was aware this could be an ambush, and Thania had a strong urge to use the toilet.

Soon, it started to look as if they were just pursuing a lone craft down an empty road. Right in the centre of the town they saw the raiders' Duck parked across the entrance to a big old redbrick pub. They halted just as a volley of shots rang out from an upstairs window, gravel chips flying up from the road in front of them. Thania heard a grunted curse from the front vehicle, someone hit.

Their crews turned the two Ducks side-on and dove behind them, returning fire with their assortment of weapons. She saw Siward crouched behind the front vehicle with a rocket launcher, and then two of the rear crew dashed out, hugging the walls of the old buildings. She recognized Sergeant Scott, whom she'd met only a few hours before, just as the defenders turned their fire on her and she spun, catching the momentum of the bullets in her body.

Then Thania saw Siward stand up, fire a rocket and dive back behind the vehicle. With shock, she watched the front of the big pub disappear in a flash of flame, and that was it, the battle was over.

It was getting light now. Thania let the absence of gunshots sink in for a full second, then jumped over the side of her vehicle and ran through the drifting smoke. Scott was dead, her eyes open to the sky. Thania turned aside briefly to vomit, before forcing herself over to the Ducks to check if everyone else was OK. She kept looking round for Duncan, and then she saw him swagger towards her, bright red neckscarf and curly red hair framing his grin, which struggled for supremacy with a frown of disapproval. Thania wanted to look professional, and refrained from hugging him, but let the wave of relief show on her face. His expression settled down to some kind of acceptance, seeming to say: *You may still be my little sister, but you're grown up now, and you're here.*

They looked over the ruins of the pub. There was no-one left alive in the rubble and they checked out the other large buildings along the street, selecting three for a base camp. Right next door a row of beautiful old cottages started, now ruined by war and the carelessness of troops. She hoped it wasn't Wessexers that had been so disrespectful as to shit on the floor.

Corporal Ward bustled round with a clipboard allocating quarters. Thania's care room was in the central building, another pub, but her one charge, Private Evans, was walking wounded, so he would berth as usual. She sat him down and dipped a nanoculture strip into the blood on his arm. 'Any fever?' Evans shook his head. 'I feel fine.' She gazed at his face while she dressed the wound. Like most of them, he was peppered with mosquito bites, any one of which might have infected him with vonnie seeds or other toxic nanites.

'What's your Raven-Kowalski rating?'

'Ten.' He smiled, enveloped in the aura of her professionalism.

'Same as me.' She finished tying the bandage and checked the culture strip. A faint blue line showed above the pale orange of the blood, like a watermark. It barely touched '11' on the numbered paper. Evans had none of the high-level, more dangerous vonnies in his system, but he might just get a reaction. She reached into her bag and drew out two white capsules.

'Take these, to be on the safe side. Elutol, a vonnie-purge. Come straight back if you get any fever.'

Evans swallowed the pills. She smiled. 'OK, we're done.'

When she was alone, she checked her stock of nanoculture strips and elutol pills. That's good; enough to train everyone to use them themselves. If the unit got split up (or I got killed, she thought, frowning), at least no-one should go down with vonnie fever.

That was it, for now. Her responsibilities towards Maisie Scott had been discharged when she'd signed her death certificate half an hour before. She was arranging her equipment round the room when Corporal Drake came in. She smiled, admiring his masculine good looks, and he announced that the supplies team had found a fairly fresh rainwater tank on the roof, good enough for washing in, so she found the upstairs bathroom and took a lukewarm shower. She'd just dressed again when a beep under her skin told her it was coming up to six o'clock, so she joined the morning briefing in the main bar room.

Prince Siward, tall and sturdy in clean combat fatigues, blond hair pushed back over his broad shoulders, announced there would be reconnaissance missions straightaway, to check how secure their position was. Then they would honour Sergeant Scott and there would be two hours rest. They filed out, Thania catching Duncan's eye, and he winked at her as he crossed the cracked pavement to his motorbike. The scouts were so important to the expeditionary forces now there were no helicopters. The whole skill-base of air transport was nearly lost, it was so long since the fuel had existed to feed such monsters.

After the brief burial ceremony she went back into her empty care-room and gazed out of the window. The whole town was deserted. She'd had a moment of horror when Siward had fired on the pub like that – she was used to the swarming towns and squatter camps of her homeland, where every tiny terraced house, every hovel, counted as accommodation for at least one family. In Wessex, fire a rocket into any building the size of that pub, and you'd kill fifty people. Here, the terror of the long war surging back and forth through their streets had driven everyone out of the southern end of the Chiltern archipelago.

Being excused watch duty, Thania dozed in a chair in the care room, hypnotized by the patterns of the sunlight on the shiny, yellowed walls.

The shrilling under her skin woke her with a shock. These high-performance vonnies would take some getting used to. She shook out a numb foot and went over to the reconnaissance briefing in the main bar.

It didn't take long – scouts Duncan and Terry both reported an empty archipelago as far as Tring. No doubt Berkhamsted and Luton were still in Pure Light hands.

Siward stood up. 'We shall reconnoitre for one more day. If we find we've secured this part of the Chilterns for now, we go home.'

He turned slowly, gathering them all into his level gaze. 'That means we won't be on home soil in time for Harvest Festival. I say we have our very own Harvest party, here in Missenden, tonight.'

He dismissed them, and Thania found herself yawning in Freya Ward's face as they left the bar. Ward grinned. 'Tired?'

'And wanting to party,' said Thania. 'What was that you were on first thing, cocaf?'

'Vonnie settings,' said Ward.

Thania's eyes widened. 'Whoa, full metabolic control! So what's your R-K, 14?'

'I'm a 15. Want me to do an entrainment on you?'

'Sure – it'll be a first. My experimental subjects talked about entrainment, but none of them succeeded with me.'

They walked up the street in hazy sunlight and entered Thania's care room. Ward frowned thoughtfully at her. 'You've gone from doing vonnie tolerance research to joining the Army; what's the appeal?'

Thania sat down and was silent for a beat or two, choosing her words carefully.

'I believed in my research. Then it ended.'

'What were you working on?'

'High-end stuff. I was trying to find people who were tolerant beyond RK15, in the super-vonnie range. You know Raven called them becters? He believed they could amplify quantum effects in the human Bose-Einstein field. I wanted – or dreamed of – something to give us hope again. Since the floods and the gigadeaths, since the loss of that glittering world, what do we have left? Vonnies is about it. I thought if I could isolate the features of nano-assembly that led to intolerance, we might be able to test Raven's claims about those other powers that his becters were supposed to bestow on those who could tolerate them. But I hadn't found anyone with unambiguous becter tolerance by the time they...' she exhaled, her breath deflating her.

'You've tried high-end vonnies yourself?'

'On a regular Raven-Kowalski, I'm only tolerant up to ten, so I wasn't a good subject. I'd inject myself with vonnie seeds in an ascending scale, a hypo of eluter to hand, but every time I got above ten, I'd go straight into fever. I'd leave it a day, then try again, hoping my immune system would get used enough to the vonnies to give them a chance to start growing nets. But it never did. It wasn't that that did it though.' She looked at Ward, unable to hide the bitter disappointment of the memory. 'Wessex's research base is cunked. They just withdrew our funding, as if there was any other hope than becters on the horizon. And if those Pure Light idiots take over, there'll be no more vonnie research, no more dreams. So I went to fight for what was left, using what I know. I'm going to be checking the vonnie profiles of any PL we capture.'

'Yeah, any that let themselves be captured,' muttered Ward.

Thania reached into her side pocket and drew out a gold coin, old but still glorious, the inverted T of the Thor's Hammer on one side and the profile of the young King Edwin on the other. 'Wessex is practically all that stands in their way. And what is Wessex? Wessex is a dream. One man's dream.'

Ward eyed the gold, gleaming in the weak sunlight. 'A man who everyone loved,' she said.

'My Uncle Ambrose gave me this. He scripted Edwin's coronation back in '93, when he handed these out. Minted from the gold he raided from the flooded Bank of England.'

She put the coin away and looked up, mixing a tired smile into her bleak expression. 'So, this entrainment. What does it involve?'

'It's simple.' Ward stood up. 'You sit up straight, but comfortable. I'll be doing it around your head.'

'Doing what?'

'All I know is my Bose-Einstein fields can influence yours, and the effect lasts for up to a few hours. Now shush and let me do it.'

Thania sat quiet, feeling nothing but the warmth of Ward's hands on her skull. 'There. That should keep you going for a bit.'

'Thanks.' Thania smiled and stood up, stretching her legs and arms. She had to admit she felt a bit livelier already. A thought crossed her mind and her smile broadened. 'You know, I've never tried flash-flesh, I was always in such a hurry to flush one batch out and get the seeds in for the next experiment.'

She looked towards the door then turned back, grinning, to Ward. 'Thank you, Freya. Tonight should be fun.'

At dinner in the mess hall in the end building, Thania couldn't sit still. Irrepressible energy, party thoughts and sheer lust; she started eying her companions, male and female too, and imagining what sex would be like with each of them. Drake caught her eye over the potatams and it was all she could do not to run off somewhere and make herself come. She wondered if it was the vonnie induction amplifying her usual urges or if it was some side-effect of military service. She bit her lip. *Oh Goddess, what's happening, am I getting absorbed into soldiering*?

After the meal, she showered again, and changed into her cleanest uniform. She pouted at herself in the cracked mirror and decided she was going to have strong-thighed Corporal Drake tonight.

The evening started with the unit's little theatre company giving a 'concert,' which turned out to be a chance for everyone to do standup routines, with points for audience laughter.

Duncan did well, holding a tiny vonnie-speaker in his

hand, pretending to get frustrated at the weak signals from NeighbourNet, the patchwork of radio that propagated between everyone who hosted basic vonnies. 'Dammit, I want to hear the news!' he shouted, waving the little device about. 'I want to hear about the bandits!' Then the speaker blared into life with a news report from Marlborough: '*Wessex constabulary today broke up a Guest Camp demonstration in support of notorious murderer Diamond Head Morningstar...*' The sound broke up into fragments of voice and blasts of noise as Duncan turned his field strength down.

'Give me the damn news! Isn't my life force strong enough for you, you useless piece of crap?' He hurled the speaker down, catching it on his foot, and pretended to stomp it into the floor. The sound died out into a final series of squawks and splutters, and Duncan took a bow.

Bruno was the top act. He was dressed in green and sported a green hat, split down the middle, with a golden feather in it. His oddly hooked nose had a down turn at the end, giving his face a distinguished cragginess. Warm brown eyes looked out from crinkled skin. He had one of those faces that could be any age, as could his clear, deep voice as he played guitar and sang seasonal songs – 'The Bright Harvest,' 'When the Time Comes,' and everyone's favourite lament, that troops everywhere sang – 'Before the Waters Rose,' wistful voices joining in for the final few verses.

I knew that our love was forever
Stronger than sinew or breath
But I lost my love in the turmoil
Of the waters that brought London's death

The Goddess of London's daughter
In her heart was a hungry flame

She watched from the skies,
the whole world in her eyes
And then the waters came

Now we live on in the twilight
Of a world that is shrunken and poor
I mourn my lost love, as I know you mourn yours
Since the waters took three billion more

Bruno banished the mournful mood with 'Darius Barleycorn,' something everyone could join in with. Then the party broke up into smaller groups. Thania made sure she got seated with Will Drake, and a shy, slender boy whom Will introduced as Ronn, 'With two Ns!'

Duncan stopped by their table for a few minutes, with Bruno and another handsome boy, and chatted for a while before leaving for the door. Then Siward came by, on morale-boosting rounds of his fighting force, every inch the fearless young hero. Thania fancied him something terrible, but he was married to Princess Hettie, fierce royal witch.

Siward drifted off on his rounds, the rest of them stocked up on drinks and went outside to smoke. Will twisted his muscular body between two of the crates stacked by the main door, sat down and got a smoking pouch out of his pocket. Ronn looked around at the lack of seating and continued standing. Thania leaned against the door jamb, looking out at the soft, moist night. Will finished his preparations and waved a simple, wooden pipe at her. The pungent fumes of hemp bud rose up to her nose.

Thania hesitated. 'Are you sure... couldn't we get, er, disciplined for being intoxicated on duty?'

Drake took it back and inhaled, then flicked back his dark hair and spoke. 'Two things: One: This is our second pass in a week through Missenden. The pass before that was a deep expedition that took out a PL supply line. So this is our point, for now. Second: You're all right. Maybe because you're a girl, which is rare round here, as you may have noticed. Three males to one female, and my friend Maisie Scott is dead. So, I'll cover for you if you can't take your smokes.' He glared a few seconds, then grinned.

Thania pretended to the boy's twentieth-century film machismo. She frowned, leaned forward and took the pipe. She inhaled deeply, did a great shuddering exhale, then took a few more for emphasis. She stood forward, raised her arms above her head, thrust out her breasts, exhaled with a loud, owlish hoot, and swayed in front of Will, her belly a foot from his nose. He opened his mouth to speak, but shut up. She caught his scent, and underneath the pride she detected the pain of his loss.

Empathic as ever, she was moved. Shy Ronn wriggled a bit in the corner of her vision, aghast, ecstatic, out of his depth.

She stepped back and looked at Will, then at Ronn, and said, 'You can come, too,' as she turned and walked away, up the steps into the central building.

They piled into the cosy room that had been allocated to Thania and another woman she'd not met yet. Either her roommate was still in the bar, or having fun somewhere else.

As she'd hoped, her entrainment leaked over into her two lovers, raising their vonnie-assisted senses to the level known as flash-flesh, the crossload where people swim in each other's sensations. They felt sudden and shocking tastes of what it was like to be inside another's body, like a revolving hothouse of hungry lust. Eventually, they pushed the two beds together and fell into them for some sleep.

They woke when Ronn's vonnies bleeped at four o'clock, for his watch-duty. He jumped about anxiously while Thania and Will ribbed him from the bed. When he'd gone out, they fucked again, then dozed. Luxurious in the half-sleep, Thania surfaced to a feeling in her body, then was vaguely aware the motorbikes had left, Duncan and Terry speeding off on their Triumphs. Unease haunted her dreams. They both got bleeped at six, and just had to get up and go. Thania didn't bother showering off the sweet stink.

The dawn briefing was the same slot as breakfast, and the news from the scouts was worrying. Siward had ordered Terry back to base after they'd realised that Duncan might be missing. Terry was already on his way back, thinking Duncan was following him after they'd split up. From Terry's report and the radio fixes they got a fair idea of where Duncan had disappeared. Everyone ate on the move, getting to their vehicles and moving out into a windy morning, long rags of cirrus scudding across a bright sky.

Chapter 2: Folly

They drove north over the hill, where they heard the sound of a bike engine, then met Terry returning. They continued downhill towards Tring, moving in their usual formation as they sighted a cluster of low, red-brick buildings on the edge of the town. They stopped and surveyed them carefully from their vantage point. Maybe the PL had used them as a temporary base, but they looked empty now. Cautiously, they moved in, the two Ducks flanking the group of buildings, the big vehicle hanging back till they'd checked all round the area. Thania heard a shout from round the back of the low central building, and their craft moved forward, but then there was another shout, and she knew with a lurch in her belly that something was wrong.

With a sick feeling she jumped over the side of the vehicle and ran round to where some of the Duck crew were coming out of the building, grim-faced. Duncan's motorbike lay in the mud. She pushed past the troops through the narrow doorway. The floor was awash with blood, trickling into the water which still dribbled out of a loose pipe where a section had been wrenched out. On the floor, in the wet, lay her brother's naked body, locked in a twist of pain, arm looped round a pool of soiled gore. A length of copper piping was sticking out of his mouth, and another piece stuck out from between his legs. Her body buckled and doubled up, she swayed violently back and forth, her hands to her head, not knowing how to let out such horror. She was hardly aware of Freya Ward leading her away, an arm around her shoulders.

Ward took Thania to a room in one of the other buildings. She had stopped trying to look professional. She heard a shrill keening coming out of her own mouth. There was no-one else for her to care for but herself.

Freya brought her medical supplies in from the mobile base and went through the bag, eventually finding some laudanol pills. Uncomplaining, Thania swallowed two of them. Freya went out, returning with Will, who stroked her hair while she shook, her keening eventually dying down to a snuffle. She squished damp surgical lint, repeating herself in a loop. 'We're soldiers, we kill, but this was done with hate, with hate.'

Around her distress, they were making a new camp. The water was off, no surprise, and Siward sent the engineers to link their taps to something with a head of pressure. The roof tank was still connected to most of the system, and they'd started filling up tanks and bottles before one of the supplies team climbed up and saw the corpse in it. The milky gaze of dead eyes stared up at them from the water. The ears were missing, rags of grey flesh where they'd been cut off.

The engineers shut down the supply and emptied their tanks, but it was too late. A few people had been careless, numbed by the horror of Duncan's death, and they were down with some gastric infection by that evening. Thania kept herself on her feet with a cocktail of tinctures, and ministered to cases of vomiting and diarrhoea. Will worked beside her, handing out rehydration drinks, to a background smell of excrement.

All in a day, the condition of their unit had slid into danger, and there was an unspoken feeling that maybe they weren't so elite after all, but more like half-trained, wide-eyed youths. Just before the evening briefing, Thania went to report to Siward. In her glazed state she blundered in on him alone in his command post, sitting forward in a chair, staring down at his hands. He was gazing at a tiny photograph in an oval of faded Perspex, talking to himself, or, to be more accurate, to his grandfather, old King Edwin, dead now these thirty years, asking his advice on whether to move on and punish the PL, or limp back to Wessex. Thania stood silent, spooked by his vulnerability. But Siward seemed to get his answer, and he looked up and nodded wearily at her.

She made her report and they went in to the briefing together. Siward announced that they would bury Duncan, rest until tomorrow, then they were going forward, to clean out the rest of the peninsula. The mood of the unit was hard and vengeful, everyone nodding grimly. They dug a grave in the dark, flickering fluorescent panels hung from the back of one of the Ducks, slapping at mosquitoes, burying Duncan with the fullest military honours they could muster in that miserable place. Then they sat down to a skimpy supper, and turned in for an early night.

The next morning, they followed Duck tracks down the old metalled road to Berkhamsted. They were alert, not knowing how near enemy positions they were. When they caught sight of the waterside compound around a farmhouse, the shattered town behind, they moved to destroy it. Two rockets blasted the central farmhouse to rubble, and they pushed ahead. Then, shockingly, a final expeditionary force emerged from the smoke of the wrecked settlement. Something about the mad way they drove the Duck and their conserving of bullets, suggested to Siward that this was a suicide mission, and something urged him to capture alive, if possible, whoever would do such a thing.

'Force them into the water,' he shouted. A well-hurled grenade blasted out a crescent of road just in front of the careering vehicle, which swerved over and plunged down the shallow bank into the water. They raced their two

Ducks down and pulled three men out of the mud, all in a bad way. The driver and the main gunner died immediately, but the commander Thania reluctantly saved, ligaturing the gushing stump of his leg with a length of cable. There was ample blood for her vonnie-test samples from all three men. Siward stared down at the short, middle-aged man. 'This one should have some interesting things to say.'

They returned to their last encampment and secured the area. It started raining, and the day was dark. Thania trudged heavily along the cracked and slimy tarmac to the care room. Mud plastered her fatigues up to the thighs. She leaned briefly against the shattered stump of a concrete post, maybe once a street light, and blew her nose with a muddy finger, onto the muddy ground. She breathed in, and gagged on the stench that rose up.

She climbed the six steps up to the doorway of the low building and stepped through the lobby into the small care room. Jervis crossed by her, going into the signals post next door. Bruno and Siward stood, mud-splattered, around the filthy camp bed. The prisoner lay on a mattress in a pool of blood, the bare, purple stump of his left leg staring accusingly up at them, a look of defiance leaking through the opiated vagueness of his face.

'Who is he?' she asked.

Bruno looked up, his eyes ringed with shadow. 'It seems he's Paul Logan, ex-General of the British Army, now high command of a PL unit. But I'll say this for him – he has guts – there he was, right in the front line.'

Thania frowned. 'Did you say *British* Army? How old is he?'

Siward nodded. 'There hangs a tale. If we're to believe his ID' – he waved a dog tag – 'he is 110. He just let slip where his supply of Rejuve is.'

Thania swayed with emotion. This was the commander of the men who'd tortured and killed Duncan. Her heart pounded in her throat, and she felt sweat beading her upper lip. She fought down her urge for instant vengeance as she looked down at the prisoner's face. Allowing for his present state, he looked a vigorous forty. Her Uncle Ambrose was the only other person that old she'd ever met.

She kept her voice under control. When it came out, it was husky and menacing. 'You killed my brother. Not like a soldier, but with hate. Why do you set an example of hate, little man?'

Logan pulled himself up, gaining a couple of inches at what looked like considerable cost. His eyes were rolling with the drugs, but he held his gaze steady for a few moments.

'You Wessex people are devil-worshippers and lovers of pleasure who tolerate perverts and sodomites in your midst. You all deserve to die.'

There was only one person moving now, the slow sway of anger in her tall body, as she reached for her brother's Webley, drew it, leaned forward and pointed it at Logan's lower belly.

'Ah, a little fear. Good. As I'm sure you know, abdominal wounds are very painful. But you – you deserve much worse than a quick death. I shall watch you die of septicaemia, and we won't be wasting any more laudanol on you.'

She put the gun away and turned to Siward. 'I'll make sure someone gags him when he starts screaming. Sir.'

She walked out through the signals room without looking round. There was an overlapping crackle of short-range radios and converted NeighbourNet patches. Jervis gave her a glance she couldn't quite read. Sympathetic, conspiratorial, lustful?

She went and stood under the narrow porch, gazing out into the drizzle. Her mind was empty, everything was filling it up. She overheard Jervis talking on some comms device, and a weird phrase stuck and revolved in her head, *folly at Chiltern.*

That evening Siward outlined a plan to loot the Rejuve stocks from the last PL position, the farm compound.

Freya Ward spoke up. 'How do we know it's not a trap, the lure of valuable drugs leading us into an ambush?'

Siward shook his head. 'There's no way they could know we're returning there. At worst, we'll meet a force who'll be at least as surprised as we are.'

Ward nodded assent. 'Might as well take what we can, then; we've paid dearly enough to win this point.'

Siward asked for volunteers. Thania stuck her hand up immediately. They didn't want her to go, and Siward could have ordered her not to, but they understood her need for vengeance. Will Drake, Freya Ward, Bruno and Ronn made up the six. They set off straightaway in the faster of the two Ducks.

The compound was still oozing smoke into the drizzle. The mud in the farmyard was churned up into deep ruts, and they parked between two barns, the smouldering ruin of the farmhouse in front of them. The barn on the right was padlocked through a massive hasp. Probably the one with the goods in, but they decided to check the other, open barn first. The door was unlocked, and Siward stepped in, the others following. As their eyes accustomed to the gloom, they saw a pile of crates at the back. Thania went up and prised off a lid, marked with North American stars. The cartons inside were marked as antelosin, with the Rejuve brand.

'Yep, this is the stuff,' she called.

They'd loaded all twenty-eight cases of the drug onto the Duck and Ward was walking across to the other barn to see what that had inside, when there was a mighty noise of tearing metal and the door crashed down on top of her. A Duck drove out of the barn over the flattened door, and two men leaned out and started shooting. Too late to save Ward, the rest of them leaped back on their craft and set off.

Will drove at full tilt, the tracks spinning in loose mud, as the others crouched down, shooting over the lip of the Duck. Their pursuers were fast, though, and a grenade, thrown at the last possible moment, exploded as it dropped into the body of the craft. The concussion knocked Thania sideways, to where she saw half of Siward's body was twisted over the side of the craft, raw flesh catching the mist of rain. Ronn was missing. Bruno dived for their case of grenades and took over at the back. Then the vehicle swerved, and she realised Will had been hit. She jumped into the driving seat as he fell to the side, and drove as fast as she could. Screams and explosions from behind indicated Bruno had scored with a grenade and they made it back to their base a few minutes later, the enemy Duck motionless and burning on the roadside behind them. Only then did she realise her leg was leaking blood onto the deck.

Someone hauled her out onto a stretcher. She was aware of some commotion around the back of their camp, and then gunfire, but she was lying down getting her leg bandaged at that point. She surrendered to her incapacitated state, and her mind raced, joining up what had just happened. Who had betrayed them and let them be caught like that? Their attackers had arrived only just in time to set up their ambush. Which meant they had a live link to her unit. Then the soft rush of the painkillers swept away her thoughts.

The rest of it was a numb, exhausted return home. They had to abandon the vehicle that had taken a grenade hit, and they all piled into the other two, this time taking their dead with them. Up in the front of the mobile base, Jervis told the story of how he'd discovered and executed the traitor. It seemed he'd caught Private Evans leaving on one of the bikes with a case of Rejuve strapped to the back. The gunshot round the back of the buildings had been Jervis stopping him. Bruno, the acting commander, seemed satisfied with this story, but Jervis kept on complaining.

Thania had heard unpleasant stories about Jervis, his cruelty in particular. Apparently, his father King Marcus had been killed in a Pure Light action, back in '26. Jervis had always claimed it was so-called friendly fire that had killed him. He seemed to need to blame his stepfather, King Peredur, for this.

Everybody has loss and grief, thought Thania, *but Jervis lets it all hang out, and it affects everyone else. Maybe he's a little unbalanced,* she thought drowsily. *Folly at Chiltern.* The weird words cycled round her head again. Next to her, Bruno shifted his long body on the seat. He was making an effort to appear conscious and available a little longer, but his heart wasn't in it.

Back home, it was obvious that Thania had impressed everyone. She'd come into her own, in a way she'd never expected to. The King awarded her the Wessex Medal, and offered her a commission. She said she'd think it over, still new to this life and not being sure what she wanted. She needed to sort through her memories, and decide what to do with them. The one she clung on to for now was of Bruno sitting in the mud, writing a song. There was hope, always, in music.

Twenty Months Later:

April-May 2171 c.e.

Chapter 3: Poison Light

The launch bobbed on a tilting sea, the horizon formed of a buckled hill of brown glass. The glass threw back flashes of light from on high, sharp as swords, presumably the sun. Sick with sea travel, porous with exhaustion, he could not escape the sordid edge of the world, the dirty, poison light, the flecks of nuclear fire inside the sun-spangles. The wind swung round, blowing out from the shore now, a simoon of rotting minerals, fresh plaster mixed with burning pepper, a smell that said the solidity of steel and bricks was subverted, broken inside. A lurch of nausea confirmed the presence of hard radiation, playing hell with his vonnies.

His memory obligingly re-ran a worse vonnie disaster: last summer, holding Julia's spasming, exquisite face, dosing her with whisky and xenothane, screaming out for help, feeling the shriek of her terror crawling in his own flesh. Julia was just an eleven on the RK scale, but that was enough for flash-flesh, enough to mirror each other's ecstasy, or pain.

He took a deep breath. There'd been risks in the fun they'd had, but that time they got away with it, and student life was carefree and pleasant. From a weekend of saying goodbyes to that life, here he was, laying at anchor off a melted city. The launch rocked, and he threw up over the railing, into the slimy sea.

The wiry, compact older man could have been inserted from a family boat trip in the 1950s, with his roll-neck pullover and navy jacket, a touch of cold severity in the wire-rimmed glasses. He nudged the other with a small bottle.

Alex drew his tall, athletic shape upright, mashed sun-bleached hair aside from a fine-boned and somewhat haughty face and gazed blearily at the other man. 'You got no vonnies, Hendry,' he managed.

Hendry twisted his mouth into a faint smile. 'Why spend your life submitting to others' signals. Other people carry that burden for me.' He proffered the atomiser. 'Have some xenothane.' Shakily, Alex took the bottle and sprayed gummy stink into his mouth. Within a breath's span, a cold wave of relief sprawled every way from his throat. The collapse of vonnie-sensitivity was so delicious he groaned as he offered Hendry the vial back. 'Keep it. Exposure to a little hard radiation is part of your education now.'

Alex huffed. 'As you may recall, Uncle, my education ended when you withdrew your sponsorship of my research project.'

'Vonnies are a dead end for energy research. You know that by now.'

Alex was too exhausted to re-launch his argument. He went quiet, recalling his spectacular failure to retro-engineer one of Raven's dangerous becter experiments.

Hendry held out a pair of ancient Zeiss binoculars, the black casing chipped, some family heirloom. 'Go on, take a look.'

Alex took the glasses, bumped an eyepiece against the scar tissue over his cheekbone and got them focused. The simplified lines of the horizon went messy and complicated.

'The top of that lump of glass is Vatican Hill,' said Hendry. 'We're lying over a place called Infernetto, aptly enough.' He was smiling faintly, his eyes bright and ambition-hard as ever. Alex felt empty and fragile.

Hendry was still talking. 'Incredible. Nobody in Vatican security knew what was happening until there was a twenty kiloton airburst over St Peter's Basilica. Jemima Tyson put them all into another reality, then vaporised herself. The last bit of camera footage to come out of there shows alarms shrilling, the radar pointing straight at Tyson's plane, and everyone just smiling and going about their business.'

Hendry turned. 'And why?'

Alex shrugged. Hendry continued. 'Desperation, Alex. The end of the old civilization.'

'So you think it's because the oil was running out a top scientist went mad and vaporized herself and Vatican City?'

'Basically, yes. And she was of course mad. You know, eco-fascist, follower of Linkola, the green nearest black. She believed that humans should be culled, eighty percent of people sent to death-camps.' Hendry paused, paying lipservice to deep thought.

'I went to look at the other attempt at a Burned City. Salt Lake City centre is a bit bleak, but the rest of the town is as functional as ever.'

'What were you in America for?'

'The big carve-up of assets after the North American Alliance government downsized. Anyway, all those places are someone else's problem. What you'll see on Sunday is a bit nearer home. By Tuesday you'll have the whole picture. Hell of a tour, eh?'

Sometimes, Hendry stirred real fear in Alex. He hid his alarm by turning away and gazing over the top of the boat, relentless heat throbbing over the slick, black solar panels. 'Hell of a choice of phrase, Uncle H.'

Hendry seemed to find this reply as unsatisfactory as he found most of Alex's comments, but he nodded and patted the young man on the shoulder. 'You'll see, you'll feel better when we get ashore.'

He turned and gave instructions to the crew. They steered towards the mudflats of the coastline, the tycoon's compact frame swivelling as he scanned with binoculars the edges of the destruction, where slimy vegetation smudged the dead sand with yellows and oranges. The steersman leaned out of the bridge holding a Tyson counter at arm's length, the sound spitting over the cabin's speakers, his face screwed tight with vonnie-nausea. 'Getting a bit warm, Cap'n sir.'

Hendry spoke without turning. 'Very well, take us out. It's about lunchtime anyway.' Solar motors thrummed.

They went below deck as the launch rode the swell away from the poison land, down into the cedar-panelled dining room, where the chef served a cold lunch. Alex managed a few mouthfuls of bread and retreated to his cabin, where he didn't have to look at the swaying water and the sick light. He lay on the bunk, rubbing his scar. It kept him in mind of his instructor, who'd studied in Heidelberg, and developed his own starkly beautiful style of ritual fencing. When Alex had acquired the scar under his left eye he had not given ground, flinched or cried out. He hadn't even realised how courageous he was capable of being until that moment.

Be that as it may, he needed a new kind of courage to deal with the future he was being shunted into. His carefree student days were over. He was about to pay for those innocent few years. Alex's passion for nanochemistry was a valuable asset to Hendry, who had stoked it and then supported him through university, and supported him well, with enough cash for a social life he was fast appreciating with each day he left it behind. Hendry had attended his graduation ceremony, of course, applauded him and pressed a wad of New Pounds into his hand, telling him to go off and celebrate his starred first class degree.

After that weekend, Hendry had turned up at his lodgings. He'd had Alex pack anything precious in a shoulder bag, leave everything else and go straight down the steps into Hendry's car and then to Bristol's commercial docks. At first, it had been exciting, like one of those old stories about the Devil valuing you enough to come and take your soul, then the sea sickness had swept him up in its miserable embrace. He'd lost all curiosity about where they were, or where they were going. Every time he surfaced, Hendry was there, talking about his future. The thing that had stuck with him was his uncle saying: 'How else would you ever make a living, in this backwoods century, as a bloody chemist, if not working for me?'

Alex had to concede the point. He'd seen them running down the chemistry department in his final year. The inevitable job prospects were all in commercial nano-production, fermenter lines that brewed vonnies for NeighbourNet, for sex-enhancement, for tooth gel or skin colour. That was all anyone spent money on these days. Raven had called the von Neumann transceiver, his Nobel-wining invention, 'the disappointing miracle,' just before he disappeared. Alex rubbed his head. Who needed chemists in a world which had squandered its hydrocarbons and run out of electricity? Hendry did. He was calling in the value of his asset, and Alex needed to get a job somewhere.

Somewhere in his doze there was shouting, gunshots then some other vessel bumping against their hull, then laughter. On the way down to Rome, they'd floated over lost, flooded Pisa and Livorno and heard the night sounds from the coastal settlements in the hills beyond, seen safely through binoculars, out of the range of grapple-arrows and blowdarts.

He woke to a change in the sound of the engines. He felt slightly better. He rose and showered, put on a fresh t-shirt and shorts, and went up on deck. Two of the crew, looking like security men in nautical gear, were eating strong-smelling pickles and sausage and playing around with a vonnie-speaker, but all that came out was blasts of noise. 'Like Wessex NeighbourNet,' Alex said, greeting them more cheerfully than he felt, and they laughed, well-paid hired hands indulging the boss's nephew.

Alex turned and looked round. They were running against the flow, entering a broad waterway in low, flooded lands. He gazed out over the waves, churning with rusty mud.

Hendry came up. 'Used to be the Canal du Midi, this. That pile of stones back there, that's all that's left of Sète. Good thing too, filthy place.' Hendry often said things like that, vendettas that hung over abysses of unexplained enmity.

He looked Alex up and down, frowned and nodded, presumably approving of his improvement in personal hygiene. 'It was a chain of canals, started centuries ago, to cut across France and avoid Spanish pirates. After the floods, it fair cut the old girl's throat, chopped the Midi into two lands. There, that mud'– Hendry swept his arm to the right – 'is Languedoc. Over there,'– sweeping to the left – 'Pyrenées. That's where we're going, to Carcassonne. You'll like it.'

The crew were singing along to a pop song in Français, their vonnie-speaker working fine now, and the Spring light was fading in the West as they chugged up to the well-dredged port. Carcassonne's battered, busy dock lay at the foot of a ziggurat of history, layer upon stone layer of ancient town rising above them. They disembarked into a mediaeval market scene. Squawking modal music sounded over crowd clamour, the timeless song of festivals mixing with the blare of a market that sells everything in the world.

Alex stood on the greasy cobbles of the quay and watched a tall, dark girl striding proudly by, shoulders strutting, bare belly swaying, singing in an ornate, dead language, trailing an airy wake of crimson silks and awed admirers, angelic feathers sprouting from her wild hennaed hair. His heart lifted in his chest. This was life, and the breath of life, after the dead towns they'd passed on the coast. Carcassonne was as busy as Wessex, bustling, buzzing with guests and business. And by the look of it, wealthier. Everyone seemed to be a full Citizen or maybe they didn't even have that distinction here.

Hendry's crew hauled their luggage out onto the quay and up the steep, cobbled streets. Alex watched Hendry's man tip the harbourmaster with a case of clean plastic, then followed up to the heart of the town, a retro-fitted square floodlit from tasteful diesel Tilleys, rescued stone hotels, smug, pampered beauties, towering around them.

The retinue flowed into the largest and most glittering of those portals, its arch declaring it as La Reine du Midi. The hotel's staff, lavish in their gold-braided uniforms, greeted him by name and fawned over his uncle.

It dawned on Alex that this trip was no longer about him. Hendry had selected the hotel to be near the meltdown site, obviously, but this was more than a sightseeing tour for Alex's benefit. This visit was something more, that the master of intrigue had set up. Alex felt a tightening in his chest. To blow it off, he strode on, forcing himself to breathe deeply. This was going to be good, one way or another. The staff cooperated, pointing him the way, getting out of the path of this angry young Briton.

Alex liked it that way. That was one of the appeals of power, that people left you alone if you wanted them to. He ran up the staircases to his floor, found his door, and let himself into a lavish, Oriental-styled mini-suite, complete with upmarket vonnie-speakers and, exotically, an exovid with TV channels. He locked the door. The en suite bathroom was enormous and he filled the big, marble bathtub, splashing strange little packages of strong smelling things into it, enacting some enclave of self in his brittle sense of the real.

He emerged and did some lazy stretches in the steam, then opened the dark wood wardrobe to an array of new clothes. He chose the brightest shirt and trousers, dressing to have fun, and strolled down to meet Hendry for drinks.

The spry old tycoon was seated alone in a broad alcove window, in immaculate tuxedo and blue silk bow tie, gleaming snack bowls and his fruity-coloured drink poised on a semicircular Moorish table. Alex wondered, half-interestedly, what the significance of this arrangement was, having got used to Hendry's ceaseless jockeying. Well, sod it. He settled into the alcove and ordered a cocktail, strictly of the alcohol variety, slouching in accord with this deliberate debauch. Why give Hendry the idea he had any ground to give?

Hendry scanned him and nodded, with no visible affect. With the clarity of youth, Alex saw that there was little that could be discussed with any profit, so he didn't bother saying anything.

His drink arrived, a tower of delicious stuff, a tribute to someone's idea of lavish sophistication in an age of chaos. Alex decided that the only reasonable response to this fragrant cornucopia was to swallow it as casually as possible. Three gulps later, it was finished, and he joined the older man in staring out of the thick glass window.

They had a clear view over the hills to higher land: an arc of pitted wall, maybe taller than a man and crumbling with neglect. It was topped with what might be rusty barbed wire, and behind it a dome of hillside, uniform at this range, dotted with clumps of red and yellow vegetation.

Hendry raised his fruit cocktail and gestured at the concreted-over hilltop. 'That's where a gas-cooled fast reactor, the sleekest and best of its kind, ruptured, tilted over and started melting a hole in the ground before the electric company got lucky and managed to put it out.' He took a swig. 'We've got some people to meet, Alex. People who are changing the world.' He swigged again.

Then, with a slothful, reptilian deliberation, he put his

drink down and turned on the younger man. Hendry didn't need to be out of control to succeed in communicating intimidation. He was well known to eschew all intoxication except that of power, which sometimes requires a decent facsimile of feral abandon. 'They told you nuclear power was evil, Ambrose and all those Asgard Hall types. That somewhere, in a parallel universe, the earth is burning in hell, because we took it up again. But what about this one, this bloody parallel universe? Three fifths of the planet's people dead in two generations. Waters rising, to swallow the corpses of those we abandoned.'

Hendry stopped abruptly. 'A religious man once told me that when we stop trimming the nails of our dead, then the end of time is near. He was a few steps behind – that has already happened. We're just surviving, not living, and we're not in the shadow of nuclear power but in the half-arsed aftermath of timidity.'

Hendry swigged the rest of his juice down. Alex managed to look unimpressed, but wasn't convincing himself.

Hendry wiped his mouth. 'And what about this, the Pyrenees. It's not just me, you know. Look at these people, compared to Wessex. They suffered the fifth worst disaster on the planet, and look at their standard of living now.'

Alex turned to the bleak view outside. *Hardly fucking inspiring*, he thought. But it hurt to think of what he owed his uncle.

'Raven nearly got there, you know.'

'Raven was quite possibly as mad as his lover, the Burning Woman of Rome, by the time of those flaky later papers.'

'Glad you mentioned Tyson, whose process for 'nuclide extraction is a mainstay of what you do, Uncle, yet you seem unconcerned that she was obviously mad.'

Hendry viewed him coolly. 'Well that's all pie-in-the-sky. The Arctic economy's booming, and nuclear power is priming it. In Alberta they're running the fracking extraction off nuclear and trading the plastics they make for 'nuclides from Murmansk and vegetables from Greenland.'

He looked at Alex for a while then shook his head. 'You lack vision, my boy. You've got your head in the sand. We're not living, not as people used to. Getting the electricity on again is the only game in town. It's the only thing that matters. You'll see.' Hendry nodded. 'Anyway, tonight's for fun, at least for you. I think you'll enjoy the party.' He glanced at his wristwatch, that pre-vonnie affectation. 'Food?'

Alex was back to his usual hungry self after the sea-sickness. 'Yeah.'

Hendry led the way through a ballroom at the rear of the hotel, and into a high-ceilinged ante-chamber where a sumptuous buffet was laid out on long tables. They were the first guests there, the only company a brace of waiters fussing over the hot dishes. They filled porcelain plates and sat down opposite the big doors, open to a garden laced with coloured lights. By the time they'd finished eating, the long room was filling up with diners.

By the way they greeted him, most of them making their way over to Hendry at some stage, it was clear that they were all his guests. *Once again, the Big Man is making something happen*, thought Alex, as he helped himself to a flute of champagne. It felt good in his mouth, and he finished it quickly and got another.

People were finishing their plates, topping up their glasses and moving into the main ballroom when a band arrived. A man in motley carried a lute, and a tall, olive-skinned woman in a red silk ballgown, raving curls spilling over her elegant shoulders, drew the gaze of the whole room. As she swished proudly by a few yards away, Alex couldn't take his eyes off her, and she'd joined the lute player up on the little ballroom stage before he realised that this was the beautiful singer he'd seen earlier on the quayside. He began to plot how to meet her, his champagne forgotten, as were the conversations around him, while she sang out the mournful arabesques of an Occitan love song.

To Alex, the woman's face seemed as if under a spotlight, every detail burning into his hungry gaze. When she finished, there were a few seconds of clapping, whistling and cries of 'encore!' and 'more!'

She dipped her head graciously at the crowd and spoke in a husky, commanding voice. 'Thank you, I shall sing again later, but now it is time for your party band for tonight.' Three more men in leather jerkin and hose stepped up to the stage, carrying hurdy-gurdy, shawm and naker drums.

With the lutenist, they kicked off into a full-tilt *estampie*. Conversations resumed around Alex, and the singer mingled in the crowd.

Hendry had done his bout of glad-handing, and he turned back to the enraptured Alex. He did his little nod of satisfaction as the woman approached them.

'Maira, my dear,' murmured Hendry as they cheek-kissed. 'This is Alex, my protégé and best hope for the future. Alex, this very special lady is Maira.'

She proffered a slender hand on which sat two great rings, a giant star sapphire flashing its six rays in a cross of yellow gold, and an octagonal emerald in white gold filigree. Her perfume was of night flowers set in deep musk. He couldn't take his eyes off her mouth, a straight slash with corners that kept writhing into barely-repressed sardonic life.

He touched hands with her. 'Good to meet you. You're a great singer.'

'Thank you. It's not my profession, though.' She smiled. 'I heal and I counsel.'

'That sounds great,' said Alex, feeling rather lame.

The ironic mouth twisted. 'You should see it from this side.'

She turned to the older man. 'I shall leave you for a while, Hendry.' She kissed his cheeks again. He gave her an almost proprietorial squeeze.

'And you, Alex, I shall maybe see later?'

'Absolutely,' he said. Their hands touched again, and she held his gaze for a second longer than someone would who was completely uninterested in him, or so it seemed. She stepped away and swept off into the crowd.

Alex watched her go before turning to Hendry. 'How do you know her?'

'I know everybody worth knowing, or will do when they become worth knowing. She's special, eh?'

'I have to see her again,' said Alex.

'You will,' said Hendry, giving one of his little nods. 'Now I'm going to mingle,' and off he went, shaking hands.

Alex helped himself to another glass of champagne. He felt he needed to prepare himself, find a way to impress Maira. He needed to think.

He took his drink out into the garden, onto a terracotta-tiled terrace surrounded by tables and chairs, multicoloured fairy lights draped over a oval border of miniature cypresses. Burning electricity just for display might have impressed him in itself on any other night. He wandered out to the boundary of evergreens, then stepped through into a deeper dark, where his eyes had to adjust to a few Chinese lanterns hanging from low branches. It smelled of trees, and of perfume here. Strolling couples must have left the scent, and it occurred to him to beware of disturbing any lovers in the dark.

But it seemed as if he was alone, as he stepped deeper into the lovely garden, until he came to a maze, a small labyrinth of head-high hedges. As he stood in the entrance he caught a hint of perfume again. It reminded him of Maira's night-flower scent, and he stepped into the maze and followed the trail of aroma round some turns to the left and then one to the right.

The clouds blew away, and the just risen half-moon came into view. He was in the square central area of the maze, and Maira was standing in front of him, her gown black in the moonlight, her eyes flashing in the icy glow.

She raised a finger to her lips; her other hand swung over her head, seeming to draw a lazy thread of light behind it. She twirled theatrically, up on her toes, whirled close to him, her skirt rustling against his thigh, her perfume carried on the hot scent of her body, then she stood in front of him, her breast rising and rising, her lips just-parted as if singing silently. Slowly, she raised her arms above her head and this time Alex was sure he saw milky radiance arcing between her palms. His breath coming fast and deep he stepped forward and placed his fingertips on each of her hips, leaving a trail of soft, cold light in the wake of his movement.

She groaned operatically. Alex pulled her to him. Their eyes met, then he bent to kiss that incredible mouth. Time stretched into stillness while the taste and scent of her sank into him, marking him, linking him to her at a level deeper than cellular. In silent, careful urgency they undid each others' clothes, and knelt face to face on the soft ground. They moved together so that she sat across Alex's thighs, and then she sank down onto his erection. Time snapped, the world stopped moving, he couldn't be sure he was breathing.

At some stage they unwound from each other and lay silent on the tiny lawn at the heart of the maze, drenched in cold light and soft air, sweat cooling on their hot skin, then she said, 'Come, I've got something to show you,' stood and picked up her gown. They dressed and she led Alex through the maze and out the other side.

The ground fell away here, and across the rooftops he saw the oily glint of the waterway. She stepped down into a sunken alleyway half-choked with broken bricks. They descended the slope between patched ancient walls, down to a balustrade of crumbled stone lapped by the heavy, black water. She raised her arm, pointing across the channel where the other edge of the water blended imperceptibly into the darkness of the land. 'Watch,' she whispered, and he saw a meandering line gradually appear where the water touched the black shore, sharpening up like a vonnie crossload getting cleaned up in an exovid. In the near-silence, with just the soft slap of the water, a crow squawked, distant but clear. The picture sharpened still further and he caught sight of a ragged shape rising, silhouetted against moonlit clouds, from broken razor wire above the shoreline.

Maira slipped her hand under his arm. 'The dump there, it's radioactive. Part of the story of the rise of the Pyrenees.'

She looked at him. 'How are you feeling?'

It dawned on Alex that he had none of the nausea of hot vonnie interference. 'Fine! What did you do to me?'

Her mouth crinkled at him. 'You've forgotten already?'

Alex laughed. 'You... you're becter-tolerant.' He shook his head in wonder, a different kind of excitement thrilling through him.

'And fucking, or even lying close to me usually results in – I don't know the English for it – my benefactor called it *embarquement* – kind of gathering your Bose-Einstein fields to mine.'

'Entrainment,' muttered Alex, gazing at her face, the glow of her skin in the augmented light. Her mouth was moving again, in one of her silent songs, and out of the corner of his eye he saw white spray sparkling over the black water, saw a tunnel of spume rise and spin into a twister until it was yards taller than them. Maira laughed a wild, dirty laugh then grabbed his arm. 'Come!' – pulling him away from the water's edge, still laughing – 'It's falling!'

They ran back up the rubble-strewn path, the foaming water crashing behind them to the shriek of Maira's laughter. They emerged by the maze and followed its perimeter hedge round to the lawn by the terrace. She looked up and down at their clothes, jewelled with spray in the suddenly fierce light and said, 'I'll come to your room, midnight,' and that was it, she had gone before he could give her his room number, joining the greater throng spilling in and out of the ballroom, a river of frivolous light bearing her into the party.

Chapter 4: Dreams of Power

His sensitized eyes amplified the ballroom's glitter, silky heat prowled under his skin. He noticed little but Maira's singing, blind to a world taking shape around him, taking shape in ways he would have hated. At ten to twelve he was in his room, wondering if she would come, aware he couldn't do anything to bring it about. He just had to wait. He checked around the room for distractions – no books. A little chilled cabinet of booze and tinctures, but the last thing he wanted was to dull his senses. He switched the exovid on and set it to random tuning, but the sound irritated him in his listening for the door, so he left just the picture on and paced around the room. He gazed out of the window, but the sight of the domed hill to the West just made him think of Hendry and his schemes.

At twenty five past, there was a knock at the tall door. He opened it and took in the change in her, the different way she lit up the space around her, the brittle glint in her eyes. Her kiss was hungry but also distracted by some strong emotion.

'You're angry.'

'Hendry's business associate' – she spat the words – 'that fucking Menard. Two years ago I saw him sell a child into servitude to a 'nuclide reclaimer from Murmansk.' She pulled away from him. Sometimes I think it would have been better to become a fighter, like my benefactor, not a healer.' She stood, hands clenched tight, glaring across the room. The becter-light intensified and Alex heard creaks and groans like straining boards. A tumbler on the sideboard shattered, spraying bright glass onto the carpet. She turned to him as a picture flew off the wall. 'I'm all mashed up, Alex. Fuck me, now.'

He stepped forward and fixed his eyes on hers. Her hair was stirring in a wind from nowhere. He slipped the gown off her shoulders then undid the zip at the back. He dropped his own clothes on the floor and led her away from the broken glass and rippling curtains, to the comfortable bedroom. Gently, he got her to kneel on the bed, grasped her hips and pushed into her. She bucked in ecstasy, the glow of her flesh lighting the tattoo on her long back. His body was a tense arc, sweat bursting from his skin, as he moved inside her. The air in the room felt sharp, heavy, as if brewing a storm, then they both came, ripples of cool light flowing along her skin.

They fell onto the bed, the tension dispersing, and he gazed at her back, where a coiled dragon, its single eye like a black star, reared up from the roots of a tree whose leaves were nibbled by four deer. A bushy-tailed rodent clung to the trunk of the tree. A great eagle spread its wings in the shadow of her shoulder-blades, with a smaller bird of prey, maybe a hawk, sitting on its head.

'That's beautiful. What's it about?'

She didn't turn, but he got the impression she was doing one of her twisted smiles. 'I had it done when I realised the nature of what my benefactor had given me.' She turned to him. 'That's another story, and I want to sleep now.'

Sleep was deep and came suddenly. His body was plastic, his arm twisted impossibly round Maira's shoulders, with no pain or cramp when he woke. Dawn bells chimed a Beltane tune in eternal brass. The soft becter glow was almost-eclipsed by day, the hybrid light making everything translucent, so insubstantial it looked as if you could pass through matter like a ghost. Her eyes opened and met his, and his cock rose. She took it in her hand and he lay back and let her mount him. Their lovemaking was slow and silent, and when they finished he lay with his arm around her, gazing at her back.

'Tell me about your tattoo.'

Maira gazed off into some arcade of memory. 'I broke into this old woman's house. I was living on the streets of the Nouveau Perpignan shanty, orphaned after one of the vonnie-plagues. She was like a spider in its web – she made it easy for me to get in then froze me on the spot. She made me stand there while she ran her hands over me, then wiped her finger across my mouth and tasted my spit. I'd never met a becter person before. I'd never been so scared in my life. Then it was as if I'd passed some test, and she let me move my arms and legs a bit and asked me what my RK rating was. I didn't know, so she did her own version of an RK trial right then. It took a day and a half, pausing twice for stew and coffee. I came out a 15-plus, and that's when she told me what she wanted me for, to try and pass her becters on before she died. She'd tried it on two others, who'd overloaded and burned up, but she said she knew I would be OK. I was.' Maira went silent.

Alex said, 'Where did her becters come from?'

Maira turned and eyed him as if he was confirming something she suspected. 'You too dream of power. My benefactor called becters the cursed prize. She used to say she'd won it in the fairground. I always had this picture of desperate people queuing at some shabby marquee as guinea-pigs for whoever made the stuff in the first place. She believed, and I think she was right, that she was one of the originals, one of the first people its creator tried it on. No-one who dreams of power could resist that gamble. I couldn't. I did as she told me, sucked blood from a cut on her skinny old tit, while she cut me in the same place. I held down the blood for a few minutes, then threw up. It worked. There was no fever. I was a –what's it in English?'

'A BT, becter tolerant. What do you mean about dreams of power?'

'The first thing I learned I could do after she gave me the blood was to see someone's – the word my benefactor used was *poursuivant,* pursuer. I can see it, usually when they're moving, like a mist of light following them. Sometimes it takes a shape, a face, an animal. It seems to be a pattern that shows through in the, you know, becter-field –'

'The Bose-Einstein Condensate,' supplied Alex.

' – thank you, that I can see. It's not a becter thing in itself –the shapes it makes run in families. It seems to be something to do with the person's genetic gift and what they can make of it. Usually one of the offspring of the family has a stronger pursuer than the others, they are marked for power of some kind – intellect, money, war, art, something in the public eye. You have a very strong and complex pursuer, as does Hendry, but they are very different. They're like chalk and cheese,' she twisted her mouth at the funniness of the English expression, 'but you are both people who act, and the world wraps itself around your actions.'

She paused then spoke again. 'There are people behind the appearance of this world. I'm not talking conspiracies in the twentieth century sense, but people who've gone missing, loners who've got all that missing technology.'

'All those things that should have been invented by now, but we never see them?'

'That's it. Ever wonder what happened to the super-rich? There aren't many of them going about their bare-faced business in the world like Hendry is. Most of them, when they realised the boat was about to go down some time in the last century, retreated into their Alamouts, their hi-tech castles.'

Alex grinned. 'Sounds like the plot from one of those old James Bond films.'

Maira looked keenly at him. 'OK, some details: there's a

black pyramid on the Gilf Kebir plateau in the Sahara that absorbs enough solar energy to power whatever goes on inside it. It's e-m-proof, nanite-proof and becter-proof. It's got no doors and no-one's been seen going in or out of it for about forty years. That's probably just one family. There's a heavily-defended farming compound by the Wilkins Coast on the Antarctic Peninsula. That's probably six hundred people. Greenland is now Pure Light, and do you know what they consist of? A consortium of Christians and Moslems who managed to agree on the nastiest features of their religions. They bankrolled the building of the nuclear plants that keep the hydroponic lights on through the Arctic night. The North American Alliance thinks it owns the American Arctic coast but NAA citizens get abducted and sold in the slave markets in Newfoundland.

'And then there's the Thule Teardrop. A very gifted and strange Scandinavian BT told me about the radio-dead teardrop-shaped area in the Arctic you can't sail or fly into. Everything looks weird. Thorvaldsson described it as like elf-land. Navigational instruments break down or give you readings that steer you round the edge of it. If you sail straight for it, you bounce off and go in a circle. No-one's been able to update a map of the area since the satellites came down. You know all the money that Rejuve makes? The Swiss consortium it's licensed to consists of individuals from all over who all buy expensive metals which find their way to the port of Hammerfest, where they leave for a journey off the map, presumably into the Teardrop. Is that enough examples, or do you want more?'

Alex shook his head, overwhelmed with new information, then, musing out loud, asked, 'Why can't I tolerate becters? I once tested as a 15-plus, I should be able to. But I can't even tolerate 14s, which is crazy.'

Maira said, 'Come here so I can touch your face and feel your breath.'

Alex moved to sit in front of her, face to face, her eyelids closed and flickering. She held her hands behind his back, as if feeling for something in the air behind him, her breathing so shallow that it made no wind on his face.

For a couple of minutes they sat like that, her brow flexing from time to time, then settling into a frown as she opened her eyes.

'Strange... first I feel the, the Bose-Einstein layer, then behind that is the person's – I think of it as the ocean and the face – there's an ocean of possible selves in that person, but one comes back again and again, their main face. But you ' – she paused and gave a short shake of her head – 'I've never seen anything like it. There's something in between the becter layer and the ocean... It seems to be to do with your becter sensitivity. That's all I can say.' She bit her lip. 'I think someone or something put it there.'

'What do you mean, put it there?'

'When you tried out becters, did you have any weird disasters?'

Alex shook his head. 'Not exactly weird, just a shockingly intense intolerance. I blacked out and was convulsing by the time another student found me and shot some eluter into me.'

'I think someone wanted to change your becter response.'

Alex sat back, puzzled and spooked. 'Why would anyone want to do that?' he asked no-one in particular. Maira gazed at him.

He shook his head and changed the subject. 'How come you speak perfect street-English?'

'I've been everywhere. You don't need to know how old that makes me.' She grimaced. 'I need a shower. Get us some breakfast, cheri.' She swung her long legs off the bed and strode to the bathroom, spirals of her hair catching crimson flame in the slanting light. He found the hotel's information booklet and worked out how to use the unfamiliar phone. Not sure what to get, he ordered everything then lay back and thought about Maira's body.

A waiter arrived, with a trolley and a conspiratorial smile. Alex pulled a robe around him and tipped the smart young guy. He was getting into the spirit of this world of money and impulse.

He lifted lids on the tray, and saw smoked bacon, poached eggs, German sausages, blood pudding, grilled tomatoes and mushrooms, thin-sliced black rye bread, English toast, porridge, coffee, green and black teas, cocoa, cocaf, all the condiments, a selection of cereal flakes with milk and a bowl of fruit. He'd never seen so much breakfast. He lifted a little silver jug and sniffed the unfamiliar tang of cow's milk. A gene-probe sealed in a branded retro-plastic wrapper lay on the side of the tray.

Maira emerged into the room towelling her hair and sat at the table.

'Mmm, hungry, eh?' She tossed the towel aside and flashed him her lopsided smile as she sat down. She spooned French mustard onto a plate, picked up a sausage and dipped it in the fawn mush, squishing it around. 'Let's eat, Alex. You need it.'

He took bacon, eggs and toast and set to. He ate in silence, ravenously hungry.

After a while, he looked at the left-overs, feeling guilty at the waste as Maira poured coffee.

'Will you be around the hotel, around the town?'

'No, I have a promise to keep, a long way from here. When does Hendry need you again?'

'Some time today.' He made a false smile. 'Yeah, needs me.'

She pushed her face nearer to his and frowned into his eyes. 'Of course he needs you. Do you think he does this for fun, even with a family member? Don't ever think he's doing you any favours.'

'You know Hendry,' stated Alex. 'What do you think of him?'

'I think he's an evil old fuck, but it doesn't matter what I think, because he's a dreamer of power. In his case, it comes from pain, and I think that's how it will end.'

'What you said about mine and his 'pursuers' being different, does that mean I was wrong when I used to wonder if he was my father? My mother disappeared when I was seven and I was shuttled between my two 'uncles.' Maybe that's where my need for power comes from, wanting to make things better again.' He shook his head, banishing self-analysis, and asked, 'How come you know him so well?'

Maira looked coolly at him. 'Before you even think it, no, I don't fuck him and never have. And neither am I some kind of corporate favours girl.' Alex opened his mouth to apologise for any offence he might have given then noticed she was smiling, teasing him. She pushed him playfully and gazed into his eyes, complex thoughts in her own.

She stood and gathered her ballgown, dressing with evident pleasure in each sensual moment. Then she turned to him, smiling, looking almost vulnerable. 'Alex. We will absolutely meet again.' She gathered herself up, centred, with no accoutrements to distract her, and out she went, head high and proud.

Alex bit his lip, out of his depth. Craving distraction, he switched on the exovid's TV reception, a fantastic novelty for a Wessexer. He settled down with his Swiss tea and tuned into a news channel. He turned the volume down, and watched the flow of images. Two posh people were being rescued from a flooded promontory somewhere. Languedoc military police had apprehended a suspect in the year-long hunt for the killer of a young girl. He had been shot dead whilst resisting arrest. Alex nodded and supped his tea. Auvergne was inviting Wessex to join in a shared currency area. *No chance*, thought Alex. Then he saw the energetic, compact shape of his uncle striding across the screen and shaking hands. The film was from last night's party. He didn't remember seeing anyone filming. Must have been crossloaded from some reporter carrying high-end vonnies, the kind you can use to record through your own eyes. Then he watched some adverts, mostly banned in Wessex with its anti-consumerist laws, and dozed happily.

Sounds from the corridor woke him. He got up, dressed and went down to the bar for lunch. The place was, he supposed, tolerably busy, but it seemed empty after last night. He got a menu, a seat and settled on something that looked light and tasty. It was a nice novelty, not having to think about the price of anything. He was a few minutes into enjoying it, when, as if he'd been watching from some carrion-stoked eyrie, Hendry joined him. 'Ah, Alex, there you are. Well? Thirty minutes? I'll come and get you.'

The sun was high in the sky when he met Hendry out the front of the hotel. The two of them and a driver climbed into a new-looking electric Citroen truck.

'We're meeting them at the site,' said Hendry. They drove out on the uphill road, the wall Alex had seen the day before coming into view as they crested the hill. The road twisted round some more, until they were the other side of the crest from Carcassonne, and climbing again. It was getting hot in the cab. Now they were right by the wall, and they followed the cracked concrete block structure round a long curve, a steep drop away to the left. There was an open gate in front of them. The enamel sign said STOP and below that was rusted into illegibility. They bumped and rattled through the gateway onto the road behind the wall, no more than a cracked dirt track, grit spraying out from their tyres. Another truck was parked over the other side of the road, three men standing by it, two in combat fatigues and one in a flamboyant shirt. Behind the truck, Alex could make out another two men in corporate suits, looking hot and bothered. Their driver pulled over, switched on a Tyson counter and got down from the cab. Hendry jumped down and approached the other group. Alex followed.

Hendry strode up to the big man in the loud shirt. 'Lucife! You're looking rich!'

Lucife laughed hugely, his red beard bobbing, and shook Hendry's hand. 'I am, my friend, and now even more so, with buying this place.'

Hendry turned to present Alex. 'This is my nephew, Alex Tyler. He is a chemist. Alex, Lucife 'Tokamak' Menard is the man who salvaged the Cadarache fusion reactor in '97.'

Menard briefly touched Alex's hand. Alex thought about what Maira had said. The red-haired man's widely spaced, tiny dark eyes held him in the same calculating way he'd seen Hendry do with others, at war with all the world, assaying his value. 'Chemist, eh? Can you improve on the Tyson extraction?'

Before Alex could answer Menard turned back to Hendry, took his arm, and walked him off the road into the concrete wasteland. Hendry's driver darted ahead of them, swinging the radiation counter. Menard's men, wearing ID lanyards tucked into shirt breast pockets, followed, one of them also carrying a counter. The crackle from the Tysons was a little over background, by the sound of it, but not alarming. Still, Alex felt very alert, and listened for changes. Maira's entrainment seemed to be holding up, but he checked the 'thane atomiser in his pocket.

The two security men flanked them. Alex walked behind, still smarting from the way Menard had dismissed him as being of no account. The counters crackled a little more.

Lucife continued. 'You wouldn't believe how cheap I got it, I had those idiots from the Pyrenées government eating out of my hand, when they saw this' – he made an abrupt hand gesture, and the tall blond aide with the counter trotted ahead and stood at the edge of a crack in the concrete. The crackles of the counter had blurred into a single blast.

The man called out in a shaky voice, 'Sept cents quinze, Monsieur!'

Lucife turned to Hendry. 'Over seven hundred counts per second pour out of that crack, my friend, so they sold it me for fucking peanuts! I am indeed a rich man!'

The two men laughed, Menard with evident joy. Only then did he recall his sweating aide from the edge of the crack.

They shook hands again. As they parted, Alex noticed that Menard's security wore white, long-stemmed crosses on their fatigues. He hadn't seen that symbol since school lessons about Wessex history and news reports of clashes with Pure Light insurgents. *So Menard's also in league with those maniacs.* The flamboyant engineer strode off, trailing images of degradation.

Hendry led his party back to the truck. The driver pulled the vehicle round, and they set off back to the main road.

Hendry was gazing straight ahead and nodding as he spoke to Alex. 'I'm showing you a new life – the problems, the rewards and next the solution. Stick with me and you'll have a great future.'

It sounded like all the other pep-talks Hendry had tried on him, but he felt different this time. His uncle's appeal to something in him that wanted to grow up, wanted to make his mark on the world, was working, but he still doubted that Hendry's work was the kind of mark he wanted to make.

‘So where are we going next, Uncle H?’

‘You’ve seen where this is leading. There are radionuclides lying around all over the place. They’re what we need to get the electricity on again. So, we’re going to the Kent flood-zone, and we’re going to salvage a decommissioned reactor core from the Dungeness site.’

Alex felt sweat prickle on his upper lip. With every day, he was getting more repelled by the future his uncle wanted for him. He fell silent, losing himself in his body’s memories of Maira.

Back at the hotel, they got their stuff. Alex chose a few of the clothes Hendry had put in his room and gazed for a moment at the rumpled bed. Hendry was waiting impatiently under the Pyrenées-Nucleaire sign across the square. They got back on the launch, and set off up the Western limb of the Canal du Midi. Alex slept fitfully on the gentle rocking as they ran the wide watercourse towards the Atlantic coast. The night seemed endless. They hugged the Charente coastline, avoiding the military colony around the La Rochelle submarine base, now run from a floating island, and then turned east around Cape Finistère, past glowing, bulbous silhouettes, the nanite-grown towers of the Breton defensive array. As Monday dawned they began a slow crossing of the broad Wessex Channel, then east across flooded Kent. As the sun sank towards the horizon, the crump of distant explosions sounded through their feet. Shortly after that, they dropped anchor in a featureless acreage of still water.

A few hundred yards away, a pair of cranes faced each other, jibs hanging over the same stretch of gloom. They rose from columns of steel rigging like drilling platforms sticking out above the churned, muddy water. They were hauling something up, foot by straining foot of cable, out of the murk.

They were running late. Hendry rushed around annoyed, complaining at the crew, shouting down audio links. 'This was supposed to be a daylight show.' The explosives team had only just blasted the core free, so it could be lifted out. Now, the sun had gone down, the last Spring light fading fast, but Hendry was making sure they saw it through.

With a series of loud pops, a bank of klieg lanterns came on and flooded the scene with hot light. The tension mounted, the only sound shouted commands. The two men leaned closer to watch as the cranes began to raise their burden. A massive, rough ball, chain-wrapped, broke free from the water and swung there.

Hendry hissed a triumphant *Yes*, and turned to face Alex. He could smell Hendry's armpit sweat as he passed the binoculars over. 'That's it. Power. What you're looking at is the future.'

Alex trained the glasses on the object, now being swung gently over to the stripped-down coal barge in front of them. It hung in silhouette against the pale sky, a rough, grey oval with spidery fans of broken reinforcement sticking out. Droplets of water caught the merciless electric light and, for a moment, Alex fancied that he was seeing radioactive poison dripping into the Kent basin. He handed the binoculars back, after-images from the klieg light striping his vision. 'That thing out there'– indicating the swinging ball –'would be a bad bollock to drop.'

Hendry poured Scotch from a very old bottle, the Gaelic label faded to near-illegibility and handed a glass to Alex with his usual lack of comment. Alex sipped the whisky. 'Where is it going now? Not Wessex, I hope?'

The grey eyes regarded him expressionlessly through round lenses. 'To a well-guarded place, where we can strip it down in safety.'

'I expect you've got those Pure Light mercs too, what are they called, supplying your security,' said Alex.

'The White Cross are good soldiers, and come well-equipped.' Hendry sounded a touch defensive. He turned away, picked up a speaking tube and gave the order to head for Wessex.

'But what is their real price, Uncle?' pushed Alex. 'A cut of your nuke for some religious fanatics?'

With a foot-stirring bass echo the engines thrummed into life. The backwash from lifting the reactor core reached them, dark water slapping against the side of the rocking launch.

Hendry turned and faced him again. 'Everyone is going to want a cut of my nuke, as you put it.' His arms rose from his sides to an expansive gesture. 'I'm making sure I'm on the winning side, Alex. As always.'

Alex found that thought chilling. He covered a yawn. Glancing at Hendry, he saw the first signs of tiredness in that tight old face.

The barge and its cargo set off to the West. Alex gazed at the receding lights of the salvage cranes, retracting and settling now, and sipped the ancient malt. His thoughts were full of worry. *Could that really have been radioactive water I saw dripping there? Wessex has been four generations away from nuclear technology now. We don't want that poison again.* He thought of the teams that loaded the decaying, shattered reactor core onto the barge, the teams that would strip it and recover radionuclides from the searing poison of its heart. They would be ordinary people, desperate for work. Would they have adequate safety clothing? Decent health care? Or just a lot of cheap xenothane and a short life? *Glad I don't work for my uncle,* he thought as he put the empty glass on the side and rubbed his hands over his face. He noticed the vonnie-speaker then, and switched it on for distraction from his thoughts. It crackled into ghostly life, the hum of insect-borne vonnies overlaid with shards of conversation, the bubbling and thrumming pink-noise of sex-vonnies and then a just-about-acceptable signal patched through NeighbourNet from the transmitter at Marlborough.

Hendry stood up and put his glass down. 'Go to Ambrose, Alex. Finish whatever part of your education you feel you need to finish with him, and come back and work with me. You've got a life in the real world in front of you.'

He turned to go, but stopped as the Radio Wessex newscast began and the newsreader's distraught voice cracked. '...has confirmed that, following an accident this morning, King Peredur died in his rooms at Marlborough Palace at 4.20 p.m., Wessex time. Queen Gwendoline made a brief statement, in which she declared that she and Wessex would be mourning together the loss of her beloved husband. There will be a two minute silence. Gods prosper Wessex.'

The newscaster could barely control her emotion at the end. Alex had less passion for the restored Wessex royalty than most of their Citizen subjects, but he had to admit that Peredur had fought bravely in the Chilterns and had restored to the beleaguered Resources Commission its powers to judge what was relevant technology for Wessex. He felt a chill foreboding about what might come next.

With all the wooden sincerity of a politician, Hendry spoke. 'A terrible tragedy. I'm to my bunk. Good night.'

The news resumed, fragments of signal bleeping in and out, whistling ghosts, fed through from vonnies under someone's skin on a dock at Thatcham, or maybe off a vonnie-infested seagull. The threat of civil war in our allies Languedoc, the recapture of bandit chief 'Diamond Head' Morningstar, the granting of Citizen status to five hundred Wessexers born to Guest parents, passed through him without thought. He stood up and turned away from the darkness outside, to the bulkhead door out to the cabins. He found his berth, the door with a cloud-shaped label and the legend *Nirvana*, and slumped onto the bunk. He wondered for a moment in what sense he didn't work for his uncle, and then, who wasn't on Hendry's payroll, as he fell into blackness.

Chapter 5: Law Tuesday: Hettie

Claws of splay-foot sky-devils, a snag-hearted murder of ravens, scratch about on the roof-tiles and shout dark, magic words that rip the veil of sleep. The world is a conundrum of pain, negotiable only by detachment, by systematic cultivation of the remote inner, the aerial self. It is she who is the raven and her heart has descended upon the battlefield of the world, plucking juicy images, the soft eyes of dead strangers to gaze through, to see the world from other viewpoints.

Then it ends. From light-sleek fluidity she is decanted into the shape of herself, the mask she wears against boundlessness. Her body's eyes are closed. She lets herself surface slowly, a skill she never lost when she grew out of childhood. The dream mind and the waking mind overlap in unbroken sequence as she watches herself at the conclusion of her dream, when the raw hunger of her need is spun into a narrative, and maybe an answer.

This morning, the production was lavish, and her narrator told a tragic story. As she repeated it to herself, to fix it in her waking mind, she started to evaluate it. Her father has died (*true,* she thought), the world is being poisoned (*yes, but that's nothing new*) and her mother came back from the dead (*she's still alive*) to avenge (*that would be appropriate*) her rape (*I hope that's not true*) in a radioactive desert (*that's two mentions of poison*).

Then she could not hide any longer, and came awake, wrapping her arms around herself, assaulted by the massive realness of things, the solidity of the world, the relentless tragedy of her family. Her violet eyes opened in grief. She rolled over. It's an ache of physical loneliness, since Siward was killed.

But now she was sure she knew something new. Later, she would process the dream and unpack its vital core of insight. Today, she would be a step nearer to finding out who was behind Siward's death, who it was who'd betrayed Wessex to the Pure Light. And that meant that she would be a step nearer to fulfilling her oath, to paying out vengeance.

She gave herself a few minutes breathing deeply from her belly and training her mind. She visualized the next room, little Siward's bedroom, as if she'd gone in there herself. Susannah had taught her this exercise when she was only a few years older than the boy. She imagined the walls of the room in dim, dawn light. She imagined him sleeping, curled up, and then stirring, sliding off his bed. Then with her physical ears she actually heard his little voice through the wall. He was cooing, quite tunefully.

She snapped back into her body-attention and thought: *Another musician,* as she got up out of the big bed. She shrugged on a deep blue silk gown, tied it round her waist, twisted her tousled blonde hair into a thick rope and speared it in place with a gold comb in the shape of a coiled dragon, sapphires for eyes.

She went into the boy's room and little Siward ran towards her. She hugged him in her strong arms. She enjoyed his warm, biscuity smell and he enjoyed the cuddle for a few seconds then started struggling, and she let him go. His eyes, fierce as a snake's, were his father's. Would the pain never go away? Every time she thought of her loss, it sucked the joy out of her life. But she had to go on living, for the sake of Siward, and for all the other people who would soon depend on her to be strong. She'd been sunk in mourning for over a year and a half now; she made a decision: *At Beltane, at Avebury, I shall take a lover.*

It was full daylight now, and a guitar strummed lazily somewhere. As with many of the customs of the royal household, Granddad Edwin, Wessex's first monarch for over a thousand years, had started it, decreeing that music be played from dawn on Law Tuesday till the end of Beltane Week, with the continuous mutter of vonnie-speakers shut down. She picked up the tune and sang a few lines of Warton's 'Everyone in Wessex is a fiddler and a fighter.' Singing was no hardship for Hettie, but balm to her troubled mind.

Siward trotted ahead of her down the carpeted wooden stairs to the warm dining room. On the sideboard was breakfast. He asked for creamy porridge and she took poached eggs, ham and toast for herself.

Sunlight streamed in through the thick glass windows and spilled over the age-glossed table. As she ate, she watched the beautiful Beltane light, the dream-processing surfacing in images. *The rape: what did that mean?* Somehow tied in to revenge, but then, everything involving her family's history was salted with vengeance. It would come; she trusted her subconscious to find the answer.

The music continued, a voice joining in.

A man may favour idleness and fishing by a stream,
Or rolling with his own particular girl
But if someone takes his pleasure from him, what is he to do?
But fight to make it right again, to win him back his world

She finished her food, wiping buttery toast through the bright yellow yolk. She walked with Siward through to the music room. She would have a few moments with him before the boy's tutor arrived. She nodded and smiled to the guitarist, patting the air to indicate he shouldn't stand for her. She didn't recognize the forty-something man, thick-set in dark woolens and leather waistcoat.

She looked down at the boy. 'Now,' she said softly, 'there can be no civilization without music.' She spoke as if to an adult, half to herself.

He watched his mother adoringly, curious of her tone. She caught the intelligence in his eyes, bright as a snake's. Again, she saw her man's body, torn open and broken on the amphibious craft as they brought the dead in from Chiltern. Would it never end, this grief?

She banished the image and sang along with the guitar for a verse.

If he just lies down and takes it, then the wicked man can win,
And rob the folk of all they have for joy
So it's watch your little freedoms, chaps, don't let 'em slip away
For there's always one who'll steal 'em from a careless girl or boy

Then she gathered little Siward up in her arms and kissed him and the tutor, punctual and enthusiastic, strode in and led him away.

Hettie turned back to the guitarist, who was taking a break. He stood and gave a short bow. 'Peter Mansfield, at your service, ma'am.' As his head bent down, the heavy, grey-streaked hair flopped aside to show purple scar tissue instead of an ear. Hettie blinked and sought the man's gaze as his head rose. 'Was that from Chiltern?' she asked.

Mansfield straightened up in military style. 'Yes, ma'am. And from Savernake, and Berkhamsted.'

She noticed then that two fingers were missing from his right hand, and there was a deep burn scar down the forearm. She whispered, 'You survived the first Berkhamsted battle?'

'I was one of the twenty, ma'am.'

She was silent for a moment. This man had fought alongside old King Marcus, her mother's first husband, before she was born. Then he had returned to service and faced new Pure Light brigades, even more brutal fanatics based in the Chilterns. Those were the PL that cut off the ear of the living enemy, because he is not listening to the Word of God, and the engagement known as Chiltern was where Siward had fallen, where Wessex had been sold out by an enemy within. 'You are a brave fighter, Peter Mansfield.'

'Thank you, ma'am.'

As Hettie walked away, picking up the old tune again, she knew her life had changed in that one conversation. Her father Peredur's death just yesterday, at the beginning of Beltane Week, left a gaping need for someone to rise to every occasion. Mother was stricken and weak, and Jervis was – well, Jervis. Someone had to play the responsible adult, and it had fallen to her. She pulled the robe round her breasts, smiling at the thought that, from now on she should perhaps finish dressing before greeting her people.

She returned to her room, showered and chose a silk blouse and a smart red day-suit. She undid her hair then coiled it up again, more neatly this time, and speared it in place on top of her head. When she was ready, she took a final look in her gilt-framed mirror.

Her deep-set violet eyes, her broad forehead had made Siward call her 'My elfshine girl.' She bit her lip, seeking in her reflection what she used to see in Siward's eyes.

She reined in her thoughts. Soon, she would see that admiration in the eyes of other beautiful young men. But now, for family, and the business of sovereignty. She picked up her diary and set off purposefully, out the door and along the landing.

She turned into the corridor with its row of windows that faced east over the quadrangle, the heart of the Palace like a traditional university. A young woman in green Palace work overalls was raking the gravel paths and singing. She thought she caught the tune of 'Beacons of Wessex,' which the tutor would have been singing with little Siward by way of a geography lesson. At the end of the corridor she went through a wooden arch. A big, dark door led to her mother's suite of rooms. Hettie noticed with grief-fresh eyes the brightly-painted hex sign, and remembered Ambrose decoding its runes for her when she was eight.

And now… She knocked softly, heard a faint 'Come in, Hettie,' and stepped into the old Queen's chambers.

Gwendoline was curled up on a leather chesterfield, looking doped. She wasn't actually that old, but aged by tragedy. The life of the Wodening clan didn't suit her, thought Hettie, though she'd buried one husband of that line and now needed to bury Peredur. She was dressed in black satin. She sat up a little unsteadily, brushed a wisp of greying blonde hair from her brow and held out her arms. The two women embraced in silent mourning.

After a few moments, Gwendoline patted her back, disengaged and wiped her eyes. She mustered a smile. *Brave mum*, thought Hettie, forcing herself to smile back as her mother poured tea for her.

She sat in the identical facing settee. Gwendoline leaned back and appraised her daughter. 'You're looking more beautiful than ever, Hettie.' If there was a subtext of *And when are you going to find yourself another man?* then she didn't voice it.

Hettie picked up her cup. She knew there was no point in beating about the bush; this needed to be done.

'Mum,' she took a sip of tea, 'the issue is, when to have Dad's funeral. I've had a think about it, and –'

Gwendoline cut her off with a gentle gesture of dismissal. 'I know darling. I feel terrible but I can still think. Perry would wish us to get his funeral over with, so everyone can get on with Beltane Week, which is, after all, the highlight of the Wessex calendar for most people. For sure, to delay the funeral might make for more dignity, but then it would cast a pall over Beltane, and could be considered to have insulted the King by its tardiness.'

She took a drink. Hettie thought she detected a fine tremor in her mother's long, beringed hand. But her voice was steady, and she had thought it through.

'What does that leave us?' She put the cup down and ticked fingers off. 'Beltane cannot be postponed. Big festivals are bigger than any of us, however royal. And,' she smiled humourlessly, 'he will get a good turnout, what with everyone being in Avebury for the week.'

She paused and nodded. 'We'll do it Thursday. It's a rush, but Friday's out, tomorrow's too soon, and Hanging Wednesday is inappropriate anyway. Agreed?'

'Dear mum, you can indeed still think. Let's get it moving for Thursday.'

'Hail Thunor,' said the older woman, raising her cup. Hettie echoed her brief prayer.

There was a hurried knock at the door, followed by the knocker striding straight in. Hettie turned in her seat to face the tall, heavily-muscled man. His blond hair was brushed back over a red, meaty face. He was dressed in the latest imported Pyrenean fashion of high-collared canary yellow silk jacket and trousers of rare, sleek grey synthetic. Hettie noted his eyebrows were plucked. 'Good morning, Jervis, you look as if you just took two hours to get ready.' She was cut short by a vivid thought, a voice in her head that added '*you traitor.' Shut up*, she told herself, but it was too late: her subconscious had spoken.

Jervis turned a cold stare on her. 'Your back-handed compliments are as pungent as ever, cunning sibling.' He turned to his mother and spoke words of condolence over the death of his stepfather, and then some other stuff which

Hettie was deaf to as she thought about what had just surfaced from some depth of her mind. *Is that really it? Can it be Jervis who sold us out?*

She paid attention when Gwendoline addressed her again in a voice hardened with anger.

'You're still with me on this, aren't you, Hettie? Wessex will never have a nuclear programme.'

She nodded, dumbstruck at the turn the conversation had taken while she was elsewhere.

Jervis said, 'Why not let Hendry go ahead, mother? What's the problem with a few carefully-sited and well-guarded power stations? We've learned a lot about safety since the meltdowns. Why not think again?'

'Jervis, I can't believe you've invited Hendry here, specially on the day after my Perry died.' Her voice cracked. Hettie moved to the other settee and put a protective arm around her mother's slim shoulders.

Jervis shook his head and ploughed on. 'You're backing the wrong side. This is progress. You'll come round.'

Gwendoline was weeping now, and Hettie flared up in fury. 'Oh just fuck off, Jervis. Have you no respect for our mother's grief?'

Gwendoline rallied, nodding her head. 'Yes, leave now, Jervis. We'll talk about this later.'

Jervis stood up, lips pursed, looking as if he'd something more to say. Instead he shook himself, turned and walked out, with a distinctly peeved flourish. He slammed the door behind him.

Hettie paid scant attention: her heart was pounding, her crazy thoughts back.

Her mother reached for a brown glass medicine bottle and let a number of drops fall in her teacup. She swigged the mixture and grimaced, then sighed.

'Jervis just flounced out.'

Hettie spoke abstractedly. 'Jervis has never flounced,

mum.'

'Well, he's started,' said Gwendoline, her eyelids fluttering.

Hettie squeezed her mother's shoulders. The older woman slumped a bit. Hettie whispered, 'Rest now, mum. I love you.'

She stroked her for a while, images streaming through her mind. The older woman began to slump more, and eventually curled up on the chesterfield. Hettie let herself out quietly.

Back in her rooms she summoned Alenor on the house acoustic network, big, old-fashioned electrics powered by the acreage of solar arrays on the roof. Her factotum, petite, with pale skin and a coiled mass of dark hair, took notes as Hettie gave instructions for the funeral.

'Lots of purple and black, the best horses, flowers, valknut flags...' She glanced at Alenor and almost said, 'Look it up if you have to,' but felt stupid when she noticed the older woman's hair. Alenor had wound it into the triple knot of mourning, copied from a lake sacrifice, reminding Hettie of the instruction she'd received at the older woman's knee. 'And a cattle sacrifice on Friday at the Sanctuary.'

Alenor passed on a message – a woman from Avebury called Thania Roberts, some relative of Ambrose's, wanted to see her.

Hettie smiled. 'Everyone in Avebury is related to Ambrose. I'll see her at eleven.'

She picked up her current book, Octavia Ward's 'The End of the Line,' and with a supreme effort of will, stopped the churning in her mind for long enough to read a few pages. She found that the best way for her to understand a dream was to set the process of questioning going then abruptly repress it until the insight burst through fully formed. She reviewed the history that had absorbed her for the last few days, about the breakdown of the civilization of the age of power. Ward had a personal, intimate style that Hettie found engaging:

> My great-great grandmother lived through the end of the Oil Age, in the early to mid Twenty-first Century. She never killed anyone, had two children, both of whom survived to adulthood and beyond. She lived to at least 115, after which point the family lost track of her. Her life was extraordinary for any age, but its circumstances were not unusual for that golden age of innocence. The climate meltdown and the end of the Oil Age happened so quickly, just as nanotechnology was promising a new technological era. As the waters rose, the tide of scientific innovation receded. In the decades that followed the collapse, two inventions, the rejuvenation drug antelosin and the subcutaneous nanosystems known as vonnies, took on an even greater significance. No other innovation was to have anything like their impact until the release by unknown agencies of the mysterious and dangerous so-called super-vonnies or becters.

As she read, she made notes. *Why do I love history and philosophy so much?* she asked herself. She had returned to study since… *since Siward had become a hero*, she said firmly in her head. *Make a coherent, heroic meaning out of it. Your man was exceptional, great-hearted, fearless – and naïvely trusting, as his name might suggest. He fought when others languished at home. He won a great victory for his people, but was killed by treachery, the extent of which is still not revealed or worked out. Never doubt the significance of his sacrifice.*

Then she heard diesel motors in the courtyard. Hendry and his crew had arrived. She went up to the window and saw the tight little man with his gaggle of experts behind him, all in the slickest suits and ties, like a retro fashion show. She heard the buzz of Jervis's servants escorting the guest up the stairs to his rooms in the west of the Palace.

The sound eclipsed the Beltane singing for a few moments. She watched them go by, and stood brooding on Hendry's endless attempts to get Wessex into the nuclear stakes. *Those maniacs with their passion for the nuclear poison. Let matter be, in it's May radiance, don't rip it open and burn it to power stupid consumer trash, like they used to do.*

At 11 o'clock precisely Alenor knocked, bringing her visitor to the door and leaving with an order for tea.

Hettie put her books aside to rise and greet the young woman. Thania was tall, strong-boned, red-haired and dressed in a black jacket and trousers. She made Hettie think of a tough pioneer-type and was wearing the Wessex Medal. Then, subtracting a year, she recognized her from when Peredur had presented the medal to her, here at the Palace. That in turn stirred memories of a coltish, adventurous girl, from her childhood visits to Asgard Hall, hunting squirrels in the badland ruins of Savernake Forest.

She stepped forward and took the other woman's hands warmly. 'Hello, Thania, long time etcetera!'

Thania smiled. 'Too long!'

Hettie motioned them to the leather armchairs each side of the empty grate. By design, little in the Palace was modern. Nodding towards Thania, she said, 'You're wearing your medal. I know the story, you know. You don't have to impress me.'

Thania turned serious. 'It's not that, Hettie. It's something more. I know about what happened at Chiltern. The medal is my protection in your household.'

Alenor came up with the tea, and placed it between them on the little table.

She left, Hettie gave the slightest nod, and Thania swallowed and began. 'You know I live at Asgard Hall. Yesterday, Uncle Ambrose was holding forth in the kitchen, you know what he's like, and he mentioned those bandits that were captured, with the call-signs for Pure Light arms dealers. The call signs go back to the identifiers used at the time of Chiltern. They're the lowest level of PL security, designed for an outsider with something to offer who's seeking first contact. They were all of a type: you take a double-barreled place name, such as Chipping Norton, and turn it backwards. 'Norton Chipping' would have got you the ear of the PL until last week, as long as you were calling from the right area. Anyway, just after Prince Siward had got the location of the Rejuve out of Logan, I was outside the signals room. I heard Prince Jervis talking on some kind of comms, and this weird phrase 'folly at Chiltern' came up twice. All the time I was sick, I couldn't get it out of my head.'

She looked beseechingly at Hettie. 'It's not 'folly at Chiltern,' you see. It's 'Foliat Chilton,' Chilton Foliat in reverse. It was the right PL call sign for the area, Hettie. Prince Jervis was talking to the enemy.'

In the silence Hettie heard the soft *fft* of an insect burning out on one of the electrostatic mosquito plates. She was breathing fast, her stomach churning, her heart pounding, her eyes closed tight. The meaning of her dream came to her, all at once, with a freight of final authority: *Images of nuclear poison means those associated with it are those responsible for the betrayal. The reference to vengeance is to your own. Your mother's rape refers to the fact that Jervis is not your brother, and may for all you know be guilty of rape himself, as some say he is. Jervis was, and is, the betrayer. I must destroy Jervis, before he destroys Wessex.*

Of course, killing Jervis would not be the end of her problems, far from it. For a start, she would be accused of dynastic assassination, of killing him to put herself next in line to the throne. And the Wessex throne was the last thing she wanted, but few would believe that. Few understood the burden of sovereignty.

She opened her eyes, gazing into some distance and said, 'Yes, you're right. You have my protection, Thania.' She faced the other woman, her thoughts racing, remembering what Ambrose had said to her years before: 'The common people have the benefit of the law. Royalty have to make do with marriage and assassination.'

Chapter 6: Law Tuesday: Alex

Alex's wind-up alarm woke him at six. He showered off stray wisps of dream – some sun-drenched holiday paradise of childhood, his mother's face how he always remembered her, blonde hair pulled back, wisps escaping in a breeze now frozen in a faded photograph. He dressed in t-shirt and shorts and made his way to the galley, where the chef's white hat was just visible through the steam. He shouted a greeting and his breakfast order over the music from the vonnie-speakers and sat down to eat while they ran the Kennet Channel. He went out on deck with the pot of strong Swiss tea and watched their approach to Thatcham Quays, a busy dock with hills rising behind covered in slabby prefab dwellings. The Quays still boasted a trophy of the 2090s, the gutted hulk of a Russian ZUBR class hovercraft, ancient even then, which Anderton's Christian brigade had used to try and land an invasion beachhead against the young Kingdom. In its shadow was a bonded warehouse where a solar-powered trimaran with the red and black stars of the Atlantic Collective was unloading sealed pallets stamped REJUVE under the eye of a bored Customs inspector. Hendry strode over, looking energetic with a towel over his shoulder.

Alex picked up his bag and stuck out his hand. 'Thanks for the ride, uncle. See you at Avebury. Happy Beltane.'

Hendry shook his hand and nodded, purse-lipped. 'See you at the weekend, Alex.'

Alex felt a wash of relief as he got off the boat. He had Wessex cobbles under his feet on a fine morning, and he was waving goodbye to Hendry, at least for a while. With an automatic gesture, he checked his short sword (better than nothing, at least in daylight, and not too far from towns) and crossed to the bus stop. He stood in the queue for Thor Wilson's old bus, loving the clotted-cream Wessex accents that surrounded him. The bus was ready to leave at seven, and Alex got a seat near the front, the battered interior filling up with festival-goers heading for Avebury.

They set off through head-high stands of early oil-hemp, first crop of the year, to their second stop, which was for fuel at the Woden's Wain compound on the outskirts of Newbury. A long-haired young boy peered around the Victory Brand Biodiesel sign that stuck out over the wide, high gateway of the farmyard. Thor Wilson, big and grim-looking in battered black leather trousers and jacket, carrying a short sword at his side, and, it was rumoured, a battleaxe under the driving seat, leaned out of the window and glared down at the boy. 'All right Boggart? Any news?'

The boy said 'Hi Thor,' shaking his head slowly, his eyes wide, his expression distant and distracted, 'Nothing that's not on your vonnies, it's well clear today.'

Thor said, 'Nothing for you, then Boggart,' leaned out and tipped the vonnied-up newsboy a silver coin then let the clutch in and drove into the muddy yard. The space was cluttered with pallets which served as seats for a dozen travellers amongst oil drums, acid carboys and curious children. Thor, well-known as no-one's fool, was careful to collect fares before spending any money on diesel, and called for volunteers to help hand-pump the fuel into the bus's fat tank.

The few places left were scrambled for. Alex gave up his seat to a harassed mother of two and squatted on his bag against the side of the bus. They got going again. His long legs were pushed against the side of the seat, over the edge of which spilled the two infants, presently squalling. The old vehicle skirted the mud-choked streets of Newbury's centre, abandoned since last year's floods. Thor turned the radio on, and they got a patch to the Marlborough transmitter.

Through the noise of the engine and the children, Alex caught snatches of the news. More on Peredur's death – the Palace were expected to announce a date for the funeral today. Cause of death was uncertain, and probably natural. Peredur was a hero, who had given his health in the defence of Wessex, etc etc.

Alex wondered idly what they knew, and what they were hiding, over in the Palace. Some dynastic struggle, maybe, even though the Percevals and Wodenings were supposed to be elected royalty, chosen by all Full Citizens of Wessex.

The rest of the news concerned the border patrol treaty with Shemeld Protectorate and the capture of a troupe of bandits, who were in possession of real guns. Not airguns with diesel pellets, but genuine ballistic bullets. The newscaster evinced concern about this new development.

Alex mused about where bandits lived. In an overcrowded world such as Wessex, it was hard to believe that someone didn't know every square foot of land. Not for the first time, it occurred to him that the bandits must be people who lived amongst everyone else. Maybe there are bandit villages, he thought, where they all go out raiding after dark.

Ambrose had once said to him, 'Law is a precarious thing in a stressed society.' And he should know. Today, Law Tuesday, Ambrose would be presiding over the Beltane Assizes in the great courthouse at Marlborough. Alex was on his way to sit in the public gallery and watch him at work, then have lunch with his old mentor.

It was a radiant day in the high hills. They rode through fields of supermaize, gigantic young buds shimmering in the sun. Dark towers of hop bines shone over on Windmill Hill and windmills turned along the land's ridge. All the solid brick houses they saw along the way had solar roof panels and rainwater tanks. He thought again of how he was qualified in something almost completely useless in Wessex. What was he going to do, to avoid working for Hendry? The only thing he could think of was to return to Shemeld Protectorate, where he'd done a metallurgy placement in Sheffield's special steel furnaces, but it felt like a retreat.

It was getting hot on the crowded bus now. They were toiling up the old A4 past the fenced-in Royal enclave that was all that remained of Savernake Forest, and everyone was swaying into each other. Some people were loosening up, others looking irritable. Alex noticed quite a few swords and knives, but most people had the amused tolerance of travelers sweetened by Beltane, the benign undertow of excitement about the festival and beautiful Avebury.

Alex thought of Maira, and how he would probably never see her again, despite what she had said. He scanned the women on the bus. The young mother he'd given his seat to had relaxed now. She was brushing out her long black hair, and her red hemp dress contrasted nicely with her deep brown skin. Then there was a big, blonde girl of whom all he could see was her ample thighs. Pink and naked, they suggested sex, without really being Alex's particular kind of turn-on. Up the front by the driver he could just make out an animated head of red hair, but couldn't see her face or figure.

He sighed, looking forward to the Sanctuary ritual, where last year he had ended up in a crazed, delicious romp and rut with at least two of the priestesses. *Roll on Friday!* he thought, and smiled. He looked around as they passed the raw steel tanks of the biomass fermenters on Forest Hill. A father was scaring a small boy. 'Y' see those, son. Well, really bad people get put in there, and they make fuel out of 'em.'

Then he heard the children laughing behind his head. He turned round to see a short, wiry man in a black leather jerkin and a slender young woman in an elaborate, flouncy black frock crouching in the aisle between the rows of seats. They were animating large, flamboyant glove puppets – a black birdlike figure with an enormous beak and a pink, sheep-faced man. With the shock of remembering something from long ago, he recognized the children's story of Old Crow, the wise one who knows all the secrets of the world, but will not tell them, because he's so mean. People go to him, and he tricks them and leaves them to die. Then he disappears, leaving his magic pot, but no-one can get the pot to produce anything, except one drunk, who can always get it to produce booze.

Alex was always intrigued by this story, the way that Old Crow said things nobody could explain, such as his catchphrase 'He's not a child, he's an Englishman!' There it was – he heard this version of Old Crow say it!

The masque ended, with Old Crow cackling like a maniac and the sheep-man falling over dead. The children were round-eyed with amused puzzlement when the mummers stood up and started going round the bus for coins. Thor watched in his rear-view mirror, no doubt calculating his cut of the take.

Idly, Alex wondered where the story of Old Crow came from. He thought of asking Ambrose and an image swam up from childhood memory – Ambrose in an absurd felt hat that had looked like a tower to Alex's young eyes, dandling him on his knee and playing a set of Northumbrian pipes, the swirling, out-at-sea music all mixed up with the goatskin-smell of the instrument. It was the day he never went home again, the day he realised his mother wouldn't be coming home. Ambrose's crazy household had taken the boy in, and the ageless man had sponsored Alex in quite a different way to Hendry's remote paternalism.

A bump brought Alex back to the external world. The bus was coming into the edges of Marlborough, through a squatter camp, long since permanent, on some brownfield leftover from the Age of Oil. Grubby, thin, sunburned children ran, tussled and begged alongside the bus. Behind them, stood well-maintained shacks of reclaimed landfill materials, their bright synthetic colours faded by decades of sun.

The houses on this row had small plots of land, big enough for a vegetable garden. Some of them were well-tended, with proud new green shoots. A couple of them had been converted into chicken runs with walls of rewoven waste plastics. A few were unkempt, choked with junk and weeds.

They pulled into Marlborough High Street, up the wide, military road lined with a graduated series of shops. At the outer edge of town, there were little markets with no electric light where recycled goods were sold for a few pence. Two hundred yards along, they saw new clothing shops, where there was less filth and rubbish clogging the gutters. By the time they reached the bustling heart of Wessex's capital, the shops were the consumer cream of the land – posh outfitters, glittering hardware stores, radiant jewelers, imported food shops and restaurants with gleaming gene-probes hanging over the vegetables so customers could assure themselves of their suitability and places that sold just ornaments and hard-to-categorize gewgaws. The bus waited, negotiating pedestrians who were ambling across the road. Alex watched a brightly-dressed middle-aged couple emerge from a gadget shop carrying boxes and laughing. *Even poor Wessex has a few people who buy stuff other people don't even know the use of.*

Thor pulled the bus over by the town centre stop, turned and scowled at his passengers. There was a ragged cheer, led by three uniformed conscripts who'd been drinking beer on the back seat. Thor opened the doors, and a few people squeezed out down the aisle. Alex got off, and was stretching his cramps out when the army boys rolled off, singing and waving bottles. At this range, he could see how poorly made and badly patched their green uniforms were. Wessex kept a sizable standing army largely to absorb the energy of unemployed young males, a route to full Citizenship many in the Guest Camps took. Ballistic weapons turning up in other hands meant that there were better-equipped militias out there, and closer to home than a Wessexer liked to think.

Alex shouldered his pack and strode over the main street, clean here and smelling of the sweet grease of biodiesel exhausts. The sun was shining above the roofline. He squeezed through the morning's crowd, down Kennet Passage to the grounds of the Law Courts. He was a bit early, the Assizes kicked off at nine. Ambrose would be busy with pleas, supplicants and deals, and wouldn't want social obligations as well. Alex stood for a moment in the elegant square, casting around for the tea stand he remembered from his last time in town. There he was, the wizened old tea seller with the little cap, his stall brightly-plastered with adverts for drinks and, oddly, one for generator parts. He strolled over.

The old man brightened at the approach of a customer and poured a clay mug of Swiss. Alex smiled as he dug for coins and took the drink. The old boy seemed to have recognized him. All of a sudden, Alex felt as if he really belonged in Marlborough, and wondered if he could ever leave his native land.

'Alright son?' asked the old man, smiling.

'Absolutely,' said Alex. 'You seen the Chief Justice yet?'

'Oh yeah, the old boy's in there, doing his Chief Justice

magic, I expect.' The old man's gravelly voice ended on a cough.

Alex drank his tea and watched the workers going into the court, sweeping the square, pressing into the offices around the administrative heart of Wessex. At five to nine by the great solar disk of the court clock, Alex handed his cup back and crossed the square to the Courthouse.

The steps up the front resumed the self-importance of all such buildings. The frontage had a more specific message, spelled out in blond wood, red wood and Portland marble. The steps led up to a deep portico like a cloister, faced with a series of square, carved yellow oaken posts. The east-facing aspect gave deep shafts of light and shadow that played upon the wall behind the colonnade, where a flat stone façade showed embedded cross-beams of red heart-yew. None of these geometrical patterns was the same as the next, because they formed a series of inscriptions, encoded in entwined runes. Ambrose had decoded it all for him a few years before. 'Three Ages' magazine called it 'the best example anywhere of neo-traditionalist style.' Ambrose called it, less respectfully, 'lavish ancestral.'

Inside, it was pleasantly cool, the whole floor an expanse of marble, looted and recycled from sunken London. The uniformed doorman showed a flicker of recognition, and nodded, acknowledging that Alex knew which way to go. The judges' chambers were at the back of the building, through a long corridor lined with portraits and smelling of beeswax polish.

Alex stopped outside the oak door to the judges' chambers and listened. He heard soft singing from within. He knocked. 'Come,' called a strong voice.

Ambrose was sitting at a large desk, facing the bay window that looked out onto a tiny garden at the rear of the courthouse.

He turned and boomed, 'Alex, my boy!' in a mountainous voice. His weathered face had a big, fat nose, his small, piercing dark eyes hid in a nest of wrinkles, his greyed black hair was brushed back in a lion's mane and worn down to his broad shoulders. This morning, he wore the ritual scarlet of a law-lord, and his goatee beard was combed neatly, rather than plaited into two forks, as usual. It was Law Tuesday, and the cases he would be hearing could be very serious. As a youth, Alex realised that he had 'got' Ambrose when he'd said to him, 'You have to dress right to hang people, or they get insulted.'

He dumped his pack on the floor and embraced the old man. 'Happy Beltane, Ambrose.'

The older man looked him in the eyes for a few seconds. 'You need to talk to me, dear boy. As for now, leave your bag here, and tell me the superficial stuff. We'll get into the rest later.'

Alex told Ambrose of his trip with Hendry, which just about filled the time before the court usher came and knocked on the door, summoning the Chief Justice. As he swept out, he said, 'Bugger off into the public bit, Alex, or people will talk.'

Alex wound his way back to the front rotunda and up the shallow stairs to the public gallery. He arrived just as Ambrose walked to the bench, resplendent in his scarlet robes.

'Court will rise for the Chief Justice,' shouted the usher, and everyone complied.

The usher continued. 'The Court will hear any new Laws to be spoken by the Chief Justice.' This phase of the proceedings was a vestige of a time when the Law-Speaker had had to make a few announcements every Beltane, things were changing so fast in the way Wessex did things. Not so now; Ambrose declined, as he had for most of the thirty years of his role, the privilege of speaking a new law.

There was nothing grand about the courtroom itself. Ambrose sat at a bench only a few inches higher than the rest of the seats, around and to the sides of the central table. An enamel coat of arms of Wessex, the wolf, goat and wildcat, with the Valknut, an escutcheon of three linked triangles, adorned the front of Ambrose's bench, and the flag of the Perceval-Wodenings hung above, on the wall behind. And so the regular court began, which was far from regular today. The Chief Justice was expected to pick a selection of cases that would provide opportunities for interesting precedent law. Ambrose, when out of judge's robes and being irreverent, had described Beltane Assizes as 'the Grand National of the court year.'

The first defendant was a short, muscular man, with eyes like a dead fish, and a sour, downturned mouth. Playing a guessing game to occupy himself, Alex had him as a rapist.

The defendant's history was read out by the court usher. Simon Jones had escaped from Kingston Island, the long-term prison for sex offenders, colloquially known as Nonce Island. Jones was a serial offender, who had been convicted of rape twice, including that of a thirteen-year old girl. Kingston Island was regarded as a secure enough facility to let incurable sex offenders live out their days. It was an easy exile, if you could defend yourself against the predations of your fellow inmates, and it was extremely rare that anyone went to the trouble of escaping; or rather, that anyone on the mainland ever learned of it.

'How did you get to Purbeck?' asked Ambrose.

'I swam, y'r honour,' said the short man, looking down at the floor.

'And why did you go to such effort?'

'Objection, my client should surely not have to explain his motivations for escaping?'

Ambrose looked towards the rapist's counsel. 'Mr Tarbuck, Mr Jones has chosen to present himself at this rare Assizes in order to argue a particular slant on his sentence. In law, he has no recourse other than the court admit his sentence was passed in a climate of poor understanding of his predicament. Does it not seem to you that Mr Jones can only temper the severity of his crime by reference to its and his own circumstances?'

'Yes, Your Honour.' Jones's counsel dipped his head and sat down.

'So, Mr Jones, I repeat my question: What motivated you to swim from Kingston to the mainland?'

'They're mad, Your Honour, terrible people you, pardon, this court, put me with.'

'Worse than a rapist, Mr Jones?'

Jones hung his head.

'Your welfare as such is no concern of this court, Mr Jones. You forfeited the care of this community when you did such thoughtless damage to the life of a young woman.'

Ambrose drew a breath. 'You are declared an outcast and an outlaw, beyond the protection of the Kingdom. You will be injected with a dedicated von Neumann seed which at all times will transmit your location on the NeighbourNet. Then you will be taken to Purbeck shore, where you will be given lunch. You will have the choice of either swimming back to Kingston Island or taking your chances on the mainland with the fully-informed relatives of your victims.'

He smacked the gavel smartly. 'Next case.'

This plaintiff was a smallholder whose neighbour's goat had escaped into his garden and eaten some of his crops before the farmer had shot the animal dead with a crossbow. The plaintiff, Mr Stone, was a gigantic man with a tough, uncompromising face and a woollen overcoat slung over his arm. The defendant, Mr Young, was mild-looking and ill-nourished, in patched clothes. It turned out that after Stone had shot Young's goat he had thrown most of the dead animal back over their fence. That night, Young had poured diesel over the fence and set fire to Stone's crops. Stone had managed to put the fire out.

Ambrose asked, 'What did you do with the rest of the goat, Mr Stone?'

The plaintiff looked embarrassed and glanced towards his counsel. 'I would like the answer to come from you, Mr Stone' said Ambrose.

Stone pursed his lips. 'I put it between my land and his.'

Young shot up and shouted, 'He stuck Polly's head on a pole and set her facing my house, the bastard!'

'Calm yourself, Mr Young. We are getting to the facts of the case here. Mr Young, how many livestock animals do you graze?'

'Your Honour, I have, or had, only Polly and a few chickens. I am a seasonal worker.'

Ambrose turned to the plaintiff. 'Mr Stone, did it never occur to you that your reaction to the depredations of Mr Young's goat were perhaps excessive?'

'My crop is my livelihood, Your Honour.'

'Quite so, Mr Stone. And what kind and size of crop did you rescue to license for sale at the Avebury festivities this week?'

Stone's eyes narrowed, then he puffed himself up, the proud farmer. 'About twenty pounds of hemp bud, Your Honour.'

'Misters Stone and Young, you will stand for my judgment. Mr Young, you will have to be more careful. The loss of your goat is punishment enough. Mr Stone, you will have to learn to control your temper. I award costs for this court against you, for having brought an unnecessary and malicious prosecution. You will deliver ten pounds of your most profitable crop, under seal of the Avebury magistrate, to the Poor Relief stall at the Friday market, to be sold for relief of the indigent in Beltane Week.' The gavel rapped. 'The court will recess for lunch.'

Alex met Ambrose round the front of the Courthouse. Across the square in the far corner was a tiny pub, the King Edwin. They headed there, as they had many times before. They ducked through the low doorway into a bright room hung with long mirrors and polished brass. A bluff middle aged man in shirtsleeves, a shiny steel gene-probe clipped to his waistcoat pocket declaring his pride in the pub's food, presided over a busy bar, just filling up with lunchtime court workers. He looked across at Ambrose and said pleasantly, 'Clear the best table, here comes the Hanging Judge.'

Ambrose strode past the bar with an airy 'Your turn one day, Gregory!'

They sat down at an alcove table, a couple of lawyers behind them talking loudly and drinking cocaf from little silver cups. One of them, middle aged with a red face, waved at Gregory and called out, 'My friend here looks as if he's running out of Rejuve, you couldn't sell us a month could you?'

Gregory spoke askance, his round face a study in perfectly tuned contempt. 'I'm not running a nano-pharm here squire, you'll only find proper mollycules that behave themselves in my pub.' He handed menus over to Ambrose and Alex.

'What are you going to poison an old man with today, then?' said Ambrose.

'I can recommend the pork steak, and the chicken. Will you be lining anyone up to hang this afternoon, Chief?'

'I sincerely hope not, unless it's your chef, Gregory. I'll just have the leek soup today, and two pints of best.'

The landlord nodded. Alex ordered the chicken, remembering Ambrose eating much more at lunch.

The soup arrived. Ambrose was morose, even when Alex praised him. 'I love watching your work on Law Tuesday.'

'Yes, but I wonder how relevant it is today. Look at all the people out there in squatter camps, almost as many as there were in King Edwin's day, long before you were born.'

He took a mouthful of greenish soup and continued.

'Encouraging the people back to our old religion was a terrific shot in the arm for Wessex, hence Shemeld's tribute when he followed suit in Sheffield. It was perfect for an era of low material expectations, it was the right decision spiritually, and it worked, as well as any set of ideas could at the time.'

Ambrose took a drink, his eyes hooded. 'And that's just the barefaced monetary aspect of it. Given a half-decent rate of economic growth, curse that filthy old notion, everyone would be cheering and Wessex would be half way to paradise.' He stirred his soup. 'And if we had just a third of the population, it would be even better. Look at the bandit gangs; some of it's driven by the Pure Light, but even they and their lies wouldn't have half a chance if we could feed our own people better. And if you can't feed people, they turn to something else they believe can. The Pure Light cobbled together a religion which acted as a beacon of hate and vengeance for the dispossessed.'

He put down his spoon. 'There is always a wolf in the woods. Maybe we should have spent more on the people in the squatter camps, cut back on something else, back in the 'twenties, but how long would that goodwill have lasted?' He took another desultory mouthful of soup and frowned. 'You heard about those bandits with proper guns we captured yesterday?'

Alex nodded.

'Know who sold them the guns? The Pure Light. The

bandits had code signs for PL contacts going back two years. Two years, Alex. Since Chiltern, our enemies have been infiltrating here, trying to bring us down from within.' He shook his head, an old man sorrowful at the ways of the world. He pushed his plate aside. Alex finished his chicken, which was good, and washed it down with the rest of his beer, wondering at the old man's lack of appetite. He'd always seemed inexhaustibly healthy, even now when he must be well over a hundred.

Ambrose spoke again. 'Our culture, like all cultures, is on a spectrum, with civilization at one end and barbarism at the other. I and a few others are holding up a dyke against the waters. We're in decline, young Alex. Our dream is dying.' He stood up, signalling Gregory to put the meal on his tab.

Back at chambers, Ambrose slumped in his big chair.

'As for you, dear boy, I expect you want me to say something to save you from the nightmare of working for Hendry. Well, I've nothing to say. You have to make your own way in life, make your own mistakes. As you can see, I'm nearly finished with this life.'

'Don't talk like that, Ambrose!'

'How should I talk, Alex? The world is not fair or trustworthy; matter is a cloak for a blind fire-giant, and the god of mischief makes his home in the hearts of men…'

The old man slumped even lower, his breathing laboured.

Alex dived forward. 'Oh fuck, Ambrose, don't do this.' Ambrose's face was grey, his breathing shallow, his eyes flickering behind closed lids. Alex searched the pockets of the old man's waistcoat and came up with a brown glass bottle, the label faded to illegibility. He tipped some blue capsules out onto his palm. There was no brand on them.

Ambrose stirred with a groan and reached for them. 'It's Rejuve, dear boy, give it to me.' He dry-swallowed two of the pills as Alex looked round and found a glass of water. The old man revived a little.

Alex still had the pills in his hand. He waited until Ambrose was sitting upright again, with some colour back in this face.

'This isn't Rejuve. What is it?'

'It's generic antelosin. I ran out of the stuff we captured. This seems to be working.' His eyes wouldn't fix properly on Alex, as if he was drunk.

'Ambrose, you're not well, and I bet it's because of these cheap drugs. Let me get you some decent Rejuve. I'm getting a job, and I'll be working with people who can get anything.' He tailed off into the nightmare world of his own employment prospects. He was about to speak again when the usher knocked to start the afternoon session.

This was the big case. The man who was being led into the dock was distinguished by being the only one of five men not to be in Wessex Constabulary blue. His tailored clothes were torn, his face was bruised and scarred, his eyes dark and angry, and the way he pushed back when his escort moved him along told you just how he got some of that damage.

'Diamond Head' Morningstar had been recaptured after his previous appeal had failed and he had escaped from Marlborough Prison. He and his six companions had been convicted of killing three people in the course of a robbery, plus a Wessex Constable who tried to stop them. The other gang members had been shot dead in the gun battle leading to Morningstar's capture. Diamond Head was something of a mythic figure, a bugaboo to scare children with.

He had admirers too. Whilst most of the stories that criss-crossed Wessex on the overlapping patchwork of NeighbourNet denounced him as a violent thief, there were some that lauded him as a swashbuckling hero. Alex imagined the appeal of such an idea to unemployed youths in the squatter camps, prime recruitment zones for bandit gangs.

Morningstar insisted that his appearance today was a fresh appeal. This was irregular, and would have taken months, if it was granted court time at all, any other time of the year. Ambrose had picked the case, because he wanted to show exceptional even-handedness by allowing Morningstar's appeal at the Beltane Assizes.

He addressed the prisoner. 'You are very lucky to be standing in front of this court, and not rotting in the ground, Mr Morningstar. What do you have to say for yourself?'

Morningstar stood tall and faced the Chief Justice. His hands were cuffed, and he shook a strand of dark hair out of his face. He spoke in a deep, steady voice.

'Nothing regarding the law, Chief Justice. I have little doubt that I shall hang, and that, by your heathen values, is what I deserve. I want to say that you built your fine Wessex on the ruins of a Christian society where there was no death penalty. So I stand here to curse you and yours, your failed heathen society deserves to die. Death to Wessex!'

The court was shocked into silence. Ambrose took a few seconds to answer, in a calm voice. 'This is not the first time I have heard a merciless murderer call on the name of gentle Jesus in his defence. I am glad you stand before me today, Mr Morningstar, because your behaviour demonstrates what a sham your newly-adopted faith is. By your callous multiple murders you deprived yourself even of the honourable sentence of outlawry.' Ambrose picked up the square of black cloth that lay on the bench and placed it carefully over his wig, one of the corners drooping forwards. When he spoke again, his manner was even more grave. 'You will be taken to Marlborough Prison, and there, at six o'clock tomorrow morning, you will be hanged from the neck until you are dead.' The gavel rapped. The gaolers took the struggling Morningstar down into the cells.

Ambrose faced the court. His voice was steady, but his face was pale again, and the effort seemed to cost him pain. 'Court will adjourn for today. Gods prosper Wessex!'

The Chief Justice rose, and his court with him. Alex wound back the way he'd come in, round to the rotunda and out the front to wait for Ambrose, who was forswearing his student-driven biodiesel car for this special day, joining the court officials.

The minibus they shared was round at the front of the court. Another five minutes passed, various Court workers boarding, then Ambrose emerged from the main entrance. Alex thought he had a little more colour in his face. All were aboard now, and the bus set off towards Avebury.

Most of the Court workers were chatting. Two junior clerks had slung their jackets over the back of their seats, opened bottles of beer and were making party plans for Beltane Week. Ambrose slumped silent in his seat behind the driver.

Alex gazed out of the window at the hills in warm, late afternoon sunshine. They climbed west, through the circle of squatter camps round Marlborough, then a bit north onto the Downs Road. They dropped down into the megalithic splendour of Avebury town, the whole area preserved as a ritual site for over half a century now. Everyone except Ambrose and Alex got off outside the Red Lion in the centre of the circle. The minibus continued on up the north Downs road, stands of hemp, wheat and barley dark-green in the evening light, then turned sideways on to the sun, so they had to shade their eyes. They crested the first rise and the roofs of Asgard Hall came into view, trapezoids of hemp-thatched gables, golden straw-coloured in the slanting light. Then the walls of the house came into view, half of a two-story hexagon of Purbeck stone, soft grey divided up by columns of dark oak.

The bus let them off by the main entrance, a square portico of weathered, knotty beams. A flag snapped in the evening breeze, an equal-limbed vertical red cross on a white ground, with the Valknut in blue. Ambrose dismounted with barely a gruff 'thanks' to the driver, walked quickly up the steps and let himself in. Alex followed, into the rectangular entrance hall lined with blond wood, rooms and a staircase branching off the sides.

Directly across the hall, through windows that brought in a western light, he could see the roundhouse, the heart of Asgard Hall, around which the other six sections of the great house were built. This opulence was a remnant of the young Ambrose's vast wealth, derived mostly from his popular writings, but partly in gift from Edwin when the King had carved up Church of England lands. Looking out into the soft sundown, Alex was caught by an image of his mother, as if she smiled at him in the sunlight.

He looked round from the view to see Ambrose lurch against one of the wooden pillars. He rushed up and got his arm around him, supporting the old man towards the stairs. He repeated his offer of finding a source of proper Rejuve, anything to preserve this beloved life.

Ambrose stopped and stood leaning against the wall at the foot of the stairs, his breathing laboured. Somberly, he said 'It's not a question of money or contacts. I won't use licensed Rejuve, because it is all supplied through PL fundraisers now. If I buy that stuff, I'm supplying the enemy.'

Ambrose coughed and there was a dripping sound. Alex looked on in horror as bright spots of blood speckled the pale wood floor.

Chapter 7: Becter-Space

Alenor, wiry and light-footed, crossed to the wardrobe and took a shawl, tying it sarong-style above her breasts. She bundled up her long, dark hair, smiled at the sleeping shape of the man sprawled across the rumpled bed, then stepped out along the landing. Rainbow light from the stained glass eastern window patterned the dusty air as she trod barefoot down the old, creaky wooden stairs, and round the hallway to the kitchen. She knew this house so well, knew it as her own home for more than half of all her years. Nothing changed here. Nothing that mattered, anyway; the solid substance of her long life, the impact of the bright world on her flesh, was vivid every day.

She stepped into the walk-in pantry, terracotta tiles cold and smooth underfoot. A large, fluffy ginger and white cat slipped in and ran between her naked legs, erect tail sending shivers up her thighs. She lifted the thick earthenware lid of the cheese cooler, cut a chunk of rind off the fatty, white wedge. She put it in an old terracotta saucer with a splash of milk from the bottom of the ladle, the saucer made by her at school, in her tenth spring, in the boredom of the village's tiny circle of life; another world, long since gone. She stroked the cat's long, scruffy fur as it ate, gathering its furry beast essence to her. Its purrs were short and abrupt with the pressure of her hand as she whispered a small prayer of thanks for the gift of life.

She took the milk, cheese and bread to the kitchen table. She stood and waited for the water to boil, gazing out of the window. That was west, the direction of Avebury, where the lovely riot of Beltane was just getting going. Suddenly full of a giant feeling, she began to sing 'Avebury the Heart,' that song so full of religious yearning.

She calls us on, she calls us on, she calls us on to birth
In the sweetest, softest flesh, in the sacred joyous earth

She made the tea and carried the tray of breakfast up the stairs, still singing.

Over and over and ever and on
She calls us on, she calls us to birth
I don't want to leave, and to here I'll return
In the softest flesh, in the sweetest earth

Late morning, she was back in the kitchen helping peel gigantic potatams for lunch and being ribbed by the garrulous cook, forty years her junior but looking every one of her sixty years. Her massive hands stripped a boiled leg of goat with practised ease as she elaborated. 'You've been scarfing bleedin' Rejuve from somewhere, look at you showing off your young stud before I'd had me breakfast.' She looked grim but Alenor knew there was no disapproval in Gemma's words, only an attempt to pump her for salacious details. She was opening her mouth in rejoinder when little Siward ran in from play, scouting for anything to eat right now.

Gemma smiled indulgently. 'Hello love, it's lunch in an hour and I wouldn't want to draw down your mum's disapproval, but I think some apple chips would be all right.' She hefted a jar down from the big shelves and handed it to Siward, motioning the boy to sit down. Siward joined Alenor on the wooden bench, smiling and pushing against her. She put her arm round his shoulders, broad for such a young lad. He'll be big like his father, she thought.

'I bet you'd like to hear some tales about the Old World.' Siward nodded, his mouth full of dried apple. Alenor let her memory bring back the TV set they'd had in the old Palace when she first came to live there, just after most of the factories had closed but you could still get a second hand set and they still bothered transmitting programmes from Marlborough. 'You used to be able to switch on the TV any time of the day and night and there's be some programme on.'

'Like what?'

'Oh, football, the Wessex Cup, news, old travel shows from the Oil Age, gardening shows, religious programmes with lovely rituals at Avebury, even dramas with real actors and wonderful old films.'

'When did they stop?

''2100 I think. Not enough people had sets any more, you couldn't get new ones or spares, the satellites wore out or fell, and King Edwin started a big drive to help the people in the Displaced Persons camps.'

'That was when everyone was a Citizen?'

'That's right – everyone had the same rights in law. Then there were too many people coming into Wessex from other countries where they hadn't managed so well after the floods and there was no land for them, so they went to live in what we now call Guest Camps.' Alenor thought back to her first husband, clever, gentle Andrew, and how he'd fought and schemed his way out of the camp. She'd always had time for those who by bad luck had ended up in those grim enclosures for years, even to die there. She changed the subject. 'You know how NeighbourNet started?'

Siward had probably heard her tell some version of the story before, but he shook his head. 'Well, it was after the floods in 2109, when half the people in Wessex got bitten by mosquitoes with vonnie-seeds in their stomachs from other people they'd bitten. So all of a sudden nearly everyone had vonnies. Some got sick and even died, but among those who survived, some started noticing that they could hear radio programmes or sometimes even feel what each other was feeling.'

'Is that when you got your vonnies, Alenor?'

She started a little, wondering again at how she'd managed to keep her becter tolerance secret for so long. 'Yes, I got bitten and was fine.' She'd been a well-Rejuved sixty when the bec-plagues came, when Rejuve was still plentiful and cheap enough for a household manager to afford. She had been honoured by what she came to think of as the becter-oversoul, an intelligence that must have emerged from the vast spaces of becter quantum processing,; she, Alenor, had been chosen to receive the most powerful seeds of all in the saliva of a mosquito. An exquisite alien soul had come to live under her skin, and granted her life for as long as she wanted it, analyzing what the Rejuve drug was doing to her body and mimicking it perfectly, so that she never had to take another capsule.

Siward was smiling. 'Vonnies – funny word!'

She smiled back. 'Snappier than 'subcutaneous von Neumann nano-transceivers' though! Anyway, some people were able to tolerate more powerful vonnies than others, and that meant they could do all sorts of things, such as pick up signals and send them out again. My Andrew, he was like that. They used to call him 'mozzie-boy' in the pub and ask him to stand by the speakers to improve NeighbourNet reception. So NeighbourNet just grew, as a replacement for radio and TV news and entertainment.'

She remembered sad times with Andrew towards the end, the dementia eating up his mind, the obsession with mosquitoes and flies, the repetitive hand-washing, the way he sprayed everything with this stinking juice he boiled up from cigarette ends he collected in the pub.

Siward was restless, kicking his legs under the bench. 'Tell me about great-granddad Edwin and the gold, Alenor.'

'Ah, now that's a good story, and I got it from an eye-witness, Jeremy Wilde, who was nine years old when young Prince Edwin came to Thatcham.' Alenor didn't mention how she'd got the story; early on in their reign she'd been deeply curious about the Wodenings and had trawled the informal Net of becter-tolerants, crossloading every eye-witness account of them she could find.

'That was before it was Thatcham Quays,' she said, 'when it was just plain Thatcham, with the floods right up to little Jeremy's back garden. He was in bed when the noise started, and he looked out of his window to see Edwin's barges pulling into Thatcham.'

'So how come they could just take the gold?' asked Siward.

Alenor drew a breath, marshalling her story.

'It turned out that the head of the Bank of England, Mr Chalmers, was loyal to your great-granddad, and was eager for them to get the gold out of the flooded Bank vaults before someone else did.' Alenor remembered the crossload she'd got of Chalmers' memories of meeting the young Prince. With a banker's instinct, Chalmers had favoured the Wessex faction in the House of Windsor as the best bet for the government of whatever emerged from the collapse of Britain. With impeccable logic, it therefore followed that he must go and pledge all the Bank's gold to the proposed new Crown of Wessex. He'd turned up at Windsor, in the dead of night, after demanding audience with the young Prince. Edwin had asked him how much the gold was worth. This was Chalmers' moment. 'It's value in old pounds, Sire, is of little account. It is better thought of as more than enough to buy the whole of Wessex, in that land's present lamentable state, and to re-issue that tarnished value as bright, new coin.'

Alenor continued. 'Young Edwin – because he wasn't King yet – took thirty men in helicopters, but many of them were killed as soon as they arrived, shot out of the sky by the forces of Colonel Anderton, one of the fanatics who founded the Pure Light. So they were in a very sticky situation, a third of their number killed already and the rest of them under fire in the fortress walls of the Bank of England. It looked as if they'd left the transfer of the gold to Wessex a little late, though and given their enemies a chance to ambush them. Those enemies were well-equipped and well-organised, up to a point, but they hadn't the firepower to storm the Bank directly. So, either they were bandit opportunists, ignorant of any plans to strip out the Bank's gold or, much worse, a break-away military force, in other words, someone known to Edwin and his CO, Colonel Geddes. Did they know of the plan to transfer the gold, and how would they have found out? No-one knew the answers to those questions until we heard the name Pure Light a few years later.

'Anyway, they needed a new plan, and fast. Prince Edwin located the enemy's command post, in one of the tallest buildings in the city, and sent a team of men to set charges under the buttressing struts. They brought the building down, made quite a splash they say, escaped in the confusion in Mr Chalmers's boats and docked at Thatcham with the gold. Jeremy said it was in open steel pallets held down with webbing straps and covered only by rough old tarpaulins. You could see the gleam of the yellow metal in the light of the old fluorescents. The Upper Kennet channel was blocked, the last dredger abandoned for lack of fuel, and they had to unload there. Jeremy perched on the remains of a garden wall that served as a bulwark and watched the engineers get the little dockside crane hooked onto one of the pallets and start to lift it. The crane lurched and threatened to tilt over, and Colonel Geddes had the harbourmaster brought before her, in his nightgown and somewhat drunk, to get them a bigger crane. She said to him, 'Keep this secret, man, it's about the security of

Wessex.' The Colonel was a clever woman, and understood that the news would be all over the Kennet valley by breakfast, which could only be good for the reputation of herself and her commander, Prince Edwin, the King-Unelect.

'Well, the dock was soon alive with would-be helpers and onlookers as the pubs emptied and more children escaped their bedrooms. Edwin and his tired troops had the whole of Thatcham as an audience while they loaded the gold onto army trucks. When the loading was done, and they were ready to set off for Marlborough, Edwin mounted the back of the amphibian at the rearguard and raised his hands. People nudged each other into silence. They waited for him to speak, looking up at their tall young Prince in his dirty fatigues, a stray hank of blond hair stuck to his brow.

''Come and see me at Avebury, my friends! And I swear I'll share out the booty we have won today. Gods prosper Wessex!'

'The way Jeremy tells it, there was a pause of about two seconds, then a swelling roar of approval. Judging this to be the right time, Edwin signalled the off. The convoy began its slow, careful trail up the cracked old road that rose out of the river channel it had never been built to avoid, skirted the edge of what was left of Savernake Forest, and then towards Marlborough and the old Royal palace, the makeshift one your family used before this one was finished.'

She smiled at Siward. 'And with that speech, your Granddad Edwin passed into history. For years people would say things like 'The King himself was right here at Thatcham dock with three boatloads of gold! Or was it ten boatloads? Anyway, after that, life got good again!''

Siward sat chewing, his eyes wide, gazing into history, a faint smile on his smooth, young face.

Gemma's big voice interrupted his reverie with 'Better wash your hands for lunch, young man.' The boy shook his head in stylized exasperation but jumped up and obeyed. Then he came back over to Alenor and stared into her eyes with his wide-open gaze. She wondered for a moment whether he could see the traces of becter activity somehow... She blinked and smiled, but he held eye-contact for a bit longer before turning away, saying, 'Thanks Allie!' as he charged off.

'That one loves you, don't he?' said Gemma. Alenor laughed and stood up to help the cook shift a vast soup kettle, still thinking about how Siward had gazed right into her… he was a subtle and complex child. She returned to her vegetables and thought about this morning's vision. Her flight into becter-space had been triggered by a chain of orgasms, each better than the last. To Alenor, everything had a soul, a living sentience, and the mighty, alien-hearted soul that lived in her becter-network loved it when she fucked.

She was a fallow falcon, soaring and stooping over worlds both familiar and strange, dipping to view some fascinating place or other. Then she'd found herself gazing down at The Map, one of the places the becter-soul had made for her, a map of the world where pictures swam, hazy portraits of the few hundred BTs worldwide who were alive at this moment, the few hundred people like herself. She recognized some of the little icons the becter-soul provided: old Bruno the musician and informal ambassador for Wessex, with his ability to induce visions and hallucinations in people; that beautiful dark woman, almost as old as herself, who could heal anything and do powerful things with bodies of water, she who'd been becter-infected in some witch-line blood-ritual; another blood-line initiate, that dangerous-looking (and sexy) shaman from Arctic Finland; (she'd left a brightened-up picture of herself wearing a black one-piece hanging in the space next to his image). Then that strange cluster of icons in Sheffield, where they called BTs 'subbits,' like other clusters around holding camps near the mosquito-infested flood zones, where there were more becter infectees, a tiny percentage of whom survived and made their own deal with the becter-oversoul. Some of whom even broke out into a new life, like Arctor Trent had, before he'd disappeared. Like his, some places were blank, just holes in the becter-space where the person behind them had cared a lot about being invisible.

And weirder still were those mean-faced men who ran the Old Crow stalls up and down the British Isles, something terribly broken about them, their souls all mashed up and twitching to the vibrations at the empty centre of the web. The heart of becter-space was a void which the becter-soul placed at the far North of the map and labelled 'Thule.' Threads spread out from this empty place, touching all the Crow-men and other BTs the world over. Alenor was tough, adventurous and skilled at navigating the becter-space, but she had always had the feeling that it would be a very bad idea to try to break through the becter-ice of Thule.

The sound of Gemma ringing the bell for volunteers to set lunch and serve brought her out of the memory and back to the kitchen. She stood and got busy as, with practised ease, she asked the becter-oversoul to surf any open becter-net-spaces and find the kind of music she liked. A few seconds later the squawk of a hurdy-gurdy playing in a bar in the Republic of the Pyrenees filled her head.

Chapter 8: Beltane Wednesday: Alex

Alex woke at first light to the clamour of the great bell in the north tower. He showered quickly, the water from the roof tanks just barely lukewarm. He dressed in shorts and work-shirt and let himself out into the bustle of the great house. The rare and delicious smell of coffee was on the air, and everyone was up early, either for the execution or to prepare for the day of meetings. He made his way down to the big kitchen in the east wing. A student was stirring a pot on the range. Ambrose was already down there, seated on a pine bench, tucking into a bowl of porridge and listening to the NeighbourNet reports on the kitchen's audio. Alex couldn't believe the change in the older man.

'Good morning, dear boy. Sleep well?' Ambrose inquired in his affectionate boom.

'Yes, and what about you? When I put you to bed you looked on your last legs. Now you're fine!'

'Those pills aren't so bad, are they?' Ambrose finished his porridge and sipped coffee. Alex felt immensely relieved. He got a bowl from the side, took porridge from the pan on the stove, and filled a cup with aromatic coffee. He ate steadily and didn't say much. It always took him a while to wake up enough for conversation. Ambrose put his cup aside, stretched and yawned.

'I'm off to Marlborough Prison now, to witness the execution of Diamond Head Morningstar. I can get you in if you'd like to join me.'

Alex shook his head. Ambrose seemed unsurprised, was used to his family and guests turning down such gruesome invitations. The old man got to his feet, picked up a small pocket book and headed for the outside door. 'Perhaps see you at the meetings later.' He saluted and stepped out. Alex liked the idea of staying around the house today, Beltane Wednesday, the day when Ambrose's Wednesday Club ran seminars and discussions. He leaned back from the table, and the student volunteer cleared his bowl and spoon. Alex looked up at him. 'Your first year here?' he asked. The fresh-faced young man nodded. 'Been here since Yule. Mr Swords invited me when my mother died.'

'Sorry to hear that,' said Alex. 'Where were you living before?'

'Cricklade Guest Camp.'

'Thought I caught a Border accent. Congratulations on getting out of there, I'm impressed.'

'I took a Wednesday Club test paper and next thing I knew, Mr Swords had sent for me. I'll be reading Philosophy at Bristol this Harvest.'

'Ambrose is a one-man conspiracy to nurture the best minds in Wessex. Good to meet you.' They shook hands. 'You like it here?'

The boy grinned, shook his head in disbelief, eyes wide. 'Love it. Can't believe Asgard Hall, just never met any of these kinds of people before – philosophers, scientists, artists, mystics, magicians, and...'

'Generic oddball geniuses,' completed Alex. They both laughed. 'See you later!'

Alex finished his coffee, stood and stepped outside. A rough lawn, kept short by a few placid goats, ran a little way down the hill to where fields of wheat started. The sun was low, behind a thin haze. It would be hot later. He noticed a figure down on the lawn, dressed in white and going through the precise moves of a t'ai chi form.

In the moments before he recognized Susannah, he remembered his mother the last time he'd seen her, at age seven, her face rich in painful messages. Dry-mouthed, he walked down the lawn until he stood behind the figure, a slender, middle-aged woman, tanned, with red hair in a thick plait. She turned, in the course of the form, and saw Alex. She smiled faintly and continued her exercise.

Alex started his own sequence of stretches. It was a joy to feel the flow of a martial form again, and after he'd finished he wanted to do something else immediately. Susannah was standing poised and still, facing him. 'Long time no see, Alex! Welcome back to Asgard Hall!'

They embraced. 'It must be a year. It's great to see you, Susannah. You're looking as young as ever!'

'Flattery will get you everywhere. How about some sword-play?' She grinned fiercely, the deep wrinkles creasing, the irises low down in her eyes like rising suns.

Alex nodded briskly, and she turned and walked over to a row of picnic tables. She picked up a pair of wooden swords, turned and tossed one to Alex. He caught the hardwood and got into stance. They circled each other, low and cautious at first, feinting and lunging, then jumping back. Then Susannah pressed forward suddenly. Alex, a decent sword fighter, was taken quite by storm by her speed and fierceness, and only just managed to beat off her attack by using his superior height. However, she got through his defences enough to land a painful blow. She stood still, the point of the sword at his upper belly, not far from where a knife had gone in two years ago in Bristol.

He tossed the sword aside and conceded the bout. They were both a little out of breath. 'Still so fast and keen!' he said as they walked up the lawn to the house. 'And how come you had a pair of swords to hand?'

She laughed, a big, shrill sound, and said 'You know me. I love a bit of a fight after breakfast!'

Alex laughed too. 'I do indeed, and I'm so glad to see you.' Their hands met as they walked, and she gave his a squeeze. 'Things are changing, young Al. And Ambrose... Well, you've seen the state he was in yesterday. That's happening more and more often.'

'How's Thania?' asked Alex, remembering Susannah's tall, gangly daughter, the redhead with the very direct stare.

'Well, thereby hangs a tale. She's over at the Palace, believe it or not, but if anyone asks, you don't know where she is. I'll fill you in on it all as it develops.' Susannah shook her head, then turned to him and smiled. 'Time for music!'

They were at the door now, and Susannah led them through the kitchen, up a few steps at the back and through a corridor to the other side of the east wing. They left the building and took a short path through herb gardens to the Roundhouse, the centerpiece of Asgard Hall. Wide double doors were open to air the chamber out for today's seminars and meetings, and the great circular room was flooded with light from the high windows. Tiered rows of cushioned wooden seats for maybe two hundred people surrounded a central area, at present with just a table and a blackboard in it. The floor had been swept clean, and the space smelt of pine resin.

Susannah stepped behind the central table and lifted out a harp. She took a seat and arranged herself and the instrument. Alex sat down in the front row. Susannah said, 'I want you to tell me if this works.' She plucked a few notes to tune the harp, then began a figure which seemed to climb up and fall down, climb and fall, again and again. She began a soft droning song, a chant in which Alex heard lines he remembered from school, the story of the god of wisdom, from an old poem:

'I know that I hung on a wind-swept tree
All of nine nights
Wounded by a spear and given to Woden…'

It went on, and he was lost in it, the sweat of combat

drying on his skin, the scent of the wooden roundhouse, and Susannah's strong, ringing voice holding him there.

She finished, and turned to look at him. 'Well?'

Alex shook his head in wonder. 'Awe-inspiring, Su. What else can I say?'

Susannah looked perplexed. 'Yes, you appreciate it, but will our guests tonight? Won't they just be bored with more of the same old traditional stuff they learned in school? Or that's how it seems to me, in this changing Wessex.' She made a disappointed moue.

'Fuck 'em if they can't take it, Su. It's great,' said Alex.

'Thanks, Al. I've mutilated another bit of *Havamal* to use on them if they're really boring. Listen.' She started a plodding, heavy figure on the harp, and sang in a stage whisper:

'Who travels widely needs his wits about him,
The stupid should stay at home:
The daft man is often laughed at
When he tries to keep up with the wise.'

She kept a mournfully straight face throughout, then turned to Alex and did her big laugh. 'Yeah, fuck 'em. I'm off to stir up the other musicians. See you at lunch.' And with that, she was up, hugging Alex and off.

He spent the rest of the morning making himself at home in the big house. He could hear people arriving from time to time, and just after midday, there was a commotion outside and the court bus pulled up. Alex was leaning out of his upstairs window overlooking the main entrance, and he saw Ambrose get out and come into the house. He didn't do his usual booming 'I'm back!,' and Alex wondered if it was the sobering effect of witnessing an execution, or the old man's medical state again.

He took a shower and went down to the dining room. Lunch was starting early, to fit in extra sittings for those who'd come great distances, and the long table was filling up with diners. As was the custom of the house, Alex as resident brought jugs of water to the table and served the guests. Then he sat down, near the head of the table next to a frowning man who kept glancing round. He introduced himself. 'Alex Tyler, Marlborough, lately of Bristol.' The dark, well-groomed man frowned at him and blinked a few times. Then he extended a hand, while continuing to frown.

'I am called Patrick Marcier, and I came from Languedoc. I should not be 'ere. I came to meet Mr 'Endry, and he is not coming now.' Alex was catching up fast, not aware that Hendry had planned to come.

Alex rose to the duties of host. 'I'm sure we're all sorry for your inconvenience, Monsieur Marcier. Perhaps Mr Hendry will be along later.'

'No, they say he's not coming because the Queen is not 'ere.'

The question mark over Alex's head must be becoming more visible by the second, but he bluffed on. 'Ah, she has been bereaved. King Peredur.'

'Oui, d'accord. These things 'appen.' With that, Marcier appeared to close the discussion.

Wondering what was cooking with Hendry's plots, Alex looked round at the new arrivals. A dark, sturdy man in an immaculate blue uniform, a peaked cap under his arm, black hair greying at the temples, looked around him, and Alex stood to make him welcome.

'Alex Tyler, occasional resident. Please take a seat.'

The big man extended a massive, hairy hand and smiled as he sat down. 'Joshua Herz, Free American Airforce. Pleased to meet ya.'

'I'm afraid I'm ignorant of...'

'That's OK, you British Isles people must have given up

on North America by now. But we're not all under the heel of the PL.'

Alex brought a jug of water and some glasses from the sideboard. 'I'm enormously relieved to hear that. The PL started in the old USA, didn't it?'

'And that's where the war will end. My Tribe defends a few thousand acres in Kansas, and there are a fair few other Tribes who've started levying fighting personnel and equipment. That's why I'm over here; we're getting to the stage of looking at strategy.'

Ambrose strode in, looking fresh, and came over to sit at the head of the table next to Alex. Two Asgard Hall students came up from the kitchen with hot tureens and Alex helped serve out the soup. When he sat down again, the main table had filled up, and a sombre man with lively eyes, all in black, was seated across from him.

Ambrose leaned forward and introduced them. 'Neil, my ex-student and friend, Alex Tyler. Alex, this is Bishop Neil Smith.' Alex shook hands with the intense man. 'If I may be so bold as to ask, what are you Bishop of?' said Alex.

'I serve the Diocese of Wessex in the Anglican Catholic communion,' said Smith, in a soft, precise voice. Alex didn't know what to say. He'd never met a high-ranking Christian priest before. He smiled and nodded at Smith and refrained from saying 'Wow!'

Next to Smith sat a small, muscular man in administrative grey, so alert as to seem on the edge of his seat. Ambrose continued with the introductions. 'Alex, this is Mr MacLeod, until recently the Loyal Lothian Ambassador to Wessex. Mr MacLeod, my ex-student and trusted henchman Alex Tyler.' Alex shook the man's cool, moist hand. MacLeod's smooth face allowed a pinch-lipped smile and he spoke in a clipped Lothian accent. 'My circumstances here perhaps warrant the excuse that I am in exile. Since I have worked for my Government in Wessex, things have rather changed in Lothian. I rather fear that, if I were to go home, by the time I arrived I would have my ears cut off for ideological impurity. So I'm stuck in fair Wessex. To you and yours, Mr Swords!' MacLeod raised his glass and toasted, as if it were filled with liquor. It occurred to Alex not to trust MacLeod too easily.

A tall, muscular man dressed in a green kilt, his hair a vivid red and his chin the first thing you noticed about his face, took a seat across from Ambrose. The old man called out, 'Riagáin, how goes fair Leinster?'

'From Tipperary to Dublin it is still fair indeed, but we have heard that further north has lost some of its charm to our white-jacketed friends.'

Ambrose shook his head. 'Bad times, Riagáin. Meet my current genius Alex Tyler. Alex, this gentleman is Riagáin ó Flannagáin, of the Kingdom of Leinster.'

Ó Flannagáin shook Alex's hand. 'And what is your area of genius, young Alex?'

'I'm a chemist,' said Alex, used to the embarrassment attendant on Ambrose's exaggerations, 'though as yet unemployed.'

'Have confidence,' said the big man, blue eyes piercing and bright. 'We live in a world which is changing shape every day.'

The student stewards gathered up the dishes and piled loaves and bowls of salad on the table, followed by cheeses, pickles and cold meats. Everyone fell to, and the conversation waned for a while. Alex was leaning over his plate enjoying an enormous sandwich when he noticed Ambrose turning away from the table and knocking some pills out onto his hand. They weren't the blue, generic antelosin Alex had watched him take yesterday, this was something else, and equally unbranded. Ambrose caught Alex watching him, and looked shifty for a moment.

After the lunch people started to wander across the herb-garden to the Roundhouse for the opening ceremony. Alex followed and sat near the front, but he didn't pay much attention. He'd seen it before; Susannah burned some incense, enjoined everyone to seek their highest consciousness for the days ahead and led a brief, silent meditation.

Ambrose gave a short keynote speech, this year's a passionate defence of the Wessex Crown.

'My friends, some have said that we need a written constitution, a rule-book or manual to regularize the making of justice in Wessex. I disagree. The only way you can hold together a swarming rabbit warren such as Wessex is by appeal to the transcendent, by the evocation of utter loyalty to an eternal power, the living myth of a sacred Kingdom. Shorn of Her Majesty, we'd be at each others' throats in minutes. The idea of the Queen is in our minds, minute by minute, giving us a direction to gaze in, and a glory to gaze upon and love. She is the compass of my heart, a far more basic and indestructible part of my citizenship than any public morality I serve. And that is my case. Gods prosper Wessex!'

People divided for their meetings then, consulting the running order on the tall flipchart stand by the podium. Alex didn't fancy the sound of 'Population control – new perspectives,' or 'Foreign policy and the collapse of Lothian.' He was more drawn to 'Alaric Tate & Monotheism – an appreciation,' and decided to start there. He wasn't obliged to attend anything, but everyone who was anyone in the Kingdom of Wessex passed through the doors of the Wednesday Club, and he'd meet interesting people. Maybe even someone who could offer him a job.

The North Studio meeting room was full. It seemed that historian and activist Tate's muscular condemnation of monotheistic creeds was popular. The speaker, a bespectacled academic in a shiny waistcoat, introduced

Tate's work in breathless quotes designed to make sure that no-one was left in the dark as to Tate's position.

Having got his audience warmed up, he threw out his big question, sweeping his glasses around and frowning at the people in the front row. 'How shall we deal with the Pure Light threat to our liberty? Perhaps the best way to characterize this problem is as a virus, an infectious pathogen that spreads from host to host. As such we need to contain, to isolate the infection, to prevent an epidemic. In short, we must segregate and quarantine the actively-converting monotheists in our midst. We must be vigilant to the activities of well-funded groups. Any entryism in education and politics must be exposed and ousted. Any buildup of military strength in such groups must be flattened without hesitation.' The speaker paused for emphasis. 'And what means shall we consider?'

The room exploded with questions and statements. The chairman just about achieved order. One man shouted, 'They try to destroy us by sneaky means, seducing our children with life extension and nuclear power!' A woman agreed. 'They wouldn't flinch at invading and enslaving us, like they did before. We should consider ideological cleansing.' A man yelled out in opposition. 'Since when has our way sanctioned the extermination of an enemy? Only monotheists do that. We can't stoop to their level of dishonour or life isn't worth living.'

Alex found it depressingly ugly, and after a while he left. Last year, these people wouldn't have been talking like this. He wandered through the Great North Hall, out into the landscape of giant stones, horizon and sky, in the blazing Spring light. He lay down on a warm stone bench and dozed.

Starlings, and people moving about, woke him up. He'd slept for a couple of hours, and the afternoon meetings were turning out. Time to freshen up and get down to dinner and the Symposium, which would surely be more fun. He stretched, rose lazily and went up to his room.

The Symposium was the social highlight of the conference, so the dinner that night was a showpiece. Susannah ran the household rotas of students and volunteers, but outside caterers were brought in from Marlborough for the Wednesday feast. He did his stint of stewardship, serving wine, beer and fruit juices, and tried to talk to as many people as possible as he circulated, alive to the faint possibility someone might have a job for him. Then he settled in his place to enjoy the magnificent food, but distracted and worrying.

The music started. The man sitting three down on his right stood up and moved his chair away from the table. He stood and looked around, then picked up a lute, introduced himself as Bruno and requested silence. Dressed in green, he sang an old hymn to the Goddess, 'Quean of the Meadow'. There was a burst of applause, and conversation resumed, but lower, as Bruno strummed an interlude piece.

Alex looked round and recognized a long, fleshy face with strong features, from his placement year at Sheffield University. 'Professor Regudy! Remember me? Alex Tyler.'

Regudy grinned. 'You don't have to remind me, how could I forget your making that bathtub liquor for your leaving party. I think you had to leave after that, or face prosecution for poisoning. I hear you got a First, congratulations.' He turned to the younger, blonde woman on his left, who was holding a child of about two years. 'May I introduce Iduna, and Thora.' Alex leaned over to shake Iduna's hand and smile at Thora, who turned away in shyness.

Regudy smiled warmly. 'How are you, lad?'

Alex had to think before answering. He wasn't enjoying

today much. 'I'm OK. Needing a job now, of course.'

'There's not much doing at the old Uni these days. There's no funding, what with all the border clashes with Lothian since the loony faction took over. I expect they'll be trying to take Sheffield's armaments factories next. But you're bloody good, Alex. You could always get a job as a metallurgist.' He paused for emphasis.

'After all, we've got a weapons boom on.'

Alex nodded. 'There could be worse fates. And how is old Shemeld?'

Regudy laughed. 'The blighter's been trying to find his idiot son an aristocratic bride. The present front-runner is none less than the gorgeous daughter of the Khan of Bradford. Lass'll run rings round that boy.'

Alex reminisced. 'I enjoyed Bradford, friendly, busy place.'

'Not so much now. Their economy is imploding. That's why the dynastic marriage. Khan gets guns, Shemeld gets a ruthless ally.'

Alex refilled his glass and looked glumly into it. 'Our economy is buggered too. Some people here are saying that any dictator with enough guns could just take Wessex. And others say it's already happening.'

Regudy leaned over and got a refill, then opened his mouth to speak, but Bruno was on stage, raising his arms for hush. 'Dear friends, I wish to tell you a tale of the history of Wessex. Please relax and open your minds...' As his melodious voice tailed off, music swelled from somewhere.

Alex peered at the stage, but the vonnie-speakers were yards away from the tall figure, the music still rising in volume, wrapping them around as if it came out of the air itself. Hunting horn brass, tense strings, the crash of waters and what might have been a muted choir. He looked over at Regudy, whose mouth was hanging open. The hall was dark now, even though it would still be light outside; they had been sealed into an enclosed space.

Bruno's voice, eerie and massive, spoke out of the air around them. 'In the beginning, came the waters, and thus ended the old world. Out of the chaos of dissolution and battle, swooped the ravens of war...' Suddenly, the air was filled with the slap of helicopter blades and the deep thrum of long-vanished engines. Across the table, little Thora stuffed her tiny fist into her mouth, frozen in fright.

Then the war-sounds dissolved, fading into the chiming of distant bells. Bruno's voice soothed them. 'And out of conflict, arose a new Kingdom, where people could live their lives in the true joy of the flesh and the earth. King Edwin was crowned in the first official celebration at our sacred Avebury for over two thousand years, in a ceremony that broke the strings binding the British Crown to lost London and to the old state religion. ...' A new soundscape rolled over them, bells, birdsong and laughing crowds, then, inexplicably, the darkened hall around them faded, and a vision, as if projected onto the very air, took its place. They saw the figure of the young King, in his baggy white shirt and red trousers, climbing the great mound of Silbury Hill, to receive the power of the Sun at midsummer.

Then they saw, at the base of Silbury, Edwin take his place at the head of a singing, dancing, drinking and capering throng for the procession up the Great Avenue, ending in the newly-cleared green in an arc around the middle of the inner circle of megaliths.

Here, a wooden deck had been set across the dips of the earthwork. Here, King Edwin was crowned, with the blessing of the Goddess, in the persons of his sisters Effan and Faina and Asgard Hall's priestess Susanna, and at the hands of Ambrose, his mentor and priest.

He then mounted a stage at the centre of the deck, and spoke out as King. The festival frenzy of the revellers quietened down.

The listeners in the hall heard his speech in a voice they knew was Edwin's. He spoke passionately of the true, traditional faith of Wessex, which held in trust the traditional religion of Britain, in case that sunken land should ever rise again. His reference to Britain sent a thrill and a shiver through the crowd.

He declared, in no uncertain terms, that he, Edwin Wodening, King-Elect, would defend all the Gods of Wessex and Britain. He further declared that all men and women were free to worship as, whom and what they wanted, but there would be no more state religion or state funding of Christianity.

The crowd cheered everything he said, and the applause reached fever pitch when Edwin stepped down from the stage and strode over to a row of bulky steel chests. He flung open a lid, and started handing out leather bags to a platoon of the Wessex Royal Guard. The red-jacketed household troops marched off through the crowd, opening the satchels and distributing the commemorative gold. Each one who reached out his or her hand to one of these men got a coin, stamped with a simple profile of their new King, and the inverted T of a Thor's Hammer.

The images began to fade, and Bruno's voice sounded softly. 'King Edwin had kept the oath he made at Thatcham, and won the hearts of the people of the Kingdom of Wessex.' Golden evening light slanted in low through the hall's high windows. The great room was filled with hushed silence and a few muted sobs. The stunned watchers looked around at each other, dabbing tears from their cheeks. Bruno bowed low, and returned to his seat, as a stunned trickle of applause rose to a climax.

Regudy reached for the bottle and poured, shaking his head in amazement. He gazed a little blearily at Alex. 'What a history you Wessexers have got, man.' He took a swig of wine. 'But we've all had it easy for too long. Just like in that kid's story, when Old Crow says, 'Serves you right for being smug!' Always made me laugh, that, though when you think about it, it's about something pretty frightening.'

Alex frowned. 'What do you mean, it's 'about' something? I thought Old Crow was just a kid's story.'

'Well, I heard it like this from one of the folklore chaps at the Uni: Old Crow is actually a folk memory of a particular person, someone who went missing. As it happens, someone who used to work at Sheffield university, back in the 2060s, Darius Raven. Won the Chemistry Nobel in 2071 for von Neumann nanites.'

'Yes, of course I know about Raven. I just never connected him with Old Crow.'

Regudy nodded and continued. 'Before he cracked up and disappeared he was supposed to be pretty close to the old Holy Green Grail, a source of clean, free energy.' He took another swig, and waved his arm unsteadily. Alex noticed that Bruno had come over and was listening.

'Gentlemen, please don't mind my butting in. You are speaking of the missing immortal, the wandering wizard.'

Regudy nodded in drunken friendliness. Bruno sat down and continued. 'Old Crow resumes the tale of the Faustian madman, and I agree that it is indeed frightening to contemplate the depth of inhumanity that Raven must have sunk to when he surrounded his house with landmines.'

Regudy frowned. 'How d'you know that? I never heard anyone'd found his house.'

'I saw the site, in Caithness. There was just a circle of defences. Somehow, he left, and took the whole house with him.' Bruno paused. 'I think the only way he could have done that is if he had succeeded in his quest, and discovered a radically new source of energy generation. Ever heard of the elekilpo generator?'

Regudy nodded. ‘Kaz Tazhin, early 21st century.’

Bruno said, ‘No-one knew how it worked, or even if it worked, and it was either lost or suppressed. Raven was playing with the idea that the elekilpo process involved something like void-energy, and tried to replicate it with von Neumann nano-devices. Which is how he stumbled on the vonnie, and eventually the becter. He suggested that the becter was a vital component of the system, that only someone with ‘becter powers’ could cause the assembly of elekilpo generators.’

Alex shook his head. ‘So the generator system needs someone with becter powers to work it at all. He’s hiding out somewhere with two wonderful technologies that could maybe save the world.’

‘And that maybe can only be operated by a few in a million, those who can tolerate becters.’

‘‘Kin’ell,’ said Regudy. ‘‘Scuse me, gentlemen.’ He rose to his feet and wove off.

‘So Crow was Raven?’ asked Alex.

‘In more ways than one, I think. He must be over 150, you know. He’s still out there, fishing for information, for some grand scheme of his. People don’t just disappear.’

‘Oh yes, they do,’ said Alex. Suddenly, he felt confused and emotional and found himself telling this person he’d just met his most private sorrows. ‘My mother did. She left when I was two. I got up in the night to look for her, and she was gone. Lights flooded the place, and winked in the sky. She came back. Then she disappeared, when I was seven. I was told she’d gone to the coast to find someone, and I never saw her again. No-one knows what happened to her. She must have been abducted, twice. What does that mean…?’ He trailed off, saying, ‘I feel lost. I don’t know why I’m telling you all this. I suppose I need to tell someone.’

Bruno said, 'Listen, Alex, and then get some rest. You need to find out what happened to your mother. I don't know, but I know how to find things out. We'll talk tomorrow. Now go and sleep.'

Chapter 9: Thursday, Hettie

The morning went on forever. Hettie was up at dawn, severe and elegant in black goatsilk, seeing that everything was in place for the funeral, inspecting the servants, lending a helpful ear to Gwendoline rehearsing her eulogy. The Queen seemed busy and effective today, which was something.

The cortège set off at eight, the streets already lined with mourners waving black-bordered Wessex flags, the worn hempcloth left over from Siward's funeral, a weave that outlasted death. At the centre was a long-disused gun-carriage brought up from Thatcham, its steely shine cloaked in a great flag, drawn by four black-plumed, high-stepping horses. Marlborough's main roads were closed to other traffic for the morning. Their slow progress took them from the Palace on the edge of the centre, in a loop round the heart of the city to their destination in the military ground of Thor's Field, down by the Kennet Channel. To onlookers craning for a view of Peredur's body, it looked as if the big man in Wessex green was sleeping on a great bed, his grey hair combed out, his grey hands rigid by his sides, the stock of an ancient automatic rifle resting against his left hand. The body and its wooden trestle were taken off the hearse and placed reverently on the funeral pyre. To one side there stood a steel platform, and the Royal party climbed the steps, Gwendoline, Jervis, then Hettie and little Siward. Gwendoline stepped forward and took the microphone, delivering her eulogy, praising Peredur's courage and loyalty, his love for Wessex and his hard work. The sound of her voice pulsed and swirled through the crowd's vonnies, picked up by the surrounding ring of vonnie-speakers.

When she finished, her voice unwavering, she picked a torch out of a sconce at the front of the platform. Susannah stepped up and received it from her. She raised it over her head and her strong voice rang out. 'Cattle die, kinsmen die, you yourself shall one day die. But fair fame never dies, for the one who wins it.'

Chanting, she walked sunwise around the pyre. She finished her circuit in front of the platform, and plunged the torch into the base of the oiled wood. The flames caught and rose, licking around the body. The Army band struck up 'Glory,' the Wessex national anthem, the crowd picked it up and sang along, and Hettie saw the orange firelight catch her mother's tears.

It was soon over. Once the central tower of fire collapsed into swirling cinders, and only the faintest outline of the body was left in the flames, the crowd began to surround the beer-wagons. Palace staff breached the kegs and passed goblets up to the royal party on the platform. They all drank, Gwendoline weeping freely now, and the beer was passed out to the crowd. Then Hettie had to wrap things up. She touched her mother's hand, and escorted her down the steps. She and Susannah were the last to leave, making sure that everyone was in the old diesel carriages.

Back at the Palace, Hettie saw that Gwendoline was fairly all right, and then she let herself feel exhausted. Normally, on a Beltane Thursday, she'd be off to enjoy the testosterone-drenched rough-and-tumble of the wicket match. But she didn't have the energy, and she did have the perfect excuse, so she went up to her room, lay down, and was asleep within minutes.

She woke with that dull, creepy feeling brought on by daytime sleep. The edge of her dream recall was blunted, with only confused and directionless wisps of imagery left as she pulled herself up. It was the sound of Siward's voice that had woken her, and he was climbing up onto the bed.

'Come on mummy let's play come on mum come on mum let's play.'

She smiled at him bouncing up and down, took his hands in hers. 'Yes, let mum get a shower and we'll go and play.'

She heard him wittering to himself as she washed, and when she came out into the bedroom again he was in some inner play-world, pushing things round the floor. She dried her hair and dressed in plain blue hemp trousers and shirt.

Outside, the sunshine was hot, and they were the only people on the lawn. Everyone else would be at the wicket match. Last Samhain, and then again at Imbolc, Avebury had beaten Marlborough at the big football matches, and Marlborough would be desperate to win the Beltane wicket cup. She and Siward played a toned-down version of wicket, the little boy defending the sanctuary of the Goddess while she threw the hard, wooden ball at him. They played slower and slower as the heat got to them, and then Hettie announced that she wanted to go inside.

She sent for Alenor, who set up the old computer for her, unrolling the screen, now frosted with age, and fetched a data-stick from the archives. Alone, she watched Ambrose's commemorative film of Edwin's coronation. A hailstorm of pixels darted across the old picture, but they were just part of the familiar counterpoint to her grief. Ambrose's voiceover began, his tone almost unchanged in the sixty or so intervening years.

'...The coronation of elected King Edwin Wodening was the first official celebration at Avebury for over two thousand years...'

Hettie sighed, *All that wood, and all those horses...* Those that drew Peredur's carriage today were the last in the palace stables; few had been bred after '35, when most of them had been eaten during the drought and famine. She watched in a daze, to the end, when Ambrose recited the familiar history of the Wodening dynasty, added years later when he'd donated the film to the Palace.

'In pursuit of Anderton's forces at Oakley, Edwin was killed by enemy fire. His son, Marcus, was elected King on the strength of his father's illustrious record. He reigned during a few short years of peace, which ended in a sodden field outside the ruins of Berkhamsted.' Hettie switched the machine off, her tears falling quietly as the dinner gong rang.

She trudged down to the formal dining room with its long oak table. Tonight it was set for four, including Siward's high chair, but only Gwendoline was seated. Dinner was the only remotely formal meal in the royal household, and the family almost always met for it. Jervis's absence probably meant the avoidance of more unpleasantness with his mother for a day or so. She greeted Gwendoline, who looked unnaturally serene and detached in her widow's weeds. She thought of Jervis, and the heaviness of her oath of vengeance settled on her as she watched the handsome young household volunteer serving the soup. Hettie fed herself and kept an eye on Siward with part of her mind, while with a bigger part she began to shape the destruction of her half-brother.

They finished the soup, and roast chicken with herbs followed. To volunteer in the Royal kitchens was the launching-pad for many a great chef, and they seemed to have a good one at present. Only little Siward seemed to be appreciating the excellent food, though. Gwendoline took a couple of bites of the white meat and dabbed her mouth.

'I'm going to lie down, darling,' she said.

Hettie nodded supportively, then went back to asking herself what she needed, what resources must be in place. She needed proof of his betrayal, a confession at least. She needed a plan. She needed friends. She swallowed hard. Tonight, tonight, she would call to her spirits, from the burning ground.

After dinner, she sang with Siward before putting him to bed. To please the boy, they sang 'Everyone in Wessex' twice, but another song kept running through her mind. She kissed Siward, then went to her wardrobe and wrapped herself in a woollen cloak the colour of dried blood. Already she was singing under her breath the call to her ancestors that old Queen Maeve had taught her, as she followed the wide stairs down to the Palace's main entrance hall then turned aside into the Northern gallery.

The daylight was fading, a bronze glow from the western windows filling the long chamber. She stopped before the oil portrait of Maeve, King Edwin's Queen. The woman's immense personality and personal force flooded into her mind like bright sunlight; in the painting, she was dressed in white fur and red silk, a necklace of emeralds at her long, white throat. She stood with her hand resting on a wolfhound, in front of a window which gave onto a forest. Maeve's soft, steely voice carried down the long room, carried down the years, to Hettie, aged seven, eavesdropping from behind the curtains. 'Come out, little bird, come out…' This tall, serene woman whom Hettie had witnessed both weep and order the death of a traitor, had taught Hettie her bittersweet magics, witcheries of bone and moonlight, menstrual blood and nonsense rhyme, trance and psychic domination. And she it was who had taught Hettie how to use the portrait gallery as a shrine to the ancestors, to awaken the female soul of the clan. Hettie sang her name, in the childhood chant Maeve had given her. With her pleas, she reached out to the image of the old Queen, and it was as if cool, elegant fingers touched the back of her hand.

Then she stepped before the portrait of the mother of her own mother. Sif towered in front of her study, chaotic with books, a tall easel, and a guitar and a mandolin hung on the white wall. Her powerful build concealed a riot of creative brilliance and painful feeling. In Hettie's mind's eye, Sif walked towards her, picking her way through a landscape of war, heaps of broken bricks and rusted steel struts, the ruin of her own mother's home. She walked and reached out and caressed the air with elegant, tragic gestures, their arc following the outlines of long-vanished furniture or flowers, contours of memory from her broken life. In her eyes was a fey look, but she came up to Hettie and clasped her hands. Hettie felt a shock of power from the ghost, a promise of terrible magical assistance, the oath of the justified dead.

Then she stepped down the gallery to the picture of her other grandmother, Peredur's dam, Titania. That statuesque redhead leaned over the prow of a steel-armoured boat, like a living, voluptuous figurehead, the very image of female power reaching out to her in sympathy. Singer, party-host, bon viveur, she too was tragic in her own way, that beautiful body, that powerful will broken by unidentified, unknown fevers. Hettie swallowed and touched her fingertips to the canvas, Titania's lovely eyes bearing her message of help.

She stood silent, feeling the presence of these mighty women, then drew her cloak around her and stepped out into a spring dusk filled with distant sounds, as if the world had already retreated from her. She made her way around the Palace, through the south-facing gardens, towards the flat field where she'd burned her father's body.

The pile was much smaller, and still giving off wisps of smoke. Palace workers had raked the ashes over, letting the outer edges of the pile cool and sequestering the bone-fragments into a central heap. Hettie stepped across the warm ground, up to the central pile of Peredur's remains. She looked around and located a rake. She stepped back to the charred bones and gently raked them over, sooty shards of skeleton blending with grey ash, back and forth, into flat plains and ridges as she chanted her old song, into hills, into valleys and gulfs and seas of death, until she began to think of it as a landscape of the future, a place where everyone was fated to go. She sang on, almost lost in her grief even as she held her mind still, still enough to pay attention to the spirit world she invoked.

Then she drew a series of long, slow breaths, moving the rake back and forth so gently, so softly above the ash, and called on all her dises, the group-soul of all the unnamed women of the Wodenings, back to the beginning of time.

With that army of bright darkness about her, she voiced her plea. 'Give me what I need for my vengeance, give me everything I need, the knowledge, the allies, the opportunities....' She let that desire lodge in her chest, as the tears ran down her cheeks.

After a while, she felt cold and exhausted. She had done all she could, for now. She gathered up a shovel-full of the warm bone-ash and poured it into a pocket of her robe. Next year, at Beltane, she would scatter it at Avebury, and there would be a totem ceremony for Peredur, a year after his death, and a great carved tree trunk would be raised in the Sanctuary. She trudged back to the Palace.

Chapter 10: Beltane Thursday, Alex

Alex slept late. He didn't remember much about the end of the Symposium. He got up feeling a little shaky, showered, and did some qi gong on the lawn. Susannah wasn't there today; in her role as High Priestess, she would be helping with the Royal funeral. He didn't regret missing that event; his feelings were still too raw to spend the early morning sunk in a funeral crowd. After his stretches and some breakfast he was starting to feel better.

Ambrose was out too, as were many of the household. Alex realised he would have to lend a hand in the preparations for the Beltane rituals the next day. He made his way over to the roundhouse, where Susannah had pinned series of To Do lists around the circle, with helpful estimates of how many pairs of hands each task would take to achieve it all by the deadline at the bottom. Alex was filled with admiration for her efficiency; she balanced Ambrose's immense, creative scattiness. The final list was directed at Alex himself, and instructed him in how many people he had to find and assemble for all the tasks to be completed, and by what times of day. He went to work.

At about five, Alex packed the last of the checked-off boxes onto the mule carts by the stables, and went back into the roundhouse. Four students were just finishing tidying up. It looked as if all the lists had been ticked off. Alex showered, went to his room, and picked some fresh trousers and a bright shirt, dressing with pleasure. Remembering that he was leaving the safe enclave of Asgard Hall, he belted on his short sword, then checked himself in the small wardrobe mirror. Good enough. Then he remembered he'd better take some money too. And then, he was off out. He strode impatiently out of the main entrance, facing down towards Avebury. He stood for a moment munching the sandwich he'd put together hastily in the kitchen and looked out at the raucous, inviting sprawl of Beltane Fair. The Wicket match would be long since over, but there would be girls, and beer down there. He dusted the last crumbs of bread off his hands, and set off down the hill to have fun.

The sounds of the fair reached up to him, but there was a short span of fields before he came to the open space of the fairground. He headed for the Red Lion, around the edge of the market. He found himself walking between bivouacs and bender shelters. Avebury was always like this in Beltane Week. It was well worth a long tramp or hitch to get to the festival even if you hadn't got a penny. People would feed you and get you smashed, and you might find a lover, or, much less likely, a job. So people slept in fields, in temporary shelters, in the warm soft nights of early May. Sometimes the rainstorms came, but there were always a few big canvas pavilions and marquees up on the land inside the outer Avebury Circle. Some people didn't give a damn, and slept anywhere they fell after the hospitality they'd been enjoying ran out. This looked no different from previous years, when everyone mingled freely, rich with poor, and little harm was done in the good-natured fun of Beltane.

Alex bought a pint of beer, leaving a deposit for the glass so he could walk around. He couldn't help but think that it felt a bit different today. Nothing specific, just a less easy-going atmosphere, somehow. He checked his sword as he plunged deeper into the crowd. He saw a large, busy stall on trestle tables in front of him. Two men, big-built and covered in dark blue tattoos stood behind it. One of them reached out to straighten up the stall's wares, and Alex noticed the long-stemmed cross on his forearm. He reached down and picked up the pale rectangle the man had just moved. It was made of plastic, not like the low-tech stuff on other stalls. As the sunlight caught it, and it powered up, Alex saw a stylised picture of Diamond Head Morningstar, the black hair framing a face which must have been meant to represent righteous anger, the common man's indignation at the plight of the poor.

'Five pounds,' said the big man. Alex looked up into his contemptuous glare, and replaced the picture. He held the man's gaze for a second, then turned to go. Another large man moved out of his way. On his sleeve, he wore a White Cross armband. Alex put some distance between himself and the Pure Light-supporting bandits.

A stall drew his eye, loaded with knotted leather talismans and strings of bright beads, the kinds of thing someone might buy as a lover's gift. He picked a choker of red thonging, fat drops of cracked green glass plaited into it, with a complex bindrune beaten into a tiny, old copper coin. He imagined it hanging round an elegant neck. The stallholder said, 'Luck in love, and the power of sweetness in a bitter world. You like it?'

'Yeah, it's pretty. How much?'

'Two pounds, squire.' He leaned forward. 'Add another two, and Old Jambo will charge it with his mystic arts. Never again will you be without love, whether you keep it or give it to the first girl you see.'

Alex smiled. 'Where's Old Jambo then?'

'Right over there, squire.' The man pointed with a grubby finger that protruded from a grubbier sleeve. 'He's a cunning man, if you follow my meaning.'

Alex looked over to a booth, ripped leather curtains hanging from a decrepit frame. He didn't see anyone, just a dead crow lashed to the front pole of the shanty, eyes sunken and feathers mostly gone. Crow-men again; the previous night's bizarre conversation with Regudy and

Bruno came back to him. 'What is it with this Crow stuff?' he asked the talisman-seller.

'Just somefink for the kiddies, innit? You want the choker or what?'

'Sure.' Alex fished in his pocket and handed two coins to the man, who immediately turned away and started calling to another passerby. Alex strolled over to the Crow booth. He still couldn't see anyone; then, as if he'd crossed an invisible boundary, he did: the man was seated in front of the booth, skinny and hard-looking, his clothes grubby but with immaculate white gloves on his hands.

'Nice, aren't they?' The man let his mouth hang open, to show a mass of gold teeth. 'It all comes from the dead, like everything we own. Eh, posh boy?' The shrunken, mean eyes regarded him. 'You gonna make me do a show, or are you gonna fuck off?'

Alex shook his head in bewilderment, and was casting around for a reply, when he heard the row break out. By the time he'd turned round, the two men were staring each other down, then one of them was wielding a sword, and the other was falling to the ground, clutching his belly, blood oozing between his fingers. It was instantly obvious which man was of Citizen rank and which Guest. People were gathering round, and Alex drew his sword, just in case. The assailant turned round, sword still drawn, and faced Alex. He screamed, 'You saw what happened. Filthy squatter scum pushed me. You saw it!'

The crowd, obviously sympathetic to the squatter, were closing in on the better-armed man. Out of the corner of his eye, Alex saw a big man pick up a heavy wooden pole. In one of those accelerated moments, he understood what he must do to prevent a riot happening. He stepped forward and brought his sword up in a feint. The shocked, unfocused toff parried, and Alex got under his guard and flicked the sword out of his hand.

He turned around to face the crowd. The scar on his cheek felt taut, like a suture holding his self-image together. 'Fight's over, and I'm making a citizen's arrest of this man for using excessive force. Get that man a doctor.'

Heart in mouth, Alex motioned in front of him with his sword, and got the toff to the edge of the crowd of squatters. The immediate danger was over, but Alex had no idea how the damage to the goodwill of Beltane would be repaired. It felt like a powderkeg now.

Chapter 11: Friday Fun For All

Friday morning Ambrose was already holding forth in the kitchen. Released from court duties, he'd reverted to ageless peacock, red waistcoat and blue jodhpurs clashing with purple shirt, his beard freshly plaited into two waxed forks. He had a enormous, battered old book open on the table and was just finishing reading out loud from it when Alex came down for breakfast, in plain work-clothes.

'Eat well, dear boy! Much to do, to worship Our Lady of Ecstasy!' he boomed, the capitals evident in his tone. Then he was up and off while Alex helped himself to food.

The book was Julian Cope's twentieth century classic, 'The Modern Antiquarian.' Alex turned it over in his hands, for the pleasure of handling such a well-made old volume, then opened it to the page the marker was in and read:

> At the great Avebury temple on the Marlborough Downs in Wiltshire, ancient visitors were presented with a distillation, an overview, of their entire megalithic culture set down in one place. For at Avebury there appears to have been an example or analogue of almost every type of monument found in the European megalithic world.

There was little time for reading though. He closed the book, finished his breakfast and went to look for the source of the clamour racketing through the house.

The storeroom by the kitchen looked as if it was being raided by bandits, provender being tugged out and stacked on carts at the entrance to the main stables, shouting children weaving between painted screens, totem staves and ballast barrels. The roundhouse was the evident centre of operations, streams of people swarming in and out of the multiple doors. Fruit and fowl, cups and carts, swords and shields, platters and pigs, herbs and flowers in shimmering sprays and bulging bouquets, clothes, cloths and clobber, and a variety of objects inscrutable to understanding in a mere glance flowed in and out of the room, processed by men and women, girls and boys, and people dressed so that it was hard to tell their age or sex, weaving back and forth and flirting as they went, the whole thing with an underlay of garbled vonnie-noise, like all the radio stations in the world babbling, singing and muttering at once. Alex shouldered through to Ambrose's central trestle-desk, and the grand old man looked up at him, his frown cracking into a smile. He launched into a commentary on the ritual order for the day. The new arrangement meant that, not only would the sacrifices be able to feed more people in the big marquees outside, but those who weren't going to join in with the fifth rite wouldn't be, as Ambrose phrased it, 'Put off their grub by people doing sex magic in the corner.'

He went on. 'It always happens anyway, and I thought we'd structure it a little, for everybody's benefit, this year. If it doesn't work, we'll just go back to the free-for-all next time!' Ambrose guffawed, hugely amused at human chaos. 'Oh yes, since I imagine you'll be doing the full business, I've a special mask for you. Over there, by the urns.'

Alex reached over the stacked table and hefted the lightweight full-face mask, silver-white, with big eyeholes. It looked like a sinister frost-imp. 'Yes, that one. Bring it here.' Ambrose appraised the mask. 'Yes, that's for you. I call it The Thuler. It's from the old places that used to be frozen, and it's almost human. There, take it.'

Alex put the weird mask on. It was easy to wear, and he could see well. Ambrose peered at him. 'Good. It doesn't obscure your eyes. That's what the girls will go on. While you're dressed, that is!'

He nodded and looked round at the queue of people waiting for instructions from him, and picked up a clipboard. 'Alex: Boxes of crockery and stuff, on the carts. Then back here.'

A lot of lifting and three cartloads transported later, Alex was glad of a quick bath, and glad of the fact he'd kept fit with swordplay at university. He sagged into the bathtub, watching the hand-wound tower clock through the bathroom window. Asgard Hall had had the clock put in at the beginning of the dynasty, it was the oldest thing there. It was called the Eternity Clock, based on the idea of winding something up generation after generation, passing on responsibility, as Ambrose had taught him. The great Sheffield steel hands said three o'clock, and people were gathering for the ritual at five. Alex could hear that the sounds of the day had changed from bustle to revelry, as people began to drink and smoke and get merry, getting their blood up for feasting and sex. The singing was getting ruder:

Hooray hooray for the month of May
Outdoor cunking every day!

He hurried back to his room and ransacked the wardrobe for something suitable. Eventually he settled on baggy silk trousers. He clipped his sword belt on and looked at himself in the wardrobe mirror, standing tall and posing a bit. Not bad. He slipped on his canvas shoes and stepped out of the room, out of Asgard Hall and into the stream of festive people making their way to the Sanctuary.

The crowd slowed down as they neared the Sanctuary entrance. Alex was happy to pass the time with the people he was pressed close to, all dressed, or undressed, for pleasure. Girls wearing only thongs or little more, girls in robes that opened down the front, girls in just body paint, girls in every kind of sexy retro from all ages. Girls singing and laughing and capering, the whole crowd giving off a steam of sexual anticipation. *Wow, I love Beltane*, thought Alex, as he put his mask on and plunged into the throng.

Chapter 12: Friday Frolics

On Friday she woke early, as usual. Her mind was clear, a feeling of something in preparation rather than the crowding imagery of recent nights. She rose and sat writing her diary in the lovely stillness, windows open to the sounds of Beltane, the calls of cocks and goats a familiar and soothing soundtrack to her thoughts. Then she heard little Siward waking up, and she went and fetched the boy. She dressed in simple clothes for play. She would make the most of her time with Siward today, because she was giving herself some special time tonight, the night of the Sanctuary ritual. She led him down to the breakfast room, getting him to sing 'Beacons of Wessex' along with her.

Light a tall fire,
Upon the high ground,
Call your friends in the beacon's sight
It's days from Shaugh Moor t' Blewburton Hill
But you're safe in the ring of the beacons' light

They ate and sang, little Siward spluttering his porridge over the table as he tried to copy his mother's phrases. Then the music tutor arrived, and Hettie sat in with her while they all sang that lovely old song, and the tutor's version of 'Good King Spring At Last,' with its rousing tune. They finished with Iles's restoration of 'The Holly and the Ivy,' all laughing at Siward's pronunciation of the unfamiliar words. Then she led him out onto the big front lawn, and they kicked a ball about as the sun crept over the avenue of cypresses. He wanted to play sword-fighting, so Hettie got him to race her back into the house and across the clattering corridor to the play-room, where they found two play swords. He wanted to do it outside, because he'd seen the men's morning practice on the lawn, so they ran outside again.

Playing, fighting and singing filled the morning, then the gong went for lunch. They joined a whole queue of guests at the buffet, which was a bit more lavish than usual for Beltane. No sooner had they sat down than a massive choral sound erupted from the music room as the Beltane choir launched into 'The Poet's Share,' complete with fancy harmonies. After she and Siward had eaten, she took the boy through to listen to the music for a few minutes. He needed a bath, but Dora could see to that later.

Dora took the boy away for his afternoon nap and activities, and Hettie sat down at her desk to read again. She noticed the advance leaflet the ever-communicative Ambrose Swords had sent out ahead of the Beltane ritual, so everyone knew what to expect. She put her work aside and picked it up.

Sanctuary Night
Welcoming - Pledging - Honouring Ritual
The Fifty-Fifth since the restoration of the Sanctuary!
The Rituals:
This year, there will be five stages to the rites.
First Stage: the Labyrinth Greetings, in the New Labyrinth
Second Stage: the pledging of the Ancestral Totems.

Last Beltane, Hettie had set up a great carved oak for Siward. Ever since it had occurred to the people of Wessex that they loved the Sanctuary ritual, it had occurred to Ambrose that those that could, should pay for the rites, just like in the old days. If you wanted to honour your deceased mother at Avebury, you could get a big tree trunk, carve it, transport it to Avebury, pay Ambrose's team to set it up in the Sanctuary, and it would get a consecration that was considered the best you could get in modern Wessex. It would cost more than a few pounds, and would help to feed those poorer than you and to sustain the rites for another year. She focused back on the leaflet.

Third Stage: the Sacrifices, Pigs for the Living and Cattle for the Dead.

Fourth Stage: the Feasting. This year, the roast will be with the other foods, in the outer Sanctuary. This will be an end to the rites for anyone who does not want to take part in the:-

Fifth Stage, the inner Sanctuary Working. This will consist of rites of a sexual nature.

Ah, here came the new development: Ambrose was asking 'those that did want to take part in all the rites to be masked throughout, to preserve the anonymity of those who wished it. Those who didn't give a damn about their anonymity were also requested to be masked, to add to the general confusion and therefore the anonymity of those who did.' Ambrose's prose was a little tortured at times.

Thinking of sexual magic and old Ambrose Swords made her smile. The old shagger has probably had half my family. Almost certainly my mother, and maybe Maeve. For that matter, he probably had Edwin as well.

Anyway, a mask for her, of course. Hettie was staying on for the whole trip. She would pick the best from the cream of Wessex manhood in the labyrinth-working at the beginning, then in the sex rite she would find him and take him somewhere where no-one, especially him, would recognize her, somewhere of her choice, and fuck his wits out.

Yes, that's what she would do. It was too long since she'd felt the heat and forcefulness of a man's body on hers. She hadn't been able to think about sex, not with mourning Siward, had not been able to open herself up to that sacred impersonality.

Yes; she'd wear the cat-mask, in honour of her patroness, Freya. And beneath the neck? Sky clad? No, she didn't want anyone to recognize her by her witch-tattoos, though few had seen them. The elf-garter round her thigh would raise a lot of questions in the gossiping classes. *Which is everybody, in news-starved Wessex.*

She opened her wardrobe and selected a simple black silk robe that opened all the way down the front. She dressed in the robe and some thonged sandals, added a belt with a long, thin dagger, then threw a cloak over it all and picked up the mask. She looked around her, saying goodbye to the room, as she did when she expected it to look different when she returned, when she was going out with the intention of changing her life. She found herself speeding up, moving fast and eager, as she cut through the quadrangle to the stables, where she packed the mask in a saddlebag. Her big black stallion Gram greeted her, and she saddled him up and rode to Asgard Hall, across the beautiful North Downs track.

The sun was low in the sky when she left the horse at Asgard Hall's stables. She didn't want to speak to anyone, in the midst of preparing her mind for the evening's rituals, and Ambrose was probably already down at the Sanctuary. Instead, she set off on foot down the Avenue, joining the people who were surging between the twin rows of ancient stones.

Close to the outer edge of the Sanctuary complex, the crowd was compressed, and movement slow. She passed the time looking around her at the splendid, hot throng packing the cracked, old metalled road in front of the

Sanctuary. A girl pressed against her and they smiled at each other. The girl was dressed only in a leather thong. The woman she turned back and chatted to was slim, gleaming brown with oil, totally naked. A man stumbled in front of her, tripping up on his shining black robe covered in stars and moons. His companion, a tall woman in a silk robe that showed off her enormous breasts, cracked up laughing as she steadied him. In front of them was a couple in bright cotton kilts, and at the front of the crowd, where they were entering the Sanctuary itself, a petite girl standing aloft on a crate swung her body to the mad pace of her violin, her only dress the rainbow hues of her dyed body hair and painted skin. To this rhythm, a naked, athletic young woman danced, sinuously, muscling a fluorescent hoop up and down her body, the hyper-real colours blending into a cylinder of vibrating light, as if her aura had taken on solid form.

Hettie pushed down a surge of guilt about leaving little Siward behind. He would be cared for lovingly by his governess, whom he adored, and he was too young to go to something like this. She recognized her rationalization in that thought, but a more sensible part of herself, recognizing her own needs, let her quash the guilt and look after herself. If Dad had been here, he would have insisted she go, would have pushed her out of the door.

Now she was inside the complex. The entrance was given over to the new labyrinth, low stakes of wood driven in a swirling double-circle. Everyone was waiting at the edge when Ambrose stood on a box to deliver one of his knowledge lectures.

An old hand in the crowd shouted, 'Make it short, please, Ambrose.'

The old man smiled. 'In deference to the Goddess, and Her impatient devotees, I shall indeed keep it short. But not too short.' He took a deep breath and launched into his speech.

'A labyrinth is not a maze. It's not for getting lost in. It is a vortex of balanced flow, bringing people together in a state of concentration, as in any good dance. It harmonizes the two sides of the brain. It allows us to focus on the immense Other of the Earth-Goddess. Our labyrinth is Cretan-style. There is a cross, for the Earth. The round belly of the Mother. Breasts above Her belly. Hands of the Earth Mother, resting on Her belly.

'You don't need to know consciously what happens with this pattern. It will happen as you walk it, as will many other wonderful things. That's it.' Ambrose stood down again.

The crowd were almost shocked at this brevity, at least, those that had actually been listening, and not simply eyeing up their neighbours, making conversation or fondling each other. The band struck up 'Sumer Is A-Cumen' In,' that stirring song that Hettie had believed was from a film in the age of excess, until Ambrose had told her it was much older.

The people at the labyrinth entrance started to form into a queue, cheerfully putting up with the shepherding part, as everybody got loaded into the magic diagram. Ambrose and his student assistants fussed around until everyone was in the spiral sections and being led round by the chanting priestesses.

Hettie saw the relief on Ambrose's face as they swung past each other smoothly on the first whirl of the dance. The labyrinth was a fantastic opportunity to get a good look at everyone else, a chance to check each other out without staring rudely. They all passed in front of her, close enough to catch a glimpse of the person's face in action, get a snapshot of their soul in the circling.

Some of the dancers were already masked, ready for the sexual rite. She paid particular attention to those bodies and their masks. There was a huge, dark man masked as a bear, a tall, slender man with a bird head, an elegant, capering man with the head of a snake, but the man who held her attention was tall, slim and strong-looking, and she liked the eyes she glimpsed through his curious ice-giant mask. *That's the one for me.*

When everyone had been right round the labyrinth, the masked priestesses ushered the crowd through the arch, a pair of stone columns covered in climbing vines twining up and over to meet in the centre. The dreamy fragrance of early honeysuckle mingled with pine resin, sweat and perfume as they streamed into the circular enclosure and flowed round the space to surround the central trio of carven trunks. That circle was the first layer of restoration of the complex, way back in Edwin's day. The crowd kept drawing up to the centre until everyone was pressed together, leaving barely enough space for the new totem-trees to be carried through to the middle.

There were three this year, all royal oaks from the tiny remains of Savernake forest. The first was presented by Cymru Assembly-leader Gwyn Ap Rhys, with a fine ritual incantation delivered in Cymraeg, in honour of Gwyn's father. The richly-carved totem was anointed with oils and all who wished to, came up and touched it, adding their power to the memory of an ancestor. Then it was carried to its pit in the second circle, and hauled upright by six strong youths. The second was blessed by a small, tough-looking woman with swarthy skin and shiny black hair. In a lilting voice, she sang an impassioned song about her husband. Many were moved, and paid their tribute; this was a world where everyone had lost loved ones before their time. Hettie was surprised when the third tree was presented by Hendry, and dedicated to all the dead from the Wessex wars of the previous century. This was a transparent plea for public support, surely everyone could see that. But many placed their hands on the totem, thereby adding their power to Hendry's gift.

Hettie was taken up with the beauty of it all. Drunk on freedom as only a mother on holiday can be, her heart went out to her fellow celebrants. She looked round, thinking: *This sexual celebration, life and death all mixed up and thrilling through us... The naked, gorgeous priestesses oiling the wooden Frey figures, the dignified and shocking sacrifices to come, the honouring of the living and the dead... We're living such a rich, rich life, this Spring evening, the Goddess dances in the soft light, all the world is a-glow. I am so glad that I can live through this age when people can finally, at least for a while, love life as it is, without wanting to change humanity, just to live with depth and truth, with such a hum of blood and seed.*

Then an unfamiliar sensation gripped her. The light might have shifted, but it hadn't; something had gone off, profoundly off. She didn't know why she seemed so suddenly suspicious of everything; things had just turned, instantly, sour. Looking round at the smiling, flirting, caressing people, at a happy, middle-aged couple gazing at the spectacle, she thought, *Their reality is so fragile, I could destroy it with three words or so... anything powerful and only a little malign could.*

She mentally slapped herself. *Get a grip, Hettie! Have a bit of fun!*

The doubting, troubled voice continued unabated in her head. *They don't know it's going to end, anyway... it's all poised to fall apart, this Wessex golden age! Here, you Wessexers, you need to wake up and see what's happening!*

The voice went on, with its own momentum, *Can't you see, this perfect society is just a temporary phase, everything passes, don't you know that? Can't you see the writing on the wall?*

She steadied herself, took a few fast, shallow breaths and then a deep one. She tried not to listen to the mental noise, not to pay attention to it, but it was overwhelming, this dark rant. So instead she formulated an intention, imagined it succeeding and felt its success intensely. Then she imagined it failing, and felt that too, keeping the breath rhythm going.

Then, having created a space of detachment, she was ready, her inner voice quiet, slender and bright, like serpentine golden script in a dark room.

Her prayer began: *Let there be a time when people will all be vigilant, unlike our ancestors, who let in the darkness of Christianity...*

Then, in a flash of insight it occurred to her what the price of such mental vigilance is. The happiness she had just glimpsed on the people here would be wiped out. Vigilance is a warrior virtue, and these people were having time off from their worries and pains. Their lives were hard enough as it was, without depriving them of their innocent recreation.

She re-scripted the intention in her head and began: *Let us make a society as naïve as the elder one, where our lives would be real enough to be eternal.*

But then again, she reflected, *nothing lasts.* She scrapped that one, too.

Drawing a long breath, she settled on: *Let me understand what it is we need.* Something about that felt right, and her mind steadied again. She watched as the last stages of the Giving rite closed.

Then came the blood sacrifices. Those who didn't wish to witness them left, and the crowd thinned out a little. Hettie found the sacrifices a big, exciting thing, with the undercurrent of dubiety generated by bloodshed, the sacred terror that comes with killing. The masked butchers stood by Ambrose, by the great stone slab just off-centre of the circle. They looked impartial, lifted out of their gruesome role by the solemnity of the sacrifice.

The animals were led in one by one. Three boars were first, each bathed clean and decked out with wreaths of flowers. They skittered about but didn't squeal. *I expect they're tranquillized*, she thought. The butchers slit their throats expertly, and the animals died as quickly as anyone could make them.

Then a bullock, large and sleek and decked with ribbons and flowers was led to the centre. The pampered animal was stroked and petted up to the moment of its death, glorious and terrible to behold. Most people were silent as they watched, stunned by the reality of flesh, blood, and the death that gave life. The carcases were strapped to poles and carried out of the enclosure for butchering, and those who wished to, left behind them.

What Ambrose had planned as the fifth stage of the ritual got going seamlessly, as soon as the sacrifice team had left. Two priestesses spun round the circle whirling thuribles of pine resin and hemp bud.

Fucking was breaking out all over. She saw a slender redheaded woman kneeling in front of the tall bird-headed man, her half-mask facilitating the wrapping of her mouth around his long cock. The massive, dark-skinned man fucked a tiny, shrieking woman against one of the totems, then pulled out of her and spurted over the tree-trunk. Hettie wondered if he was honouring his own ancestors or just anyone's.

In the centre, the sacrificial altar was even livelier, two women sandwiching a man in the slick blood congealing on the great stone. Over by the shadow-hut on the edge of the Sanctuary, what looked like three big-built men were going at it hammer and tongs.

Then she saw her frost-giant man. She moved round so that she was in front of him, demanding his attention, and began to saunter in measured pace, her intention clear in the attitude of her every step.

Behind her cat mask, Alex could see how widely-spaced her eyes must be. The eyes were violet, and deep. She radiated sexual power and authority. She put a finger to the lips of her mask, seized his hand firmly, and led him through the crowd, out of the crowd, out of the Sanctuary and up the hill towards West Kennet Longbarrow.

Chapter 13: Darkness

She pushed through the leather curtains that hung over the entrance to the passage-tomb. Some warm nights it was hard to get time on your own in West Kennet, but tonight nearly everyone was off to the pubs and booths of Avebury. It was almost completely dark and silent, with a lingering sweetness of hemp smoke, perfume and sex. Hettie knew the space well, and she led them through the soft darkness to a low arched entrance on the left. She knelt down and listened to the emptiness, then led the way inside. The chamber was tiny, with a massive rounded rock rising up from the middle of the floor. It was so dark that their movements became spare and tentative, their accidental touches soft and yielding. Hettie unbuckled her dagger belt and laid it by the entrance. She laid her cloak and robe on the gritty floor. She felt the man laying out his clothes too, to make a soft space for them. Her eyes had adjusted enough now to see him remove his mask and place it aside. Her heart pounding in her neck, she did likewise, and met his eyes in the gloom.

Alex had strewn his clothes around him and sat watching the faintly-visible girl across the rock take her mask off. Her eyes gleamed, a little like a cat's. He stretched out to reach her, over the rock, and it too felt warm, and smooth, like firm flesh. His fingers touched taut skin, his face moved into the stream of her breath. He shifted his weight over the stone, as if he was flowing. Her face was in his hands and their breaths mingling. He wrung the pleasure out of every moment of the touch of their lips, of moving and pausing, of sticking and sliding, of pushing and yielding. In the near-darkness her body seemed to glow. He followed the aura with his lips, kissing and turning her, nuzzling the softness and sniffing the feast of her body's scents.

She gazed at those faintly-glowing eyes until his breath was on her lips, then entering inside her, his body-scent catching in her blood. She moved close to him, letting the delicate dance of his kissing draw her into slow movement, turning and presenting each part of herself to his lips. Then they were both twined round each other, the space they were in could have been any size and there was no sense of up and down. She felt like she was drowning, but willed it to go on.

He had got to a place where everything that happened was perfect. He found himself lapping between the fur of her lips, and his cock sliding into a hot mouth. Time slowed right down, then sped up again, and they were seated somehow, she on top of him, her hair like a cool burn on his skin. Entering her was shockingly intense, and then when they came, he couldn't tell if his eyes were open or closed, or where that light was coming from.

When he surfaced, the smell of their sex filled the space. They held each other, their boundaries permeable, the stone itself alive with soft light. Her mind was wide open when her vision came. At first, it was like the beginning of that cerebral panic she'd felt at the ritual, but more forceful this time. She knew there was no fighting it, this time she just had to let go. She took a deep breath and fell into a darkness bursting with energy. There, her dises found her and spun her head into a whirlpool of spiderwebs, every thread carrying droplets of imagery. She let the vertigo of ecstasy bear her along until it had run its course. There she sat, her arms still round the man, letting her mind process it all, alert for any developing meaning.

After some time, he knelt upright and took her hand. He leaned forward and whispered, 'Main chamber.' It felt good that his invitation used so few words.

In the circular central chamber they spread their clothes out on the straw matting someone had covered the floor with, and lay down in each others' arms. She was still waiting for the answer from her deep mind when she found herself drifting into a dream. Oddly, she couldn't remember anything about it when she woke up. She was resting on the chest of the man, her hand over his belly, and there was a faint grey light in the chamber. He was asleep, but she would have to decide if she was going to let him see her face. An authoritative female voice in her head said *Yes.*

She drifted back to the edge of sleep for a while, while the man's strong arms held her gratifyingly as he slept. He snored softly. She smiled and drew in a luxurious breath. He smelled of bronze and cinnamon. She smiled some more. She liked the look of him even better with his mask off. Short fair hair, a high, squarish forehead, a fine, intelligent face, stubble on his prominent, dimpled chin. This one was worth showing herself to, because she would want to see him again and again. He stirred against her and his blue eyes opened. Their breaths met, like earlier, and that made her want him all over again.

When they'd disentangled their bodies again, it was almost broad daylight. He smiled. 'Let's walk up Silbury.'

She nodded; it was so pleasant and easy to agree, in her holiday, in her freedom. They dressed, buckled on their slim weapons, picked up their masks and stepped out, into a glorious dawn.

Golden light slanted across that god-infused landscape. They sauntered down the footpath, past the three protected oaks at the bottom of the slope, and then jumped down the bank of the Kennet, into the stream, to splash water on each other and laugh in the shock of that intense cold. Then they crossed the bridge and the old, cracked trunk road to reach the foot of Silbury. They climbed the path up the west side, a breeze clearing the sky and combing the grasses into brindled hair-patterns, rippling, alive, under fast, cloud-dappled light. At the top, they stood holding each other, she shivering, suddenly sneezing and laughing at the same time, shaking her head, savouring the feeling of emptiness, like after coming, the pure, animal unselfconsciousness, there on the highpoint of the Avebury complex.

When they'd had enough of the wind, they ran back down the hill, joining the wide path by the Kennet. Here, they came to the bend in the tangled, overgrown lane that led into Avebury. They could hear raised voices just round the bend. As they approached the sounds became clearer – a woman in distress, and more than one man's voice. Their glances met. They both drew their weapons and stepped forward slowly and quietly.

Two well-dressed men held a struggling woman against a car, while a third stood in front of her, his back to Alex and Hettie.

Alex raised his sword. The two men let go of the girl and stepped towards him. The assailant turned. The victim rolled to one side and ran off up the path, clutching her torn clothes. Alex sidestepped the drunk-looking man nearest him and ran towards the would-be rapist.

In a moment of shock, the world slowed down. Hettie realised she was facing Jervis. Her dises had brought her to this moment, to this opportunity. She charged at him, dagger extended; Jervis turned aside and pulled a real-looking handgun. He pointed it at Alex. 'Your commoner boyfriend gets it if you touch me.'

Alex was almost upon Jervis by the time this happened, and Hettie saw him rushing into the gunshot as Jervis pulled the trigger.

The gun clicked, jamming, and Alex slammed into him. The gun tumbled out of Jervis's hand and Alex grabbed him by the hair. In a rage, he slammed the man's head against the car bonnet, again and again, until he stopped moving.

He let go of Jervis, who slid down the car bonnet and crumpled on the ground. He gasped and staggered back, his blood-splattered arms out to the sides. The other two thugs had run off.

Hettie went to him. Part of her had wanted to stop him, the part that hated violence on general principles, but the stronger part was aware that she might be getting what she was working for – the traitor's death. They held each other, then Alex got his breath and said, 'I take it you knew him.'

Hettie drew away from him a little and looked into his eyes. 'I've got you involved in an old battle of my family's making.'

Alex sat down stiffly on the overgrown bank, incredulous, as she told him who she was and why she'd tried to kill her half-brother.

When she paused, he stood up and said, 'Come on, we're going to Asgard Hall.' He took her hand. They both looked down at the body. It seemed there was nothing anyone could do for Jervis now, and if there was, it was the business of his friends. They set off up the track.

Chapter 14: Trial

Asgard Hall looks down over a long slope: a student in wellingtons and ragged tweeds pauses in her feeding of the goats to gaze over the arc of giant sarsens in the shifting morning light. Two figures are coming up the path, their heads down, their hair flicked about by gusts of breeze. She is about to start singing her morning Goddess song, when the couple reach the top of the path and look up at her. The song dies on her lips.

They sat in the kitchen. Alex made coffee and they sipped it, but neither of them wanted to eat. Ambrose appeared in a dressing gown, about to start his usual rumbustious greeting, when he noticed who was in his house.

'My dear Hettie, it always a pleasure to see you, but I fear something has happened, and it's probably not as bad as you think. Let me get some coffee and we'll adjourn to my rooms.'

They spread out around the armchairs of Ambrose's private study, and told their tale, up to leaving Jervis for dead.

'Oh fucking hell, my dears, you really have stirred things up.' He shook his head, then smiled. 'But really, although this may be of no help right now, you've probably saved Wessex! Alex, we've got to get you a decent lawyer, you'll plead self-defence, and Hettie's witnessing will make sure you are exonerated. Now, I'm going to make a call. I'll get the kitchen to send you some food up.'

They were eating porridge when Ambrose returned. Stiff and formal with perplexity, he stood by Hettie, his hand on her shoulder. 'My dear, I have to send you home. I have just heard that your mother Gwendoline, Gods bless her, is sick. My dear, she may even be dying.'

Hettie looked at him, numb. Ambrose said, 'I know... I'll get my driver to take you.'

Hettie shook her head decisively. 'No, Ambrose, I'll ride Gram, he's in your stables.' She stood up and embraced him, holding him tight and hugging him like a child. Then she turned to Alex. 'Alex, last night was...' She shook her head. 'You are dear to me. Be lucky.' She kissed him lightly, turned and left.

They sat in gloom, finishing their coffee. Ambrose stood up. 'Your lawyer will be round after lunch. You'll be fine, Alex. Things will change for the better. Hettie will be chosen, everyone loves her, she will rule, and she will have cause to thank you for removing the most hated and murderous member of her family. Get some rest now, dear boy.'

Alex went and lay down in his room, but couldn't sleep. He got up, washed, ate a skimpy lunch and went to sit and wait in the downstairs study. He pushed the door open and bumped it against an apologetic student who was reaching for some high-placed book. Another student was laying drawings out across the only table, absorbed in some task, and a third was muttering softly into a vonnie-recorder. The only space available was a decaying leather chair wedged tightly in an alcove opposite the high window. Alex squeezed in and sat down, his mind blank, his senses pricked into uncomfortable intensity by sleep-deprivation. It was hot in the alcove, and the books emitted smells of oxidizing paper. Their spines stank of animal-skin, of fish-glue, of rusting steel wires. Then there were the exotic chemicals, the plasticizers that keep old synthetic leather soft, the sebum of vanished cyborgs. Underneath that, the shelves bled oaken sweetness, and from somewhere came a hint of ancient cigars. Alex sat and chewed the inside of his cheek, swallowed up by unwanted awakeness. He was starting to wish he smoked.

The lawyer arrived, a stocky man with deep golden, pock-marked skin, a colour only a wealthy person could afford. Alex stood up and shook hands, watching him, fascinated. 'Racheby,' the man said, looking genuinely open-hearted. 'I charm courtrooms, Alex. And we have right on our side, which, while it does not guarantee victory, at least will always make us feel better.' Racheby's smile seemed to say that defeat was highly improbable.

Racheby heard out Alex's version of the morning's events, nodding sagely, then stood up and said, 'I have my instructions now. Do not worry.'

Alex drifted back to his room and lay down. He'd never killed a man before, and he felt as if he was in a dream. The events kept running, taking up the whole volume of his thoughts. He smashed Jervis's head in, over and over. Prince Jervis Perceval-Wodening, half-brother of Princess Hettie, the woman he'd spent Beltane night making love with. He saw the body on the ground, limp and motionless. Jervis was a bad man, he needed to be stopped. *But I've never killed a man before. And I smashed his head in.*

He slept fitfully.

He woke in half-light, amplified sound booming in the distance. It was the Avebury Fair music stage, the big one with solar panels, old-school amplifiers and big name bands. Wrapping himself in his numbness, he drifted across the room to the chest of drawers, on which someone had left a small brown bottle and a jug and glass. Laudanol. He let three drops fall into the glass, topped it up and drank.

He slept.

The next day the images of Jervis's death, the bloody face, the body crumpling to the ground, had receded into the background. Instead, his mother's smile hovered in his mind. He looked at the tincture bottle, then crossed to the writing-bureau, opened it and slipped the drug into a tiny drawer. *I've slept enough.*

Inside the bureau was an old photograph album. He hefted it out, opened it at random, and his heart skipped a beat. He was viewing a faded colour photo of his mother, standing with a toddler's hand in hers, her hair blown by a sea breeze, the stones of some quayside under her feet. The boy had his large eyes and proud forehead.

He took the album down to the kitchen and helped himself to porridge and tea. He was alone, until a student came in to start on lunch. She smiled at him, a strong-looking blonde girl with a pleasant face, and he smiled back, but he didn't feel like talking, except with someone who might be able to help him find answers to give his old ghosts. He went looking for Ambrose.

The grand old man was lounging in his study, doing what he loved to do when on holiday, working. He was dictating a letter to a student, a skinny, bespectacled dark-skinned youth, who was clearly in awe of Wessex's cultural icon. Alex nodded and smiled to indicate non-urgency, and sat in a deep leather chair.

'So we shall not know how it all turns out until after it has all happened. Yours etcetera, etcetera.' Ambrose exhaled. 'Bring it to me in writing, so that I can see how truly badly-written it is. Thank you, er...'

'Winston, sir.' The boy packed his shorthand pad and pushed the pencil into the top pocket of his work-shirt. He opened his mouth, then remembered not to say 'Thank you,' because it annoyed Ambrose. The old man never explained why; it was one of those things the student had to work out for him or herself. Winston left.

Alex hefted the photo album. 'Sofie, Ambrose. Tell me everything.'

The old man rang a little bell. 'We shall have tea.'

Another student knocked and stepped in. 'Earl Grey, my dear.'

Ambrose remained in half-profile to Alex, who saw one brown eye gaze into a tunnel of old memory.

'She said she was from the Northern islands, you know. She had that accent, almost Scandinavian.'

The student came in with tea, placed it on the side table and left.

'Becters? Did anyone in my family use them?'

'Not that I'm aware of. What makes you ask such an odd thing, old chap?'

Alex frowned, remembering what Maira had told him. 'I... I don't know... A woman I met in Carcassonne told me...' Ambrose cocked his head, willing to listen.

'She said that the reason I can't use super-vonnies, becters, is that someone has put something in the way, something deep in me.'

'And this woman, given to mysterious utterances, is a BT?'

Alex nodded.

'Hmm, can't tell you what that's about. But some of the people I've met – not judged, we never catch them – special people, BTs – your mother thought you were like that. But all mothers think their sons exceptional in some way. She kept some seed vials, she said were becters. Couldn't find them, I looked after... she finally went away.'

'Yes, yes...'

'You know, the second time she went away, she took you with her. Or, at least, you went missing too. Anything could have happened to you.'

Alex opened the photo album. 'What about my father?'

'Chester Tyler, a true gentleman. He died at Savernake, you were twelve months old. You came to me. Sofie got ill and went to a retreat, where she was supposed to be cared for by some kind of healer. Who died very soon after.'

He sat up. 'Here, I believe I have a snapshot of Chester. Over there, Alex, you'll have to use the steps.'

On the top shelf, covered in dust, there was a little solar-powered photo-viewscreen, a luxury from just before the end of the electronics age. Alex passed it to Ambrose, who blew dust off it and chuckled. 'Present from one of my first students, a long, long time ago.' He fiddled with the display. 'Still has some battery power, well-made piece of stuff. Here.'

Alex took the tablet device. It showed a blond, handsome man in his twenties. Any more than that was impossible to tell – the old plastic screen had gone patchily opaque, a cataracted eye on the past. 'What did she do, my mum?'

'She had her own money, came to Wessex with some kind of inheritance. There's not a lot more I can tell you, old chap, and I don't think any of it would be of interest.' His brow furrowed. 'Or maybe just one thing: Hendry was always besotted with her. Which is probably why he showed such an interest in you. Though I can't imagine you're Hendry's son. I've never known the apple fall that far from the tree.' He smiled and squeezed Alex's hand. 'Keep the tablet.'

'That's something else Maira, my BT friend, said; I can't be Hendry's son.'

There was a knock at the door. 'Ah, my eleven o'clock,' said Ambrose, as the Asgard Hall clock chimed.

Alex went back to his room. He stared out of the window, remembering his mother kissing him goodbye, and saying something he never caught, her words blown away on the wind as she stepped onto the ferry. She wasn't going to the Isle of Wight, like she'd said, she was leaving him. He paced the room, turning abruptly, thinking about Chester, about Hendry, about Ambrose – who was his father? *Who else did you screw, Sofie? Who else did you fall so passionately in love with?*

There was an astonishing range of alcohols and tinctures in the glossy old sideboard, and Alex chose an old bottle of brandy. He paced the room drinking, catching himself in the act as he passed the wardrobe mirror, observing the drama he was making. After a while, his mind seemed to dull over, and his anger seemed like clarity. He stood up, cold as ice, and punched the ancient oak door.

His other hand dropped his glass, which rolled on the floor, spilling an inch of liquor. He looked at the crack in the door and the damage to his knuckles. It hadn't made any difference, no catharsis had come about. All that had happened was that he was a little ashamed and contrite. He sat down on the floor and wept, pointlessly, for a few moments, aware he was trying to empty an ocean with a teaspoon.

The rest of the day passed in a daze. At some stage, he found himself looking at the half-empty bottle and the tinctures. But there was no hiding from this, he had to make it into something. He forced himself through some qi gong stretches, showered, then went seeking music, down the hill into Avebury Fair.

A woman sat on a small sound stage, vonnie-speakers powered by solar panels, the sound sweet, only slightly fuzzed by the unshielded pickups. She had a gentle, yielding style, that opened up for incursions of vonnie-noise; the wind through a seagull's wings, the gasps of lovers, it was like the world was taking part in Zara Holmes's performance today, not getting in its way.

She was blonde, and not young – forty, maybe, or older, if she was well-off enough to be on Rejuve. *She could have a son my age.*

He felt his attention splitting into two, the basic meditation his fencing instructor had taught him. He let be the violent ache over his mother, and the cool self that perceived it. *This feeling cannot hurt me.*

He heard Zara's performance out, and suddenly felt tired. He was tired of holding together this edifice of anger. He trudged back to the house, and at some point the chain of thoughts that held up his wrath collapsed, and the feeling popped like a bubble. It occurred to him then: what if she'd had no choice? What if he was the fruit of rape? What if his mother had been abducted, and then maybe killed?

And maybe what Ambrose was protecting him from, with his reluctance to commit to an explanation of Sofie's disappearance, was that she might have been an adventuress, always needing a new thrill in her life, and that in the end, one of those thrills had destroyed her.

At some point, he found himself in his bedroom. He poured a glass of water and drank it, then another. He sat on the bed, and then lay down and submitted to sleep.

He dreamed of leaving Wessex. When he woke up, the sadness filled him, but he was watching it play through his body. It didn't matter all that much if he had to run. It occurred to him that he was less upset than he would have expected.

He was already getting breakfast when Ambrose appeared. 'My boy, we have a new development. Did you realise you hadn't killed Jervis? No? Well, he's in a coma, up at the palace. His cronies scooped him up after you left, and discovered he still had breath in him, if not consciousness. As long as he stays unconscious, your position is little altered. If he wakes up, then what he says could make all the difference.'

He pushed aside his bowl. From outside, he heard the horn of one of the house minibuses, announcing they'd be leaving for Marlborough in a few minutes. He stood up, and joined Ambrose on the drive. Their silence infected the bus.

At the courthouse, it was clear that the word was out –

there were already twenty or more people in the public gallery, waiting to get some entertainment with their justice.

This was just the magistrates' hearing. Alex was remanded on his own surety to be tried for grievous assault. The public were disgruntled. A reporter closed in on him as they left. 'NeighbourNet, Mr Tyler, do you have a statement?' Ambrose stepped in front of him. 'My nephew will speak in due course. Thank you.'

That was it. He was free, for the time being. Ambrose took him for a pint in the Red Lion. Neither of them bothered ordering food, but sipped their beer and listened to farmers making deals. Some people wanted to get back to work now, and were selling off everything they could before the closing ritual that night. The latter was a mongrel tradition, a bonfire with a firework display and some dancing, at dusk on the final day of the Avebury Beltane week. Some would stay on; the agricultural show would continue as long as the farmers had things to sell and buy.

Back at Asgard Hall, Alex allowed himself to cheer up a bit. He wondered how soon he would see Hettie again. Dinner was a more pleasant affair, lubricated with beer, and they were all sitting round in the dining room when there was a loud banging at the door.

A student went to look. She came back hot-foot, tripping over herself to get the words out. 'Armed men, Jervis's men, for- for Alex!'

Ambrose jumped up and went to the door.

There were raised voices, then he returned. He stood in front of Alex. 'Jervis has recovered. He is charging you with malicious assault at the behest of Hettie. You are to be arraigned as an accessory to attempted dynastic assassination. Because it is a Royal matter, I cannot stand surety for your bail. You must go with Jervis's men, dear boy.'

Ambrose led Alex to the front door, where he handed him over to Jervis's constables. The three men, in Palace livery of deep green and black, handcuffed him, none too gently, and pushed him into the back of a cramped diesel van. The back window was painted black, and when the van stopped and the doors opened, they were on the gravel drive at the side of Marlborough Palace. The tallest of the guards took his arm, this time more gently, and nodded grimly at him, then led him into the house and down whitewashed basement stairs to a black painted steel door, which even in the dim light Alex could see was dented and battered. The guard unlocked the door and slowly pushed him forwards until he stood in the brightly-lit space. The door closed, and the lock clunked, hard. In front of him stood a tiny bed on a pallet, and a washbasin with no tap or jug.

A few minutes later, he heard footsteps outside, and the light went out. The darkness was total. He felt his way over to the bed and lay down, despair filling him up like a cold fluid, numbing, sleep-inducing. He closed his eyes.

Some unmeasured minutes later, bright light flooded the cell and the door swung open. He sat up, shielding his eyes, and wondered if Jervis had come to gloat, or worse.

A tall silhouette loomed in the glare. Nothing else, no other sight or sound. Then a gentle voice. 'Alex, it's me, Bruno.' The figure in the doorway stepped forward, closing the door completely. The light dimmed a little.

Bruno's eyes sought his; Alex was silent, full of questions. Bruno put a hand on Alex's shoulder, and a second later, Alex slumped, and Bruno put his arms round the younger man. 'It's OK, you'll be fine. And I think I have some answers you want. Sit down.'

'First, we have plenty of time. Remember last Wednesday at Asgard House, my history lesson? Well, your two guards are living in another reality, a bit more enveloping than that, until I bring them out of it. It's a lot happier reality than this one, so they'll be in no hurry to leave, and it'll all seem straightforward when they return.

'So yes, I am becter-tolerant, like the woman you know as Maira. Do you want to know what I know about your mother, Alex? It isn't everything, it will not give you closure, but this might be the last chance I get to tell you.' Bruno looked carefully at him. Alex nodded.

'Sofie disappeared or was abducted three times. The first time will have been when Raven impregnated her with you.' Bruno tried to catch Alex's eye. 'I am fairly certain he is your father.' He made a long pause, but Alex squeezed his arm and nodded.

Bruno resumed. 'The second, I believe he was trying out becters on her. I think he was trying to create a dynasty of BTs, those who could tolerate the most powerful BEC-transceivers. That is something you may treat as a speculation, but I warn you that it is difficult to account for Raven's history in any other way. That is the occasion when you went missing too. I suspect that is when he adjusted your becter-tolerance; we are talking about a master of von Neumann nanotechnology.

'I believe it's also possible that Sofie was Raven's daughter. That would make him both father and lover to her.

'The third time, which is when she may have left of her own accord – is when she never came back. I believe she was in conflict with Raven, and he may have killed her.'

Alex's mind had long been stretched beyond anything he'd previously endured. He felt as if he was articulating a dream... He asked, 'Why did you seek Raven, Bruno? How come you know more than anyone else about him?'

'Because he threatened the life of someone I loved. And somehow I saved that person.' Bruno's voice was a whisper. 'And because he is the key to becters. Do I need to say more?'

'Do you think Maira knew Raven?'

'I think she was very close; her benefactor was one of the originals, Raven's first test subjects. Step this way for death or power.'

'Where do the Crow stalls fit in?'

'They seem to be information-gathering portals. I suspect they are actually much more, though, involved in some long-term goal of Raven's.'

Bruno stood up straight and closed his eyes. 'I have to get moving, Alex.'

They hugged. Alex felt bad. *What next?* Bruno picked up the thought, it seemed. 'War. Read the classics. We're not so different from our ancestors, despite vonnies. And, with becters, we're just imperfect gods, like our ancestral ones. I think all we have left is tradition. It's survived a couple of civilization collapses already. It's a runner, man!'

Bruno left, and with him that good humour. Alex slumped back on his bed. Bruno had left the light on, just a little.

He lay down and got ready for sleep. The light dimmed. *I did that – I've been entrained!* He lay there, thinking about the mystery and power of the becters. *I have a friend with that power.* He felt a flicker of hope, which brightened as it occurred to him that Hettie would support him. *Surely she will. It was only one night, but we were so close...*

Then it occurred to him: She'll be in line for the throne. Or Jervis would. But it's not a hereditary monarchy... or is it, have things changed that much, has it become that corrupt and lazy? Would whoever came out on top simply seize power? Surely people wouldn't stand for it. Or would they? He fell into a fitful sleep, punctuated by a dream of running, and of the cackling of ravens.

Then there was the other dream. He is on horseback, he seems to be at the head of an army, but he looks down at his hands and, under the dirt, they are yellowed bone, the hands of a dead man.

Chapter 15: Exile

The court was preceded by its noise; his was the star case today. Reporters, low-budget genetic speciality-acts, high-level-vonnied-up for full visual transmission, stepped in front of him and peered to get close-ups, wide-eyed and unblinking. Idlers jostled for free entertainment in the public gallery. Seven days before, he'd been one of them, sitting in exactly this courtroom; but today he stood, and it was not Ambrose on the bench, but another judge. The courtroom mutter said he was up before Judge Rowlinson, a staunch Wessex Royalist.

The crowd's vonnies were buzzing; in any group that size, there'd be enough people with high-end transception to saturate every receiver in the place. A potentially explosive enhanced crowd-effect, everyone feeding on each others' emotions. The cloud of mental mutter washed over Alex, and it seemed to average out to two possibilities: *exile*, said most; *execution*, said a few, excitable souls.

So much for public wisdom, thought Alex. He turned his attention away as best he could, distracting himself by looking at women in the public gallery.

The judge came in, resplendent in scarlet and purple, and the usher shouted. Rowlinson thwacked his hammer and threatened the rowdies. 'I shall have no hesitation in emptying this court unless...' *Blah blah blah,* heard Alex, soaked in the vonnie-noise. This time, the crowd was subdued. A hush fell, with vonnie whispers washing back and forth: *He's for it... He'll walk...* On balance, they sounded negative.

Alex was accused of assisting an attempted dynastic assassination. Because the arguments consisted of the words of one member of the royal family against those of another, it was impossible for the court to doubt either story. It was a deadlock, which, in a certain sense, was to Alex's benefit.

Judge Rowlinson spoke. 'Alex Tyler, what you actually did will remain a secret between you and your Gods. This court cannot sentence you to anything worse than exile.'

Alex was aware of the subtext: exile is outlawry, as long as he was within the borders of Wessex, and not much law prevailed just the other side of that border. Jervis's party smiled mirthlessly in his direction.

The usher ordered Alex to stand for the sentencing. Alex rose to his feet, time stretching out. He felt calm, and bent to brush imaginary lint off his black woolen trousers. Across the courtroom, in the public gallery, a large man pointed a finger at him, smile spreading across his thick-jowled face. Alex recognized one of the assistants to the attempted rape. The court was silent enough to hear a cat screech outside. It was too late to hide; instead, it was time to show whatever mettle he could. Alex stared his would-be killer in the eye as the judge spoke his sentence.

'Alex Tyler, you will be released into the custody of Ambrose Swords. From sundown tonight, you will leave the Kingdom of Wessex or be counted beyond the protection of our laws after that time. Your outlawry shall extend throughout your life.'

Alex swallowed, a lump in his throat. *My beautiful Wessex*. Ambrose walked before him, clearing the way, as he stepped down from the dock.

They hurried back to Asgard Hall to get a head start. Ambrose had spoken to the right people, and it looked like Alex was getting quite an escort for the dangerous journey. Ambrose supplied horses, rare and expensive, but giving them a better chance than cars, which could run out of fuel or get broken on the rough terrain.

'It's a terrible thing, to be forced to leave your homeland,' said Ambrose.

'I lived in Shemeld before, remember? I'll be fine.'

Ambrose looked him in the eyes. 'You have the power of stoicism, of letting things happen and not being destroyed by them.' The thought had never occurred to Alex before; maybe he had never needed to know what he was capable of.

He smiled mirthlessly. 'At least I won't be working for Hendry.'

Susannah and Bruno had also been busy. Bruno was coming along for at least part of the way, and he'd raised four other volunteers, students who were coming along for the adventure and the story. The tall, muscular lad stuck his hand out. 'I'm Wayland. I'm confronting my limitations and making myself more conscious.'

Alex recognized the style. 'Susannah is your teacher?' Wayland nodded. 'She's the best,' said Alex.

Freya had jet-black hair scraped back off a high forehead. She smiled, eyes narrowed, and shook Alex's hand. 'Glad to have you along.'

Alwiss accepted Alex's hand shyly, and Fitela just nodded and smiled.

Susannah stepped in, dressed in combat camo. She smiled and touched Alex on the shoulder. 'I'm coming too.'

They were seven now, and Alex was moved that so many people cared about his welfare. His spirits rose even more when Thania appeared.

'We're both in exile now. Jervis is after me. I blew the whistle on his treachery.'

Their eyes met; Alex felt a rush of gratitude in his chest, and grasped her hands in his.

He explained his plan to head for Sheffield. Cirencester was the nearest town along that route where the friendly

Birmingham militias held sway. This meant they'd have to cross the badlands south of the Thames channel. The hope was that his pursuers would give up before then.

Ambrose found some century-old high-performance body armour for all of them, and they took the few ballistic guns for which any ammunition remained, and diesel-enhanced airguns. They agreed a couple of tactics for various situations, and talked them over as they set off on the North Downs Road. They rode steadily in broad daylight, on the old metalled road past Broad Hinton, then via the smaller roads between the big farms round Binknoll Castle. Wayland rode ahead, on point, and Freya brought up the rear, checking and re-checking for signs of pursuit. They talked, but not much; any lapse in alertness could be fatal.

They skirted the edges of the Swindon sprawl and were dropping down towards Cricklade, with Wayland, Alex and Thania in front. The road plunged between two steep slopes of rubble, made of some demolished factory estate, the perfect place for an ambush. Wayland and Alex checked both sides, and met again on the old, muddy road.

'We'd be sitting ducks down there. I say we go round this rubble, however far away that takes us.'

Everyone agreed. 'We'll split up, to provide cover.' Alex, Wayland and Thania led the way, the horses pickling their way over the brick-strewn terrain to the left of the great mounds. Freya, Bruno and Fitela hung back.

The front six of them were a couple of minutes ahead when a crossbow bolt nicked Alwiss's horse. The animal reared up, neighing shrilly and the next bolt caught the rider in the shoulder. Alwiss was managing to stay on his horse, so they all rode as hard as they could, away from the slope. When Alex felt a bit safer, he turned round and checked to their rear. Four or five shots rang out, someone cried out, and he saw two figures jump out from cover and run up the slope, black fatigues against the dull orange of the rubble. In the distance, Bruno stood up and fired more shots after the departing attackers, then waved the all-clear.

The party regrouped at the foot of the ruins. Two of the ambushers lay dead, sprawled in front of the cover they'd used. One of the horses was cropping some grass nearby, and Bruno captured it. Alwiss was in pain, but staying calm. Susannah pulled the quarrel out of his flesh, and got the youth up on the horse in front of her.

They moved as fast as they could, down to the pontoon bridge over the Thames channel, which was narrow here. Freya, Wayland and Bruno formed a rearguard, and they rode in silence; surely Jervis wouldn't give up this easily.

Then a shot rang out from the rearguard, their signal to run for cover. About a furlong ahead, an up-ended pontoon section marked the Shemeld Protectorate border. Thania, Alex, Susannah and Fitela reached it first, and as they did, three green-clad figures stood up from behind the barricade and let fly with large, black automatic rifles, shooting over the heads of the rearguard at the distant attackers.

Alex and Thania joined them and turned their own weapons on the four men still standing on the far reaches of the pontoon, covering the rearguard as they joined them. One more of the attackers fell; three bodies were bleeding into the marshes now, and the remaining three fled. Everyone stayed in defensive position for another few seconds, then Alex stood up and crossed over to the Shemeld troops.

The one who stepped forward wore the crossed guns insignia of the Birmingham brigades and a sergeant's stripes on his dark green sleeve.

Alex greeted him. 'I can't thank you enough. We' – he indicated Thania –' are exiles, who wish safe passage into the Shemeld Protectorate. We offer as good will this horse.'

He waved his hand and Wayland brought the nag forward. 'And we have Wessex gold deposited in Birmingham.'

The quiet, wary sergeant inspected the horse, then turned towards Alex and nodded. 'Sergeant Poliakoff, Second SP Militia, out of Cirencester.'

Alex extended his hand. 'Alex Tyler, and this is Thania Roberts.'

'Our boys'll get you to Birmingham, Mister Tyler. After that, you'll be on your own.'

The sergeant took his men aside and there was a whispered discussion, from which Thania thought she caught the word 'gold.' Then the sergeant returned and said, 'Private Burslem will accompany you. He will be pleased to draw our reward when you are delivered to Brum.'

Alex and Thania checked their kit and made sure that the others had enough for the journey back. Hopefully, Jervis's ire, or at least resources, was spent for now, but no-one was happy until they'd checked their ammunition.

'Goodbye Wayland, Freya, Fitela. And you, Alwiss, you took a shot for us. Thank you is not enough.' He turned to Bruno and Susannah. 'I know I shall see you again. That's... it.'

Thania saw the tears in his eyes as she turned to make her farewells. They had left Wessex, and their exile had begun.

*

The palace dripped with a painful, waiting silence. Hettie sat and stared at the silk handkerchief she twisted in her hands. Her mother was dead, the doctor just withdrawing. The servants were standing helpless, not knowing whether to tidy up or weep for their beloved Princess.

She stood up and turned around, orienting herself. The

room smelled of tuberose and disinfectant. Her mother's death had been soft and gentle, at least from the outside. The doctors said her heart had given out. Broken, thought Hettie. Broken by the Perceval-Wodening clan, broken by the exercise of royal power.

She looked again at the silk in her hands. It was Susannah's, painted with the runes of memory and ecstasy, of ancestry and glory. She, Hettie, had played the role of priestess at Gwendoline's dying, speaking the words of the litany for entry into Freya's halls as her mother's breath stopped. Someone had to give that final bit of love, to hymn the spark of consciousness that still lived in the dying brain, living on in what Ambrose had told her was the hallucinatory, accelerated reality of the near-death state.

She clasped and unclasped her hands. *There is no end to it,* she thought. *I have lost all my family except the one who deserves to die, and my new lover is in exile, probably dead by now.*

She turned and walked over to the deathbed. One last time, she clasped her mother's hand, then let it go. She spoke words of instruction to the servants, then let herself out of the room of death, into the great corridor that led to the west wing. On the way, she stopped by her rooms then walked on through the silent corridors of the palace.

She buckled on the belt with the long-bladed dagger she'd worn on Friday night, three days ago, when her life had tilted over into an abyss. Now she had to go to the bottom of that abyss, she had to finish the job.

*

Burslem led Alex and Thania up the long rise onto the spine of the Cotswolds. Down on their left, they saw the spires of flooded Gloucester sticking up out of the Severn Channel, then rode on past New Cheltenham, a favela of recycled stone and prefabricated recrete slabs that straggled uphill from the flooded city. They followed the road north-east, uphill past Chipping Campden, where a stone cottage overlooked the Vale of Evesham, two bored Birmingham Militiamen sitting on crates out the front. Burslem rode up and saluted the sergeant of the little post. Alex heard him giving a brief report. Without mention of the gold reward. The sergeant looked over at them and nodded. Burslem returned. 'Tide's in at the minute. The causeway opens at seven. The sergeant says we can join him for tea.' He looked round and spoke softly. 'I'd be careful what you say. This is a Brum Militia, but the other side of the channel we get PL infiltrators.' He tapped the side of his nose. Alex and Thania nodded. 'We're government contractors,' whispered Thania. 'Nobody expects them to have any money.'

They all dismounted and went to greet the sergeant, who stood up. He was a thin man with red hair and freckles, and a thick Birmingham accent. 'Welcome, travellers. Henry Wirth, West Heath Militia.' He raised his chin and spoke to the man behind him, dark and taciturn, still seated on a plastic milk crate. 'Travis, put the kettle on.' The man rose slowly and nodded at the newcomers, slit eyed.

Alex, Thania and Burslem tethered their horses at a hitching post formed from the broken stump of a telegraph pole. Travis emerged from the house with three extra crates, faded orange polypropene, and threw them on the ground. 'Thanks,' said Thania.

They sat down. Wirth extended his hand, and they exchanged greetings. 'You trading folks then?'

The inquisition had begun. Alex hoped it was a purely commercial one. 'We're surveying the Wessex-Shemeld border for Wessex Crown Properties, crossings and channels of military importance.' He blinked at Wirth. 'PL trouble, y'know.'

'I do. So do you, don't you, Trav?' Travis's face was set in stone, his eyes bland and dull. Wirth turned back to the others. 'We've all had trouble with those bastards. And some more than others.' Wirth nodded. 'Any of that ol' trouble this trip?' His blue eyes held nothing.

'Gang outside Cricklade. One of our apprentices got hit, and we sent him home with the other two. We decided to suspend the survey and go on to our meeting in Brum. We're hoping to raise interest in a collaboration with Shemeld. Tomorrow we're meeting, what are they called, Thania?'

'Protectorate Borders Agency,' she improvised. Alex dived back in. 'It's a fantastic opportunity for a collaborative venture between our two great nations.'

The story had worked. Wirth looked as bored as Alex felt. He nodded. 'Well, fine thoughts.' He looked at the low sun. 'But if you've got to get to Brum tonight you'll need our causeway, and my help.' Wirth paused for the implication to take root. Alex nodded cautiously. 'Best part of fifteen miles to the Redditch peninsula. You'll need my guidance and protection. It'll cost you twenty New Ones.' His eyes searched Alex for a second. 'Each.'

Alex held his gaze. 'Fifty, the three of us. Best offer.'

Wirth broke eye contact, a trace of smile on his lips. Alex regretted not offering less. Wirth stood up. 'Seven we go. Where's that fuckin' tea?'

The tea arrived. Wirth pulled out a battered pack of cards. 'Pontoon?' He smiled, showing cracked teeth, and no sweetness.

They rode downhill, to a stone pier at the edge of the Vale of Evesham, a wide channel with low, bare hills rising on the Redditch side. The first stage was, as advertised by Wirth, a stone causeway, built on the remnants of a system of walls that ran under the water for the first few miles. That comfortable road ended abruptly, where a tall concrete pole jutted out of the muddy water. The tide was out, and the draining tidal waters rushed between struts formed from broken buildings and sagging motorway lampposts. Strung between the more robust-looking uprights were cables, and a wooden pontoon, in sections which were flexing in the flood. Alex looked at Wirth. Wirth raised his eyebrows and pulled a face. 'S'fine, just watch.'

He spurred his horse onto the first section of lashed-together planks. The animal danced and skittered across to the first post, where the structure was more stable. Wirth turned round and gestured. Alex had to admit the man was a good horseman. He swallowed and rode forwards.

The pontoon was in fact more solid than it looked. Making it less likely that people would cross without a guide. Well, a man has to make a living, Alex thought, looking into Wirth's cold eyes as he rode up to him.

On the other side, Wirth stopped. 'You're all right now. Over this hill, and you'll see Redditch on the left. Keep it on your left, you'll come into Brum from the South. Good day to you gents.' He rode back over the pontoon, quick and easy, no longer bothering to play up the danger.

The three of them set off up the metalled road, fairly well maintained. At the crest of the hill, looking down to the left, they saw the remains of some low, redbrick buildings stuck up out of the water. 'The uphill end of Redditch,' said Burslem.

Burslem led them along the edge of a sunken roadway, one of the motorways of the Age of Oil. Tall banks on either side contained the floodwaters. In the distance, Alex spotted a barge. 'Birmingham's got good water transport then?'

Burslem nodded. 'Everywhere's joined up by water. The

centre's split into two sides. Seems to work OK. Downside is a porous border, with the PL all over round here.'

The road sloped up, then down, and they rode up to the entrance to Birmingham Centre, a wide, stone bridge with a civilian police post by it. The streets here were lit by low-hung fluorescents and methane lamps, producing a sort of cold, unpleasant light. The two police officers glared at them but let them pass. When they were well clear, Alex leaned over to Burslem and asked, 'What was their problem?'

'I don't know, but they looked like PL scum to me. I bet they heard about you and Miss Roberts, and... well, whatever kind of rubbish those mad buggers think. This is Centre. And we've got to find you somewhere to stay. The banks won't be open till tomorrow.'

'What about you? Where do you stay?'

'The Militia House, down in Canal, the other side of Centre.' Burslem frowned. 'I could probably get you two in as well, as long as you don't mind barracks conditions. And you put some money in the pot.'

The barracks consisted of two long cement-block buildings with the glittering black of the wide central waterway behind them. Burslem presented himself at the tiny comms post and introduced the others to a tired Sergeant in creased, dark green.

The sergeant coughed with a deep, bronchitic honk and pointed at a plastic box. 'Charity box, matey.'

Alex reached for some change. 'What's the charity?'

'Beer for Troops,' said the sergeant. Alex showed the man a twenty then dropped it in the box. The sergeant seemed satisfied.

The bunk was hard, but at least it was flat. The other occupants of the men's hut were already asleep. It was warm; Alex stripped down to his pants and got under the cool blanket. His first night of exile. His thoughts began to turn to Thania, but within seconds, they were interrupted by sleep.

They breakfasted in a café on the edge of Centre. 'All the banks are down there.' Burslem pointed down the crowded thoroughfare, lined with tall stone buildings. He led them to the finest of these, the Shemeld Bank, where Alex's signature enabled him to draw five Gold Edwins, which he passed to the boy. Burslem was dumbstruck.

'Don't forget to share it out, Private!' said Thania.

'I won't, ma'am,' said the breathless soldier.

'Lunch, then. Where's the best pub round here?'

Fortunately, Burslem – 'Call me Kenneth' – was well-informed about the geography of the region, and he sketched a map on a table napkin. 'You need North Centre via Walsall, then up to Cannock. Then the only water you've got to cross is the Stafford Crossing. Then to Upper Stone, you pass by with Stoke on Trent to the West, then up to Leek, over the peaks to Bakewell. Then you're in sight of Sheffield.'

They ate well, said their goodbyes and set off at an easy pace. The day was fine, they could see far ahead, and as they crested the rise and dropped down towards Cannock, Alex noticed they were being paced ahead by a tall man in shining black. They advanced cautiously, but at the distance Alex was expecting to make him out clearly, he seemed to vanish.

Then suddenly he was there again. Then he vanished right in front of their eyes. Alex was still looking around, hand on gun, when his horse started. He looked down and there was a grubby-faced, wide-eyed child, of indeterminate sex standing in the road. For a moment, Alex had the distinct impression that the mosquito-bitten hand had been holding a sickle, then the girl-boy disappeared, and a flock of crows flew up.

‘What are you?’ Alex whispered, beginning to feel like something he had been waiting for, for years, was starting to happen. It was not a pleasant sensation.

The air in front of his face formed itself into a toothy grin. He spoke softly. ‘I think we just met the most powerful BT in the Midlands.’

*

Hettie knocked perfunctorily and let herself into Jervis’s rooms. Jervis was in bed, his head bandaged, his face bruised. He looked levelly at her, a hint of fear in his eyes. She walked across the room slowly, drawing with her to the bedside a small ormolu chair, ram’s heads of German silver on the ends of the arms. She didn’t hurry to speak; with just their breathing overlaying the silence she imagined as best she could that she felt enormous and powerful.

Finally: ‘You ready to be King, Jervis?’

He looked nervous and greedy. How come he was so stupid? She remembered clearly the voice of Hendry, overheard talking to one of his cohorts about Jervis: ‘Perfect combination of a rigid, intolerant child and a frightened debauchee.’

She let the silence fester some more, then: ‘I need you to tell me, J, because it is just we two now, and you have the upper hand. Why did you join the other side?’

He looked her up and down but spoke as if to himself. ‘As it makes no difference whether you know or not, now: eternal youth, my nasty half-sibling, Rejuve, that’s what it’s all about. My doctor says I have accelerated ageing genes. I’ll be lucky to reach seventy without the drugs. And some powerful friends of mine have a good supply.’

‘And for this, for your stupid life, you betrayed my Siward, betrayed Wessex?’ She knew it was more than that; limitless depths of bitterness lay in him.

‘I prefer to think of it as taking the long view. The dream of heathen Wessex is dead, Hettie, and you are the only one who doesn’t know it.’

Hettie remembered the somber voice in the midst of Friday night’s revels, the voice that had told her much the same. That didn’t matter, though; her oath did. ‘Your call signal for your PL contact was Foliat Chilton,’ she stated flatly.

Jervis jerked a little, and looked fearful. Hettie wondered how she would work herself up to killing a defenceless man lying in bed. It seemed wrong, seemed cowardly, by the code she subscribed to.

There was an apple on the side cupboard. Hettie reached out to it with her mind, imagining for a moment that she could move it with the force of her will alone. That moment ended and something inside of her snapped.

She pulled Jervis to the edge of the bed, stepped over to the sword hanging on the wall and said ‘Now, kill me if you can, Jervis, because that is what I shall do to you.’ She slapped the sword across him and drew her long dagger. He was weaker, but she’d given him a longer weapon.

‘Do it, Jervis, you piece of shit,’ she hissed, ‘Do it!’

Rage twisted his face, and he grabbed up the sword and lunged for her. She was caught a little by surprise at the speed of his response, and the blade sliced into the flesh of her waist. The sight of her own blood gave her the momentum she needed, and she ducked under his clumsy guard and sank the dagger into his thigh. He howled, and she drew back and stabbed him again. He slapped the sword down onto her back, but she felt nothing, and kept stabbing him till after he was still, and the dagger finally slid out of her hands, slippery with their blood. She leaned there a minute, against his corpse, then got up and staggered to the door. She pulled the cord for the servants to come. She checked the pocket of her trousers. There it was, the little vonnie-rec, the power light still on. She replayed it and, with a flood of relief, heard Jervis's voice confessing his crimes. She had what she needed to face the people. She tucked the tiny box away, and then it hit her that there would have to be an election before Midsummer. She'd unwittingly manoeuvred herself into the position of a candidate who'd murdered her way to within a view of the throne. She was still throwing up when the servants burst in from the corridor.

*

Two ravens circled them, the old English kind, magnificent large birds, not the new, smaller migrants. They were riding slowly, and Thania looked up and snorted. 'This is a cartoon from a religious education comic, isn't it? '*And the great god of consciousness, Woden, is accompanied by two ravens...*' I've never seen them do that.'

Alex shook has head. 'Four miles now, I've been tracking it.'

'I don't do omens, honey. I just want to get to Sheffield and have a bath.'

The road ran up out of Leek and over the high moortop. The ride was slow, and pleasant, and finally they looked down into Derbyshire's cool, moist valleys. Deep down there, they could see a modern, water-powered forge and mill, ringed with its defence emplacements, then another, then another. These ancient valleys were alive with the steel and the skills that made the greatness and stability of the Shemeld Protectorate's heartlands.

On a final rise in the moor, the light was failing, the evening still, even at those heights. They turned and watched in silence, where the sun had gone down, and they rode to within view of Sheffield, where it seemed as if the horizon behind them was leaking the bloody light of open furnaces.

Above them, the ravens circled and circled, then flew off.

Ten Months Later:

March 2172

Chapter 16: The Shemeld Protectorate

'Look! They've got a *crow*!' He heard the child's shriek, as if addressed to him. He turned from looking out at the smoking Crescent across the valley to see a little girl looking his way. She sported a tutu and a star-topped wand, and was hopping from one foot to another, her brow furrowed with fierce excitement.

He smiled down at her. 'A what?'

She yelled 'An *OLD CROW*, stupid!' and then turned to a well-dressed young man behind him. Thania laughed and they watched the girl tug the man towards the arch that led out of the café. Thania and Alex looked at each other, and set off to follow the pair.

The weather was turning, dark clouds scudding over, as they dropped down the staircase of the Town Hall café-bar into Old Sheffield's main square. They turned right down Castle Hill, keeping up with the young father.

Just before Sheaf Valley Bridge, there was a low-budget fair, stalls of recycled plastic signs, layered brilliance in the fading Spring sunshine. The little girl was riding on her father's shoulders now, shrieking, 'There he is! It's Old Crow!' They turned into the expanse of cracked paving, broken into shanty streets, that led to the edge of the mud-clogged channel. The Crow stall was in a cul-de-sac. Thania, the seasoned soldier, checked their exits. Alex had never been in this level of Sheffield society in his ten months here. He thrilled with the seediness of it. They ducked under a flap of patchwork nylon tarpaulin manned by a barker, unshaven and enveloped in the gummy stink of xenothane. They paid him and stood before a stage of motley plastics, like a Punch and Judy stall.

The glove puppet of Old Crow was glossy black, with a great beak and yellow glass eyes, dull and blank. He produced a purple plastic bowl, and flung a few sweets out to children in the audience, representing the bounties of his magic pot. He kept on going through the motions of flinging out his empty hands, and began to complain to the audience. 'You want it all, and then more. You're not happy with the world as she is. Well, I pronounce a curse on your greed and stupidity, ha ha ha!'

This was the cue for his first foil, the sheep-faced man, who prostrated himself in front of Crow.

'Baah, we're all just poor people and need help, please help us Mister Crow, baah!'

Crow cackled. 'Why should I help you when you won't help yourself?'

'Baah, I don't know, Mister Crow, baah, please have mercy on us!'

Crow appeared to consider this, nodded and said, 'Very well, Mister Sheep, I shall give you the mercy you deserve.' He reached down inside the stage-box and came up with a gun-shaped object, encrusted with plastic jewels. He pointed it at Mister Sheep and a red light came out of it. Mister Sheep said 'Baah, baah!' and fell over, clutching his chest. Crow cackled, a practised, ugly sound that sent a thrill of disgust through the little audience.

He was still cackling when the next puppet rose up, a man in a dark green uniform, with a big pink face. He flapped his arms, waving an oblong of gold and said, 'Mister Crow, I bring you all the wealth of Wessex and Shemeld. Join with us, and with your magic pot and my money we will change the world! Please, for all the little children!'

Alex found himself smiling, the puppet's words reminding him of Hendry's relentless ambition. Crow said, 'You speak of children, Mister Power, but you are not a child.' He turned to the audience, cupping a black wing to his ear 'What is he? A child?'

The audience was primed for this and picked up the refrain. 'He's not a child, he's an Englishman!'

Crow nodded, satisfied, and shot Mister Power, who shrieked and fell down. Crow grabbed the gold bar and tossed it into the audience.

The final supplicant was a female caricature, masses of blonde hair around a tiny, neat face. In a falsetto trill, she said, 'Mister Crow, is there no room in your heart for love and beauty? Come into the warmth of my arms.'

Crow seemed discomfited by this, and approached the woman shyly. Then, with an uncharacteristically gentle gesture, he extended a wing. The woman raised her arm to join his, and they waltzed back and forth, Crow humming a popular dance tune. The audience were transfixed, knowing how it would end. Crow drew back from the blonde, still touching her with one black wing and spoke. 'No, there is no more room for love. I would rather boil your skull to have as my cup.' He reached for his gun, and shot the blonde, who looked beseechingly up at him, then died twitching on the little stage.

Crow did his horrible cackle, then reached up his magic pot and threw a few more sweets out to the children. The audience applauded, in the dubious way of puzzled people. Alex turned to Thania, assuming the show was over, but Crow's voice rang out again. 'That is all you can see of my powers today, unless...' the puppet turned this way and that, as if searching the audience '…unless you care to come into my parlour and ask me my secrets in person, good bye to you!'

Alex had never heard Crow invite the audience in like that. He felt Thania's hand dragging him through the exiting crowd, round to the side of the stage. They were in a narrow passage between flapping sheets of dirty plastic. In front of them, the well-dressed man and his little daughter, still hopping about with excitement, were just going through a door flap into the stage-box.

Their interview with Crow lasted only a couple of minutes, and the man came out, holding the hand of the now-quiet girl, her face pointed at the ground, her wand dragging in the mud. 'He can't mean it, can he, dad?' she asked, as they squeezed past. The man picked her up and comforted her as they left the booth.

Thania and Alex stepped through the flap into a dark room. The gently undulating walls were hung all around with the pelts of various animals, not well cured, to judge by the rancid, urinary smell. As their eyes accustomed, they saw a shrunken man in the corner, the Crow puppet on his hand. 'Yes?' he inquired, in a low, menacing voice. Alex felt the pressure of Thania's hand on his arm. 'Ask about your mother,' she whispered. Alex gave her a pained look. 'What for, it's just...'

'It's just what?' said the Crow-figure. 'I can hear very well, you know. You were going to say it's just nonsense, weren't you? Why not ask, and find out if Crow has something for you?'

To get it over with, Alex cleared his throat and spoke stiffly. 'If you can tell me whether my mother is alive or dead, I would appreciate it.'

Crow held out his hand. 'Two pounds.' Alex fished out the coins and passed them over. Crow paused, as if he was listening to something no-one else could hear, then said, 'She's dead. Another question.'

Alex stood stunned, then exploded in anger. 'What the fuck do you know about it? Come on, tell me, you little fuck! How could you know anything about my mother?'

Behind him, he heard the man from the front of the booth enter the room. Thania touched his sleeve and said, 'Let's go, Al.' They pushed out, past the xenothane-drenched barker, brushing against what looked like the skin of a dog, into the shanty street. The sun had come out again, but the joy had gone out of their holiday.

Up on the furnace platform the noise was audible only for the first few minutes of the shift. After that, deafness prevailed, and Alex's technician had to come round in front of him to tell him he'd got a call. Alex gave the boy the thumbs up, then hefted the tongs and picked the cooling frustum of fresh steel out of the bucket of water. He scrawled a note of the time on his wristpad and hastened off the platform, down the steel stairs and onto the thick dust of the melting-shop floor. He took his usual short cut under the furnace stage – saluting the fire-watcher, old man and ancient wooden chair welded into one by the grey dust – then between the giant scrap bins and out to the edge of the vast workshop where his lab was, a small steel shed welded to the wall of a great one. The phone – yet another antique brought up with everything else when the steelworks were shifted out of the flood zone – was lying on his cluttered desk. He dropped the now-cool steel into the sample box and picked up the receiver. Regudy's voice yelled down the line. 'You lucky bastard! It'll be an orgy!'

'Explain please, Leonard.'

'I have in my hands an envelope, an envelope with the Manor Castle crest on it, an envelope which no doubt contains an invitation to the weekend's nuptials at the Castle. There must be a mistake, because it's addressed to you, c/o the Department.'

'Leonard, please open it and tell me,' said Alex, exasperated. There was a short pause, then Regudy spoke again.

'Yes, I was right: 'Alex Tyler and one companion', blah blah, "Manor Castle on Saturday the twenty-first of March, party in honour of the wedding of Frey Shemeld and Zakia

Khan", blah blah. Like I said, you lucky sod! Any chance I can be your 'one companion'? No, didn't think so. Ah well. You in the Department tomorrow?'

'Yep, I'll pick it up then. Thanks, Leonard, that's made my week.'

'Allright, see you tomorrow, party boy.'

Alex finished his work for the day, grinding a flat edge on the steel sample and dropping the swarf in a beaker of acid. The night shift's duty technician would do the analysis, and everything else would keep till Friday, when he was next in. He updated his shift log and went and washed off. His way out took him back through the melting shop, and he sat at the edge of the casting pit to watch the white-hot steel gush out of the furnace and into the ladle, great arcs of yellow fire burning across his retina. He'd come to love steelmaking, the sheer scale and visual drama of it. When the moulds were full, he strolled out to the company bus for his ride back to the other side, to Old Sheffield, a nice place to live for a young man with a job and money to spend.

Everyone in town was watching the wedding. Alex and Thania saw it on a screen in the crowded Town Hall Bar, Alex in a dark lounge suit, Thania resplendent in a brand-new backless green frock, her unruly red hair disciplined into a neat bob. The show started with a panorama of Sheffield Old and New, the stately drift of Shemeld's gigantic red airship across the Sheaf Valley to the Old Town underlining how secure Sheffield felt these days. People raised their glasses and cheered with pride at their city. Next, they saw the arrival from Bradford of the bride's party. The elephant with its pink and gold howdah drew gasps of incredulity from the viewers, and when the bride, veiled and glittering, was helped down and joined her father on the forecourt of the Cathedral, the crowd oohed and aahed at the lavish costumes. The scene continued inside, and Alex doubted that Sheffield's cathedral had ever hosted such an extraordinary mixture of ceremonials, a nod in just about every religious direction other than the Christian. At the altar, young Frey Shemeld, adorned in red silk, clasped an ancient jet and gold necklace around the elegant throat of his bride, and she slipped onto his finger a massive platinum ring blazing with diamonds.

The whole town was on its way to getting roaring drunk by the time Alex and Thania stepped out of the bar and met the cab they'd booked. The driver made slow progress through the singing crowd, down to the edge of the Old Town and over the bridge to New Sheffield. It was less crowded on the other side, all the steelworks closed for the day. They drove along the great flat arc of land known as the Crescent, past Alex's place of work, silent and shuttered like he'd never seen it, up past the great coal yards in front of the mineshafts and then onto the approach road to the outer yard of Manor Castle. The rebuilt complex was ringed with black-uniformed guards carrying automatic weapons. Alex showed their invitations at the great steel gates and they stepped out and paid the driver.

They stood in the stronghold of the Shemeld Protectorate, looking around at the walls of young stone looming over them. A nearby doorway let out a wisp of smoke, some furnace in a workshop had that had only just closed. Engraved on the lintel above it were the crossed guns of Birmingham. Stone buildings stretched in every direction, along a grid that filled the arc-shaped enclosure, bearing every coat-of-arms in the British Isles. This was the heart of New Sheffield's industrial success story, the arms-making bailey of Manor Castle. The effect was oppressive, the bare young stone underlining the bareness of the streets, scoured of all human dimension by the ubiquitous surveillance, old-fashioned optical cameras in steel mesh cages.

Silently, they joined the other guests streaming through the inner bailey of the complex, up to the red-carpeted entrance to Shemeld Keep.

Two guards flanked the high arch of the doorway, their uniforms distinguished by gold braid and the Shemeld arms, an eagle grasping crossed hammers, in red. One of them checked their tickets and directed them politely into the tall lobby, a square, vaulted chamber giving onto a vast ballroom.

The last time Alex had seen this much electric light at once was in Carcassonne. He was glad that stage of his life was over.

The buffet was gigantic. They piled their bone china plates with vaguely-familiar rich foods plus dishes they didn't even recognize, helped themselves from the fountains of champagne and found a table.

Thania looked round slowly at the circles of reproduction antique wooden chairs, then turned to Alex. 'There's a forest's worth of wood in here. Where the hell did they get it all from?'

A man behind them interjected in a cultured American accent. 'Caledon, I believe. They still have forests in Caithness.'

Alex turned to face the man, strong-featured brown face above a soft black silk shirt, who smiled and gestured to his companion, a proud-faced dark woman who seemed to be wearing almost nothing. 'This is Nahida, and I'm Charis.'

Thania eyed the woman and gave her a big grin. 'I'm Thania and this is Alex.'

Charis said, 'Are you staying for the house party?'

'I don't know,' said Alex, fishing out his ticket.

Nahida looked over at it. 'Ah, gold border. It seems you are. Excellent!'

Charis said, 'It's a special party for people whom

Shemeld wants to reward for services rendered. I guess he didn't get round to telling everyone what it was about.' Charis offered a smile. 'What did you do for him?'

'I solved a problem in special steel manufacture,' said Alex.

'Oh, very close to the old boy's heart,' said Charis. 'No wonder he loves you!'

Alex asked, 'What was your contribution?'

'Ha, I wonder myself,' said Charis. 'Import, export, information….' His friendly face closed up for a moment, calculatedly leaking vague information. He asked, 'You two are from Wessex, yeah?' Alex nodded. 'The PL aren't getting any weaker down there, are they?' He searched Alex's face as he answered.

Seemingly satisfied, he nodded. 'I see you waste no love on those maniacs. Be careful, you two. There are some dangerous undercurrents in these sweet waters.'

'What are you saying?' asked Thania.

'Nothing, just… be careful! But don't neglect to have fun!'

Charis looked around, then back again. 'Ah, here's Gudrun,' as a petite woman picked her way over to their table.

'Have you three met?' asked Charis. Thania and Alex shook their heads. Gudrun was in a purple silk two-piece and her spiky blonde hair was woven through with silver wire. She gave them a raw, direct gaze, seeming to be aswim in the sensual details of the scene as Charis introduced them. An impossible amount of energy was compressed into her slight body and Alex and Thania were both smitten.

'What brings you here?' asked Alex.

Gudrun spoke in a northern accent with a hint of Scandinavian. 'I deal art. I've been working out of Goathland' – a swift, sideways glance at Charis, whose face was bland and impassive – 'I brought The Shemeld some salvaged sculptures down from the Northeast.'

Thania smiled. 'I grew up in a house full of reclaimed artworks, and we all got lectured on them by my Uncle Ambrose.'

Gudrun said, 'You are a niece of Ambrose Swords? A great man!'

'Well, the Asgard Hall family tree is a bit convoluted; all us kids called Ambrose "Uncle", though he probably fathered half of us. Where are your sculptures?'

'Ask The Shemeld, he loves showing people round,' said Gudrun.

'I will,' said Thania.

An orchestra struck up what the scrolled, calligraphic playlist behind them announced was a selection from Malcolm Arnold's 'Machines,' lots of brass and percussion. Gudrun excused herself and got up to mingle.

They ate and drank and chatted, time flying in that sumptuous room, then around eight o'clock, the music livened up again. Guests began to drift out, until maybe fifty people were left; the ballroom looked empty. To mark the start of the private house party, waiters came round with trays of shot-glasses and tall silver coffee-pots.

One leaned towards Alex. 'Cocaffee sir?'

Alex nodded, accepting a tiny glass of the hybrid stimulant. Underneath the coffee fragrance the liquid tasted metallic and bitter, but almost instantly the fumes of alcohol cleared from his brain.

As Alex sipped, old Shemeld appeared, decked out in a lavish uniform of black and gold. All eyes were upon him as he made his way round the room, looking every inch the glad-handing dictator. In his wake, strode the dynastic couple, Frey and Zakia. Frey was attended by a couple of his own guards, whose uniforms lacked the eagle-and-hammers insignia. The three made their way over to Alex's table and he and Thania stood up and faced the stocky, red-faced Shemeld.

'Welcome, my friends!' he shouted in a deep voice that was well-used to command. 'So you're my prize metallurgist! You've made Sheffield and me' – his meaty face creased with pleasure – 'a good deal of money, Alex Tyler. And your lovely companion?'

Alex introduced Thania, who shook Shemeld's hand. Thania's facial expressions were well known to him now, and he read an amused contempt behind her elegant warmth.

'A doctor, eh? You know, the Shemeld Protectorate has only one proper doctor per five thousand citizens, so you are more than welcome in our capital.'

Zakia, no longer veiled, stepped up to them. She had a long jaw and fine large eyes in a strong, wilful face. She spoke to Thania. 'You are a doctor? I studied medicine, but matters of dynasty proved more urgent. We must accommodate ourselves to a world in crisis, mustn't we?'

Thania caught a hint of regret. 'Absolutely. May I offer you my congratulations?' Zakia's face became a mask of polite boredom.

Shemeld moved towards the picture-windows that overlooked the Crescent and said, 'Come over here, my friends, and tell me what you see. Isn't that beautiful?' The question didn't require an answer. The old dictator was in a familiar rapture at the sight of the Crescent, lit up in a blaze of security floodlights.

His chest swelled with pride. 'That is the most valuable piece of real estate in the British Isles. D'you know how we built it?'

Alex nodded, but had the feeling Shemeld was going to tell them anyway. The stocky man launched into his speech. 'Shemelds have been making knives here for a thousand years. Poured steel was invented just down there' – he swept his arm towards the dark swathe of the Don Channel – 'in 11,742 Interglacial.' Most people dropped the additional hundred centuries from the cumbersome Interglacial dating. Shemeld said the whole number, conjuring great spans of time with it.

'All my father had when the floods came were a lot of unemployed and some explosives. We blasted away the hillside until we bit right into the Silkstone seam.' He clenched his fist. 'You know how we turned it into energy?' The big hand gripped Alex's shoulder. 'Muscle power, Alex. Ten thousand desperate men and women on treadmills pulverized a cubic mile of low-grade coal for the producer gas plants. Human power, driven by need. Beautiful, isn't it?'

They gazed out at the Crescent, letting the moment fade.

Thania said, 'I was talking with Gudrun, and she says you have quite an art collection here.'

Shemeld's face glowed. 'The best in the British Isles, I dare say. Come over to the old Lodge and see for yourselves.'

Their proud host led the way deeper into the Manor complex. Next to the ballroom they passed through a domed octagonal gallery with wide balconies to the outside. 'The Pleasure Dome,' said Shemeld. 'You'll be staying in the rooms off here tonight. I hope you'll make yourself at home in my house.'

The gallery was in a suite of ancient rooms, the remnants of the original Sheffield Manor House. They swept through the first, where tarpaulins and ladders bespoke new hangings, into a room crammed with sculptures. Alex & Thania recognized a few famous pieces from the great days of art. Thania ran her hand over the rough bronze pelt of one of Moore's giant goddesses and Alex gazed at the weird tensions of a Beuys installation, then Shemeld hustled them through to what he really wanted to show off. The room beyond was smaller, with tiny spotlights and glass-fronted cases.

'Silver,' declared Shemeld. 'We still export to North America, not to mention our prosperous brethren in Bradford.'

He touched Thania's elbow and indicated a large, circular tray. 'D'you know how we get that final polish? Pearl ash. Pearls from the ocean, burned to a silky dust. What d'you think to that, then?'

Thania shook her head in wonderment, feeling oppressed by the secret, secluded light emanating from the silver. *Imagine the days of your life bleeding into this pointless, pond-flat surface.*

Shemeld waved around in genial hospitality, as if showing them everything at once, then headed back the way they'd come. 'The others'll be freshening up now, you might as well check out where you're staying.'

They followed through the Pleasure Dome, Thania wondering at the name for a moment. Their room was warm and comfortable, with a huge bed and mirrors. Thania put her arms around Alex's neck and smiled. 'They're nice, aren't they, that Nahida and Charis.'

'Not to mention little Gudrun,' said Alex, running his hands over the long arc of her back and down to cup her rump. They slipped their clothes off.

Washed and dressed, they emerged onto an upper balcony, relaxed and sweet, and made their way down the steel stairs into the centre of the Dome. They helped themselves to cocaf from an urn. Carrying their drinks, they followed the faint sound of voices out to a deep balcony. A curved leather settee backed onto the parapet, under the night sky and warmed by the obscene expense of overhead heaters.

Charis and Nahida were sprawled on the couch, Charis

running his long hands over the woman's elegant, net-shrouded body. Their eyes glittered in the gaslight, and the warm air was balmy with their sexual perfume. Alex and Thania sat down nearby. Nahida turned and leaned out, kneeling on the seat, facing the blaze of the Crescent. Charis undid his trousers and leaned forward, lifting Nahida's filmy skirt and kissing her dark rump. Then he parted her pubic bush and mounted her, their necks arching in bliss.

Getting into the spirit of the party, Alex let his clothes fall to the ground. He was seated facing Thania, who hitched up her skirt and sat across him, impaling herself with a coo of pleasure. Alex caressed her arched back and kissed her breasts as she shuddered, her eyes rolling.

Alex saw Charis watching them, his dark eyes glittering again. Without any intervening thought, Alex leaned over and kissed him on the lips. He pulled gently out of Nahida as Thania rolled off of Alex, touching the other man's cock and guiding him gently to Nahida's behind. Alex entered the dark woman, pushing the dress up further to kiss her moist, gleaming spine.

Holding himself back, trembling with delight, Alex felt another touch, a hand between his legs. In the side of his vision he saw a trim white shape. Gudrun's tiny body and bright hair shone in the distant arclight as she moved round to his side. She took his face in her delicate hands and kissed him on the lips, her hot breath all over his face, her eyes vivid and complex.

It seemed an eternity before they slowed down, and sprawled back on the couch, arms around each other, catching their breath. Thania's scent was blended with the dark couple's aroma, and it made Alex feel good all over.

Thania was the first to notice Frey Shemeld leaving the upper balcony, swinging a small, grey film camera. One of his guards followed him, a curl of disdain on his lip. Thania nudged Alex in the ribs. 'I expect he's been stood up there, watching with his creepy minder. What a shithead,' she whispered, then burst into a fit of giggles as Nahida rolled onto her lap. 'No vonnies and no style,' said the dark woman.

Later in their room, Thania was asleep, only the softest trace of light showing her outline on the big bed. Alex got up and went out into the Dome to look for a drink. Under the balcony there was a big refrigerator, with quite a range of booze and tinctures inside. He selected a beer and turned, almost bumping into Frey Shemeld. The chunky man, his shirt dishevelled, loomed up to him, with what looked like a nasty expression on his face. Alex smelt the whisky on his breath as he leaned close.

'You Wessexers are so fucking snooty, you think you're it, because you've got borders and a fucking Royal Family. See that?' he pushed Alex back clumsily, until his shoulder was pressed against the ormolu frame of a portrait.

'My granddad. He had much worse to contend with than your fucking Wodenings.'

His stinking breath blew over Alex's face, small red eyes glaring out above the broken capillaries of his cheeks.

'You think you know what's going on, but you have no idea of the forces that are about to change it all…' His face lost focus in some dreadful epiphany and he lurched away. 'No fuckin' idea…'

With a chill feeling in his chest, Alex took his drink back to the bedroom, Charis's warning echoing in his thoughts.

Chapter 17: The Shoot

Dawn light blooms through the bedroom's arc of tall windows. Sounds surface from the busy world beneath them, then that discreet bustle is drowned in six deep chimes.

Thania's eyes opened and met Alex's. She touched his face with her fingertips. 'I feel as if my whole body is smiling.' Alex kissed her fingers, one by one, savouring every touch. A single long trumpet blast interrupted their silent bliss.

They showered, smiling but not talking. In the long wardrobe they found neat khaki suits with lots of pockets. They dressed for the hunt, a discreet clatter of plates rising from the main Dome room.

The room was busy. Charis and Nahida, buffet breakfasts in front of them, stood up and embraced Alex and Thania, big smiles and glowing eye-contact all round.

Charis spoke in both their earshot. 'Stay close to us.'

Thania looked into his eyes and nodded. 'A countryside ramble requires a decent few calories,' she said as she helped herself to fragrant bacon and eggs.

They sat down together. Alex, munching eggs, tilted his head in question at Charis.

'This might seem like Shemeld's thing, a hunt, but it's really for Frey's benefit, a show of ostentatious expenditure.' He looked round. 'And a perfect opportunity for an accident. Keep an eye on who's shooting, and where.' He smiled and filled glasses with fruitjuice cocktails. There were two long blasts on the trumpet.

'What are we supposed to be shooting?' asked Alex, trying to appear nonchalant but concerned at Charis's redoubled warning.

'Last shoot I was on, it was pheasant and grouse, but they're way out of season, so I guess it'll be a specially set up captive game event in one of the Shemeld's parks.' His voice was light, unconcerned.

A long series of trumpet blasts announced the off. Outside, three Ducks were revving up on the gravel drive. The vehicles were polished, shiny, leisure-military, like their costumes. Alex saw Thania look down, her eyes going into memory.

Shemeld stood in the front of the leading Duck, scanning round him, stiff-bodied, taking pleasure in his realm. Zakia looked up at the sky, heartbreakingly elegant in fatigues, her hair covered with a vivid golden scarf, her eyes shielded by dark glasses. Frey, his hand resting on her lower back, looked crude and unformed in comparison. Two men in the dark, anonymous uniforms of Frey's bodyguard held shotguns behind them; three gundogs sniffed the air and strained against leads. The second Duck held some faces Alex didn't recognize from the party, three men and two women in Shemeld's fatigues, with a gun each. A bland, dark face turned and frowned quizzically at him.

Alex and Thania climbed aboard the rear vehicle behind Charis and Nahida. Thania noticed the gunwale benches were done out in khaki cushioning. Zakia's father stepped on board, resplendent in glittering turban, his eyes fierce under massive, iron-grey brows.

The lead Duck turned, spinning, scattering gravel, and set off up the swooping curve of the main drive. A servant dragged the long steel gate out of the way and the convoy crunched out onto well-maintained, metalled road, all dark retro asphalt and original granite kerbstones.

The old Khan stepped up to the front and placed his hand on the driver's shoulder. 'I wish to drive.' The driver stepped aside, letting Khan take the controls. They headed west around the curve of the hill, past well-scrubbed brick houses and across another old road to the edge of a steel-fenced park.

Two gamekeepers opened the gate and closed it behind the rear Duck, then trotted downhill into the trees. Alex had no idea such a large game-park existed so close to town. Grassland sloped down towards a cluster of ruined brick buildings. The whole thing gave the impression that it had been a public park in the Age of Oil; the ruined municipal brickwork, the crumbling, vine-wrapped statues. They all took guns from the rack at the rear of the Duck and dismounted onto the grass. Shemeld fired a shot in the air, a signal to the beaters. Within seconds, some large birds flapped up over the ridge of bushes downhill. Shemeld shot the first, then stepped aside for his son. Frey brought down another before standing aside for Zakia.

After the first party had all taken shots, the Labrador and the spaniels were sent out. One of the springers trotted off to the side and sniffed behind the plinth of a vanished statue, barked, then reappeared, wagging its stump of a tail. For a moment, Thania saw a scruffy figure stand up behind the plinth, then disappear again.

More birds were released, and the Khan stepped forward and took his shots, bringing down two. He broke his shotgun and fished in the pockets of his fatigues, bringing out two cigars. He proffered one to Alex, who shook his head. Khan turned towards Thania, who smiled. Khan clicked a lighter and lit his cigar, leaning back against the side of the Duck. Alex and Thania stepped down. There was a pause in the proceedings, dogs returning with pheasants and Shemeld sitting on a shooting stick down the hill. Alex turned to Khan and said, 'I hope you don't mind my asking, Mr Khan – '

Khan interrupted. 'Not 'Mister,' Alex, just Khan. It is my title as well as my surname. Now ask away.'

Alex resumed. 'Everywhere I go, religion seems to divide people, except in Bradford, yet your city is renowned for its religion. How do you hold it all together?'

Khan's broad face creased into a smile. 'My people can cry to Allah from a Sunni minaret, or a Shia tower. For all I care, they can eat pig and drink beer, fornicate and gamble, as long as it's in secret. It is of no consequence. I am a Pathan, an exception to these rules. I have vision, and an army.'

Alex nodded. He thought he saw a figure move from behind the nearby plinth into the cover of a dead elm. 'What about bandits?'

Khan inhaled blueish smoke and raised his cigar slightly. 'Bandits hang just as high as other mortals. I think we disposed of more than one hundred last year. But of course they keep coming, there are always disaffected people who will turn to crime.'

'What about BTs, subbits as they call them here?'

Khan flashed him an arch, quizzical look. 'What interest is that to you?'

Alex frowned. 'It's the weirdness. You know those Old Crow stalls in the markets and fairs? Do you get those in Bradford?'

Khan shook his head as if he wasn't sure. Three of the dogs ran up and dropped the dead pheasants. Plump, cage-reared and released just for this occasion, they bled onto the grass.

Khan threw down his cigar and they set off downhill, into the interior of the park. They took new positions under a gash in the land which showed wind-rubbed anticlines of cracked strata, the lichen-spotted arm of a statue sticking out of the loose soil.

Shemeld motioned Alex and Thania to the front, and fired his signal shot. They took aim at the birds, Alex wasting his shots but Thania bringing down two. More birds rose up, and it was the turn of Charis and Nahida. The dogs ran out again, and the remaining group took up their positions.

There was a respectable pile of feathered corpses stacked up by the time Shemeld called everyone round. 'Now for something special,' he shouted, and fired three shots off into the air. Everyone watched down the hill to where the forest cover began, and suddenly a deer ran out, its head high and its feet pounding as it wove away from the wood. Shemeld took aim and fired, and the beast tumbled over, rolling to a halt. Everyone started surging down the hill, when Alex felt a hand on his arm.

'It's started. This way,' hissed Charis, urging the other three back towards the vehicles. The front Duck was empty, and Charis jumped in it and started the engine.

He shouted, 'Take the middle Duck, you two. Wait here if you want an escort to Bradford, otherwise, get the hell out!'

Alex ran up to the Duck just as one of Frey's minders stood up from inside it and trained a handgun on him. Alex dived sideways, the gun went off and Alex heard the round whistle past his ear as he hit the ground. He looked up in time to see Thania shooting the minder in the face, and another figure, the skinny, scruffy man who'd been lurking around, who'd pushed the minder off-balance and saved Alex's life, standing in the Duck.

Thania jumped on board and Alex followed, as the skinny man tossed the dead minder overboard. Their eyes met in a fury of indecision, then Thania shook her head and said, 'No, Bradford's too risky, drive round to the southern end of the Don Basin. I'll explain later.'

Down the hill, shots and screams rang out, then they

caught sight of Zakia supporting her limping father up towards the front Duck. 'Now!' shouted Thania, and Alex started up and ran the Duck at full tilt, crashing over the closed gates and out onto the tarmac.

They followed the old road uphill, away from the battle. Thania picked up the pair of Zeiss binoculars hanging from the gun rack and scanned round. There was no pursuit, so she turned to the small man, who was shivering and panting, gazing about him, looking into every corner. Suddenly, he dived for something under the opposite bench, straightening up with a small aerosol. He thrust the little cylinder into his mouth and squeezed, eyes closed tight. After a few seconds, his whole body relaxed and his eyes opened, streaming tears of relief. Red-rimmed eyes gazed at Thania; he nodded, unsmiling.

'Are you vonnie-sick?'

He nodded again. 'PL weapon, an overloader, a tuned EMP that makes yer feel as if yer skin's on fire.'

'What's your R-K rating?'

'Can't measure it, mine. I'm offscale, I'm a subbit.' He stared at her, guarded, vulnerable.

Thania frowned, then said, 'Subbit, SBT, super-becter-tolerant, OK.'

'Thane does the trick.' He sat up a bit straighter and extended his hand. 'Scargill Twigg's the name, call me Scar.'

Thania took his hand and shook. 'Thania, and this is Alex. Thank you for tipping it for us.' There was something familiar about the man, and not just the stink of xenothane.

Alex stopped the Duck. They'd reaching a vantage point, the hill dropping down and then rising again to Manor Castle. There was a series of distant explosions, and a plume of smoke was rising over the Castle heights. He reached for the binoculars. 'It's an invasion, isn't it? They must have infiltrated the Castle…'

Thania finished for him '...and done old Shemeld in while his son's undercover PL friends took out the Castle guards. Their occupation force will follow up from the Don Channel, which is why we have to skirt them to the East. Fancy a trip to Caledon, my love?'

'Or as far as this thing will get us.' Alex took a look round the deck of the craft. A row of full cans of diesel sat under tarps at the back. 'Oh, thank you, Charis.' He smiled grimly and took the wheel again.

Scargill raised both hands. 'Something you should know. I'm a precog. What's called a spatial precog. Which means, amongst other things, that I know now what I'm going to know later, if you see what I mean, about where I'll be. And when it's a life and death situation, where I'm going to be is the best place. So we need to be on this side of the hill, right down till we get to the water. The PL militias are already mopping up around the Castle.'

Alex said, 'OK, that makes sense. Thank you for saving my life. I'll drive, and you can tell us why you bothered.'

Scar sighed. 'You got some time?' He closed his eyes. 'Yes, you 'ave. One point two hours.' He leaned back on the cushioned seat, propped his feet up on an ammo box and took another hit of the xenothane. 'Ladies and gentlemen, seat yourselves comfortably for the Tale of Scargill Twigg, the Subbit of Sheffield. Me mam were a subbit. I never knew, not till she gave me the blood. Her special talent: she could get anyone to part wi' anything, if she needed it. And she always needed summat, wi' us lot to feed. Y'did well to live to twenty, what with old Shemeld suspending the tube-tying laws so's he could get more bodies to work to death digging the Crescent and crushing rock-coal from the Silkstone seam.

'I were one of five, the rest all lasses. We all went down with bec-plague after the '59 floods. I were seven year old. Babby Sif, Betty, Freya and our Sofe all died. Just me and mam left then. Mam must've heard some old wives' tale about subbit blood healing bec-plague and thought she'd risk it, with me dying anyway. She sat by me bed and cut herself on the arm then made me suck it till I puked. I got a bad fever, survived, and then I were a subbit too, though it took a few year before I knew what it meant. At first it were just a bit strange, hearing voices that were other people's thoughts. Mam filled me in on being a subbit, her main message being 'if you want to stay alive, don't let on.'

'Anyway, I met a few other subbits from New Sheffield's criminal classes, and it weren't long before it were time to exploit me subbit talents, basic mind-reading and spatial precog. Ended up working for Skinny Lenny the Crow-man at Sheaf Market.' He paused. 'You know me, now?'

'The barker…'

'At your service. Working for Lenny really opened me eyes. Us subbits are an underworld elite. I'd gone from being a nobody with nowt to knowing everything that goes on, and I mean everything. Anywhere there were people wi' top end vonnies, we 'ad a window straight onto whatever they could see, hear and feel. And the precog: Lenny's a mean old bastard, no teeth and no hardon, like all thirty-something gasheads, but he taught me how to feel time-branches, how all the different futures branch out from all the choices anyone makes.

'Anyway, it were all because of Zanti, my beautiful piebald, mosaic skin of brown and pink and cheekbones to kill for.'

Scar took a hit of xenothane. 'She were a gun girl for Sheaf Valley Crows. Took her orders from Johnny Pain, another of the local subbits. The useless bastard sent her and two other guns down to take on Ma Knight's 'thane factory. Weren't even a serious go at taking the business over, just a 'cunk you' to certain parties. Zanti were shot through th' head.' Scar paused.

'I felt her death. Any idea what I mean? No, you couldn't have. It's like colours that burn behind me eyes and a cry of hurt that goes higher and higher, right into ultrasound. That ghost-scream, it's still there at back of everything. That's when Scargill Twigg's war started.' Scar hit the 'thane, the stink drifting into Thania's face.

'Course, y'know about Old Crow, the same puppet show up and down these islands from Wessex to Caledon, with the same boss who no-one ever met, Mister Crow, who's always after information from any punter he can get into Old Crow's back room. Like he did with you two yesterday. I smelled army vonnies on you, Thania, and me precog started twitching wi' Alex. I knew you too had some kind of important future. Then I saw you two again last night. Us subbits have our own special entertainments, one of which we refer to as the subbitnet.' Scar fluttered his eyelids, doing 'snobby people.' The effect was disproportionately unsettling.

'Like I said, anywhere there's top-end vonnies, just add a subbit and all his subbit mates are invited to the show. That's our Friday night 'business meeting', up at Frosty's, gassing up, drinking and watching th' subbitnet. The usual crew were there, plus a couple of big-cheese subbits, including Johnny Pain. He were a dead man who still 'appened to be breathing.

'We'd watched all the public shite on Frosty's exovid – Shemeld showing off his big red airship, look how secure we are in Sheffield these days, and all the rest of the bollocks. Then we settled down for the rec one of our subbits up at the Castle had sent out, fresh that day. Lots of eating. You and Shemeld, him going on about his cunking Crescent. Pretentious cunk wi' his Interglacial dates. Then Frey going off to a shagging party. That were th' only bit worth watching.

‘But me precog were itching like no cunk’s business on you, Alex. You listening?’

Alex flashed him half a glance, eyes committed to the road and the horizon, where smoke rose. Scar continued, as unconcerned as a man who knows exactly what the future holds. ‘Well, Thania, you’re cunkin’ listening so, I shall tell you: Alex is cunkin’ important. Well important, and all the subbits in that cunkin’ room knew it.’ He nodded, then his eyes darted round. ‘Any liquor on this tub?’ Not waiting for a reply, he started rummaging in the packs and boxes under the benches, then sat up, clutching a bottle with an air of victory. With a cursory inspection of the label he uncapped it and sniffed, then poured a stream of the colourless liquor into his mouth. He stuck his tongue out, his eyes bulged redly, said ‘Bwaaarhh!’ and handed the bottle to Thania, who took it and swigged a tiny amount of the fierce gin. Scar settled down to continue his story.

‘That’s when I knew something too – Pain was in wi’ th’ Pure Light, their tame subbit, selling out Sheffield, and Alex would be very, very good to have on our side.’ He paused, crinkled his brow and waved his fingers in the direction of the bottle. Thania returned it, Scargill gave a nodding bow, and took a deep draught. ‘I knew what I ‘ad to do then. My enemy’s enemy is my friend. So, as it’s getting light, I creep round the outside of the Castle and stalk you lot, feeling th’ timelines, knowing it’s soon. Shemeld’s crew are rotten wi’ Pure Light agents.’

He cast around him and picked up the xenothane atomiser. ‘And that’s pretty much it.’ He took a hit of the gas, then a swig from the bottle. ‘Except for the undeniable fact that it’s a shit life, being a subbit. But xenothane and gin do help.’ The bottle was looking quite empty when he handed it back to Thania.

Everyone went quiet. No sound carried from over the hill, they were approaching the old suburbs along the edge of the Don Basin. Scar sat up and looked around, then closed his eyes for a few seconds. 'This is the place, my friends. I know you know which way to go, because I know you'll get there.' Alex halted the craft. Scar picked up the canister of xenothane and hauled himself over the side.

He started to walk away, then turned and faced them again. 'In the shadows, there's a very likely future, which branches out from the fact I saved your life, Alex Tyler. One day, not long, you have another name. You're tooled up to the nines with some fancy new weaponry, and you're leading an army to take Sheffield back from them Pure Light dipshits.'

He turned and started walking, then swivelled again. He stood steady, his eyes wider and softer than they'd seen them. 'And by popular demand, Johnny Pain is hanging from a lamppost, his guts wrapped round his legs. The screaming in my head has quietened down a bit, my friends. That's why I helped.'

They watched the small figure wander down the road. He seemed to be singing, as if listening to an inner performance.

It was a relief to leave the cracked motorway and the overlooking brick houses for the water. The sun was still high, clouds scudding overhead, as they splashed into the Don Basin, their eyes peeled for enemy craft in the bright, shifting light. Once past the sunken ruins of Doncaster, the cathedral tower sticking up out of the water, they breathed sighs of relief. The Pure Light would be facing the other way as they took Sheffield.

Alex steered north, into the widening channel, the other side lost to sight. Thania mused, 'So many BTs, subbits as they call them, a whole criminal class with kind of magical powers…'

'And they work for Mr Crow. Who is Darius Raven.'

Chapter 18: Caledon

They woke on the floor of the Duck, a vague memory of gunfire tossed aside by the wind. Alex sat up and peered over the side of the craft. They were floating just out of the mouth of an inlet, grey-white birds clustering on brown-grey mudflats. Here and there, grain-stripped, grey wood stalks made half-hulk outlines of rotted boats, and the brown-rusted steel struts of dead vehicles stuck up out of the mud.

They scanned around, instantly alert out of sleep, but all they heard was the wind, driving ragged clouds over a low, grassy hill, carrying away any evidence there might have been of battle. They'd had an uneventful meander up the wide flood-zones inland from the east coast, stopping only to refill the Duck's fuel tank from their cans. Wherever they were now, the empty cans and fuel gauge told them it was near the end of their journey.

It was warm and breezy. Thania stretched and searched the craft for provisions, digging deep into a box and coming up with the last of some dried fruit and a little leather-jacketed steel field kit sporting a Shemeld crest and containing drug tinctures. She pulled out a vial of cocaf. They broke their fast, sitting chewing and sipping the bitter tincture with swigs of stale water from a canteen.

Thania picked up the binoculars and peered around for somewhere to land. The low hills were quiet, no sign of humans at all.

Alex said, 'Where the hell are we?'

Peering into the channel, which stretched as far as she could see, she said, 'I think we're too far north for Newcastle. Maybe the Lothian Channel. In which case, if we land on the north side, there's a good chance we're on High Caledon's relatively friendly turf.'

Alex pointed. 'OK, let's land on that hillside, and reconnoitre on foot.'

'I agree.' She slung the binoculars round her neck. 'I see you're learning this soldiering game.'

They took the Duck up the shallowest slope, as quietly as they could, switched the engine off and waited for half an hour. Then they took their guns and walked uphill.

It was a dangerously beautiful morning, torn clouds rushing across a bright sky. As they got near the top of the rise, they saw ragged smoke rising. Thania dropped silently and turned her head side-on to the wind, listening. The wind rose and fell; all she could hear was the whistle. She stood crouching and they continued up the scraggy bracken. As they crested the rise, they looked over the other side at an apparently deserted village, maybe three dozen houses knotted round a crossroads.

The smoke they'd seen rose from a couple of broken roofs. Thania scanned the horizon all round 'Nothing. Whoever did this came and went.' She slung the binoculars. 'Let's take a look, might find some food.'

The village was almost intact, though everyone seemed to have left. The main street was long and straight, its emptiness emphasized by the uniformity of its redbrick cottages. They walked, still keeping low, alert to everything around them. A gust of breeze brought a mouthwatering waft of fresh bread out of an arched alleyway. They ducked in; the bakery had golden, crusty loaves left out on shelves. They tiptoed through an open door into the rear of the shop, where there was a tiny cold-store. Heat-exchangers thrummed above shelves with steel mesh fly-screens. Alex picked up a wedge of dry, yellow cheese.

They sat on crates out the front of the bakery. A very off-white feral cat skulked around the shop doorway and

Thania got up with a piece of cheese, approaching the nervous, starving beast. When she was about a foot away from it, it pounced, digging its claws into the back of her hand for a moment as it grabbed the food.

It ran off and sat just a few yards away, growling as it ate. She watched the blood well up on her hand, then dug into her pack. No eluter. She felt a flash of fear, then thought, *We are way beyond that, now*. Alex looked over at her. 'You OK?'

She nodded. 'Yeah. May have just been exposed to vonnie-fever, so keep half an eye on me.' She went back to her meal. 'There was a battle here, and the defenders had somewhere to go, maybe were rescued by Caledon forces and taken out of the war-zone. Which is bad news – PL making inroads into Caledon. Hopefully, if we move north we'll come into friendly territory. Let's see how far the Duck will get us.'

They went and got the craft and drove through the village. The road up the hill to the north was in very bad repair, and they drove off of it most of the way, slewing over a lunar themepark of mud-encrusted asphalt chunks. At the crest of the hill, it twisted round to the left and revealed a new view. A steep hillside dropped before them, with another, larger settlement at its foot. Their first impression was of trailing smoke and shattered buildings. The road dropped steeply down to the ruined town and two roads ran out of it on the other side, up the opposite slope of the valley. Thania scanned for a long time before they set off down the hill.

The road was lined with the stumps of street lights and road signs, all the metals and electronics long-scavenged out of them. They drove past an edge-of-town industrial site, chainlink fence ripped and storage silos shattered, pale dust coating everything, smoke still drifting in the wake of a fierce battle.

At the edge of the town itself, someone must have made a stand. A thick, nineteenth-century wall of industrial brick gaped open, a hole punched in it by heavy artillery fire. They scanned the piles of rubble for survivors.

'Where are all the injured people?' asked Alex.

They rode clear through the abandoned ruins, out to the other side of the small town's center, a cracked and stained concrete plaza, still seeing no sign of casualties. 'This must be where the Caledon forces made a stand, drove the attackers back, then withdrew,' said Thania.

On the far edge of the ruined town, where the road ran out into dry, dusty fields, was a fairground, smoking tarpaulins blowing in the breeze, a few flames still licking here and there. They stopped the Duck and got out to walk around the tattered booths and silent machines, puzzled.

Thania nudged Alex and said, 'Look.' Beside them was a booth, with the legend 'Auld Corbie's Hoose,' in cracked paint. Spooked, Alex ducked behind the flap with his gun at the ready. The owner of the booth must have been killed or wounded, or taken away, because he'd left his Crow puppet behind, a crest of black feathers sticking out of the trampled mud.

Alex took the weird doll outside. 'Look at this.' The puppet felt amazingly heavy, and he tugged at the stinking fabric, then found his penknife and cut it open. Inside the head was a small device, made of some hard plastic. They gazed at it in wonder as it began to glow. On an impulse, Thania grabbed it and threw it as far as she could, then dragged Alex into the shadow of a broken wall. There was a shrill screaming noise, then a flash of purple fire *whumped* above them and shrapnel pinged off the bricks to each side.

Thania jerked aside, grunting in pain. Her right trouser leg was ripped open and blood welled up from a deep, open wound in her calf. Alex peered over the wall; there was no sign of the Crow-device, just a flattened circle of land, smoke rising through the settling dust. He squatted back down and searched their packs, coming up with a shirt which he tore into strips. He bound Thania's leg, then helped her into the Duck, made her as comfortable as possible on the deck and passed her the bag of supplies.

They set off up the north-leading road. The fuel only lasted to the next rise, but from there Alex could see an encampment in the valley, neatly-lined up camouflage tents flapping, diesel fumes rising, military vehicles kicking up dust. No white paint or long-stemmed crosses.

'I'll be back with help, don't go anywhere.' Thania gave a strained grin.

Alex walked into the camp with his hands held high. The first man he saw close up looked half-starved and ill, and no-one challenged him. A corporal took him to the lieutenant in charge, a tall, slender man in camo fatigues. He wore a green tartan cap with the thistle and knotwork crest of Caledon, had a bandage over one eye, and looked as if he hadn't slept for a week. He indicated an oildrum and Alex sat down. 'I'm with one other, we escaped from the Pure Light invasion of Sheffield, yesterday. Our Duck ran out of fuel. My companion is wounded, she's in the Duck. She's a doctor,' he added.

The shattered officer lifted his cap and ran a grubby hand through thinning red hair.

'So those fuckers have taken Sheffield. Give me some fucking good news, for a change.' He looked at Alex, as if seeing him properly for the first time. He nodded. 'McAllister, Third Caledon Infantry, out of High Crieff.'

'Alex Tyler, Wessex via Shemeld.' They shook hands.

'Well, Caledon can always use another Duck, not mention another doctor,' said McAllister. 'Corporal, take this man in a truck, refuel his vehicle and pick up one wounded medic.'

As they'd surmised, this Caledon force was limping back after a costly victory. The driver of the truck was unshaven, and the feverish intensity of his gaze suggested he'd been on cocaf for days. He seemed to want to talk. 'PL just came over the Lothian Channel, and took that wee town back there. No-one even noticed till it was too late. If we hadn't chanced upon the whole show, there'd be a PL beachhead by now in Comrie. It's all we can do, just stop them again and again. So well supplied... From North America, I guess....' The man shook his head.

'What would help?'

The man turned red-rimmed eyes on Alex. 'Intelligence. Real fucking intelligence.' He pulled the truck over at the side of the Duck. 'Or just really superior weaponry. Fine-looking vehicle you have there.'

'Courtesy of Shemeld.' Alex hauled a can of diesel off the back of the truck and set about filling the Duck's tank, then hopped on board and went over to Thania.

'You OK?' She nodded, numb and shaky-looking. 'Friendly Caledon unit. We're riding north with them.'

The convoy rolled over the sunlit hills. It was a beautiful day in the Highlands, now populated with tiny settlements, uphill off the main road, ringed with stockade walls and observation posts. They crossed Rannoch Moor and the road climbed up into the Grampians. Alex kept one eye on Thania, and the other on the landscape. White rocks stood out on fire-blackened earth which rolled down to a tiny tarn, and then they dropped down into Fort William, Ben Nevis looming behind the clouds.

The troops stumbled out of their vehicles. The exhausted lieutenant came up to him. 'This is where we get off. Our wounded will be treated here, you'll have a better chance in triage in Inverness. I'll get you a lift there. Goodbye, good luck, and thanks for the Duck.'

They shook hands, and waited for the truck to pull up beside them. Alex and the driver helped Thania onto a bench in the rear. Alex sat by her and rested a hand on her shoulder. The driver looked tired, but was friendly. 'We're taking the new northeasterly road by Loch Lochy and Loch Ness. It's fairly well-maintained.' He swung his body up into the cabin and the engine thrummed through them.

They thundered along. Thania seemed to be dealing well with the bumps. She hauled herself up and hung over the side of the truck, gazing out, silent, then Alex heard her muttering, 'Look, down at the water's edge, it's all dotted with bare houses, looted villages…' Alex leaned over and felt her forehead. 'You're burning up, what do you need?'

She faced him, her eyes big and red, unfocused as if set loose to move around of their own free will. 'Laudanol would help. And maybe an eluter, just in case.' She curled up on the bench, all her professionalism gone again. Alex searched their bags. The tincture pack they'd taken from the Duck had a little stainless-steel laudanol vial. He shook it; it felt full. He reached for his canteen and unscrewed the cap, filling the cup-lid. He dripped dark brown tincture into the water. 'Four drops. Tell me if you need more.' He held the cup to her lips.

When she was resting back on the bench, Alex read out the labels on the other vials. He got to 'Elutol.' 'That's it, give it here,' said Thania. The road was a good one, hardly any major bumps. Alex stroked Thania's hair and had to fight off an urge to lay down and sleep.

He actually came round from a light doze as they entered Inverness's busy and convoluted roads, military traffic backed up, queuing at the rebuilt bridge over the Ness.

There was a lot of traffic around the hospital, and even more in front of it. They drove up to a steel pole barrier guarded by a stocky, bored-looking woman wearing a waistcoat studded with comms devices, a new-looking AK47 slung over her shoulder. The driver hailed her then pulled the truck round sideways. Alex leaned over the side. 'Hello, we need help for a leg-wound and fever.'

'Sorry darling, they've ceased admitting patients. War and vonnie-plague. Full up.' She pronounced the two words with a bleak finality, but added, 'There's a triage point just round the corner, down the hill towards the campus.'

It was a large building that looked like a nineteenth-century church hall, identified by the giant TRIAGE sign that swung over the forecourt. Someone had taken their time to try and make the sign look nice; the letters had been carefully painted onto a square grid, red onto cream, but the E trailed a trickle of paint like an untreated wound. Alex jumped over the side of the truck and went into the ill-lit interior. There was a tiny vestibule, fawn and camo-surplus paint, a desk with a jam jar full of pencils, a few crumpled scraps of re-used paper, and no-one tending it. A constant flux of people moved in front of him, some of whom had uniforms and some of whom didn't. After a few moments, Alex simply asked the next person who rushed through the lobby.

The petite woman, hennaed strands stuck to her forehead, her right hand shaking a little as she tucked her hair underneath a silk headscarf, turned out to be the volunteer shift nurse. 'Yes, bring her in,' she gasped, eyes flicking from exhaustion. 'I'll get a stretcher.'

They carried Thania through the lobby and into the vast, ill-lit room behind. They laid her on a narrow mattress on the floor. Alex thanked the driver, who left for the Inverness army base, then sat down by Thania, held her hand and waited. She was calm, her pulse regular, her breathing slower now. Either side of her bed lay other women, and then more and more figures, on the tiny mattresses. There was a background of occasional cries.

One woman sobbed, dully, slowly, pausing for a minute, then starting again. He heard a male voice from the far end of the ward, shouting something incomprehensible then crying.

Some time later, he returned from the toilet, a grim experience in itself, to find a dark, slender woman in black overalls kneeling beside Thania. No surprise to him, she was trying to dictate her own treatment. 'Elutol, five milligrams! Now! Fucks sake, sorry, no offence. But...!'

He stood back while the woman gently turned Thania over, injected her in a raised, vaguely struggling buttock, then, just as gently, turned her back and placed her long hands on Thania's head. Her slow thrashing quietened, the healer inserted needles into her earlobes, then began to clean and stitch the leg-wound. She spoke soothing words to Thania; there was something familiar about the soft susurrus of her voice, and the shape of her back… She finished, and was bandaging the gash when it clicked. Alex whispered, 'Maira?'

The dark woman turned, her hands still meticulously in contact with her patient and smiled at him. 'Alex Tyler.'

'What – what are you doing here?' asked Alex.

'I might ask the same of you, but I'm not that surprised. Doing my bit, as a healer in Inverness. Part of the war effort here. Told you we'd meet again.'

He gazed at her, her great dark eyes, her twisted mouth, her vitality just a little dimmed by tiredness, drinking in the sight of her, unbelieving. She shook her head slowly and with her free hand reached out to Alex. They touched, and a flood of feelings hit him. He grinned, embarrassed, through sudden tears, knelt and wrapped his arms around her, looking at Thania, who was breathing slowly and peacefully.

Maira said, 'My shift finishes soon, then I'll take you to my place. We have some catching up to do.'

Alex sat by Thania, watching her doze. People cried, people moved around. Time passed.

Maira came up, carrying two shoulder bags, buttoning a long, black woollen coat. 'We can get a truck if we leave now.'

The truck took them down the slope where rubble mounds linked the heights of Inverness with the part-sunken Kessock Bridge. Maira's place was an old cottage sitting above concrete landfill and facing the plateau of the Black Isle across the Beauly Firth.

They stepped into a postage stamp of a garden, dry fronds of fern and grasses brushing against their feet. The doorframe was twined with honeysuckle that was just forming flowers. Alex and Maira supported Thania inside, and laid her on a couch in the one downstairs room. Maira made some soft, cool light come on and drew the curtains on the fading daylight. She stoked up a pot-bellied stove and put a big steel pan on the hotplate. A big black cat emerged from behind the curtains and rubbed against her legs, purring loudly. She opened the steel-mesh door of a small meat-safe and brought out a jar of scraps. She put some down in a bowl and stroked the sleek animal.

Thania twisted herself round to lift a curtain and gaze out of the window. 'What's the security situation like round here? I mean, bandits, PL militias?'

'I have some telepathy, which came with a touch of precog: I get clear ideas of when someone's got violent intentions towards me.' She turned and stirred the pot, then set a board with chunks of fresh brown bread down on the floor. She served them a bean stew, and pungent, yellow goat cheese. They sat in a circle, Thania propped up on cushions, and ate voraciously. Then Maira took their plates and brought a tray over from the sideboard. On it was a bottle of malt whisky, and three glasses. She crossed to the sink, pumped some water into a jug and sat back down.

‘Water’s still good round here,’ she said, as she served the straw-coloured liquor with a splash of icy water in it. ‘They filter it through reed beds somewhere up Cromarty. It’s a priority, for the whisky drinkers. Slainte! Now we catch up.’

For the next hour, they did just that. Alex and Thania told their story of Wessex and exile, Sheffield and the invasion, breathlessly, hurrying to narrate their own crazy few days. Maira filled in a bit of their background from Carcassonne. ‘We met while Alex was on a jaunt with Hendry. We had a… an intense time.’ She glanced at Alex, then at Thania, with a tentative smile. Alex looked at Thania, wondering if she would get possessive, but she was smiling, her eyes warm. Maira said, ‘He was beautiful, your Alex. And he’s not bad now.’

They all laughed.

‘Now, here’s how I landed up in Inverness,’ Maira said. ‘Alex, remember that party where we met? One of the orgs that had a begging bowl out there was the New Gene Foundation. They’re researching those new viruses that weaken immunity, the HIV-31 series, here in Caledon. I knew I could heal some of the sufferers, and it dovetailed with my own obsessions. The people I worked with, well, their immune systems have been through the meat grinder. Those that survive are incredibly tough at a molecular level, and I wanted to learn anything I could apply to life-extension.’

Thania frowned. ‘What kind of thing, Maira?’

She paused. ‘You know what the action of antelosin, of Rejuve is?’

Thania said, ‘Slows down telomerase, and so helps new cells to be produced like they were in your youth. And some other actions, apparently.’

Maira nodded. ‘About those other actions, nobody has a clue. It’s an incredibly sensitive molecule, which is why purity is so important. Which in turn, is how it has its political clout. This war, it's all driven by Rejuve. Your Jervis's betrayal of Wessex, Frey's betrayal of Sheffield, the fact that everyone has to buy the decent stuff, the stuff that works, off the Pure Light, who have both the backstocks and the factories...' she shook her head 'Like all monotheists, these people are promising eternal life, but unlike any of the others, they can deliver it, or at least a facsimile of it.'

She took a drink. 'I don't need it, you see, not any more. My becters read the signature of antelosin in my body, and replicated it. I haven't had to take Rejuve for... for a long time now. So maybe that secret could be unlocked without becters. Maybe it's hinted at within an older magic. Maybe other people could get off Rejuve and still live, and that would break the PL monopoly on life-extension. But...'

'What?'

Maira shook her head. 'The whole... problem, the whole question, it's enormous. A lifetime's work for someone much more knowledgeable than me. But it's all there already, inside becters. I can do it, just because becters let me. Whoever invented becters must have seen all round that, must have the answers, or some of them.'

Alex sipped his whisky. 'Darius Raven, the Old Crow man.'

She shot a sharp glance at him. 'Which is why I wanted to be up here, that bit nearer to Thule. I'm obsessed. It will probably kill me.' She drank, then got up, collected dishes and took them to the sink.

'The way you got your wound, Thania, from that Crow puppet – those Old Crow stalls are all up and down the British Isles, but there are more of them in the north, and there are more of them lately. The ones here in Caledon work differently to the southern ones – if you get asked into the back room, you might get invited to a meeting, always at night, with a prospective employer. Some people take up the offer, thinking they'll get a franchise, but they're never heard from again. The Crows are a kind of transmitter, given out to all the franchisees. Just south of here, a few weeks ago, there was just the kind of explosion you described. They never found any trace of whoever tried to open the thing up.'

She sat back down. 'Thania, your path might have crossed that of a Wessex man, a musician called Bruno Lorenz.'

Thania nodded. 'I know Bruno, I served with him in the Specials.'

'Bruno tried to infiltrate the Crow franchise, but they wouldn't have him. Probably because he's too intelligent.'

Alex said, 'Who else knows about the Crows?'

'Hendry's onto it,' said Maira. 'As you've no doubt guessed Alex, he's in bed with the PL, but I think he's succeeded in keeping the Crow story from them so far. Which is believable – they're not a British-Isles based movement any more. It seems they have powerful friends across the Atlantic, in one of the North American enclaves.'

They all fell silent and drank for a while, then Maira got up and went to the stove. 'There's some hot water now, do you want the first bath, Alex?'

He nodded.

'Just up the stairs, go easy on the water.'

The bath was a fantastic luxury and Alex lay in it until it was getting lukewarm, then dried himself on Maira's thick towels and went back down. Thania was sitting up, and Maira sat by her, holding her hand. She turned to Alex with a soft smile. 'She's lovely, your girlfriend.'

Alex sat across from them, drinking in the sight of these two beautiful, strong women so at ease with each other.

Thania spoke. 'Maira's invited us to share her bed.'

Maira said, 'That's if you don't mind sleeping with an

old, old woman. We've been telling some truths.'

Alex, transfixed, shook his head gently.

'Eighty-nine in May.' She stood up and twirled proudly. 'Not bad for an old girl, eh?'

He crossed over and knelt on the floor in front of the two of them, reaching out to their hands. The three of them sat like this until Maira disengaged gently. 'Let's help Thania upstairs.'

Thania and Maira went to bathe. The bedroom was tiny, stuffed full with an enormous bed underneath a skylight window. He lay back on the bed, gazing at the full moon. It seemed as if a lot of time passed, and he heard faint singing from somewhere. The two women entered, swathed in towels. They mounted the bed, threw the towels aside and knelt, naked, in front of him, still, hands resting on gleaming thighs. Time slowed down. The pale moonlight behind the women gave them cold, white haloes. In that eerie, suspended space, their voices twined together. Thania sang, 'Green Grow the Rushes-O,' the ancient, mysterious rhyme coming out breathless, small and silvery.

'I'll sing you one-O, Green grow the rushes-O
What is your one-O?
One is one and all alone, and ever more shall be-O.'

The words sounded quite normal, the restored pagan version, up to 'Three, three the Ribalds,' then Thania switched to the Burns version:

'The finest bed I ever did have was the bellies o' the lassies-O.'

Then the sound got funny. He thought he heard the words shift again: '*Three is three and all alone...*' and then he realised another voice was weaving in, insinuating other words and another tune. Maira's husky contralto sang half-audible words that drew him in.

'He was the hunter, now He's the prey
They are the night, He is the day

He was the flower, Now He's the seed
Spent in Her place, emptied and freed!'

The voices wove together, weaving unholy, sacred words, lewd words, lust twined with transcendence. These songs came from the depths of these two women, from the private dimensions of the souls they were baring for him, the core of the lights that flared out of their radiant flesh.

'He was the brave hunter, now the hunted
Knotted in her silvery hair
She has stuck him, stuck him fair
Where she wants him, now he's cunted!
Now he's fairly, truly cunted!'

Things warped further. The light around the women swelled, ballooned, penetrated everything in the room, including him. Everything was aswim, everything was vibrating in a soup of silvery radiance; right down to the very particles of his senses, he swayed and vibrated and sang in his bones to that pulse of energy, energy that goes everywhere. This was like the transformed light that morning in Carcassonne, but this time it was lighter, emptier. And somehow frightening, a cosmic awe that blended in its upper reaches into terror.

Alex knew he was in the presence of something older than vonnies and becters, a magic that belonged to moon and blood and psychoactive herbs that brought madness, awe and healing. The magic of Maira's lineage, in other words. His breathing got faster, and he felt fear prickle in his skin. The moon was playing peek-a-boo with scudding clouds, gulfs of light yawning and shutting in the sky. He realized he had to let go, he had little choice but to open himself to the divine madness of the priestesses. He gasped, with that feeling of taking off from the surface of a planet, something in between terror and ecstasy, as Maira moved behind the younger woman. He made himself breathe deep and even, slow and strong.

Maira's fingers reached round Thania, round her breasts, cupping the gleaming flesh, lazy light spilling from between them. Thania's eyes rolled up; Maira lifted her hand, twisted a thread of radiance round her fingers and brought the hand up to Thania's mouth. She gasped, her lips parting, the light streaming into her mouth, her body drinking it like electric milk. She shook, briefly, gave a little gasp, and a dark flush rose up her chest to her face. Still orgasming, she opened her eyes and gazed into Alex's. The light linked them, strands of cosmic moonlight bridging their gaze. Maira moved round to kneel beside Thania again, this time with her long body extended, upright. Her hand, with those heavy jewelled rings on it, reached between her own legs. Her lips moved in whispered song, as she drew a thread of light, seemingly out of her cunt, into a spiral which she showed, lifting her hand and opening it to Alex. The light throbbed and extended, pulsing and kicking like a muscle, and wrapped itself around Alex, then Thania, a cloak of silvery radiance.

They formed a triangle now, and the energy pulsed between them, settling into a slow throb. Alex moved forward, resting a hand on Maira's thigh, the light spilling all around, its pulse speeding up. Maira lay herself down between them, her body encased in pearly light. Her head rested against Thania's pubes, her legs parted wide, and Alex bent to lap at her swollen lips.

The light passed inside him; he swallowed it, and it felt as if the inside of him was a vast space, that his point of view was shared with two other presences. This was something like flash-flesh, but a few orders of magnitude more intense. And deeper; the sweetness he tasted didn't just come from the feelings in his skin, but from the deepest parts of his selfhood. He heard a voice in his head, saying 'All of this, plus flash-flesh.' He opened his eyes, to find Maira's mouth on his, though somehow she'd just spoken. He closed his eyes again, and sank into the immense inner space that was the three of them.

Alex and Thania were exhausted. The sex, haunted, ecstatic, shivery, soon segued into sleep. Maira watched the lovely long male form relax, curling a little in foetal surrender, then rolling back over and susurrating, susurrating. She traced the worn, tired, scarred edge of his eye-sockets with a damp index finger, tears pricking her old eyes, in their casing of young skin. *The crumbling empire of the flesh*, she thought, with a wrench in her chest. Then she reminded herself that even the cells have ears, and amended it to a vision of soft, sweet new tissues as she curled up to sleep.

Chapter 19: The Road to the North

They woke to the squawking of crows, drawn out by their dreaming minds into long cachinnations of warning, just a couple of feet above them through the tiles of the roof. Thania ached; Alex surfaced. They lay in silence, orienting to this new world. A cat yowled nearby.

They went downstairs. Maira was at the stove, a NeighbourNet audio on, voices sharp and clear. She turned and grinned, filled bowls with porridge. 'How's your leg?'

'Sore, but much better, thanks. All that healing sex.'

'I've got more treatments for you, when I get back tonight. And more sex, of course. I want you able to walk unaided by the weekend.'

'About six times the usual healing rate for a deep wound.'

'What's happening at the weekend?' asked Alex

Maira looked round. 'Fancy a trip to Caithness? I think we may find some answers there, a little nearer to Thule.'

There was a thud, the flap of the old plastic cat-door shot up and the big cat charged in with a black bird-shape in its jaws, a loose wing twitching. The cat released the bird, which blundered sideways, half-flying until the cat pounced again. Maira watched while she dried her hands on a towel, her throat working in a silent song. The cat stood still, growling. Maira came out with a single, odd note, a high, trilling susurrus, and the cat grabbed its prey and scooted back out of the door.

Puzzled and smiling, Alex and Thania looked at Maira, who said, 'I never tried talking to animals till Mars turned up. I think I've got his number.' She sat down and ate a few spoonfuls of porridge.

‘What’s the Thule thing, anyway?’ asked Thania. Maira put down her spoon. ‘The myth, it’s,’ – a horn sounded from the road. ‘That’s my lift. We’ll talk tonight. Take it easy, Thania, no exertion, please.’ She leant across and kissed them both goodbye, their three breaths mingling.

They took it easy, as instructed. In the afternoon, Thania lay down and was soon asleep, so Alex went for a walk. He’d learned by now how to spy out dangers in the territory, and he climbed the hill that rose behind the house, the big cat following him, miaowing, for the first couple of hundred yards.

The hilltop was a low rise on the way to the heights, and it looked as if the house couldn’t easily be overlooked. Something bothered him though. Was he getting entrained into Maira’s precog? He must ask her. He walked back, waking Thania as he came in. He was just stoking up the stove when Maira returned.

Maira went to wash, then made tea and sat down. ‘Now to do more healing, OK?’ They gathered round. Maira reached out and took their hands, and they joined up the circle. ‘Now,’ said Maira. ‘You may remember last night…?’ They all smiled. Alex felt the blood rush to his groin; Thania’s chest rose, her breath deepening.

‘Yes, Thania, that’s it. Let the breath fill you, let the energy spill out. I shall help, like last night, but not as much. Even though you haven’t got becters, you do have this energy. And we have the links between us from last night. Close your eyes and let it build up.’

Alex started to feel the pulse of Thania’s breath in his own body, and he let his own breathing entrain to it. He felt Maira do the same. Rapidly, his sense of his body changed. It was as if he had no weight any more, was made of energy. The energy flowed between them, in a vortex which got faster, until it no longer pulsed with their breath but spun in a circle, something that was beyond them all now, with its own life. Time ceased to be important; they sat in the spinning light. It ran and ran, on its own agenda.

At some stage, Alex opened his eyes and gasped – they were embedded in a disk of silvery light, like the moonlight they'd drunk and fucked with the night before, all around and inside them. Even with his eyes open, he had some flash-flesh, suddenly being on the inside of Maira's smile, feeling the energy surging into the wound on Thania's leg (*my leg…*).

Clearly, Thania was lapping it up, but eventually the energy started running down, seemingly of its own accord. Gently, Maira raised both her hands and opened her eyes. 'Let go your hands when I do,' she whispered.

Maira helped Thania onto a pile of cushions, then motioned Alex into the kitchen, where they chopped vegetables for supper. Not much was said; they sat and ate, and breathed in the glistening fog of energy that still hung in the air. Alex cleared the plates, and Maira went over to the corner and picked up a small, skald's harp. She checked the tuning, then started a simple figure, that rose then fell. 'This is a song by Bruno Lorenz. He said it came from a vision, and I think it's about Raven, our Thule-man.'

Knowing nothing in their youth,
Like bare-boughed trees awaiting spring
Few learn they're more than what they dreamed;
Most cobble lives from others' truth

But some who sense they're on their own
And common ways they cannot tread
They dream their own and deadly path
And find the strength to walk alone

Mother, lover, home and friends
When all he loves is torn away,

What can a man stripped down like that
Do with his life? On him it depends

From far above the world's dumb mystery
Beyond the clamour of the war
Comes a sound of different struggle
Minds unfettered by their history

Way beyond the mountains bare
Far off in the land of Thule
Lives a strength that few can fathom
The northern road that few may dare

She put the harp aside. 'It's unfinished, isn't it? It's like a story waiting to happen.' Alex shuddered. Maira's eye caught him.

'Bruno and I went north last summer. Thule is a myth; Bruno taught me that. It's the vanished ancestral home, it's the source of civilization, it's what we all remember in our hearts about how profoundly good life can be. But Bruno found out that it's also what Raven calls his world, whatever and wherever that is. And that myth means something different to him, something much darker than what we understand.' She paused.

'We met this amazing man and his family, like something out of the twentieth century, in a compound off one of those hill-roads. I think I could find it again, and he's well worth a visit. He may have useful information.' She crossed over to Thania. 'Alex, please fetch the whisky, and pump some water.' She undid the dressing on Thania's calf and checked the wound. She smiled and nodded.

They drank some whisky and went to bed. Once more, sumptuous sex segued into sleep.

The next morning, Thania was hobbling about the living area, wincing only occasionally.

Maira was on her way out to work. 'You need all that energy to fix up your leg. Don't squander any!'

On Thania's insistence, Alex walked a short distance up the hill with her, then brought her back and made sure she laid down. 'I'm bored,' she said, stretching out on the cushions. Alex nodded. 'Me too. Not used to all this inaction. And…'

'What?'

Alex sighed. 'I keep getting things that feel like precog flashes, and they don't feel good.'

'Since when have you done precog?'

He shook his head. 'Never, until Maira. She's entraining me, probably by accident.'

Thania frowned. 'Ask her, later.'

Maira came home loudly. 'Hey, anyone in? I've brought a visitor.'

She stepped in, ushering in a young man. The first thing Thania noticed about him was pale blue eyes set in a craggy, broad face, long reddish-blond hair brushed back over his shoulders. She took a liking to the face. 'Hello, I'm Thania.'

'Alex.'

'Duncan Lamb.' They shook hands. Something flinched in Thania's chest, hearing the namesake of her dead brother.

'Duncan's offered to lend me his pickup for the weekend. I thought he ought to meet the others who'll be riding in his pride and joy.'

'Thank you,' said Alex.

'It's a pleasure,' said Duncan. His eyes dipped, consulting some vonnie setting. 'Is that the time? Must be gettin' on, Maira.'

Maira left to drive Duncan home. They heard the diesel outside again a while later.

'Lovely bloke,' said Thania.

'He is. My favourite old flame, with a wife and child now. He wants to live to be a thousand, and it'll be a pleasure to help him, if I ever find that secret.'

Maira led their healing circle again that evening, and Thania showed off her agility in bed that night.

'You will NOT bend like that!' scolded Maira, half-stifling a crooked grin.

In the morning, Maira gave her a thorough check-up, and announced she would do. They packed plentiful provisions under tarps in the back of the pickup and squeezed into the front.

Maira knew the way, so she took the wheel first. 'Know how I learned to drive? I got a crossload, from another BT, a man called War-Fox. Sometimes BTs can share skills like that. He got it off another BT. Such a rare skill these days, everyone used to do it.'

'I can drive,' said Alex. 'Hendry paid for lessons for me.'

'Posh boy,' chided Thania. 'I got taught by the Wessex Specials.'

They crossed the Beauly Firth and climbed up the slope of the northern road. Maira struck up the old barrack-room song 'The Poet's Share' in her ringing voice, and Alex and Thania joined in the verses they knew.

You've heard of the Hero's portion,
how a big man takes his choice,
But the man or the woman who's bigger still
Is the one who can charm with his voice, with his voice
The one who can charm with his voice

He's drunk of the poet's portion
Of the Allfather's stolen drink
He might be an ugly fellow

But the women all smile at his wink, at his wink
The women all smile at his wink

She might not have two pennies
Or be sailing around on a yacht
But she makes her life from the songs in her heart
And not from the things that she's got, that she's got
Not from the things that she's got

He's a poet and singer and lover
She prattles in rhyme by firelight
He's there by your side in the evening tide
And she's gone like the smoke of last night, of last night
She's gone like the smoke of last night

He tells you a tale that makes sense of your world
Gives you costume and tools for your life
Writer's pen, jester's motley, forester's green,
Soldier's khaki fatigues, butcher's knife, butcher's knife
Them old khaki fatigues, butcher's knife

They were repeating the last verse as they joined the main coast road up to Dingwall. On the hillside above, they saw a few military encampments, tiny outposts. 'They protect the few settlements up there from bandits. So they claim,' said Maira. 'I wouldn't stop and ask the way, though.'

When they couldn't see any outposts, they pulled over into a layby that looked down over the North Sea. Alex broke out their lunch. 'What are we expecting to find?' he asked.

Maira gestured with a sandwich. 'Just up above New Thurso, in the forest, there's a clearing with the remains of a settlement. No-one has taken it over, because it's ringed with landmines. I went there with Bruno, and he showed me a route through them. In the middle of the clearing, there used to be a cabin, according to Bruno's research among the locals.'

She took a bite and shook her head. 'Rough lot, hill bandits, but Bruno's good. Anyway, the legend goes that it wasn't a cabin at all, but some kind of a flying machine. It flew off, with a great roar and a bang, about eighty years ago.' She looked straight ahead. 'That's our man, I reckon. Our immortal, off to his Thule.'

Thania stood up. 'How's your leg?' asked Maira.

'Good.' She walked over to the bushes at the side of the road, with no visible limp.

They swapped seats and Alex drove, past Tain, now a string of farm compounds relocated uphill, and Maira got out an old map. They were skirting a wide firth, Maira looking round, deep in concentration, when she said, 'It's the next inland road, runs along the Fleet inlet.'

An hour later, she said, 'Turn left, and keep your guns to hand, bandit country starts round here.' They followed the steep and potholed road into the mountains, stands of Sitka spruce on the hills to their right, the deep inlet below them. About five miles further, the road leveled out a bit, and the forest was thicker.

'That farm track, down there. Go slow, and keep your eyes peeled for wires and caltrops.'

Alex crawled the car along, lights on against the forest gloom. He spotted one of the spiked devices and managed to edge round it, just as the path swung round to the left and a tall steel fence came into view, smoke rising from a chimney behind. They pulled up by a barbed wire-topped gate, two security cameras on tall poles swivelling towards them. Maira jumped out and went up to some kind of audio input on the left pillar of the gate. She keyed in a sequence and they heard her half of an exchange. It seemed the householder was satisfied; the gate swung open to reveal a squat, brick-built farmhouse.

Maira got back in and Alex drove cautiously onto the gravel track. The steel front door opened and a tall, fat man in brown tweeds with long hair and a straggly red beard emerged and stood on the step, a rifle slung lazily over his shoulder. He sized them up then yelled in a Highland accent, 'Two friends of Maira's are, I hope, also friends of Travis Mackay, and are welcome on that basis.'

They got out of the car, Maira running up to hug the big man, who ruffled her hair and gave them a friendly scowl, then unhanded Maira and shook hands with Alex and Thania.

Alex did their introductions and Mackay said, 'You sound like you're from heathen Wessex. Come inside, into the time capsule and home of the mysteries, Travis's new friends.'

They followed Mackay into the dimly-lit hallway. A shout sounded from the left, and the crying of a small child.

'Mistress Mackay greets you in her own inimitable way,' yelled Travis, and led them through the left doorway into a big dining kitchen.

The squalling of the toddler clutching his mother's grubby print frock reached them just before the smell, which was of rancid chip fat and overcooked nappies. They stepped forward to greet Mistress Mackay, a spare, bony woman with red hair, dressed in a faded cotton dress, but she ignored them and turned on her husband.

'What're y' doin' fetching more folks up here Mackay, you fuckin' idiot? I hope they've ... ah, for fuck's sake.'

She tailed off into a despairing shake of her head and Mackay replied with wounded dignity. 'Maira and her friends Alex and Thania made their own way, I did not summon, them, so calm y'self down, woman, and let's have a drink.'

Still shaking her head, Mistress Mackay turned to the

three guests and spoke above the whining of the boy. 'Ah'm Mags, you've already met my fucking idiot husband, and this wee starveling is Connor. Say hello to the nice people Connor.' The boy drew closer to his mother's skirt and closed his eyes. Mags said, 'He's a shy one, give him time.'

Maira approached the boy and knelt in front of him 'You know me, don't you Connor? Would you like some fruit?' She fished a bag of dried apples out of her pocket and the boy grabbed a handful and gazed at her with big eyes for a moment.

Mags seemed to relax a little. 'You must think we're dead rough, but it's living up here, y'see. Mackay, stop standing there and fetch some drink for the guests.' She shook her head with a strained smile at Thania. They sat down round the greasy pine table and Mackay served them straw-coloured whisky in steel tumblers. Thania raised hers and took a sip. 'This is good.'

'The art of living has a good deal to do with knowing what it's important to spend money on, and what it isn't.'

'Like your fucking son, for instance?' snarled Mags.

'No fine glasses at Castle Mackay, I'm afraid, they always seem prone to breakage round here.'

He glanced significantly at Mags, who muttered, 'Shut up, cunt,' but seemed mollified by having the malt in front of her.

Maira felt little Connor tugging at her leg, and gave the boy more fruit. He sat down beside her on the bench, and she said, 'We've some food in the car, fancy bean stew and bread?'

She didn't wait for a reply but got up and fetched the food. Everyone sipped and smiled tightly at each other.

The food got demolished as soon as Maira distributed it. Alex reflected as he wiped up the last of the stew that it must take a lot of food to sustain a man Travis's size, let alone his family.

They sat back, more relaxed now, and Mackay excused his poor hospitality. 'Can't get down these roads for flash floods and bandits half the time, and we don't have a lot to trade, just timber.'

'And most of that you burn to feed your fucking machines, Mackay, rather than sell it to feed your son,' added Mags.

'Machines for our security, woman, as well as for my important research,' said Mackay.

Mags rolled her eyes and addressed her whisky.

When the bottle was down to a quarter full, Mackay stood up and said, 'Now for your tour of the time machine, my friends.' He reached for the whisky, but Mags cornered it and scowled fiercely at him. Defeated, Mackay snorted and led the way through to the room across the hall.

The room was lined with benches covered in computer hardware. Since the collapse of high-tech manufacturing, even old and cranky systems were rare these days, beyond the hybrid technologies based round NeighbourNet. Mackay sat down in front of a screen and made it light up with some control out of their sight. The screen filled with lists and the big man clicked on a couple of items.

A massive sound filled the room, a raging silvery trumpet over electric guitars and keyboards, a gigantic ecstasy driving the music. The sound was incredibly clear, none of the muddiness of vonnie transfers. They all sat there as it rose and crashed around them, borne up in the wildness of a bygone age, and when it ended, Mackay turned to them with tears in his blue eyes. 'Well, what d'you think to *that*?'

Maira said, 'Like being blasted into the sky at dawn.'

'Like the first time I tried flash-flesh,' said Thania.

Alex said, 'I've never heard anything like it. When's it from?'

'The late twentieth century, an American musician called Miles Davis. He shows you how to get high when you've forgotten how.' He sighed and wiped his eyes. 'Travis Mackay probably has the greatest collection of old music in the British Isles. Unless, of course, the man we seek is also a music fan. The more Mackay comes to learn about him, the more likely it is that he has everything. Mackay of course has a snapshot of the entire of what used to be called the Internet, frozen onto a thing called a disk drive. Like an old-fashioned version of that computer you wear under your skin, Maira. But Mackay's Internet drive, as he calls it, is a mere classical processor, nothing like your becters.' He turned away from the screen. 'Now tell me about the war, and about Sheffield. I hear that evil death-cult has taken it.'

Alex took a deep breath and filled in the story of the invasion and their journey north. Maira added, 'And we're looking for information about Darius Raven, the Thule-man, the Crow-man.'

Mackay nodded sadly. 'I knew it was only a matter of time. Sheffield's the key to armaments, and in turn, the key to everyone's loyalty these days is that terrible Rejuve drug. Me, I'll stick with the water of life.' He managed to get one more drop of whisky out of his tumbler.

'But of your quest, Travis Mackay believes he can help you there. We've known the identity of your man from Thule, since last Summer, and Mackay has found out something about what he might be doing. Watch this.'

He did something to the computer and a series of faces began to flash before them, each held on the screen for only a second before it was replaced, each face split-screened with columns of data. Overlaid on the images was a grid that expanded and contracted, picking out pieces of data and fitting them to faces.

'Mackay put together everything he's ever found about Darius Raven and those around him,' he said. At that moment, the search-net stopped moving. It showed a cluster of faces, one in the center bearing Raven's name. Neural nets of data jumped forward then retreated around the face. 'Darius Julian Raven, born 2007, the year the floods began, the year they began the first evacuation of low-lying lands, the Republic of Tuvalu. His first formative memory was of watching a TV news report of the murder of Kaz Tazhin, and becoming fascinated with the autistic inventor of the fabled, and possibly failed, elekilpo generator. Graduated from Merton College Oxford, top of his year 2027, the year they evacuated Fiji and the Maldives. Went to Sheffield to work under Banstead, in direct academic line from Hans Krebs, on theoretical problems in nano-engineering. Gained his PhD in 2030, the year they evacuated Bangladesh, Vietnam and the Nile Delta. In the 2050s he started taking the rejuvenation drugs. In 2071 he got the Chemistry Nobel for von Neumann nanites, vonnies. It was the year they evacuated Florida. Disappeared from view in 2089, the year that most of East Anglia was abandoned, and roughly the year Bruno's informants told him the man in the flying house left Caithness.' Mackay paused. 'The same year his ex-lover and research partner Jemima Tyson vaporized herself, together with a good deal of the Vatican.' He paused again. 'And that will be the next part of the story.'

Maira went *phew*. 'Big story. You're a genius, Travis.'

Mackay bowed his scruffy head. 'Travis Mackay thanks you. And imagines you would all like another drink.' He got up and went through to the kitchen, from where they heard a brief bout of shouting, then the sound of breaking glass.

The outside door clanged open and shut, and Mackay was back in the room with a small cut on his face and a mud-streaked bottle of whisky.

'Have tae hide it from her, y'know. Can't take her liquor.' He poured them all generous measures and toasted.

Maira took out a handkerchief and dipped it in her glass, then went over to Mackay and said, 'Let me…' as she wiped the cut on his cheek. Mackay smiled in appreciation.

'OK, the story, part two.' Mackay gestured to the screen, and a new face came into the foreground, a severe, sculpted face, blonde hair scraped back from a high forehead. 'Darius Raven got together with Jemima Tyson in 2063. She built on Raven's work, amongst that of others, in her development of nuclear fuel extraction with von Neumann nanites.

'Now here's the interesting bit. Nothing is available about Tyson's early life. The history we learn in school tells us she was a fanatic, one of the followers of Pentti Linkola, the people who believe we should cull human beings, by any means necessary. Now, does that sound like the philosophy of someone who works on nuclide extraction, someone who demonstrates hope, however misguided, about technology and its beneficial effects on the world? Well, does it?' Mackay paused and poured himself another dram.

'Of course it doesn't. She hadn't always been a Cullist. So what was she before that?' He sipped, eyebrows like briar thickets raised in exaggerated enquiry. 'Once a fanatic, always a fanatic. She was from a religious background. And which one? Well, the little Mackay was able to find out about her childhood links her to a community called Tall Pines. They in turn connect to the earliest mentions of the Pure Light.' He hit a link. Nerve nets flowered, crosses, crescents, condensed religious iconography assembling into a genealogy of the cults of control. 'There it is. Jemima Tyson's ideological DNA.'

Maira looked at Mackay, as if to speak, but let him resume.

'She and Raven must have shared a plan, something to save the world. Something that she'd abandoned by the time she decided to start burning cities. Something that he never gave up on. He invented becters, and a novel power system which needs becters to control it. He left the known world, and is plotting and working, somewhere beyond the edge of it.'

Maira nodded. 'In the Thule Teardrop. But what is he trying to do?'

'Something involving the Crows,' said Mackay. 'Obviously, they're more than just desperate, ten-a-penny fairground barkers acting as his eyes and ears. They're all BTs. An army with mutant powers. And another thing.' He took a swig and looked round at them. 'It is the opinion of Mackay that he's looking for someone, for just the right person, to complete some scheme of his. And with his technical resources, it's a big scheme.'

'How big?'

'Ever thought about what Thule means? I mean, for the world at large? If we think of it for a moment as a myth about the illuminated ones who bring high civilization from the North, then what were the great ones doing up there? It's a climate-change myth, isn't it? If you read up on the Ragnarok, the final battle gets going with Surt, the arch-demon of fire. What if we think of Surt as a comet, one of those harbingers of ill luck, who strikes and burns the earth? Perhaps it tilts the axis, perhaps it's the dust in the air, but one way or another, we get the Fimbulwinter. That's when the ice sheets re-encroach. Survivors amongst the Northern peoples all around the globe have to migrate south, into the new coastal regions opened up by the expansion of the ice-caps and the concomitant drop in sea-levels. They retain a memory of the previous Northern civilization as they move southwards. That is the Thule cycle of myths, relating to the beginnings of glaciation.'

Mackay filled glasses.

'Then at the other end of the cycle comes the bleeding of Ymir, the floods that deluge the world. Coastal settlements are abandoned and people have to migrate north again. This is the Atlantis cycle of myths – islands are swamped by rising waters or sink under the waves. That is the myth we've been living in for the last two centuries. Raven wants to shift the climatic baseline again. He wants to bring about the Thulean myth-phase, re-freeze the ice-caps. That's how big it is, Mackay believes.'

Chapter 20: The Edge of the World

'We're on our way to Caithness,' said Maira, 'to the cabin site. Tomorrow, if you'll put us up tonight. We've plenty of food to share.'

'As far as Travis Mackay is concerned, you are always welcome here, you three. We get few enough visitors, and it works on our minds, y'know. But the food will be welcome too.'

'Good,' said Maira 'We'll cook you a fine supper, Travis.'

They unloaded most of their provisions, saving just enough for two days' traveling, and set to in the stinking kitchen. Mags and Connor had disappeared, presumably to bed for their separate reasons. Rather drunk now, they all went quiet as they worked.

Alex was slicing onions, and suddenly an image hit him through the tears, as he cut the bulb straight across to reveal the concentric rings – his mother cutting onions just like that, and dipping the rings in vinegar to eat them. He must have been very small, and it had fascinated him that anyone could eat one of those fierce things. Now the tears were of loss, and behind them was an ugly rage at her abductor.

The rest of the evening was a bit of a blur, and at some point Mackay stumbled upstairs to bed. The house went quiet, and they all slept heavily on the floor of the study.

In the morning Maira aired out the kitchen and they stoked the stove and cooked porridge. The three of them had started eating before Mackay appeared, numb with hangover. *If he's like this*, thought Alex, *what state must Mags be in?*

They didn't have to wait long to find out. The mistress of the house stood leaning on the doorframe, swaying with nausea, before staggering out to the front yard. They heard her throwing up, then the squalling of little Connor as he searched for his mother. She came back in and sat shivering and feeding Connor porridge. Nobody spoke. When they'd all eaten, and drunk dandelion coffee that Mackay boiled on the stove, Maira got them ready to leave. They each clasped Mackay warmly, and Mags simply nodded at them.

They were piling their bedrolls back in the pickup when Mags rushed out with the boy, straight up to Maira. 'Take me away, I can't bear this. Just give me a lift away from this fuckin' place, anywhere'll do.'

Mackay stood on the doorstep, looking wounded. 'Go on, woman, leave Mackay if you must. Take her away, Maira, just don't give her any whisky if you value your life.'

'Shut up, you useless fucker!' screamed Mags.

Maira gave him a troubled, sympathetic look and said, 'I'll do that, Travis, and I'll bring her back if she wants to come back. Take care of yourself.'

They all got in, Connor on Mags's knee, Mackay watching them from the doorway. They saw him for the last time as he pressed a button somewhere and the gate closed behind them.

They stayed alert, guns at the ready, on the road along the channel. Maira asked, 'Where do you want dropping off, Mags?'

Mags turned her tragic eyes on Maira. 'Anyfuckinwhere… ah, sorry, Golspie'll do.'

Alex pulled over on the cobbles of the little town. Maira turned to face Mags. 'Who do you know here love, where's best?'

'Post office, Maira. I used to fuck the postman, so he's

probably worth a try.' She jumped down, Thania handing little Connor down into her arms, the two of them crossing the cobbles in the subdued morning. Alex set off, up the coast road.

Just north of Golspie, a new section of road bent west, up into the hills. Guns at the ready, they followed the steep slope, gravel scattering from under the tyres. At the top of a rise, they stopped to drink from a spring.

'That forest down there,' said Thania, 'must be part of Mackay's estate.'

Just as she finished speaking, there was a distant droning sound and they all looked up, to see a silver dart flick across the sky. It dipped straight down towards the Mackay forest and disappeared about where the house must be.

Then most of the forest was replaced by a disk of violet flame. A couple of seconds later, an ugly scream, like an amplified firework, shattered up over the hills.

Shocked, they watched the fire collapse back, leaving a perfectly-circular pit of bare devastation, with snakes of rainbow light playing round the edge.

Maira was shivering. 'That energy, becter shock… what the fuck… so alien, so weird… much weirder than nuclear…'

Alex put his arm round her shoulders. The word *elekilpo* sounded in his head, but he didn't speak it. They all looked down at the black pit, at the smoke drifting through the flattened trees around it, for a bit longer, then Alex stood up. The others followed him to the truck. Maira whispered, 'Goodbye, Travis, you fucking genius. It looks like it wasn't you Doctor Raven wanted.'

They got back in and drove on in stunned silence, trying to get to grips with the brutal power they'd just witnessed.

'How did he know where Mackay was?' said Alex. 'Was it our being there, did we bring something with us that transmitted our position?'

‘And if not,’ said Maira, ‘and Raven already had Mackay’s location, why did he choose the moment after we left to blow him away?’

They fell silent again, then Maira said, ‘Thania, I wonder if that blast last week left something in your leg I couldn’t detect, something that could have given our position away.’

Thania brooded for a moment, then said, ‘Even if that was the case, what about his timing? He would have had our position for eighteen hours before he sent his missile. It’s an uncomfortable thought, but what if it’s one of us he wants?’

Alex took his eyes off the road and caught Maira and Thania exchanging glances. ‘Which one of us, then?’ he asked.

Maira said, ‘He could have got me when I came north last year. It has to be Thania or you.’ They went quiet for a while, then she gave one of her twisted smiles and said, ‘It’s just as well we all adore each other, because as soon as we split up, the other two are targets.’

‘It’s me, isn’t it?’ said Alex. ‘He’s probably my fucking father. And the last couple of days I’ve been having…’

‘What?’ asked Maira.

‘Bad feelings, precog stuff. I didn’t mention it, because I’ve never had precog before. It must be…’

‘I’m entraining you,’ whispered Maira, ‘and you saw him coming for you.’

Silence.

Thania spoke up. ‘So let’s just get this clear. I’m in the company of two lunatics, one of whom is wanted by the much more heavily-armed psychopath who’s just wiped out the harmless Mackay, and the other is, on her own admission, obsessed enough with life extension to risk ending her own life by being shot at or blown up in the course of turning up on this madman’s doorstep.’

Alex looked at her. She was frowning, but grasped his hand. 'Guess you need me along to look after you.'

Maira reached out and put an arm round Thania's shoulder. Then she reached across and touched Alex. Everyone knew, without speaking, that this was beyond thanks, that they all wanted to stay together, whatever came of it. She spoke. 'Raven is a psycho. He stoops over the battlefield of the world, and takes what is his, which is anything he wishes.' She squeezed Thania's shoulder. 'I love you both.'

Those thoughts, plus scanning the hills for bandits, lasted them to where the road turned inland near Janetstown. They climbed the worn-out track over the crest of the land and followed the River Thurso down into the dense evergreens. The road intersected the overgrown gravel causeway of a dead railway line, steel long since recycled, no doubt for weapons. Maira said, 'Turn back, we've missed it.'

They drove slowly back along the shattered road, guns at the ready. A mile or so later, they spotted an overgrown farm track. Thania said, 'Reconnaissance on foot, folks,' and hopped out of the car, keeping low, while the others followed her.

The track twisted this way and that for about three hundred yards, then they saw the clearing. Maira came up to the front and said, 'This is the place.'

They returned to the car and brought it carefully up to the edge of the circle, Alex walking in front and sweeping the bracken-choked ground for caltrops. Maira said, 'Stop here, the rest is on foot, and step exactly where I do. Exactly.'

She led them through bracken, step by step to the centre of the clearing. Rank weeds choked the ground, but there was still a faint rectangular outline, more emphatic at the corners. They wandered around, staying inside the limits

Maira had pointed out, gazing around for any clues.

Alex's eye caught a glassy glint, and he turned over the side of a broken bottle, the label flaking off with age. As he straightened up, he spotted a dark grey shape under a limb of bramble. He hauled it out. 'Hey, look at this.' He dusted off the metal cylinder, melted in ragged blobs at one end. 'This looks like titanium, and it's been subjected to incredibly fierce heat. He must have been testing a new fuel.'

'Something like that,' said Maira.

Thania said, 'Where did he go? Where is the Thule Teardrop?'

'North of here, there's Hoy on Orkney, a couple of sad strips of land left on Shetland then nothing till you get to Spitsbergen, and we couldn't get there without a flying machine.'

'So what next?' asked Thania. 'Pack up and go home, or start swimming?'

Just then, Alex's ears caught the drone of engines, above and to the south. They all looked at each other, alarm multiplying on their faces.

Thania said, 'Maira, lead us back onto the track.'

On the path out of the clearing, she said, 'Leave the car, this way,' and led them into the dense woods. The aerial drone was louder now, and recognizable as a helicopter. They huddled in the undergrowth, guns at the ready, when a massive voice boomed down at them.

'*THIS IS CAPTAIN RENOIR OF WHITE CROSS SECURITY. COME OUT INTO VIEW. YOU WILL NOT BE HARMED.*'

'That's Hendry's outfit,' said Alex. 'Don't trust the fuckers.'

'They'll be forced to land in the clearing,' said Thania. 'Wonder if they know about the landmines...OK, they won't have seen us yet. We'll lure them through the minefield. Follow me.'

They edged cautiously through the thick vegetation, until they were about a quarter of the way round the circle. The copter was just landing in the clearing, three camo-clad figures with automatic rifles jumping out and scanning round.

Thania said, 'Split up a little, and make some noise. Now!'

They all hollered, as if calling for rescue. The three men ran in their direction, then as the first one reached the edge of the clearing there was an ear-shattering blast. When Alex looked again there were only two men left, and one of them was rolling round in pain discharging his automatic, spraying bullets everywhere. The third man got caught in the hail and went down. The clip ran out, and there was a moment's silence, then the amplified voice shouted '*I REPEAT, YOU WILL NOT BE HARMED, STEP INTO THE CLEARING OR WE WILL SURROUND YOU.*'

'Up!' said Thania, 'This way!' and led them further round the circle.

More men were streaming out of the copter and heading towards their fallen comrades when a shrill whining noise came from above. Everyone looked up. A bow-wave of rainbow colours pushed into the sky above the northern end of the clearing. In its wake rode a massive grey cylinder with a front end of faceted crystal. A beam of grey stuff that moved much too slowly to be light came out of the crystal and hit the White Cross copter, which bloomed into a rainbow fireball. The grey rod swung round, picking off the rest of the hapless troops, then retracted back into the crystal prow of the craft, which hung still, wreathed in its burning colours.

Then something else emerged from the flying ship, a hollow tube of silvery light which reached straight towards them.

‘Split up!’ yelled Thania. They were frozen in awe for a moment, then they dived in different directions. The tube of light kept advancing, and then Alex suddenly found himself helpless inside a cylinder of solid silver, rising into the air.

Thania and Maira saw the tube contract back into the crystal polyhedron, then the craft rose and screamed northwards into the bruised sky.

Chapter 21: Thule

The tube held him tight, a crude straightjacket of hard, translucent plasticky material, tiny lights flickering in its depth, like stars inside ruined polythene. Alex turned so he could see the back of a tall seat outlined against the crystal window. The rest of the craft's interior was a cylinder, featured only with steel brackets and webbing straps. He felt rocketing acceleration upwards, and the ship broke through a wispy layer of clouds into bright blue sky. The craft kept climbing, its noise rising to an ear-bruising pitch as it kept up the punishing acceleration. He was pressed against the wall of the tube, the blood rushing from his face, the corners of his mouth stretched back. The scream rose and rose, then there was a sudden pop of silence, though the acceleration didn't let up.

A few minutes later, the craft reached its cruising speed, some way beyond the sound barrier, and Alex gazed through watering eyes at the fierce deep blue of the upper atmosphere, with a haze of softer blue below them.

Just as his fear was overlaid with irritation at an itch he couldn't reach, the layers of light tilted and the craft began its descent. He found himself sliding up the tube till his head was pressed uncomfortably against the ceiling.

Minutes later, they shot through the upper cloud layer, ice crystals sparkling and boiling outside the crystal prow. Alex saw the sea, as featureless as the upper sky above the clouds, then a sudden flash near the horizon, of arcs of white and gunmetal grey, vast enough to be a land mass, resolving into an impossible island, a ring of concentric circles, circles of ice alternating with steely water, right to the central landmass, where an artificial mountain rose, terrace after terrace of shining grey stone.

The flying machine dropped lower. A wrinkled texturing of waves appeared, the cloudline tilted, peaks of foam emerged and vanished like particle pairs from the quantum void. Then the sea grew details of shining wavecrests. The craft began to level out, and they were heading towards an arc of ice-floes, and behind it, high hills covered in the stepped terraces of glistening grey. They swung round and headed for a tower in the centre of the complex. For a moment they faced the afternoon sun, and below them ran a wrinkled road of molten white gold. As they skimmed low over one of the arcs of ice, Alex thought he saw a polar bear slide its long-extinct bulk into the sea.

Then something pricked his leg, and the world spun and shattered as he slid down the tube.

He emerged from a confusing swirl of perceptions, seated upright, facing a little girl. She was standing in front of him, a pink, serious face framed in a halo of strawberry-blonde frizz, hands clasped in front of her. Behind her, the wall was featureless pale light. 'Hello,' she said, 'I'm Trivia. You must be Alex Tyler.' She reached out a shiny pink hand.

Alex leaned forward and extended his hand to shake hers. 'Yes, Alex Tyler, pleased to meet you.' Something flashed on her wrist, like a fluorescent tattoo, but wasn't there when he looked again.

The room was filled with the same cool, symmetrical glow. The child held his gaze, unsmiling, then said, 'You may take a shower. There are fresh clothes for you in there.' She broke eye contact, swivelled round and pointed to the right hand one of three doors. She didn't turn back again, but marched towards the middle door, which swung open as she approached it.

Alex stood, feeling a little spaced out. He walked over to

the door the child had indicated, and it opened. A short corridor led to a small room with a couch, and beyond that, toilet and shower cubicles tiled in pale grey, both spaces filled with the same unstructured light. He dropped his clothes on the floor and stepped into the shower. No controls were visible; guessing, he waved his arms about. Water sprayed out of the rose, unfamiliarly hot, but comfortable. A single bar of white soap sat on a ceramic shelf.

He emerged to find clean versions of the shirt and trousers he'd come in with. Back in the main room, a table by his seat held a plate of cubed fish, some kind of heavy bread and a tall glass of water. The food looked and tasted like it was made by machines, but he found he was very hungry, and eating it settled his mind a little. He stood up and walked round the room, drinking the water. Was it drugged? Maybe, with something that had no taste? He approached the other two doors. Neither of them opened. *Imprisoned, again.*

He sat down in the chair. His prison was comfortable; it was best that he stay calm, save the energy he might have squandered on anger. He looked around him. The wall in front seemed to be made of some kind of polymer.

He stood up and went to it, feeling the smooth surface. Trails of light moved through the plastic, following the path of his hand. He pressed the surface, and abruptly, pictures leapt out of the wall, now an exovid screen.

It was a silent stream of images, all from a vanished world. He watched girls dancing to inaudible music, a stiff, muscular dance that blended whorishness with fitness instruction. Then other images of that era – ships laden with plastic toys, oil gushing out of wells, good, edible food thrown away, heaps and piles and mountains of discarded consumer electronic goods, made to last only until the next fashion came along, then abandoned to clog the arteries of the world's ecosystem. The scene switched to actual war, the lavish and terrible conflicts of the twentieth century – Germany, France, Britain, Japan, Russia, Korea, Vietnam, Iraq. Vehicles migrated like ants, people swarmed like molecules in Brownian motion, dead faces, mud and blood and fire and explosions, tracer across urban skies, the empty, devastated heart of a bombed city, forests on fire, ships sinking, planes crashing, all rendered in the achingly clean video images of the pre-Flood era, the radiant iconography of the Age of Oil. Then the scene was of the dawning of disaster, the great collapses of the twenty-first century, their beginnings hidden behind new heights of consumer absurdity – larger cars, more exotic foods, more waste, while the ice-caps melted into the seas.

The wall contained nothing but relentless images of the vast stupidity that had wrecked the world. Never before had the terrible loss and folly struck him so vividly. He stood up and looked around for a control. In frustration, he waved his arms. The picture paused, just as a Humvee pulled up at a junction in a desert somewhere. Something above it glowed threateningly, then the Humvee and its occupants just blew apart in a fireball, which sucked inwards and vanished, leaving a mangled mess on the ground. Alex waved his arm, but the scene went into a loop. The Humvee and its inhabitants died again, and again, and again.

A tall, gaunt, one-eyed man dressed in shiny grey overalls stepped before him. Alex gasped, his heart racing. The man stood, something awkward in his posture, the way the forward lean of his torso clashed with the expression on his face, which was not friendly. He turned his head this way and that, so that Alex got a good look at the slick, black plastic of his prosthetic right eye. It occurred to Alex that if he wasn't already convinced he was in the hands of a madman, that face would have made it abundantly clear.

The man spoke, his voice rather high-pitched. 'I needed

to find out how easy it was to kill someone, both technically and, of course, emotionally. I targeted one of those morons, and fried him. It gave me no satisfaction at all, just made me realise I'd squandered a little more energy to no avail.' He leaned towards Alex. 'Know who I am?'

'Darius Raven,' said Alex. His throat felt dry, the words came out sticky, uneven. He narrowed his eyes, fighting down his fear, something stronger and more insistent rising within him. 'Mister Crow. Master of Thule. My mother's abductor. And killer?'

Raven huffed and bent forward a little, as if something had hit him. He stood back from Alex and waved his arm. The screen stopped playing the loop of Humvee-destruction and whited out.

Raven gestured again, and news footage of the Burning City ran on the screen. 'My ex-lover vaporized herself, together with some few thousand others. You know, some mystics say that the nuclear blast is worse than other deaths, because it extinguishes the electromagnetic cradle that would allow the soul to reincarnate.' He shrugged. 'Rubbish, in my opinion, but a hell of a sacrifice anyway. And what for? To tear another hole in the ripped fabric of history, in the hope that the future you want will gush through.'

He shook his head. 'Didn't work, did it? Jemima Tyson was wrong and deluded,' he paused for emphasis, 'but she did have a point.'

Specular reflections from the black bulge of Raven's prosthetic eye caught the blossoming mushroom cloud of Rome. 'I shall only keep you here as long as is needed, to limit the effects your hatred of me will have on what needs to be done.' He walked out, leaving Rome burning, over and over.

Alex exhaled a long, angry hiss of a breath. He waved his arm about until the screen whited over. He picked up the ceramic plate he'd eaten off and hurled it at the screen wall. It bounced off. He imagined if he went up close he might be able to see a tiny dent. He ground his teeth, shook his head; a groan escaped his lips. He was furious, but aware he was probably being observed, overlooked from some control room full of screens. He looked up and around for hidden cameras. Nothing. They must be in the screen itself. He angled his face up and spoke loud. 'Send me someone else to talk to. You owe me an explanation.'

A few seconds later, the middle door opened and a woman stepped in. She stood straight, hands open, a few inches from her sides, looking all around her like an animal scanning for predators. Other predators. She was tall, about Alex's height, slender and athletic-looking. Dark reddish hair two inches long, angled back from her prominent cheekbones; a two-piece suit, tunic and trousers of a matt black fabric, maybe cotton. The martial goddess look was completed with plucked dark eyebrows. Her eyes, wide open, drank in everything of Alex, her mouth relaxed, lips parted. Her running shoes snickered against the soft floor tiles as she approached him. She stopped, and her entire demeanour shifted; the tilt of her hip, the bright smile that crinkled the sides of her eyes, the way she extended her hands a few inches in front of her, soft, as if pleading a tiny bit. 'I am Oona.' She extended a hand; short, manicured nails, a shiny scar tracking from the wrist to the knuckles.

'Alex,' he said, almost frozen by the power of this woman, power that grabbed him in every cell. Deep breath. 'You're a BT, becter tolerant.'

She looked into his eyes. 'And you have been becter disabled. By my father, whom you just met. Because it's easier to control you that way. He will re-enable your becter tolerance when you understand the role he has for you.'

'You – are my sister? Or –' he swallowed – 'my aunt? Great-aunt? He bred us, didn't he? A dynasty of BTs…' He shook his head. 'Once I understand his plan, I shall hate it. But I won't have a choice, will I? I am… genetic raw material for my fucking father's world domination schemes.'

'Your pain is showing. It doesn't help. You'll play your role, one way or another. We're all in this together – we're the only people that can make a difference to this fucked-up world.'

'You fight as a slave, Oona.'

Her eyes narrowed. 'No more than the rest of the world. And at least we are doing something worthwhile. Making more than history, believe me. You don't know the tenth of it.'

'You sound defensive.'

'You sound desperate.' She did her seductive hip tilt and flashed her eyes at him.

Alex sighed. 'No, I don't want you to leave. I have so few choices available. Tell me about the becter tolerance blocking I've got.'

'You'd need Darius to fill in the fine details, but it's a von Neumann nanite, based on the one Darius called the glass nanite, because it's transparent to any scanning, totally invisible. It mimics becter antigens that are toxic to anyone, even someone with BT genetics.'

'So, the BT genetics – that's what you, and me, and Trivia, and how many others, are line-bred to have?'

'Yes. Jemima Tyson was my mother. Mirrorea, my daughter by Darius, is your mother Sofie's mother.' She gave a frown, then a smile. 'You are my great-grandson. Trivia is Sofie's sister. Your aunt.'

Alex palmed his forehead. 'This is frying my brain. I feel as if I'm vonnie-sick. I… I…'– he looked at Oona – 'I wasn't raised to be a fucking… genetic soldier or something.'

'No, you weren't, and you will be much more than a

soldier. Much, much more.' She looked him up and down. 'You're too emotional to take any more today. Use the rest of the day to maintain yourself. Get drunk or stoned if you need to, but relax. There's a tincture cabinet in the dressing room.' She gave him one last, searching look and left.

Chapter 22: The Making of a Hero

He woke up on the bed in the small, blank room, surrounded by symmetrical light. He waved his arms until the light increased. Might as well treat it as day. His predicament hit him, and he sank his head in his hands for a moment, then literally shook himself and got up.

In the main room there was some food on the little table, more of the dark bread, some white cheese, and a steaming pot of something. He did some stretches, using the back of the chair, then sat down and ate some breakfast. He poured some of the pale tea into an earthenware cup and sipped.

'Darius Raven. You still owe me some answers.' Nothing. He waited, drinking his tea, then went over to the wall and pressed it. A giant face filled the wall, a bland, pink skin with mouth working, head nodding forward. The picture jumped; an advertisement for industrially-produced cakes. And again; enormous expanses of flesh, shot in reddish light, resolve into a copulating couple, he kneeling behind her. And again; the string section of an orchestra sawing away frantically, all in silence. The sequence cut again, and again. It seemed to be a diverse collection of old television clips, thrown out at random. 'The fucking point, please?' said Alex.

He resumed stretching. 'Anyone out there?' After a while he got bored and faced the screen, waving his arms to try and gain some control over the display.

Something told him someone was behind. He continued his stretch, bending forward and back. 'Why did you kill my friend Mackay?'

Silence. Alex turned round and faced Raven. The slick, black bulge of the prosthetic thrust out at him. His brow was creased with a frown. His left eye looked curious, as if Alex was a problem waiting to be solved. Alex remembered Thania's describing Raven as a psychopath. 'You don't feel anything, do you? It's all about power and control for you.'

Raven's face was stony, then a smile twisted his mouth. 'What did you think you were doing, walking the length of old Britain, seeking you knew not what, on a quest that led you to me?'

He raised his hands, as if miming exasperation. 'What did you think you were doing other than carrying out a plan, someone else's plan? You're on the outside, looking in. Today I shall sow in your soul the seeds of the insider-awareness, which will bring knowledge of your true purpose.'

'Why did you kill my friend Mackay?'

'Because he just might have got in the way. Because he represented an unquantifiable risk. Because I like to keep risks low. What do you want to hear?'

'You are a fucking psychopath, aren't you? Killing a good man is nothing to you. You lack the emotions that make for a proper human. So why can't you go and fight your own fucking war, since killing is so easy for you? What do you need me for?'

Raven stared at Alex, his head tilted slightly to one side, like a bird. 'It's true, I have the MAO-A low-activity variant gene. Not to mention the Kobayashi cluster, and what would surely count as an abusive childhood, so that probably qualifies me as a psychopath to the tiny minds of the world.'

He walked over to the screen, which had frozen amidst a war scene, and stood looking in that direction, his back to Alex. 'You hate me. That is perfectly reasonable, because of what I've done to you. But you also hate me, or are repelled by me not because of what I did, but because of what I am. Everyone outside of a small circle of my family feels the same way. I am an object of disgust. People such as me cannot lead. Normal humans cannot accept us as leaders. We have our own archetypes – Hephaestus, the ugly cripple, who forged armour for the beautiful Olympian tribe who didn't want to lay eyes on his twisted form. The original arms dealer. And amoral Loki, the only inhabitant of Asgard who ever invented anything – a net for catching fish, which the Gods used to catch him. People such as me are always the backroom boys, who make it all happen for the front man – Ares, Woden, the President or whoever.'

He turned round and faced Alex. 'But you are different. You don't have the low-activity MAO-A gene or the Kobayashi cluster. You are not constitutionally unable to empathize. You bring a new constellation of genes to the Thulean gene-pool. You have the genetic profile of a leader, the greatest leader our lineage could produce.'

Alex decided his best bet was to pretend to be coming round. 'What do you want me to do?'

'All in good time. First, the rest of your education. I invented the most useful thing in the world, but realised that the twin plagues of monotheism and consumerism would have made it into a scourge rather than a blessing. The world had to change to be worthy of the elekilpo threads. Atheism failed to extirpate the monotheist poison, so I waited for the revival of heathen ways to take hold. Your Wodenings became strong heathen warriors, and your common people took up avidly their old ways of worldly joy and divine ecstasy. But they lack the leader who could save them from their present sad, beleaguered state, a leader who can withstand the journey to Thule. And the return.'

Flames from the TV images gleamed in his bulging black eye. 'With what I invented, human beings can become as gods, if they become worthy of it. That can only happen with the right war-leader, to break the power of the Pure Light. You will become that leader, which means you must change. You are too soft, too compassionate. Your compassion will be stretched. In a certain sense, you will be brutalized, but there is no alternative.' Alex felt something prick his foot. 'There are no schools that can teach you this. I have given you a drug which will heighten your awareness and I shall fine tune its effects.'

So Raven knew he wasn't really cooperating. The drug overcame him; his palms tickled with sweat, his heart hammered. As Raven spoke, cold, grey stars invaded Alex's field of vision and a sense of immensity swept over him. His eyesight sharpened as his body began to feel huge and gaseous.

'As you become hyper-aware, your defences will fall away, and I shall be able to influence you.'

Alex felt terrible, his mind gripped with abstract nausea, decorated with a border of the grey stars. He struggled with his voice, his speech centres like melted wax. 'How – long – does – this – last?'

'Until I switch it off.'

'You – shit – Raven – this – is – unnecessary – a – sadistic – fucking – flourish.'

'Far from it: until you get a real dose of cosmic terror you'll never be able to grow into your power. Increased awareness always hurts at first. We must be prepared to sacrifice a good deal of human life and happiness to forge the heroic consciousness that makes anything and everything possible.'

The voice warped, swelling and fading. 'You know the *Volsungs' Saga*; there, the hero Sigurd is himself forged by a process of magical eugenics, which takes six generations of conflict and a dash of incest. His magical sword is so sharp that it cuts the very anvil it was forged on.' Raven's voice was borne up in his excitement. 'We are talking about a consciousness and its tools which are created by non-ordinary processes, forged to be far stronger than necessary for mere functioning in the quotidian world. That is what you will become.'

Everything appeared enormous to Alex, vast and distorted. Raven's face was twisted, a hellish cartoon animation. He took a breath then plunged on. 'Let me pursue an analogy that should appeal to you as a chemist: In the earth's crust, we find substances that could never have been created here, in our Sun's nuclear heart. All the elements heavier than carbon were made somewhere else, left over by the decay of radioactive elements. Those elements could not have been formed in any stars around this part of spacetime; they are the residues of inconceivably gigantic explosions, unbelievable temperatures, that happened billions of years ago. Our bodies are made from shattered stars, and contain within them the traces of vast, ancient cosmic violence.'

Like a super-villain from some old film he leaned forward, gesturing, flecks of foam on his lips. 'Similarly, souls such as ours are not formed by current social realities; they hold within them memories of the terrible energies of cosmic fire and ice, the anvils of the giants. We are of the Allfather's brood, and were forged for something greater, something that consensus reality shatters on. You are of that bloodline, Alex, and you will come to know it.'

In Alex's warped vision Raven seemed to be achieving some horrible apotheosis. He paused and leaned forward, gazing into Alex's black, enormous pupils. 'Do you know yourself yet?'

The face loomed, bending and swelling, the yellowed border of flesh around the edge of the prosthetic, the marks of pain in the lines, the madness in the one eye… 'Sofie – tell – me – about – Sofie,' he croaked, his heart giving great, damp thuds.

'Sofie came to me, and we were happy for a while.'

'Where – is – she – now?' he said, his mouth choked

with poison stardust.

Raven flashed a ring, a great, pink diamond. 'Right here, on my hand. Her essence is closer to you now than she ever was in your childhood.'

The flash of the ring looped, like the images on the screen, playing again and again, filling his vision. Alex felt the rage gathering in him, a physical tension, then, with a feeling of something inside him ripping in half, he sprang forward,.

He surged out of the chair, lunged forward for Raven's throat. Everything slowed down then, as some force washed over him and halted his momentum. The grey stars closed in on black after-images of the diamond, and his mind fell away into nothingness.

He came round in the chair, his forearms strapped to its arms with leather bands, the screen-wall dead white. A woman, not Oona, stepped in front of him. She frowned, bent down to his chair and unfastened the straps. Still spaced out, he focused on her face. She had the high cheekbones, high forehead and frizzy fair hair of the Raven clan and was dressed in the same grey work-uniform. Something like disapproval was just leaving her face. She was stronger-built than Oona, but otherwise a recognizable member of that family. His family. 'I'm Mirrorea,' she said, in a deep contralto. She fixed her gaze on his, looked him up and down. 'Your grandmother.'

Alex's body stiffened, but Raven and his drug had knocked the fight out of him. 'It's not torture as such,' said Mirrorea, 'it's just that there's so little time, and awareness of the whole picture, as quickly as possible, with any pain that entails, is Darius's chosen method. He is partly right in that, but he lacks, as you know, the human dimension, so he makes clumsy judgments which cause you even more pain. For this, Thule is sorry.'

She turned to the screen, touched it. It was as if it had disappeared, become a gap, showing a view down over a plateau of stone and concrete buildings. Alex stood up and went over to look. 'This is my home,' said Mirrorea. She touched the window, and it reverted to a white screen. 'You try it,' she said.

Alex reached out and touched the screen. It became a window. He touched it again, and jumped back at the blast of sound, rock music as the soundtrack to an advert. He touched the glass again, and it reverted to white wall. 'I couldn't do that yesterday.'

'Becters. Darius eluted your glass-nanite blocker and installed becters, all in that one shot.'

He switched the wall to window again, and gazed out, keeping his face turned away from her, in case she saw the spark of fierce joy that shot through his chest. Outside, he saw the terraces of Thule drop away to a tranquil harbour, the water green and bright. Beyond that, some miles out, a smooth arc, a perfect concave mirror of iceberg, made the horizon. 'How long?'

'What?'

'How long is my training here?'

'That depends. A few days, maybe.'

He enjoyed a small triumph at the knowledge that Mirrorea had not done telepathy on him. He turned to her. 'Elekilpo?'

'Yes.' She reached into a pocket and took out two stainless steel canisters. She undid the lid of one of them and reached inside, drawing something wet and shiny out of it. 'We call these threads. They are colonial nanites. They pick energy from places where it's normally unavailable. You don't need to understand the physics to get them to work.' She twirled the slimy thread round her fingers. It started to glow red. 'Here.' She dropped it in his palm.

He flinched, expecting fierce heat, but the thread was

lukewarm. It lay on his hand, its brightness increasing, until it looked incandescent.

'Now you do it. Take a thread and tell it to produce light.' She handed the first canister to him and unscrewed the lid of the other.

He reached in and curled a finger, looping a slimy thread over it and drawing it out. He gazed at it. It started to glow, a dull, pinkish light, then orange. Just as it shifted to yellow, he felt the heat of it, and Mirrorea grabbed it out of his hand. She dropped it into the other canister, closing the lid over its now-brilliant white light. She held up the steel vessel. 'That often happens when people first try to script elekilpo. Without the nanites in this container, that thread would have burned a hole in your hand, then in the floor. Try again. This time, say 'light' out loud.'

That time, Alex got the thread to glow red. Then he made a green light, then he managed it without speaking aloud. He was expecting more instruction, when Mirrorea picked up the thread jars and turned to leave. 'Hey, surely there's more?'

'Of course, but you'll work it out for yourself. What matters is the transformation in you. This is just for your weapons.'

As she opened the left hand door, he suppressed a strong urge to ask her: *Doesn't it matter to you that you're all brood-mares for the same man?* In his head, he heard her voice in reply: *Not as much as the state of the world.*

To her retreating back, he whispered, 'Something truly horrible has happened to your… soul.'

All that mattered now was to stay calm and learn, pretend he was fully behind Raven's plan. Then what? Take his chances with Raven, and with escaping back to the mainland? Raven was an old hand at becters – it would be difficult to catch him off guard enough to do him, or Thule, much damage. Or maybe not; people get careless, even genius psychopaths. Stay alert. And learn how to use becters.

To pass the time, he thought about all the abilities on the Raven-Kowalski checklist above his previous level and decided to try them out. Metabolic tuning, that should be easy enough. He felt inside himself for a sense of alertness, and instructed it to increase. It took about three seconds for him to become hyper-alert, jittery, breathing much faster. He instructed it to decrease. That took a little longer; it was a couple of minutes before he stopped feeling wired. Pleased with that result, he thought of the other RK15 abilities. Immunological control? That would have to wait. Real-time signal transmission that can dominate other people's thoughts? Could be very useful, but he'd better make sure none of the Thuleans suspected he could do it. If indeed he could – he would have to find out what he could do in the real-time knife-edge of actual conflict and combat.

And then, more would emerge; all the as-yet-unknown powers that would grow in him, now he had becters. He felt as if he was clasping that thought to him, that growing in him was the power to hurt those who had hurt him and his people. It was like a glow in his chest, and it felt good. He didn't know how it would work out, but he knew he had the power. Wrapping himself around that violent comfort, he used his metabolic tuning to make himself drop off gently to sleep.

The room went bright, and Trivia's voice called from the other side of the door. 'Come on, time to go!'

He tuned 'alertness', jumped up and pulled on some clothes, muttering, 'Fuck, fuck, no time.' But part of him was glad things were moving. He needed to test his battle powers.

The main room was flooded with natural light, the window-wall showing the thousand grey-and-white terraces of Thule blazing in low sun. He had time to reflect that the room must face south, when the right hand door opened and Trivia trotted ahead shouting 'Come on, no time to lose!'

The door opened onto a short corridor. At the end of that, another door sprang open onto a stone terrace. Raven stood by a machine like the flier that had brought him there from Caithness. Mirrorea and Oona stood either side of him. Alex had the impression they were there to prevent violence. He strode forward. Raven stared at him quizzically. Alex felt anger rising in his chest, turning into power that coursed down his arms and into his brain, speeding him up, slowing time down. He saw the shock spreading across Raven's face, the mouth dropping open as Alex closed the distance in one leap, landing with his hands over Raven's face, his fingers tearing into the eyes, gripping the edges of the prosthetic.

Raven screamed. Alex had never felt such strength in his own limbs. He squeezed, and something cracked under his hand, then it was as if he had been electrocuted. His body leaped backwards and crashed into the ground. He jumped to his feet, the battle-rage guiding him, and was lunging towards Raven again when a cylinder of grey stuff came into being around him, instantaneous as light, but hard as plastic. Only one part of him was left outside of it; he raised his right hand and saw the bright blood pumping out of the stump of his little finger. He gazed at it, and something inside him said *I break myself. What does it matter. Cattle die, kinsmen die. The immortal essence powers me. This is what you taught me, Father.* He didn't understand it; it was like another self speaking in his head. Something began to lift him up, and he passed out.

Chapter 23: The Wolves

He had lost himself. He used to be able to find his way about easily, but Thule had wiped out everything that was ordinary in him. And because he had just surfaced in shock, nervous system horror-saturated, he didn't know waking from dreaming, or nightmare, for a while, only that all comfort and retreat were gone, leaving just a bleak eternal moment with no past he cared to dwell on and probably not much of a future. The only memories he could locate were of a fight, and of a tube of something grey, which sliced off the end of his finger. The stump dripped fresh black blood. The wound had got worse when he had fallen through the rotten floor into the basement. The decaying library, at the edge of the water just down from New Thurso, was the first refuge he had found when he came round in the storm.

He watched his blood splash on the soiled grey silt of images lining the floor until it occurred to him that his life was leaking away, and he had better do something about it, fast. He stood unsteadily and crawled up the tumbled remains of the ceiling to the doorway at ground level. He stuck his bleeding hand out of the arch and let the rain wash the wound clean. He tore off a strip from the hem of his trousers and wrapped it tight around the base of the mutilated little finger. The cloth had mud clinging to it. Ideally, he could do with getting some medical help, in a place at the end of the world, in the coastal hills of High Caledon. But he knew he was more likely to encounter bandits than medics out here. He shrugged off the small backpack. It contained jars of catalyst. They would start polymerizing chain reactions and spin the power-threads that will get the world started again. That was it. But first, he had to save his own life.

He considered the implications of his mission. He must travel alone, for a while. The power threads needed forming and working on before they'd yield enough power to make a weapon. And he must keep himself safe until he was ready to lead. Through the cracked stone archway he saw a great thick bar of lightning, like a tree of blue-white fire, hit the ground just a few yards away, spilling ragged arcs of blue plasma into the rank undergrowth. The atmospheric charge prickled on his skin, the ground shook with the blast. He must draw strength from memories of strength, and even more, from the solidity of his hatred. Whatever Raven chose to think Alex was, Alex couldn't care; whatever he meant to the plans and plots of the Pure Light, he cared even less about. Alex vowed that he would strike a terrible blow against the Pure Light and its zombies. He would do this by completing the task he'd been given, taking the elekilpo generator back to his people, and somehow raising its power against the insurgents. He curled up in the driest corner he could find, and fell asleep nursing his thoughts of vengeance.

Some days were better; the next morning the storm cleared. He followed the forest cover up the hill and found a deep, rocky cleft at the top. There he hooked a scrap of sun-faded tarpaulin out of a tree and made a shelter with bent green branches. Gritting his teeth against the pain from his finger, he shot a grey squirrel with a catapult he found in the backpack. He waited till dark and built a fire, eating the squirrel half-raw in his devouring hunger. He got enough energy off its flesh to set traps, and then sleep.

The next day he was a little stronger. He found chamomile flowers and rubbed them on his raw wound. Things went well, on a scale with collapse and death at one end, and wretched, precarious survival at the other. *Beasts, including humans,* he thought, *are tougher than we think, when we have something to live for.* He found a rabbit in one of the traps and cooked it that evening. His wounds continued to heal.

Another chunk of time that he had lost in the terrible days on Thule fell back into his head. He remembered Raven telling him, 'You don't need to remember any of this. Your soul will be tempered anyway.' *Tempered.* Like blade-steel.

Raven imagined that Alex would become a different person. Alex hated Raven, in a different way to how he hated the Pure Light. Raven had made his life difficult, with his crazy fucking plans. But somehow Alex would get back to Wessex, carrying the generator threads through hostile lands. Somehow. He slept again

The next day Alex woke early and ate the remains of the rabbit carcass. He began to play with the elekilpo threads, drawing them up out of the jar of slick monomer. His mind was hazy, thinking was difficult.

In his trance he heard Raven's voice again: *You are being forged for the Ragnarok.*

He rolled over and threw up the rabbit. Somewhere in his mind, a firm voice said: *Sleep*, and he did.

As he slept, he dreamt of a judgment: before the judge stands an ordinary man, who looks a bit like himself, and a lavishly-dressed man, in a purple velvet tunic and wearing a golden crown on his head. Alex can't hear what they're saying as they plead to the judge, nor can he see the judge's face. Then, suddenly the judge gets out a catapult, loads it with a lump of gold and lets fly in the face of the ordinary man. He drops down, the missile lodged in his forehead. The kingly man walks away.

When he woke again, Alex felt different, as if a weight had lifted from his mind. He played with the elekilpo threads, making them shine or heat up according to how he twined them. He snoozed in the warmth.

He woke up suddenly, surrounded by large men on horseback. The bandits had found him. *Trust yourself*, the voice whispered in his head.

He stood up, dusted himself off and faced the tall, hatchet-nosed, red-haired man on the nearest horse. 'Good afternoon, gentlemen. I am hardly ready for guests, but you are nonetheless welcome.'

The bandit leader nodded sagely, as if Alex had made a shrewd point. He rolled his leather-clad shoulders and said, in a thick Caledon accent: 'I'm glad you are at ease with me and my fellows. You will have guessed, of course, that we are gentlemen of the road, opportunists of business and robbery. First, we would like to know who you are, and where you're from, and then we will proceed to the main question: What do you have that is worth our taking it off you?'

'In answer to your first question, I am the Thuler, from Thule.'

Alex reached into his shirt and pulled out a length of power-thread, fashioned as a light-emitter. He twisted into the form of the F-rune and set it to light. It glowed a fierce red in the shadow of the rocks.

'As for what I have, I give you wealth, gentlemen. More than you have ever dreamed of. More than you can use up in a lifetime. You will need this magic thread-stuff, and my Thulean wisdom to make it work. In turn, I require an escort to the border of Loyal Lothian. What do you say?'

The big man's eyes were alight with greed. 'I believe we can come to some sort of arrangement. Come with me.'

The bandit was obviously planning to steal the secret of the threads from Alex and then murder him. By that time, though, this little war band would belong to Alex the

Thuler. He would be the king of a gang of brigands.

'Show me the way, gentlemen.'

It took Alex a series of staged confrontations over the next twenty-four hours to completely take over the Wolves, as they knew themselves.

First of all, to save his own life, he knew he had to kill Finn, the leader. It was a depressingly easy task, killing his first man. Finn's headquarters was a battered army tent that formed the centre of the main cluster of tents, upwind from the fire. A group of women were attempting to cook dinner, but people were complaining that there wasn't enough to bother with. Alex knew he wouldn't have a lot of time to make his moves. He lifted the edge of the flap and peeked inside. A skinny youth with a restless demeanour filled the role of Finn's personal assistant. He poured whisky, while a strong-looking, blonde woman stood in front of the leader. She had just finished speaking. Alex stepped in and they turned to face him. 'A word, please, Finn. In private.'

The youth turned and appraised Alex, speaking to Finn. 'Why's he want you on his own?'

'It's OK Flash, I think I can handle Mr Thuler.' He grinned and shifted in his seat, raising his legs and resting his feet on a wooden crate. He slapped the behind of the blonde woman as she left and gestured to Alex to take a seat. Flash glared as he exited. Alex sat down on the crate. He pulled a canister out of his pocket and extracted a thread. 'I can pass on to you the secret of how to make weapons out of the Thulean threads.' He twirled the thread and made it glow yellow. 'Of course, I realise that if I tell you all at once, then I have lost any bargaining power I ever had.' He paused and looked at Finn. The big man was insouciant, picking his fingernails. He looked up and met Alex's stare with a cold gaze. 'Please continue.'

That stare convinced Alex he was not far from being

tortured for the secret of the threads, and it gave him the momentum to do what he did next; he twisted the thread again and handed it to Finn. 'See the little stripes on it?' Finn brought the thread right up to his eyes and looked hard. 'What -?' he managed, and then the thread flashed a searing, intense white light, a few kilos of burning magnesium. Finn dropped the thread and cried out, but Alex was lunging forward. The knife entered the big man's heart, just as Flash ducked in under the tent-flap, foot-long Bowie knife in hand. Thuler let the body fall, and raised his hands in front of his face. The thread-stuff soaked into the rag-gloves he'd fashioned went off with another blinding flash. The bones of Alex's hands showed through his closed eyelids. He kicked the knife out of Flash's hand and the man fell sideways. Alex was upon him, the recovered knife in his hand, his knees pinning him to the ground. In the speeded-up event-time of the combat, Alex had a moment to think the word *mercy*, and to realise this was the wrong time for it, before he plunged the blade into Flash's chest.

In another two breaths, he was outside the tent, facing the ten or so people who'd realised something was up. Alex drew himself to his full height and raised his arms slowly, ever so slowly. The few men and women that had begun to approach him, drawing weapons, pulled up short and stood still. Alex's hands, streaming with rivulets of eerie, convulsing becter-light, became the arms of a V, and stayed there. Silence spread, mopping up the beginnings of shouted challenges. He stood there, the shaking, shuddering scarlet glow making a hyper-real outline for the blood that dripped from his fingers. He stayed still until his audience were still.

'I bring you the greatest fortune, my friends. A Thulean warrior has come to live among you, to bring you to victory and riches.'

Something in the Wolves understood and responded to this. They felt upset, maybe angry and frightened, because their leader had been taken from them. But maybe he hadn't been such a good leader, and the mighty warrior who'd killed Finn and his bodyguard was offering to take his place. This was worth considering, at least.

Thuler let his becter field soften a little. People turned to their neighbours and began to whisper.

The snatches that Alex caught confirmed his impression that the Wolves saw his victory as evidence of his power and luck.

They were tentatively accepting him as their new leader.

Two of the Wolves spoke at once.

'You've got the power and the initiative now, Thuler. You don't have much time to prove yourself, though. We've lives to be getting on with.' This was from an experienced old fighter, clad in leathers, short, dark and wiry. His words came out first, and the other man, a bigger, younger warrior in furs and tartan, didn't bother finishing what he started saying.

What it came down to was, he was on probation. When they'd spoken, Alex just nodded, letting his arms fall to his sides. The people in front of him, and those that had gathered behind them dispersed back to the fire and the cooking.

That was all the opportunity Alex needed to win them over. And he knew it was not only his battle-prowess that had been enhanced by the becters: for the first time, he felt the intoxicating power of controlling men's minds.

He was acutely aware now that he had revealed the power of the threads of the need for speed in getting to Wessex. Within days, someone would tell a Pure Light agent, and the hunt would be on for him. To delay that problem as long as possible, they couldn't make the threads the basis of trading wealth, so he would have to use them to make more weapons.

That evening, he called a council of war in the clearing at the centre of their encampment. They were a motley group of around thirty fighting men and women, and a few women with young children who stayed close to the main camps. Alex scrutinized the faces of the few he had spoken to, and noted a few others who stood out for some reason. He selected his staff; the older fighter who'd first confronted him was called Bel. He'd be a tactical advisor and second in command. For his sergeant-major for day-to-day command, he chose the young Fraser, a big man whose face suggested loyalty.

Bel seemed to rise to the occasion, and advised an immediate raid on a neighbouring tribe of bandits. Such raids were part of the Wolves' regular war-arrangement, or had been until Finn reduced the frequency of their attacks. Alex realised that a change in leadership to something more adventurous was very welcome in the group.

The raid on the Black Jonnies was over in no time. Alex passed out ten crude grenades, explosive balls of nascent thread-stuff. These were deployed for maximum shock effect as the Wolves' riders emerged from a wall of glowing smoke. The hapless bandits fled in confusion, and the Wolves captured a can of diesel, three horses, two barrels of beer and a goat. Alex helped himself to some trousers and a fur jacket.

That night they gave Finn a splendid funeral, burning the body on a vast pyre on Ben Freiceadan. Alex lit the logs with a long, thick power-thread, and spoke some words honouring the strength and courage of his victim. The women keened and the men bayed their tribute in the manner of their clan animals.

Then they sat in a broad oval, him and his staff bunched at the wide end. He let himself be served first with the best meat, while discussing plans for the next day's journey. He sounded out the mood of the group. The Wolves were keen to get going. They already understood that they were to be his escort to the borders of Lothian, and most of them, having nothing better to do, were already willing to follow him to the ends of the earth. He had gathered his first loyal war-band, and taken his first steps towards an unwilling kingship.

When everyone set about getting howling drunk, Alex retired to the army tent. He sat down on a folding canvas stool, exhausted from countless hours of furious, enhanced activity, and emptied his mind, just listening to the surface of the noise outside, as if it was entertainment. After a few minutes, he saw a fire-shadow cross the canvas, and knew that someone stood there. A firm soprano voice said, 'Thuler,' and a shadowed face ducked under the door flap.

'Come in, Sif,' he said.

Finn's widow stepped through and stood up. Alex motioned to a stool. Sif was a tall, dark-skinned slender Amazon in barbarian finery, great gold earrings at her stretched earlobes, spiked blonde hair, black kohl eyes and sensuous rosebud lips, with a gold torque around her long neck and elaborate gold bands twining her tattooed arms. She wore a sleeveless black top of buttery-thin leather and tailored leather trousers.

She nodded in a way that said: *You owe me, and now it's my turn*, and sat down.

Alex looked around at his band's wealth, eyes alighting on a crate of bottles.

'Whisky?' he offered.

'OK,' she said. He hadn't expected this conversation to be easy.

He found a box of shiny steel cups, poured scotch and handed it to her. To indicate solidarity, he poured one for himself. This was not the moment for a toast, he having killed this woman's lover only ten hours earlier. They regarded each other warily, sipping the Highland malt.

Finally, Sif nodded again and said, 'I demand wer-gild for the killing of Finn. Something for the protection of our mothers and children. I want a supply of those thread bombs.'

Alex turned over in his mind the risk of allowing the threads to go out of his sight, where they could be captured and maybe analyzed by PL agents. Was this woman a good risk? And what did he feel he owed her, for taking away her man? He looked at her eyes, shadowed, glinting in the waxy light as she returned his gaze. He couldn't tell if she had been crying, but some knowledge of pain and tragedy, and of the strength that grew from them, transmitted itself to him from those sparks in darkness.

He nodded. 'Before we leave tomorrow I'll give you a supply of grenades.'

Sif said, 'It's not for me, you know. Big Em will keep them. She's in charge of supplies for the mothers and kids. I'm coming with you.'

For a moment Alex wondered if she meant she was staying with him, personally, whether it was expected of him that he took her in.

As if she'd caught the thought, Sif shook her head slowly. 'You will not follow our custom and take me under your protection, for reasons which should be obvious.' At this, she just stared at him, allowing the ancient telepathy of pride to come over. After a minute, she drank up and left. Alex slumped onto the camp bed and went over what he needed to get done before the morning.

Breakfast consisted of scraps left over from the previous night, including the dregs from the barrels of beer. He chewed on cold, tough goat meat as he gathered the troupe together.

They set out south to the coast road on the first leg of their trek. Experienced at living in the high country, they made camp on the edge of an empty moor above Landhallow.

The next night, near Culmoily, they spotted a compound overlooking the road, some kind of wall with a clan flag flapping above it. Bel passed Thuler a pair of binoculars; a stone croft had been de-roofed and used as the base for an observation platform. Two kilted tribesmen stood guard, Kalashnikovs on view. Thuler felt a precog flash of serious trouble. 'Detour inland,' he ordered.

Bel led the way. 'Y'see, those clansmen are probably the only people who have any chance against the PL in Caledon. This country, as countries go, is fucked.'

The day after that they were on the Heights of Brae, looking south-west over Inverness, capital of High Caledon. Alex had the sinking sun at his back, as he gazed over at the Black Isle. Maira's house was just across from there, a short detour to the east.

'Why are we stopping here, Thuler?' asked Bel.

Alex knew he could be leading his Wolves into dangers beyond his powers, but he had to try to find Maira and find out what had happened after Raven had captured him. 'Unfinished business. There's someone I need to see down there. I don't need the Wolves with me. You take everybody round the Firth and I'll meet you on Kirkhill in the morning.'

Bel looked dubious. *Maybe he thinks I'll just abandon them now they've got me this far*, thought Alex.

'OK Bel, take the power threads. I need to do this alone. And I need you and the Wolves. Don't worry.' He unhooked the worn rucksack and handed it over.

Bel looked him in the eyes for a moment, then nodded curtly and rode off.

Alex set off down the road around Black Isle, in the

scarred red haze of the sunset. He had no idea what he'd find down there.

The honeysuckle twining round the green cottage door with its cracked, weathered paint bore magenta blooms. The latch was broken and the door stood ajar. Alex listened for a moment and then entered quickly and silently, a thread grenade in his raised hand. Inside, it was dark and stuffy. There was a disturbing sound, a sick breathing or snuffling.

His eyes began to adjust. She lay on the couch, on her side, facing away from the door. 'Alex.' Her voice held certainty. *Magic Maira, of course you'd know when I came in your room.* Tears burned his eyes. 'Yes love, it's me.' He was at her side in two strides, holding her hand, meeting her ravaged gaze and seeing with horror the crusted blood and raw wound between the two thick bunches of her hair.

'I've not much time, sweetheart.' She spoke in a rush. 'Got caught in a gun battle. The hole goes into my skull. I've stuck two fingers in. I should be dead by now, but I held on for you.'

A tortured breath. 'I screwed up. PL infiltrators using a BT-sniffer. I didn't shield myself.'

Alex's tears were flowing freely but she said, 'No tears now. First thing, darling, Thania got away. She was heading south when I last saw her.'

Her eyes searched his. 'You've come a long way, Alex!'

Alex choked out, 'I can't believe it's ending like this, Maira...' He trailed off.

'Yes, Alex, it is ending exactly like this, darling. I'm dying, and we have two jobs to do. First, I need to give you my spirits, bequeath you my powers.' She took a laboured breath. 'And second, a curse. I've no strength left to do those things one after another, so we'll combine them.'

She sucked in air again and faced him fully. 'As soon as I stop breathing, fuck me. Get as close as you can to my brain tissue. Use the hole in the back of my head.' Alex's jaw dropped. She reached a trembling hand up to his face. The touch transferred something to him, some ancient memories, the raw, terrible nobility of Maira's witch-lineage, hijacked by becters, but still rooted in ancient, organic formulas of magic. Her fingers brushed his eyes as she spoke. 'Shush darling. I'm not being crazy. I'll be conscious in there, no body any more, no pain, drunk on the lovely death-mead. That way I can pass all my spirits over to you. Those that want, can stay with you, those that don't, go to power up my curse.'

Alex was still in denial, shaking his head. Maira squeezed his hand feebly. 'Help me do this, Alex, this is my big fight. I want to be all used up in the end. I want you to use what's left of me to damage those vicious bastards.'

She tried to smile, but her leg started to kick against Alex's side. 'No time now,' she gasped. She gripped his hand convulsively and stared into his eyes. 'Swear you will, Alex of Thule. I know who you are, you see. Swear on your love you will help me.'

'I swear,' Alex whispered, 'I swear on my love for you.'

In the depths of the night, her last breaths rattled out. He held her as she convulsed, whispering his love in her ear, knowing she was in there, in the ecstasy of dimethyltryptamine, the death-mead of the high-hearted.

When her body went slack, he called up memories of hungry, tender fucking, letting the vast, impersonal authority of sex take over. At some stage, he opened his eyes, remote, hovering over the ruin of her flesh, and kept his promise.

Some ecstasies, given enough courage, have no ceiling; light and union expand endlessly into a sky without limits. Similarly, some horrors fall forever, enclosure and alienation multiplying as the heart's attachments grasp at its revulsion. All is broken, all must fall, to the bottom of the well.

And sometimes, both of these things happen at the same time.

In the rage of blood and sex, the air in the room thickened, laying heavy and choking him, as he roared out runes he'd never heard before. With his cries, it seemed he was stirring the thick darkness into a vortex. At first it was a lumbering swirl, then it was as if it gained momentum and began to whip itself into a frenzy, until it felt as if the room was spinning.

The world around him whirled and fell forever down, and then the next stage began. An ancient terror slithered into his brain, a twisting worm of dark sentience with a glittering, blank reptilian eye. The dragon force behind Maira's magic was filling him, as it had filled the bodies of a thousand others of her witch-line, back to times before the ice age. The glittering darkness crept into every cell of his body, lending him a terrible strength, wrapping itself around the core of his flesh, sparking unused genes in his DNA, waking a slumbering giant.

He shrieked and roared a counterpoint to the storm raging in him, till his whole body hurt and the deadly air was whipped into a whirlwind in the house. A glass flew off a shelf. A bottle rolled across the floor. A tall-turreted oil lamp fell over. The wooden structure of the house creaked and strained, as if muscles were about to burst from within it. With a screech of nails, a floorboard tilted and popped up. The curtains flew back and the window glass cracked and shattered, blowing out into the suddenly-howling night. He seemed to roar louder and louder still, and he felt as if he was expanding, swelling to fill the house, and then all of space as he roared, and roared.

He didn't fully return to his body until he was looking

down the hill at the cottage, watching the fireball blossom from the thread-charge he'd placed, blossom and devour the little building, the broken door, the sweet honeysuckle, the ruined body of his lover. The cat had appeared and sat a few yards away, watching the destruction alongside him.

The fireball collapsed with a weird, sucking *whoop.* He watched as the flickering flames of normal, earthly fire rose, and he let out a great, keening scream, honouring for the last time the life of brave, powerful, big-hearted Maira. Eventually, as the fire died down, he turned his back and rode south, skirting Inverness for the Wolves' camp.

He rode dead-faced into their little encampment. He found Bel, took back the pack with the threads in, checked his horse was cared for and collapsed in the tent they'd set up for him.

He slept, and dreamed of a wind, the Wind From Space: it tears up streets and houses, roads crack and roll back, bare earth is bulldozed by shock-waves, the world peeled like an apple.

The Wind now howls through space, demolishing planets, smashing suns, scattering galaxies like mad furnace-sparks. The death-screams of giant black holes shriek into the ultrasonic, carried into emptiness as the wind demolishes the universe.

All that remains is the bare winter skeleton of a tree, someone faceless hung thereon, his eyes pinwheels of nuclear spark, his smile the torment of space itself.

Chapter 24: The Thuler

When he awakes, he is dead to everything he knew. He rises out of the bed, out of the tent, as if he's never going to stop rising, something inside him expanding to infinity. He walks slowly, measured, easy paces, but his mind is full of a pressure that pushes forward, outward. His head snaps up; he sees a bird circling, then abruptly it flaps, fall a little distance then recovers itself and flies off. He reaches out and pushes against the remains of a drystone wall; he neighs like a horse, rotten stone flakes and cracks under his hands, his breath weaving vortices like braided threads.

The Wolves got up and came out of their tents, but stayed away from the figure who stood in the morning mist, snorting and muttering, an aura of altered light around him.

Bel walked up, his hands spread in a gesture which combined peacemaking with readiness to fight, walked round Thuler until he could see his face. Bel opened his mouth to speak, but was stopped short by what he saw in Thuler's eyes, a hybrid of human and something lesser, or greater.

Later, Thuler felt hunger and went to the embers of a fire. He picked a bone up, gnawed at the tough meat, his self-awareness trying in fits and starts to make up a story which would fit his new reality, something that would enable him to pull the world around him like a coat. He took stock; there was nothing left of Alex. Now, he was only Thuler, a force of nature, immovable and ruthless as the wind. He threw the bone down and looked down at himself. He needed a costume, something that would announce who he was. *What am I? I am a weapon.*

He rode into the clothes shops of smart Inverness and took what seemed right for his new identity. No-one tried to stop him when he strode about trying on the barbarous bright silks and leathers, nor when he took whatever he willed and left without paying. Riding back to the camp, his plans took form. He would give his Wolves a taste of battle against a real enemy. They would ambush a small Pure Light force.

He and Bel drilled the Wolves over the next day, trying out endless combinations of threads, adjusting the mass and the delay time before the explosion, until they could all consistently deliver effective grenades in a few sizes.

'The PL always arrive from the road by the Ness,' said Bel. 'It's one of the easier places for an incursion force to enter.' The Wolves had set themselves either side of a slender decline, the road banked into two facing slopes. Bel and Thuler shared binoculars at the top of the rise.

'Where did you learn soldiering?'

The short man snorted. 'Regular Army draft in Caledon, discovered I had a taste for it. And better ways to employ my transferable skills. Anyway, they're not yet in full control of Inverness. They have enough monkeys on the council to tilt the city governors, but their convoys from the south are still easy prey, even for the demoralized Caledon Army.'

'There,' he said. The dust in the distance, through the sun-haze, showed two diesel trucks, new ones. 'Weapons and shit.' Bel grinned.

The front truck ran over the landmine of thread charge just as the half-dozen thread grenades thrown by the Wolves hit the roof of the second one. The mine was small, and most of the truck stopped, intact, in the middle of the road for the other to bang into. Two figures, their white uniforms streaked with smoke-stains, jumped out of the rear truck and dove for cover under the chassis, rolling and giving covering fire for each other. The Wolves on that side of the road simply rained small thread-grenades onto the ground in front of the PL troops until the shocks overcame the enemy and the shooting ceased.

Thuler approached cautiously, the other men scrambling behind him down the weed-choked slope. There were no survivors in the broken trucks. The Wolves swarmed all over them. Five bodies yielded eight firearms, and two steel cases of ammo rounds in the rear truck had made it through the bombardment. They whooped and hollered as they ran back up the slope with their plunder, their first Thuler-led mission an unqualified success.

Back at camp, Bel picked five of the Wolves and started training them with the new guns. That night, Thuler conferred with him about their next target, while the others partied. Thuler exuded enough of a chilly, alien presence to make sure the celebration didn't get out of hand; he needed them to keep up the momentum they'd developed.

The Institute of Moral Education was an elegant, suburban front, a gated Victorian estate that had been turned into a defensive compound. It had a low, white, stone perimeter wall topped with a chainlink fence.

The Wolves tethered their horses at the end of the tree-lined street. Each fitted a thread-charge to his slingshot, or throwing stick, or just hefted in his palm a stone covered in moist, clustered threads. Thuler addressed them.

'Our main assets are surprise and bombs. Our shooters will lead, taking out any enemy gunmen. They'll be stunned and it'll take them a few seconds to shoot. All we want is their guns and ammo. Do not risk your own life unnecessarily. We do what we need to do to capture their guns, no more, and we get out.'

The PL were obviously not expecting any unwelcome visitors. The main gate was open for traffic to pass, and the gate-guards were standing well back from the road. The Wolves just walked in, fast. The gunners took down the guards and provided cover while the grenadiers hurled their charges through all the windows and blew the front off the building. A cloud of stone dust boiled out, the Wolves ran through it, scrambling up the tumbling masonry into the ruptured honeycomb of rooms.

White-uniformed Guards of Light loomed out of the dust. In front of Thuler, one of them held his head, nose bleeding freely, as he reached for his handgun.

There was something horribly easy about the raid, and later, he remembered how difficult it had once been to kill. The first time was when he had helped with the Yule slaughter as a ten year old. As he took his foot off the broom handle, and saw the limp goose, he felt sick and excited at the same time. Alaric the butcher had told him that feeling was holy terror, and was the basis of sacrifice.

This was a bit like that, only worse. He shot the soldier in the face. The man's hand dropped the gun, and Thuler picked it up. He turned to see two Wolves knock down another white-clad squaddie and shoot him with his own weapon.

The raid was over in minutes. They had killed the four armed defenders, giving them enough weapons to take the building. They searched the compound, encountering only terrified front-workers whom they let flee. They found another ten assault rifles and cases of ammunition in the cellar, where they also found a mountable machine gun with a thousand rounds.

Alex found the main office and, as he expected, a safe. He fed thread-charge into the fat keyhole and around the crack of the door. He set it for a timed explosion and they took cover in the next room.

The charge was a little stronger than he'd anticipated. The safe door bounced across the room and came to rest half way through the partition wall, a slug of glowing steel sticking out of the shattered fibreboard next to Sif's head.

She spat a curse at him. He still needed practice with thread-charges.

When they stepped over to the smoking, mangled safe, though, it was worth it. It was packed with bullion, in bars and coins, plus some gold jewelry. Sif looked over Thuler's shoulder and whistled. 'I know what those are. They're krugerrands. And gold Edwins. Worth a mint. So don't forget who helped you find them, Thuler.' Thuler nodded at this wisdom. Between four of them, they carried the loot back to the horses.

The Wolves were in fine mood, and would have prolonged the looting, but Thuler was satisfied with their haul and moved everyone out.

From the street, he looked back at the smoking, half-gutted house. He walked back through the gateway, tossed a final grenade into the shell of the building and turned away as the fireball whumped out.

Briefly, he remembered what it was like to feel compassion for people. He strode stiffly to the roadside, threw up and got back on his horse.

Slow as law enforcement was in most parts of the energy-impoverished world, and with Caledon no exception, after what they'd done, it was no time to rest easy. They rode hard through the night, and Thuler's Wolves made it to Rannoch Moor in a feathery dawn. A broken notice, half-fallen from its rusting steel poles, declared 'Welcome to the Highlands.' They rode up through the clouds, through charred remnants of a forest, outcrops of white rocks on blackened earth. Exhausted, washed out, it showed in Bel's face as they made camp by a tiny tarn. Thuler was still burning, impatient that they had to rest. The Thuler didn't need sleep, not with so much to do.

When they'd eaten, they tended to their cuts and bruises – miraculously, the worst injuries they'd sustained in the course of the raid. Then he called them all around to distribute the gold. He had to dispose of it straightaway. It was obvious that there was no way he could guard the hoard against them all if they wanted it. He didn't even want the distraction of thinking about it.

He selected the two best-looking armbands and a chain, and a few of the krugerrands for future bribes. He just divided the rest up, not even taking any more for himself. If he wanted more gold, they could always get some. With the thread charges, and their new weapons, they were already a raiding force to be reckoned with. He could see it in the eyes of the men and women who came up to collect their gold; their awe of the Thuler and their respect for his luck was growing daily. They slept a few hours.

That evening, they approached the Lothian border near dusk. Thuler gathered the troupe on a bracken-thick hilltop, looking south across the flooded Forth, now a sea-channel that cut Lothian off from High Caledon. They could see the partly-rebuilt and then re-ruined Antonine Wall on the other side of the water. Bel recognized the deserted guard post as the remains of the Bar Hill garrison. The waterway was crossable on a rough stone causeway made from the remains of a collapsed bridge. The border was quiet. Either the PL militias or the Caledon forces had retreated for now.

He turned slowly and faced each of them. 'You've done what you promised. If you want, you can follow me, into Lothian, and then into Shemeld. I can promise you a lot of fighting and a lot of loot. We may increase our fighting force along the way, if we can find the right people to join with us. What do you say?'

Thuler's Wolves didn't hesitate; the discussion had already happened. They roared their approval as one man. Thuler looked around at them again, an almost-smile on his face. 'So, let's get a bit of Lothian behind us before we make camp.'

That night, sitting round a campfire in the heights above Peebles, Bel asked Thuler what he was planning. For the first time, Thuler had to admit to more than his basic plan to get back to Wessex, and to articulate what was forming in his mind.

'We're going to Goathland first. There, we might find allies. If it looks good, then, somehow, we'll go to Sheffield.'

Bel's eyes were diamond-bright in the tanned, lined face as he scrutinized Thuler. 'You're at war with the PL. Sheffield's where you took a beating from them. You're going back to take Sheffield.'

Thuler returned his gaze steadily. 'If we take Sheffield's arms factories, no-one in Britain can stand against us.'

Bel gazed levelly into the Thuler's eyes. His scrutiny complete, he shook his head in wonderment. 'You know what, I believe we can do it. And if we can't, nobody else can. I'm completely behind you, Thuler, and, my arse against the world, everybody else will be too.'

Thuler couldn't help but feel a glow of satisfaction. This was how things had to be.

The next day's hard riding took them across Lothian and saw them at Hadrian's Wall by nightfall. The garrison, looking down over the drowned Tyne valley, was also deserted. They crossed the border and left the road, heading for the Allendale heights. They spent the night overlooking the flooded lands leading down to the spreading Tyne estuary, what people now called the Firth of Tyne, and to lost, submerged Newcastle. That night round the campfire,

Thuler announced his plan to go to Goathland and seek allies for an attack on Sheffield's arms factories. There was a buzz of awe at the audacity of the idea, followed by a great cheer. Thuler's Wolves were right behind him.

The following morning, he led his band across the disputed borderlands of North Shemeld. They rode down the rocky spine of the Pennines, avoiding the stronghold of Bishops Auckland, until they had to turn east, and enter the Cleveland marshes.

Everyone went silent as they entered the misted, hallucinatory twilight. They rode deeper into the marshlands, crumbling causeway sections supplemented by slippery pontoons tilting on sphagnum beds. One slip, and a rider could be lost. They rode in a close chain, wary of losing visual contact with each other, which happened as soon as one rider was a horse's length from the next. Thuler was flanked by Bel and Sif. They glanced nervously to each side.

Then a horse's skull loomed out of the stinking haze on a tall, carved pole, a remnant of an old curse. They were riding over the graves of flooded cities, Darlington, Middlesborough, and the half a million dead that didn't make it to safety after the 2112 floods and before Shemeld and Goathland closed their borders. Many swore they saw dead hands reach out of the stagnant pools in bubbles of corpselight.

Bel muttered the voice of their morbid, wondering mood. 'We live on top of the dead, as always. But the dead used to be beneath the earth. Now they are under the waters. It's not good, but there's nothing we can do about it.'

Chapter 25: Goathland

They emerged from the marshes with relief, riding up out of the mist into a murky drizzle of afternoon light. The border post at Welbury was announced by half-crushed rolls of rusty barbed wire on the road, and was staffed with an alert and battle-ready garrison. Two big-built farm boys dressed in fatigues, with the narrow, wary eyes of seasoned fighters, stepped into the road. One of them carried an ancient Kalashnikov, the other a broadsword. They conferred briefly, and the boy with the sword ran into the square stone hut. Thuler noted the short wave aerial on the roof. They were requesting backup. That was promising.

Thuler dismounted and stepped ahead of his troupe, approaching the gun-carrying boy. He opened his leather jacket in a gesture of coming unarmed. 'I am Thuler. My war-band comes in peace and friendship. We have gold to pay for a meal and a roof, weapons to trade, and important news. Who is your Jarl?' Thuler used the Old Norse word self-consciously, not knowing if it was appropriate, or even what language this youth spoke.

The boy kept that narrow frown. He thumbed the stock of his old gun in an odd sort of way, directing the barrel around Thuler's feet. Thuler hazarded a guess that he was indicating that the gun was ready to use. He was silent for a few more breaths, which seemed an eternity.

Thuler had begun to wonder about the lad's mental condition, when he shrugged, pointed the gun a little more towards the ground and spoke, in a lilting accent. 'Jarl Theodoric Darnham will welcome you soon.' He slung the gun upside-down over his shoulder, turned and stomped back to the guard hut without further ado.

Time dragged. Some of Thuler's Wolves dismounted to piss, but stayed wary.

They didn't have to wait long. A big black horse came down the hill, ridden by a young man in a baggy shirt with a wild face and tangled blonde hair free in the wind. He rode up to them with a showy finish, the stallion rearing up, the youth laughing madly. 'I am Dirk, son of Theodoric,' he grinned, 'and who might you people be?'

Thuler introduced himself again, and repeated his offer of peace, gold and weapons.

Dirk looked around at Thuler's Wolves and then back at Thuler. 'I invite you to feast in the hall of Jarl Darnham tonight. This way!'

They followed young Darnham up the spur of land onto the moor road in the fading, murky light. It was a good, metalled road, and they rode miles along it between rough sheep pastures, up to the edges of the North Yorks massif. As it began to drizzle again, Bel spotted a group of yellow lights. They approached a farm compound with a huddle of low stone buildings. In the centre was a great stone and wood hall. A stable boy ran out and took Dirk's horse. Dirk invited the Wolves to take their horses round to the stables.

The hall's thick timber door swung open and a huge woman in a green woolen dress stood there, tiny wisps of light escaping around her enormous bulk. 'Welcome, strangers, to Darnham Hall. Hang up your weapons and sit down.'

They squeezed past Mistress Darnham and into the big, warm hall. At the near end, two youths were still putting up the last of a series of trestles, and two teenage girls were bringing bread and soup. Fires blazed at intervals along the far wall. Thuler's Wolves spread themselves round the edge of the room, and fell to hungrily. Thuler stood back a little, careful of any further protocol. The Mistress came over to him and indicated graciously the high table at the far end. A big bald man, forty years and more, shirtsleeves showing off arms like inflated thighs, was seating himself in the high seat.

Thuler walked up and addressed him, giving a third, abbreviated, version of the reasons for his presence. Jarl Darnham stood up and extended his hand. Thuler shook the rough farmer's mitt. The big man held his gaze, and gestured expansively to the hall, now full up with his men and the Wolves, so that what he said was in clear hearing. 'Welcome, Thuler, to our hall. First feasting, then business.' Thuler noticed that Sif was being seated next to Mistress Darnham's seat, and Dirk to his own right.

The soup was followed by most of a sheep, roasted and packed with herbs. The girls brought round jugs of honey-flavoured ale and filled their cups of shiny Sheffield steel. Voices got louder as the tired raiders and the hard-working sheep farmers drank their fill a bit too fast, uncomfortable in each others' company.

Bel watched, and it seemed to him that under the law of their Jarl's house, the farmers were bearing silently their resentment against these outlaw scum sharing their board. The Wolves, in turn, were suppressing the contempt warriors occasionally feel for those who provide their food and sustenance. *Everyone has hung their swords and guns up in the entrance area, but most people here are carrying knives,* he thought. *I certainly am.* He eyed the red-faced farmer to his left, avoiding outright eye-contact.

The high table was also getting lively. Thuler was wondering when there would be a good time to talk business, after eating but before everyone got drunk. He suggested to Darnham they retreat for a private conversation.

Darnham said, 'Anything you have to say that's worth hearing will stand the scrutiny of us all.'

Thuler was about to reply when he heard shouting from the other end of the hall. A short, stocky young Wolf named Ramsey was squaring up to a Goathlander, about his weight, both wielding glinting knives. Two sides were forming up behind the would-be combatants. This could get very bad. Thuler stood up, mind racing with ways to calm things down, but all of a sudden there was a crash and a yell. Sif had vaulted the high table and a second later, Ramsey was clutching the side of his head and Sif was placing back on the table the steel jug she'd hit him with. 'Sit down Ramsey,' she grated between clenched teeth. 'This is too important to piss about.' She stared fiercely at him until he sat down, then turned to address the high table. 'Sorry about the jug, Mistress Darnham, we'll pay for it.'

'Call me Bridget, Sif, and let's all have another drink and forget our differences.'

A curvy blonde woman in a long, dark blue skirt and a peasant blouse showing off her bosom, leaned over to pour for Thuler. She leant far across, seemed to lose her balance and slip, just for a moment, just enough to splash a gout of beer on the table in front of him. 'Oh, my lord, forgive me!' She leaned forward again, wiping the spill up, her eyes on Thuler, her grin wide.

Thuler snorted, 'Oh please, no problem. What is your name?'

The girl straightened up and tossed a golden plait over her shoulder. 'Iduna.'

Cups were filled again, and Thuler stood to make his announcement. He glanced sideways at Darnham as he began. 'I want to show you a weapon, which could be very good for your people. Have you got something you want blowing up?'

There were puzzled murmurs at first, then laughter, then someone shouted, 'If it's a bomb you've got, you can try and open up Tanner's Hole.' Presumably, this was what passed for a joke amongst the Goathlanders. Thuler waited for the guffaws to die down and said, 'I'll try it, but only if all else has failed.' There was no laughter this time, and no sound, unless you count an audible sneer.

Thuler walked to the door at the back and said, 'Show me Tanner's Hole.'

The whole party tramped out, taking their drinks, in a mood to have a massive laugh at a fool's expense. The rain had ceased, and they strode uphill in the bright, cool night. Tanner's Hole was a disused mine, just the other side of the hillcrest from Darnham Hall. Thuler calculated that, even with the amount of thread charge he'd need to clear the rubble from the entrance, the white-hot rock chunks would fall down the other side of the hill, well away from the Hall. 'Anyone living down there?' Thuler asked Darnham. 'A few sheep,' said his host, his face unreadable in the moon-shadow.

Thuler set the ball of explosive in a pile of rocks at the head of the pit, with more than enough delay time to retreat a good distance. This was far and away the biggest charge he'd tried yet. He had no idea what would be left when it went off. He insisted everyone move back to the other side of the peak. They did so, grumbling.

Just as everyone was getting restless with Thuler's control of the situation and drifting back to the Hall, there was a deafening bang and the ground shook. The shock was followed by rumbling and then silence. A few small stones pattered past the crowd. Thuler led them back over the peak.

Below him, it was as if a giant shovel had scooped a bowl out of the earth's side, uncovering her bare bones, and a black void where the old pit-head was ripped open. Thuler felt a terrible thrill, and images spilled across his mind, images of explosions, of death and destruction.

As for the crater, he thought, in a few years, it will be grassed over, a natural amphitheatre, big enough to hold a few hundred people for great events.

He felt Darnham's big hand firm on his shoulder. 'We have some talking to do. That private discussion.'

Thuler considered saying: Well, maybe you do… but choked off his own voice. It was only reasonable that Darnham had wanted Thuler's claims substantiated. And, he needed these people; soon, they'd know that they needed him. He nodded. Before he turned away, he noticed patches of a faint, rainbow glow around the inside of the crater. Maybe he was wrong about how soon the grass would grow back.

Back at the Hall, in Darnham's private rooms, Thuler showed the Jarl the threads – the jars of monomer, the feed-chemicals, the half-polymerized thread-stuff. He drew threads out, made one light up, made one produce gentle warmth, and, a trick he had only just perfected, made one deliver a small electric potential along its length, a voltage you could feel as a rhythmic shock if you held it in your palm. Darnham asked intelligent questions (for a yokel, Thuler kept thinking). 'How easy is it to get the raw materials?'

'You need water, plus any organic substance, or any compound that's reactive at room temperature. Thread formation takes different lengths of time depending on your starting-materials. With the best kinds of mixture, after a few hours, you can start to draw the threads out. Use a poorer starting liquor, and you'll get threads within about two days.'

Darnham asked a few more questions about the capabilities of the power-threads. He understood, however, Thuler's refusal to tell him how to form the threads and set their properties.

The Jarl opened an antique cabinet and brought forth a very old-looking bottle. He poured two shot-cups and sipped, eyes screwed up in obvious pleasure.

'This liquor is two hundred years old. I did someone a big favour.'

The flavour threw Thuler. He had only tasted aquavit once before. 'Danish, is it?'

Darnham raised an eyebrow. 'Norwegian. I have business out that way.'

Something nagged at the corner of Thuler's mind. Darnham's big round face sailed on in its lunar serenity, his eyes holding some old secret. Then the Jarl turned to him, massive and stately, like a battleship facing a destroyer, thought Thuler, and said: 'What is all this about, then?'

Thuler considered his reply carefully. 'From what I've seen of your people, you don't have many PL round these parts.'

Darnham looked sideways at him, his face heated by a small coal of anger. 'You've seen our marshes? That's where Pure Lighters end up, as food for the ghosts of the Dead Cities.' Thuler heard the capitals in Darnham's tone – the wounds of the death of those cities were very much with them still, here in Goathland.

'I thought as much. What it's all about is: taking Sheffield's arms factories. You know what I have to offer: some ready-made thread bombs. In exchange for your hospitality, some radio equipment and a few lesser weapons, if you can spare them.'

He paused. 'With this thread-stuff, we can make much more than crude bombs. With a good smith or two and some weapons expertise we can build weaponry that will make it possible to take Sheffield back from the Pure Light. I know Manor Castle and the arms bailey. What I need from you is intelligence about the directions of approach to Sheffield. And anything else that'd be useful.'

Darnham was still savouring his aquavit. So far, so good. Thuler took a deep breath. 'I'm also asking you to join with us, to raise an army that will help me take Sheffield. Then to leave a Goathland force to occupy it, and keep control of the arms factories for the future. Your grandchildren would not need to worry about the PL.'

Darnham nodded philosophically. 'And if I join with you, and if we take, and hold Sheffield, what happens then?'

'I shall go back to Wessex, with whoever wants to go with me, and offer my support to the Crown. We will take the fight to the PL, and beat them. And then, and only then, I'm going to give away the secret of the threads.'

Darnham grinned. 'Ah, the Crown. Comely Queen Hettie. I admired her granddad, standing up to the Christians like that.'

He finished his aquavit and poured them both another. Briskly, he said 'Now, what makes you think that, with just a few bombs and rifles, you could take somewhere like Sheffield Castle? You'll need real superiority in weapons, or you'll not stand a chance.'

Thuler said, 'With artillery, with the range to deliver a charge big enough, we can take out their headquarters. You've seen what a thread-charge can do. What we need is a delivery system.'

Darnham nodded slowly. 'I suppose you know that Sheffield Castle is ringed with the housing for the steel workers, and the PL are not averse to using those people as cannon fodder, plus their own fanatical suicide troops. If this was a sword-battle, it'd be a slow, bloody hack-through, at best. Granted, most of them will be new to this kind of war, but most of your people are, too.'

Thuler said, 'I know we can't create really long-range, transportable cannon from scratch. We could make catapults here, though, couldn't we?' He faced the Jarl and voiced something that had been nagging at him. 'Listen, Darnham, if the artillery idea doesn't work out, how about an airburst over the castle? A charge, hanging off a balloon… I don't like the idea of something so out of control, but…' He tailed off, gazing into the other's narrowed eyes. 'Have you got any balloons or materials to make them from?'

Darnham's eyes were alight with the pleasure of plotting, and something else. 'Tomorrow, take my technical men and make whatever you need. You can announce it tonight. Don't say anything about raising an army here, though. Not yet.'

He made a toast. 'To my people, and however they view your proposal.' There was a smile on the round, red face.

They returned to the big hall and Thuler stood up at the table and called for volunteers. 'I'm developing the bomb you saw. I want metal workers, wood workers and engineers. In the main yard early tomorrow.' There was a buzz of voices and men and women started getting up and coming over. Alex shook their hands and memorized the names and faces of the most impressive ones – Chess the Darnham Hall blacksmith, his apprentice Gerda and a gunsmith, Einar, who spoke with a Scandinavian accent.

The buzz kept on round the hall, and soon people stood up and started making vows, or engaging in good natured competition. Dirk Darnham was down amongst the lower tables, boasting and blustering.

Thuler almost smiled to see Ramsey arm-wrestling his burly neighbour, no animosity left. Sif had saved the day and, like any successful rulers, the Darnhams were good psychologists and knew just what would keep or break the peace.

After a bit Thuler decided to get some rest before it degenerated any further. Darnham showed him to the back exit of the hall, shaking his head indulgently at Dirk's antics. 'He's just back from going viking. He still acts like a savage. It's good fighting experience for a young lad, though.' Darnham opened the door and pointed to another at the end of a dark corridor.

The room was warm, dark, and at first inspection, devoid of company. There was a bed over by the back wall, and as his eyes adjusted to the gloom he noticed there was a humped shape there. The woman sat up, blonde plaits brushing her breasts as she stretched her arms above her head.

Thuler crossed over and sat on the bed. Iduna gazed, big-eyed, into his face. Her scent rose up, alkaline mutton-fat soap, roses and sexual heat. Even as he spoke, he felt himself getting hard. 'I'm not looking for house favours.'

Iduna flicked a plait aside. 'I would be inclined to bed you in any house. Don't reject me because I am a stranger.'

Thuler smiled. 'I like your choice of phrase.' It struck him that he had little to lose, that the worst he could expect would be that this confident young woman had been sent to spy on him. 'Women who just turn up in my bed,' – he gauged her response, the knowing look in her eyes – 'make me think I'm being spied on.'

She twisted to one side, deliciously. 'You're not used to being a hero. Get used to it!'

'So your dad sent you.'

'No! Well, not exactly.' She smiled, eyes wide. 'I really do want you.' A duet of wild laughter sounded from another room. 'And it's not as if my dad's going to be watching. He'll be fucking that queenly dark girl you came with, I imagine. And the mistress of the house, my old mum, will have found herself a young stud or a girl, depending on her tastes for the night.'

She sat up and raised her hand, the palm outward. 'Look.' Skeins of light writhed out of her skin.

Thuler almost gasped in surprise. 'Becters!'

‘Bingo! Hurrah!’ She let a trail of light extend from her fingertips.

Three things occurred to Thuler. Slowly, a smile spreading across his face, he reached out and let light swell from his hand, meeting her light. She breathed in sharply and closed her eyes. He brought his hand to the side of her face, watched the becter-shine rippling back and forth. She groaned. The light between them expanded and pulsed. She laughed, shook herself and thrust her whole body forward, offering herself to him.

They lay in silence, in the low candlelight. Her breath played on his chest like a soft night breeze. He knew somehow that she was thinking intensely. She noticed him paying her that attention and rolled over. He looked sideways at her. ‘You want me for a breeding programme. You want to get pregnant with a becter-tolerant. What made you think of that?’

She kept her back to him. ‘It’s the elite, the aristocracy. All sensible women want to breed from an elite man. Ever read the Volsungs’ Saga?’

‘You’re not the first person to use that as a model. How much do you know about Thule?’

‘One elite technology we know about, the becters. Elite by design. Another we half-know about, elekilpo, which we imagine might be elite by accident, and a breeding programme which we surmise.’

Her voice was choked, unhappy. She turned back to him, and her face told him it wasn’t what he’d just said that was upsetting her, true as it might be. Their eyes locked, he saw a story in hers, as if they were watching opposite sides of a screen made of her corneas.

Sheffield is burning, and bodies are frying in a terrible alien light. She has taken flight into precognitive vision. She expects that Sheffield will be a horrible disaster and that they'll all die. 'So much death,' she whispered, 'so much death.'

Chapter 26: Round the North Sea

From dawn, noise filled the hall, outside and in. Iduna was kneeling upright, gazing through the window. She turned and smiled, and stooped to kiss him on the lips, then pulled a russet homespun frock over her head and was gone, an impetuous teenager who left the door open.

Thuler dressed for work and met the technicians for an early breakfast in the great hall. Over bacon, oatcakes and root coffee, Chess asked him what he wanted to make.

'Bombs, catapults, balloons, mortars if we can.'

The quiet smith nodded and addressed his food. When they finished, Chess led them across the muddy yard to the smithy, a vast stone workshop with a door you could get a bus through.

He and Gerda dragged a bench out from the wall and found seats for the three of them. Gerda waved a yellowed sketchpad in the air and made a moue. 'Not much history of innovation round here.'

They sketched catapults and mortars first, Gerda listing against each pencil drawing the components they'd need to make it. The catapults would be easy to make, and they'd have the robust reliability of low-tech in the field. They needed to be just small enough to carry on a horse but able to hurl a pound of thread a lot further than a man could. They hashed out a detailed catapult design and Chess sent Gerda to find labourers to start work on a prototype.

She came back with a posse of curious and excited youngsters, and Chess instructed them. 'All of you, get your materials ready. Gerda will have the plans by that time. Joe: seasoned yew – long, four inch trunks. Edwin: take two others and strip that hulk of a bus round the back for spring steel. Bertha: make the biggest throwing sticks you've ever seen.' The big man stared at them all till they ran off, then left them to get on with it while he rejoined Gerda and Thuler.

The mortars would consist of a long steel tube, a small explosive charge to launch, and a timed charge as the projectile. Chess fetched some steel scaffolding poles.

With their first attempt, luck was with them, in a way. They stood well back from the primed mortar, and no-one got hurt when the bottom half of it glowed red, then yellow, then melted as a fireball emerged through it, splintering the steel in white hot fireworks.

They decided to have one more go, with a length of four inch steel pipe Chess ransacked from somewhere in the supplies. They set it up away from the yard, pointing towards the hillside, with a charge carefully-shaped to the bottom of the mortar tube.

This time, the charge shot out of the breech. The projectile spun on a crazy arc into the sky, then dropped into a field near the crest of the hill. Three seconds later there was a ragged thump and the characteristic weird-coloured fireball for a few seconds. They all cheered. Greasy-faced from the smoke, Thuler and Chess strode up the hill and over to the impact zone. There was a sizeable crater, a few spectral fey-lights dancing round the edge. Nothing like Tanner's Hole, but enough to take out a large house.

They allowed themselves a moment's mutual congratulation, and walked back excitedly. The mortar tube was intact. The next stage was to try a bigger charge, to find out how much a mortar such as that could deliver.

Thuler doubled the size of the charge, and got everyone under cover. There was a throttled howl, a prolonged roar, and bits of the steel tube seemed to be spinning in opposite directions before they flew apart. They all ducked behind their wall as chunks of white-hot stuff sizzled and screeched over them.

Nobody was smiling. Thuler had to admit that he didn't have a consistent grasp of what bigger thread charges could do. Diplomatically, Gerda pointed out that it was lunchtime.

Tucking in hungrily to sheeps' cheese, dried fish, bread and honey beer, they hashed out attack scenarios. In the end, airburst seemed like the best option for delivering a major charge.

Thuler asked, 'Are there any big balloons or airships in Goathland?'

Chess did a wry shake of the head. 'There's one old thing from the last century that the Jarl insisted we keep, anyone else would have thrown it out. It's torn and probably rotten by now. And we've no helium.'

'No problem,' said Thuler. 'We can use hydrogen. We only need these balloons to work for a few minutes and get into position. Anyone shoots them down, it just brings the charge off course a bit. If we have some kind of radio-trigger, we can set it off when it's nearest to target. Can we make balloons out of anything else?'

Chess swirled the sweet beer in his mug and smiled. 'We've got an awful lot of sheepskin. Some of it is very fine. I don't know if it would be light enough for a balloon though.'

'Let's try it.'

Chess swigged his beer. 'So, how many do we need? Twenty, thirty?'

'No, just a few small ones, as demonstrations, and then two or three of increasing size. The key is fear. You saw how Tanner's Hole looked last night. This is a terror weapon.'

'You want a terror weapon,' said Chess, draining his beer, 'I'll make you one.'

At Chess's suggestion, they enclosed the thread charges in old gas cylinders. They tested a small one, below the ridge above Tanner's Hole, retreating back over the crest. The bang and shockwave were stupendous, and it was followed by a terrible, rising howl. When they checked back at the test site, they saw that Tanner's Hole now had a twin, another circular pit of bare, frightening destruction.

As they walked back to the smithy they saw people arriving on horseback and on foot. Chess set the youngsters to work under Gerda, patching the ancient nylon balloon with strips of parchment-fine sheepskin while they inspected the catapult.

The weapon was a crude, clumsy thing, and it took Chess's enormous strength plus Thuler to bend its stiff steel springs enough to secure the throwing-arm down. They stood back, sweating and send a lad to get some different-size rocks.

The first rock went almost straight up and everyone dived for cover. They re-sprung the catapult, tilted it up a bit and tried again. This time, the rock traveled a fair distance, but Chess sneered at it. 'Our best bowmen could chuck a rock nearly that far. If you can't use it from beyond the range of a mortar, it's useless.'

It was late afternoon by now, and Bridget Darnham came by with a jug of beer. They fell to thirstily while they discussed the catapult problem. Gerda said, 'I've worked out the forces we're using with the prototype, and I can easily come up with a spring size if you give me a distance.'

Chess stared at her. 'I was wondering when that maths course would come in handy. Anything bigger than that and I won't be pulling it, mind.'

Gerda nodded, flushed with pride at her boss's offhand compliment. 'Screw, worm gear, crank handle. All off that old bus.'

‘Genius. Pour her another beer, but not too much. Make it so, lass!’ Gerda glowed and blushed a deeper scarlet.

Just as they got up, the Jarl appeared and took Thuler aside.

‘People have heard. Everyone’s here, all my folks. People are going up to Tanner’s Hole.’

He paused, and Thuler looked at him. Darnham had a excited, determined air. ‘And some special allies,’ he said. ‘We’re going to have to move fast, Thuler. Couple of days, tops. You’ll understand why, tonight.’

Infuriatingly, the Jarl left with no further word. These taciturn Goathlanders.

By dinner time, there were a lot more people in Darnham Hall. The trestle tables were packed, and there were new family members and guests of honour around the high table. Everyone was pressed together and talking at once, the serving-youths had almost given up trying to weave through the throng, and pitchers of beer were passing over the heads of the crowd. Getting food was decidedly haphazard, but most people seemed to be in fine mood.

Darnham led Thuler to three men standing at the high table. Behind them, on the wall, hung new Sheffield-made guns, shiny with good care. One of the new men had thick red hair combed back from a deep-creased brow, a very weather-beaten face and neatly trimmed beard, fine bright clothes and splendid gold rings. Darnham gave Thuler’s name first, emphasizing Captain Latham’s status. The second was another Scandinavian, Thorvaldsson. His appearance was much more understated, but he also looked nautical, somehow. A thought that was nagging at the back of Thuler’s mind came to the fore; These are our new allies, nautical allies, and the possibilities gripped him.

The third man was different again, tall and wiry, dressed in bright red trousers, a soft, brown leather waistcoat over a dark silk shirt and long dark hair swept back over his high, sloping forehead. Piercing dark eyes gazed out from a pale face. His cheekbones were high over hollow cheeks, his nose was long and straight, making his face seemed pointed, vulpine. His stare was discomfiting, and he announced himself in a low, measured voice. 'War-Fox greets you, Thule-man.'

He held Thuler's hand briefly, and his gaze much longer. Thuler stared back into the black-bright orbs, aware of the importance of this transaction as he felt the layers of his history flowing into this becter-tolerant, this magic man's eyes. After a while, the tall man turned away, his face unreadable, maybe amused. The two nautical men exchanged glances, and Darnham directed everyone to their seats. The youngsters served fish soup, everyone eventually getting a dish and some beer, by which time another sheep was being carried into the hall.

War-Fox, seated on Thuler's right, started bemoaning the lack of music on their trip over, in his unaccented, sing-song voice. 'Snorre was a fine harpist and teller of stories, and we lost him on a wretched island half way between Hammerfest and Svalbard.' The narrator's eyes were hooded. 'We moored on the south side of some jagged rocks, and the northern sky was alight with strange fires. Snorre and two fighters went up the rocks, and none of them came back down.'

Thuler heard the shaman's question under the story. 'The man who occupies the Spitsbergen heights is known as Raven, and as Crow. It was there he gave me the elekilpo threads.'

War-Fox placed his knife down with an oddly delicate gesture and turned to face Thuler. 'Do you know what the Ragnarok is?' Thuler nodded slowly.

'This is a story I burn to tell. It weighs heavy on my soul. I would tell it in the open Hall, but it is too disturbing.

It would spook the men. We are in war-preparations, my friend, and it is incumbent on us, as always, to carry those who are of ordinary soul. So the telling must wait.'

After the plates had been removed, everyone expected the Thuler to say something.

He stood up. 'I intend to take Sheffield.'

The room erupted with calls, whistles, shouts and much else, not all of it welcoming.

A sturdy middle-aged Goathlander spoke up: 'What's in it for us?'

'Great plunder. Weapons and the factories to make them. The liberation of your cousins and the security of your children. Glory and renown forever.'

The questioner nodded, satisfied for now.

Dirk called out, 'And what are the women like?'

Thuler turned to his young host and gave it to him how he surely liked it, laid on thick: 'It is said even in Wessex that Sheffield boasts two beautiful girls to every man.'

Dirk raised his cup and vowed great deeds. Somebody shouted, 'A sumbel!' and an excited, informal round of oaths began. Thuler sat down, satisfied, as the men's enthusiasm bore their mood up.

When it was his turn to toast and oath, his stood again and vowed loyalty to his Wolves, to his Goathland allies and to the best of old Britain, past, present and forever. He sat down again and felt massive euphoria sweep the hall.

Some of the oaths and toasts came through the babble. He heard a Scandinavian voice toast 'To my Goathland cousins, Norwegians in blood and in spirit! And to my boat!' He heard Darnham toast, 'to Aegir of the sea, and to his cousins of the inland waters. Bless our voyages!'

The sumbel tailed off into random toasting. Darnham turned to Thuler and the three Scandinavians.

'Come and share some aquavit with me, gentlemen.'

He led the way to the back room and poured them drinks

from the old bottle. 'Now, Thuler, tell us your plans.'

Thuler turned to the Norwegians. 'I believe Sheffield Manor Castle is vulnerable to an airburst attack. Have you seen the effects of my explosives?'

Darnham said, 'We've been up to Tanner's Hole.'

The Norwegians seemed unmoved, so Thuler continued. 'We have to assume that they'll have heard they're about to be attacked and will be fully militarized, all the settlements between the Don floodplain and Manor Top, not to mention the Southern Marches, if they've got the numbers. Which they may have.'

He took a deep breath. 'The worst part will be approaching the Manor, from whichever side. There's a mile of open hillside to fight up. Support from local militias might be decisive, but my intelligence about them is from before the invasion.' It occurred to Thuler that he was exaggerating his knowledge of the local forces. He hoped he didn't sound as if he was clutching at straws.

Latham spoke. 'And what if they've got aircraft? Then, they'd really have the drop, as you say.'

Everybody went quiet and ruminated over their aquavit.

Eventually, Latham spoke. 'Scandinavia's iron ore is the lifeline for Sheffield steel. Scandinavian oil is gone. Our water power dried up. We're like that' –he clenched his hands together – 'symbiotic, is it? – with the coal that keeps Sheffield's furnaces burning.'

The impassivity of Latham's face was belied by the fierce light in his eyes. 'We are traders, not politicians, but we are also free men, free to roam the great seas, like our forebears. Those Pure Light people don't like freedom.'

He paused, seeming awkward in confessing such a strong opinion. 'I say now is the time for war on Sheffield. Others may disagree. So we must be sure we would have a much better chance if we join with you than if we wait, and pick another time.'

His long speech over, Latham went silent. They all digested what he'd said, then the silent Thorvaldsson stuck out his aquavit cup. Darnham refreshed their drinks, and Thorvaldsson said, 'To an alliance of free men!' and they all echoed his toast. Thuler was awash with relief. Now they could get into details of strategy.

Latham and Thorvaldsson outlined a plan to transport troops and back the invasion of Sheffield from the water, and the awareness grew in Thuler of how well these sailors knew the area they were talking about. They couldn't have got this knowledge just from maps of the shifting flood-lines. With allies and resources such as these, victory could be in their grasp. It seemed too good to be true. What was the catch? Or maybe there was no catch: these men were representatives of a vigorous and resource-rich conspiracy to oust the Pure Light at the first opportunity.

Thuler addressed the issue of local militias. 'I expect they'll be dragooned into home guard by PL commanders. If we can break the hold of the top brass, there's every chance they'll defect en masse to our side.'

Darnham said, 'It's possible the PL will bring everyone into the Castle compound. Or even just possible that they'll form them into a lower perimeter and prepare to sacrifice the lot.'

Thuler replied, 'If we show what looks like overwhelming force as soon as we land, we should be able to drive them up the hill and besiege the Castle complex without too many casualties. Then the balloons come into their own, and maybe catapults.'

With an approximate plan, they began to work out the logistics, the likely size of their force, how to transport them, what weapons to take with them, and the main plans of attack.

They argued to a standstill at a departure in three days. Thuler would have liked more time, to develop the thread-weapons further, but the captains had a number of convincing-sounding nautical reasons, backed by long standing impatience to get a move on. So three days it was.

Everybody got another refill of aquavit, and then War-Fox spoke. ‘Let me tell you a story.’

‘My becter powers were bestowed when my benefactor opened a vein and made me suck the blood with my lip cut open, then lock gaze with him. Blood and data mingled, stories flowed. I learned of the lineage of the power he carried. How he had sucked the becter-seed nanites out of his benefactor, the myth that she had passed on to him of the Master of Thule who’d originally created becters. How that terrible Master had abducted human women, bred from them and sometimes returned to claim his daughters. As the stories streamed into me, rainbows came into my benefactor’s hut, there in Arctic Norway, and I looked up and saw a grey disc of light which shot beams of rainbow through the window, and seemed to probe into my flesh. My benefactor said, ‘Those disks are the Master’s spy-spirits. Now he knows you.’

War-Fox looked round at his audience. ‘I saw an attempted nuclear attack on Thule, by a Pure Light commander I’d just sold my becter-rich blood to.

‘I’d been in Providence Port, the terminal for Alberta’s tar-oil. I’d had a precog blip of good business there and I’d sent out on the becter-net a ‘ready’ call for trade. The reply came from a becter tolerant. The woman looked like this:’ War-Fox extended his left hand, and a shape shimmered into being above it, a tall woman in a grey one-piece, short, dark red hair over a severe face with high cheekbones. With a shock, Alex recognized Oona. War-Fox grinned. ‘She was very confident. She was offering a dealing position with the Pure Light. I would get Rejuve, in exchange for the becters in my blood. She would get some of the Rejuve, and I was supposed to help her find someone, a Sofie.' War-Fox narrowed his eyes and nodded, almost imperceptibly at Thuler. 'My Pure Light contact was a General, Chickfeld. Oona described him as lusting for becters, as wanting to become God's *Übermensch.*'

'Anyway, I went to his ship. A ghost vessel, radiant white in the mist, white-coated sailors, no becter auras, no vonnies, and no women. All the men had that thrum of Rejuve users. He gave me the Rejuve and I passed him my blood. He said, 'Now I shall test your wares,' and walked off. I was wondering what test-facilities they had on board when a hurricane of becter-power hit me. Chickfeld had just gone and injected the raw blood, and was now linked to me in his installation crisis. I had a clear picture of him. Sweat popped on his brow, over his eyelids and his cheeks, a drop falling off his chin. His hands gripped the arms of the chair, his breath hissing and muttering a prayer, '*Not my will but Thine oh Lord*', repeated between clenched teeth. His face swelled purple, spit drooled out of his mouth, a vein popped in his forehead. I saw the glow building up, through his cheekbones, then in his temples, then it rippled, dirty-looking, over his hands and through his clothes, the becter-light.

'He started roaring and babbling. I scanned round as best I could. I scanned round for any trace of the becter-tolerant signatures anyone of Oona's lineage would have; nothing, so I got out. I could see Chickfeld in his stateroom, drooling and screaming, ordering the launch of nuclear missiles. I stayed connected to him. I knew something was wrong, and I had to know how it would play out. I scanned the missiles' comms and their destination was the Thule Teardrop. A few minutes later, they exploded over open water some miles north of the ship. Thule had intercepted them. I waited in the open sea, as wide open as I could be, scanning round again. No Sofie. It had been a red herring. It came to me what I'd been used for. Oona's people – Thule – wanted give the Pure Light something to fight about, something to split them into two warring factions. The PL attack on Thule was doomed to fail. I had been used to start a false Ragnarok.'

War-Fox paused, and let his words sink in as Darnham poured more aquavit.

He resumed. 'Oona told me that Thule had a new technology even beyond becters that nothing could stand against.' He turned to Thuler. 'That would be elekilpo. And when we did the skill-crossload, she invited me into her memories. I looked into her lineage, which is usually easy to discern in open crossload. But with Oona, there seemed to be none of that: it ended abruptly in a glare brighter than the sun. Some zipped-up data passed between us, something I needed to decompress later.

'Oona acted shocked, asked what I thought I was doing. 'Where does the power-blood come from?' I asked.

''How much do you want to know? All knowledge has a cost,' she said. 'That glare you saw, what do you know about Thule?'

'I told her I'd tried to get into the Thule Teardrop.'

'That's when she asked me, 'Do you know what Ragnarok means?' I said yes, and she said, 'This phase of the world must be brought to an end, the ice-caps re-frozen.'

'My friends, that appears to be what Thule is up to. And they have advanced considerably in technical deployment. I have not had a report on the becter-net of any spy-disk sightings for years now. I believe Thule have a dispersed, airborne technology of some kind that enables monitoring, and maybe power transmission.'

'And the Crow stalls,' said Thuler.

'The Crow BTs are part of the plan. It may be they who keep the airborne tech in place?' War-Fox ended on that question. Thuler let the silence continue a few seconds, then said, 'Since that's Thule technology, we won't be fighting against it; we have the elekilpo, and it is highly unlikely our enemy does; but I think it would be wise to keep Thule's aims in the background of our plans.'

No Iduna came to him that night. He didn't go seeking; he had enough to think about. Turning over the sheer scope of the night's plans, he revised his appraisal of Darnham and the Norwegians. They were more than just an opportunistic conspiracy of traders, much more. They represented just the tip of a resurgent, traditional civilization that spanned the North Sea.

Thuler began to understand the slick film of underground allegiances that drove the weirdness of Britain since the Flooding. He sensed the edges of the underworld deals, the sticky political stuff, the ancient alliances, of which he was now a part. Dimly, he remembered another Scandinavian voice toasting to '*the Father of victory, to our brothers everywhere, and to the Guild that never dies.*'

As he fell asleep, he remembered Darnham saying: *You'll understand why, tonight.*

Chapter 27: Taking Sheffield

The carts and the one big old diesel truck rattled down the hill into the bay of Kilburn. Most of the supplies and materiel had already been loaded onto the boats by the advance crew. The fighters had spent the night at Darnham Hall and set out before dawn that morning, ready for a long day's voyaging.

They rode down Kilburn Port's steep streets. It was a bustling hive of activity after the rural isolation of everywhere Thuler had been since the wilds of Caithness. The small town had been re-fitted as a port after the floods isolated Goathland. Dirk rode at the head of the convoy, chatting to every girl and plenty of other people too, his aide Garrick making sure that everyone got listened to and, if necessary, paid in gold.

The streets opened out into the harbour bay, Spring sunlight glittering on the busy water. There was a low stone house down by the stone quay, and as they rode up a middle-aged couple came out to greet them. The man was sturdy, grey haired, and wore a nautical cap. The woman was short and broad with a red face and wearing a woolen frock. She carried a tray with cups and a bottle.

The man addressed Dirk and the party. 'Young Master Darnham, and Thuler, be welcome. I would be honoured to tell truthfully in years to come that I drank a toast with you gentlemen. Would you be so kind?' Thuler, Dirk, Bel and Sif dismounted and the ruddy-faced woman stepped forward and poured shots for them all.

'To victory, gentlemen, for you and for our old ways.' They raised their cups and drank. Thuler asked, 'Have you any reports of the mood of the Sheffielders?'

The harbour-master nodded. 'You'll be welcomed, everyone will rush to join with you.'

'Let's hope it is so,' said Thuler, as he handed his cup back.

This was the Spring flood season. The plan was to start out today, and reach Sheffield by nightfall, ready for a night attack. They embarked, the water right up to the jetty. There were around thirty fighting men and women in Thuler's Wolves, and the Goathlanders had contributed five hundred or so fighters, fifty of whom were Dirk's cavalry. The eighty or so horses went onto the big ferry boat, the men and women onto longboats, with tall sails and oars stowed.

The boats rocked gently. Dirk took his command aboard a dragon-prowed longship, the high sunlight catching and flaring on its gilded scales. Bel shook his head in admiration. 'One look at her, and I want to go raiding. What a beauty.'

Thuler, Bel and Sif each took charge of a group on a boat. Each of the leaders checked round with binoculars, keeping the other leaders in sight.

They sat down on the hard benches. The first mate on Sif's vessel, Jon, had a concertina, and the melancholy sweetness of it made a soundtrack to their setting off. Soon they were under way, and each of them found out what he felt about sailing. Even on this gentle swell, Bel puked almost continually.

The day passed on the open water. They sailed over the flooded plain of York, the Minster spire showing where the Roman city had once stood. They turned south, avoiding the old war-zone of Leeds. As the light faded the steersmen noted the sluggish current running against them as the entered the low delta of the river Don, name of the life-giving Goddess of the waters all over Europe.

They floated stealthily over sunken Doncaster, the

Victorian Gothic finials of the Minster making a square of weed-shrouded stones, then over Maltby, past the roof of a blackened tower, the remnants of some forgotten grand house. Cautiously, they navigated the muddy channels into the Orgreave Basin and moored up by Catcliffe. This was the edge of the land mass that rose to the eight hills of Sheffield. Thuler looked west through the binoculars, towards Manor Top. He saw faint light flickering over the crown of the hill – those must be powerful lights, to carry this far. They were burning fuel, showing off their power.

There were no local people around the Catcliffe mooring. Hiding, no doubt, or garrisoned ready for a battle. It seemed likely the defenders had had news of their approach across the Don basin.

They needed to draw the defenders out. They would advance until they met with resistance. Then they would show their strength – give them a big bang and offer terms immediately. Thuler and Bel supervised the unloading of the big catapults, and they began their advance, Dirk's cavalry up the front, flanked and scouted by Thuler's Wolves, the artillery behind them.

They crested the crown of the next rise and took a look ahead. A fireball would be visible from the Castle, thought Thuler.

They moved on. They'd made it across the flat, and started up the next slope when there was a succession of gunshots, then a thud, and a cry. Thuler saw a man to Dirk's right fall off his horse, and another cavalryman clutch his shoulder. They dived for cover behind some fallen trees. Snipers! Unbelievable, pinned down before we start!

They could cower here, or they could advance, straight into enemy fire, which would be suicidal. Or they could risk a little exposure and use their artillery, for the first time in battle. Thuler gave the order, and the first charges were loaded. Three medium-sized grenades whizzed over their heads, and there were two bangs, then another, and three fireballs blossomed on the horizon. Figures were scattering, silhouetted against the flames. Under rifle cover, Thuler urged the cavalry on, up the hill into a line of defences, sand bags blown asunder and still smouldering. Further up, there was the settlement of Handsworth, stone and brick houses flickering in the dying flames. It looked as if local resistance had collapsed already.

Thuler rallied the force in the village square, and addressed his people. 'No looting. No violence, unless someone else starts it. These people will be our allies.'

He rode around the edge of their torchlit circle with the megaphone. 'Sheffield people, I am Thuler, and I come at the head of an army that will take this city. We have superior weapons, as you have seen. Join us in liberating Sheffield from the Pure Light.'

Some movements happened down in the lane ahead. A shot rang out, but Bel spun and returned fire. The sniper staggered out into the lane and fell, and Bel saw the white PL flash on the uniform – one of their fanatics. He took a few paces towards the man and shot him in the head.

Thuler took the megaphone again. 'Come out and join us now. The Pure Light is finished in Sheffield.'

Thuler kept turning, looking around. There were no more snipers. Then a white flag waved from a doorway, and three men and two women came out, lay down their rifles and stepped forwards holding their hands high.

'We're with you, Thuler,' one woman shouted. More people began to emerge from doorways, from the lane where the sniper had hidden, from the darkness at the edge of the village. In a few minutes, about a hundred men and women stood in a semi-circle in front of Thuler. He looked down at the wiry, young woman dressed in combat fatigues with an eye-patch who had spoken out. 'How many more of you are there?'

She raised her arm in something between a salute and a wave. 'This is all, or nearly all, of the Handsworth Guard. There were two embedded PL 'advisors', one of them you shot, over there' – she pointed towards the dead sniper in the lane – 'the other ran back to the Castle.'

Thuler nodded. 'And who are you?'

'Dana Pembrook, platoon leader, Handsworth Guard.' She spoke proudly. 'And I want to see the PL thrown out of Sheffield!'

'Well Dana, you can help by sending messengers to every other defence militia who are likely to defect to us.'

Dana turned and called out. Three Guards emerged from the shadows. 'Corporal! Take cars and men to Richmond and Gleadless.'

Thuler dismounted, dusted himself off and continued their impromptu council of war. 'And it would help us to know how many that might be, where they are, and what resistance we're likely to encounter between here and Manor Castle.'

'Richmond and Gleadless militias are about the same size as us. No point trying with Farleigh, they're the Castle's home guard, heavily PL.'

'And how much do you think they know about us?'

'Everyone has heard about Inverness.' Dana grinned widely. 'The PL are mad as hell. Everyone knows that Thuler is on his way here, with powerful bombs. We were put on standby a week ago, and on red alert last night.'

Thuler nodded. As expected, they'd been spotted crossing the Don Basin and the PL had been warned. He looked round at his fighters. No need to rest yet.

'So, we have no element of surprise. What can they throw against us here, Dana?'

'That, for a start,' she said, looking up and over Thuler's shoulder. He turned, and saw a shaft of fierce torchlight stabbing the ground, swaying, suspended from above. Then his eyes adjusted to the scale involved, and he saw that it was a giant searchlight, and a massive balloon, with a pod slung beneath it. The PL were sending an airship against them!

'What's this mean? Bombs?'

The young commander gave an open-eyed gaze. 'I imagine so, but I've never seen that airship before. Or bombs, or artillery, though I believe they have mortars and cannon at the Castle.'

Thuler turned to Bel. 'Snipers onto the personnel, artillery onto the gas bag. Bring it down, but try not to damage it to much.'

The catapulters loaded their range-finding, weighted light-pellets, and white tracer arced across the dark grey sky. Some fell short, others overshot. Through binoculars, Thuler could see that the airship was racing up to them. He could hear the sound of engines now, and see a man leaning out of an aperture in the pod holding a cluster of stick grenades.

The airship was almost upon them when the catapulters let fly again. This time, two of the fire-pellets stuck fast to the gas-bag and blazed brightly. Holes appeared in the fabric, the edges glowing like suppressed embers in the treated cloth. A bang to the right of their circle scattered Handsworth Guards at that end, and another bang was followed by a man's scream and bloody scraps of flesh spattering down.

The bombs started to fall thicker now, and Thuler no longer cared if they captured the airship whole. On the third salvo, the catapulters got their sticky thread-grenades all over the gas bag, and suddenly it was more holes than cloth, plummeting to the ground. The ripped bag blew aside, and the pod came down almost on its own, to be surrounded by Handsworth Guards pointing guns at the one survivor. They dragged him out of the wreckage, a thin youth in a PL uniform, and took his weapons. Thuler called his captors to bring the boy over.

'You'll do just fine as our messenger. Go to the Castle and tell them this: Thuler will detonate a series of three airburst charges. The first will be the weakest. The third will be powerful enough to melt Sheffield Castle into a puddle. I will keep on advancing, and destroying, until the Pure Light surrender Sheffield unconditionally. Got it?' The sullen, frightened face nodded.

'Go!' shouted Thuler. The boy ran, up towards the crest of Manor Top, where that boastful light was burning.

'Fraser – coordinate direction with the cavalry and scouts.' Thuler mounted his horse, swung round to face uphill, cried, 'Let's go!'

They crossed a big, old metalled road and entered Castlebeck, an oval of old streets. A Handsworth scout came running up. 'Richmond and Gleadless militias up ahead, sir!' He paused for breath, and added 'Farleigh Hill – that's the main approach to the castle complex – is swarming with troops, either loyal, or directly under PL fanatics.'

Thuler nodded in acknowledgement. That would be where they had to really fight.

Thuler rode across the centre of the oval, where the two local militias were forming up. The figure of a woman in combat fatigues broke away from the main mass of infantry and crossed the grass towards him. In the fitful gloom she looked up, and he saw Thania's face. He jumped down off his horse and stood, frozen for a moment.

Her red hair was cropped close to her skull and her eyes showed strain and tiredness. She spoke with awe in her voice. 'You made it. I knew it was you, when I heard about Inverness. Come here.' She flung her arms around his chest and he hugged her to him. He felt her trembling, then she pulled back and said, 'Plenty of time to catch up after we've won this war.' She stepped back, shaking her head in amazement still, then said, 'Come on,' and walked back towards her unit.

Thuler shook hands with Jackson, the Gleadless commander and they stood round while he outlined his attack plan. 'We need to get upwind, to have best control of the line-held balloons. That means, for the time being, we need a position to the south east of here.'

Thania, Jackson and Thuler led their forces round to Elm Tree Hill. Across the wide, broken old road, which now served as a bare no-man's land, loomed Farleigh's stone towers, and they took cover from snipers.

Thuler and Gerda inflated the balloon from their hydrogen tank, and attached the first thread charge and the radio-detonator. As they stood up, they saw in each other's eyes the same thought: I hope this works.

They paid out the line, letting the balloon rise into the gentle breeze. The dark sac and its deadly cargo drifted towards the line of deserted houses that sheltered the enemy troops. When he judged it to be just over the ridge of a house, Thuler pressed the detonation button. It took about a second, then the fireball blossomed, making a thump, and then that disquieting sucking-in sound.

They heard a scream – there must have been a sniper inside – then silence. When the smoke had cleared, they saw the fireball had annihilated two houses and bitten hemispheres of molten brick and slate out of the adjoining ones, raw, melted surfaces shining under the smoke. Thuler scanned the ends of streets across the road for any activity, any white flags, or gunfire. Nothing happened.

He waited till his becters told him fifteen minutes had passed. Nothing was happening. That was time enough for the Castle to send a signal of some kind. Obviously, they weren't frightened enough yet.

He spoke to the commanders. 'Advance cautiously, keeping the Castle downwind. Artillery – up here, clear those houses out of the way.'

They moved out, across the cracked tarmac of the old road. It was unnerving, not being able to see your enemy, even when you knew he couldn't be that near. They needed to get behind the perimeter of abandoned houses and in view of the final slope that ran up to the outer wall of the complex. Thuler wanted to see how the defenders were positioned before letting off the next airburst.

They formed up on another big old road, now perfectly upwind of Manor Top. The catapults lobbed charges into the rows of houses ahead, until there was nothing left but smoking rubble. They advanced a hundred yards, and demolished the next line of streets, and the next. Standing on warm, crumbling ground, Thuler gazed across the rubble-strewn dip and rise to where he could finally see the blaze of the Castle compound. The attacking army formed up and scouts were sent out to check how big a position they'd secured. There was no more activity from the direction of the Castle.

Despite everything having gone to plan so far, Thuler's gut feeling was very bad, on this blasted hilltop, looking across at the most weapon-rich fortress in Britain. *This is where a lot of people die. And it's my job to make sure it's not my people.*

He manouevred them round behind a row of head-high wall remnants for protection from snipers. He wondered why the defenders weren't attacking with cannon, and whether their artillery had been sabotaged by locals.

He ordered the second balloon to be prepared, and got down to check the charge and detonator. This was a big charge, smaller than what he'd used on Tanner's Hole, but not much. He hoped it would do the trick this time.

It was a larger balloon, and the wind was getting up.

Three of them held the line, against a sudden gust and squall of rain, but the balloon stayed on course. As it blew close to the castle, volleys of shots rang out from below it, and a single cannon shot boomed. The ball flew harmlessly over their heads. The bullets were breaking the balloon up, though, and Thuler detonated it, hoping it was still high up enough to give an airburst effect.

It exceeded their expectations, and went off with a ripping sound, arcs of lightnings burning after-images on their retinas. Thuler took up the binoculars. *Those little lightnings follow the splashes of water around it, as if it's burning the rain*, he thought, wonderingly. All that could be seen of what remained under the airburst was a smoking dip in the ground, and behind it, a breach in the stone outer wall of the compound.

Then he looked down, and saw the defenders streaming out of the castle, and appearing from some trench or hole, last ditch troops spilling out into the spectral afterglow of the thread fire. Led by white-clad Light Guards, they scattered and began shooting at the attackers.

The sally was so sudden and shocking that some Wolves and a number of Goathland horsemen fell before they could duck down, and the outlying infantry from the local militias were chaotic with screams. They still didn't have the overwhelming force they needed to take the Castle without massive loss of life, and that wasn't going to happen. They all dived back under cover and Thuler got the third charge ready. This was bigger than anything he'd attempted before. He was beginning to be aware that weird and unpredictable things happened with bigger charges, but this was the only card they had to play.

They slung the massive blob of explosive under the balloon and set it to rise. They let it go high, away from the snipers' bullets, for that bit more lift to get it over the castle. The wind blew up, and it looked as if they were going to make it, when suddenly the wind gusted from the west, and the balloon swung round, heading for the defending troops who were frantically shooting at it.

This was the best balloon they had, and it was sinking, and Thuler knew there was only one last chance. He hit the detonator button.

At first, there were just flashes of light of a crystalline, brutal clarity. For a moment, Bel's keen eyes picked out two faces among the defenders, as sharp as if they were a tenth the distance. Real, particular human beings caught up in the horror of war's generality, their faces transparent, their skulls grimacing in the unbelievable light.

Then it all went out of control. Horses, blinded, panicked, reared and fell. People vomited. Eardrums burst. The sky turned into jagged, overlapping arcs of rainbow. In the centre of the horror, something drifted gently downwards, and screamed.

The burning thing continued its stately descent, through people, through earth and into the ground, spilling more terrible iridescence. The sounds were freakish squeaks and shrieks, abominable in their irrelevance to the death that was eating through the world. As the wind swung round again, it carried to the attackers an obscene smell of roasted flesh.

Bel saw Thuler, silhouetted against the fire. His commander turned and looked back at him, his face melted and transformed by the apocalyptic light. Another face seemed to burn through it, something wrinkled, with a terrible shrunken eye-socket, inadequate skin stretched over the bare outline of a skull.

Thuler watched as the runaway firestorm swallowed up a thousand lives and sterilized the hilltop into a glowing desert. Eventually, the fireball stabilized and its electric outriders shrank and collapsed back with that unsettling, sucking whoop.

Darkness fell, lit only by lazy lightnings playing around the edges of the fizzing crater. They advanced cautiously. Pseudopodia of cold fire reached out to the ring of corpses around the pit. The flesh of the dead flared into brief candles, lighting an extravagant hell. The rear part of the outer wall was all that was left of the enormous Castle compound. The wall was cut off sheer and shiny by the edge of the fireball.

Fire with sharp edges, Thuler thought. He felt enormous and calm, the power of destruction filling him with ecstasy. In that inhuman intoxication, he was a god, ragged lightning barbing through his bloody hands as he looked down at the melted, iridescent earth. *Raven*, he muttered *when you broke Alex to release me, to release* this, *did you have any idea what you were unleashing?*

Words from some old crossload whispered in his head. *For I am become Death, destroyer of worlds.*

He saw Bel looking over at him, then turning away and throwing up.

Something like a moan and a gasp shuddered through the attackers. It was as if they were asking: How can anything ever be the same again, once you've been led to war by Death himself?

Thuler wandered among the rainbow-lit dead, losing his edges to the madness in him. No-one could look him in the eye.

Then he felt Thania come up to him and grab his arm. 'Finish it, Thuler,' she said 'Finish it. Bring peace.'

Chapter 28: A moment's peace, then…

Grey light dawned over the devastation. The rainbows had gone, and a rain of greasy soot fell through the damp air. Thuler called everyone – the Wolves, the Goathlanders and the militias – to move around the pit, into the now-breached arms bailey.

The shocked, shattered bands of fighters straggled away from the smoking hillcrest and packed into the broad streets with their stone workshops, bringing their wounded as best they could. Thuler called the artillery to the front, and they blasted open the outer gate.

He led them through into the Crescent and the troops spread out into the vast yard in front of the coal mines, someone's idea of a final spree-fund of compressed energy. He called the commanders up and asked for reports. First estimates of numbers of lost and injured seemed to confirm that he'd made the only possible decision with the airburst; relatively few of his force had been lost.

He drew a deep breath. 'First, we secure the Crescent. Snipers and scouts: Check the factories for holdouts.'

The teams of experienced fighters spread out around the ladder of wide streets that held the great steelworks. Most of the groups soon secured the factories, some still hot with hastily-shut down furnaces, then reported back.

Jackson's group was taking longer. They'd just pushed open the big steel door when a white-uniformed Guard ran at them, one hand held high, the other grasping the white cross on his chest. Jackson had a moment of insight and shouted 'Cover!' As they dived behind the nearest barriers the suicide bomber vanished in a clap of fire and noise. The sniper at the front was ripped apart by shrapnel.

The second fanatic obviously anticipated a straight run-through to the massed troops outside. He came running, but a hail of automatic gunfire cut him down before he could set off the belts of grenades crossed over his shoulders. He fell harmlessly in the thick dust, and everyone moved very cautiously around the corpse.

It looked as if that was it, any other PL surviving the attack must have run away.

Thuler called the commanders round again. 'Now we finish the job. Thania – triage, pick one of the secured buildings. Militias – secure the hilltop, report any fleeing enemy. Dirk – how's your cavalry?'

Dirk looked tired and his bright clothes smokestained, but he turned to his men and shouted, 'How're we doing?' They sounded as if they were trying to convince themselves when they called back, 'Ready!'

Dirk turned to Thuler and nodded. Thuler said, 'Would you do an advance sweep of Old Sheffield? We'll follow up and secure the town. We can billet there. Wolves and Goathland infantry, follow me.'

Slowly, they rode and walked out of the Crescent, down the hill to the Sheaf Bridge and across to the thronged main street of Old Sheffield. As an army, they were grubby and ragged, but victorious, and cheering locals lined the streets as they passed. People ran up to them bringing them bottles of beer and a group of young girls bared their breasts in an ecstasy of freedom. Bel spotted three corpses in white uniforms swinging from lamp-posts.

They gathered on the wide cathedral green, locals swarmed round distributing food and drink and they fell to an impromptu victory feast under the leaden sky.

Dirk's cavalry returned with news of the best hotels in the city, and Thuler announced that the rest of the day was for R&R, then they'd have a meeting tomorrow. The Wolves and the Goathlanders left to find billets, while the militia troops melted back towards their homes or stayed to party on the green.

Thuler took a suite at the top of the Crystal Tower, a twenty-first century hotel Dirk's men had recommended, kicked his boots off and helped himself to a beer from the ice-box. He slumped on the bed, and the blankness in his eyes soon spread to his brain as the bottle slipped from his grasp onto the woolen carpet.

He woke in the dark, faint sounds of carousing reaching his ears, amplified music pumping into the sky, flickers of red light behind the blinds. He fell asleep again, back to some realm deeper than dreams.

Local volunteers had laid on an impressive spread for breakfast. Thuler came down to the dining room and saw Bel and Sif tucking into enormous plates of fragrant fried stuff. He just helped himself to coffee and joined them. Bel spoke with a forkful of bacon raised. 'We've got a big concert hall for the meeting at noon, should hold hundreds.'

Thuler nodded and sipped his drink, pleasantly surprised by the aroma when he had been expecting the earthiness of root brew. He made an effort to speak. 'Treating us well, so far.'

Sif said, 'Thania called the hotel. She's got the wounded shifted to the city infirmary, plenty of paramedics and a few surgeons. She says she'll try to make the meeting.'

Thuler was having difficulty grasping the world today. Bel looked at him and saw confusion in his eyes, a military leader forced to stop fighting, suddenly out of his depth in civil life.

The wiry man said, 'I've sent word of where the meeting is to all the militia commanders. The job's done, we won, cheer up!'

Thuler gazed with unintended stoniness at Bel's face.

The hall was oval, with a low stage at one end, surrounded on all sides by tiers of seats. On the stage sat Thuler and his staff, the commanders from Goathland, the militia heads and local faces he didn't recognize, some in military uniforms, some representing public bodies, and the rest no doubt politicians and the talking heads of vested interests. In the chair was tall, middle-aged Thor Allen, one of the Goathland captains, now dressed in a dark suit. Next to him sat a big, portly man wreathed in chains of office, an ex-mayor of Sheffield from before the PL takeover.

As they took their seats, Bel whispered to Thuler. 'He's called Crookes. Unremarkable as a mayor, but a bit of a hero to his people, I'm told.'

As the great ampitheatre filled, and the standing areas got packed out, Crookes stood up and spoke in a voice trembling with emotion.

'People of Sheffield, some of you might remember the last time I stood before you. It was a time when we were free and this city was great. Today, we are free again, thanks to our friends from Caledon and Goathland,' – a scatter of cheers round the hall – 'and we're here to start the job of making our city great again, not to mention fighting the war which will secure our freedom and that of our children.'

Applause rang out for just long enough for everyone to celebrate their liberation, via applauding Crookes. 'I shan't be taking up more valuable time talking. I hand you over to our chair, Thor Allen.'

Bel leant towards Thuler. 'Interesting choice – an outsider.' Thuler looked blank, not sure what use any of this knowledge was supposed to be.

Bel continued. 'Seems the Goathlanders have got a bit of a reputation as wizards at collective bargaining.'

Allen stood up and reeled off their agenda. There were reports on the care of the wounded, discussions on local security and about broader military objectives – the tall man paused and looked straightfaced over the top of his reading glasses as he said, 'That's a big one' – and – he treated them to another unreadable gaze – 'celebrations. We will hear agendas for each of these topics, then split into work-groups for detailed planning.' No-one argued with his schoolteacherly manner. Thania stood up and reported on the wounded. Then Jackson organized a working team for the militias to thrash out local issues. Someone called for a force to liberate the PL prison camp at Wincobank. Jackson said, 'Bring it to the working group, thanks, that's me done,' and sat down. Crookes called for two more work groups, one on finding accommodation for visiting troops, and the other to plan a concert.

That left only the group charged with the war at large. Some of the militia commanders and scouts sat in for the first part, and Thuler was left with them and his team in the main hall while most people left for the other meetings. At Allen's suggestion, they took their chairs down to the space in front of the stage and sat round in an oval. Thuler fought to keep his wandering attention on the border reports from the militia scouts and speculations about the state of things further afield.

He regarded most of this as useless, and soon they moved on to weapons. He would supply electric power threads and thread-charge and the Sheffield ballistics people would make shells, airburst bombs and rockets. For rockets, they were aware they lacked the high-tech components to make guidance systems, and this brought up the big issue: did the PL have aircraft and rockets, and if so, why hadn't they used them in Sheffield?

Thuler said, 'An outfit called White Cross security have. A month ago, a copter full of them tried to capture me and my companions in Caithness. I believe they're PL troops that have been bought out with equipment and are now under the partial control of a man called Hendry.'

Thor Allen asked, 'What happened to the people that attacked you?'

'They were destroyed by a superior force that turned up. The same force that supplied me with the threads.'

The hall went so silent that Bel could hear laughter and raised voices from other rooms.

Thuler continued. 'Hendry is not the main issue. The real danger is that the PL's overseas factories could even now be churning out helicopters and rockets. We don't know how much of the world is under their control.'

He took a deep breath. 'We have to move on Birmingham fast, and destroy their presence, irreparably, before air support arrives.'

One of the militia captains argued briefly for a longer-term solution, involving tanks. Thuler said simply, 'I'll kick-start your weapons factories, then I'll remove the source of the trouble. Meanwhile, you build tanks.' That was that. Thuler gave his technicians lists of feed chemicals to commandeer, and went to fetch his horse for the ride over to the arms bailey on Manor Top. He would be spending the day with his hands dipped in the tingling slime of thread-formation, programming the gels in ways he still couldn't easily explain. By nightfall, he would be leaving them with enough explosives to vaporize the Midlands.

Thania was recovering from a fifteen-hour stint at the hospital, sitting in the front bar of the Crystal drinking real coffee when Thuler pushed through the door, grubby and tired. She got his attention by standing in his way, at which he gave a tight smile.

She looked in his eyes. 'Supper, a bath and bed is Dr Thania's prescription. This way,' and led him to the lifts.

He was harder work than some of the amputees she's been joking with earlier. She had to order his food, shove him into the bathroom and then make all the running to get him into bed. Only after a while did he seem to focus on her long, naked body, and then his lovemaking was clumsy and tentative at first, like an adolescent's.

Then, he seemed to fall into the sweet absorption of deep sex, and in his eyes she saw her old lover, Alex. She smiled with pleasure and spoke his old name tenderly, and something in him froze. His erection died, and he rolled off her, staring with wide eyes at the shadowed ceiling.

Thania lay beside him on her side, watching the tormented face and holding his hand. She fought down her own sadness and reflected that she hadn't been joking about being his doctor tonight. At some stage, she slept.

The man beside her was broken. He'd been somewhere, and what he did there was wrong or incomplete, and then some inexorable mechanism turned. He'd melted down for long enough for the other selves that lived in that body to surge up and clamour for attention.

For a while, he became Alex again, but from that angle his life looked terrible. Alex was too human to bear what Thuler had done, and must do again. He wrenched out of the Alex-frame and hovered in chaos.

He tried to return to being the Thuler he'd known, who was at least functional, but it seemed like an empty mask now, a decoration that covered something much worse. In desperation, he twisted in his mind so he came free of the old Thuler-self. As he faced it, it dissolved, and there was just a vortex of black and red flames. He asked with his thoughts *What are you?*, and the thought came back *War, endless war! I am you!* as the faceless god swallowed him.

Friday dawned, trailing clouds of glorious gold, the air ringing with victory bells. Thania checked her patient, ordered coffee from whoever was on duty downstairs and went to shower. When she returned and let the volunteer in with the fragrant brew, Thuler was still apparently awake and gazing at the now-bright ceiling. She had to be off to the hospital, so she tried various ways of breaking into his trance. Cuddling met with no response, nor did calling him Alex.

Eventually she settled on the kind of practical message the Thuler was well used to responding to. 'Birmingham.' she said. There was a flicker of attention. 'NeighbourNet patches cross Derbyshire. How about a scouting force?'

The man blinked a few times then spoke. 'Yes. Our best vonnie-people can be a vanguard. And I could…' He turned onto his side and looked at her. 'I'm Thuler again. Alex is really gone this time.'

'Do you want me to stay?' asked Thania.

He shook his head. 'I'm OK. Thanks, Thania, thanks for understanding. It makes my job a lot easier.'

She let herself out of the room and the hotel, hurting in her controlled way. She waited for the hospital bus by a field of ruins choked with dusty willow herb. Six or seven butterflies, near-black with pale orange wing-edges, scattered as the bus pulled up for her.

Thuler dressed and got breakfast in the bar with Bel and Sif. The smiles they wore as he approached froze when they saw the stony look on his face.

Bel said, 'We've had a message through from Derbyshire. Platoon up from Birmingham, should be meeting our militias this morning south of the city. Good news, eh?'

Thuler said, 'I'll be happy when we know they've no air support. How long before we can set off?'

'Re-arming, re-provisioning, recovery – two days minimum. They set the concert for Saturday, so that's neat. Sunday good enough?'

Thuler nodded. 'It'll have to be.'

Thuler and his staff met the Birmingham platoon in the

hotel's main conference room, which they'd adopted as operations centre. The ten men looked ragged but cheerful, and brought news of PL movements in the Midlands.

Making use of the regional map on the wall, dark, stocky Sergeant Sowerby described in his broad accent how all the militias from the Birmingham area had reported the same thing – the PL retreating south. Infantry had been seen heading into a big compound to the east of Redditch, near the edge of the Evesham Channel, and some copters had flown troops either in or out, no-one was quite sure. All the other PL positions had been cleared out or had fled to that fortress. He added, 'We can guarantee you a friendly journey right up to the PL's front door,' and sat down.

Thuler asked, 'Those copters, were they White Cross?'

Sowerby nodded. 'They're built locally. Everyone in South Brum knows Hendry's factory compound. He's kept well in with the militias, too well in, if you ask me – '

Thuler cut in. 'How many aircraft has Hendry got?'

Sowerby shrugged. 'Dozens of copters, helicopter gunships, long-distance transporters, seaplanes. Most of them grounded for lack of fuel.'

Thuler nodded. So that was Hendry's game – get everyone else to fight the PL to a standstill, then arm and fuel his air force with thread power, no doubt seduced away from him. It looked as if the next move would have to be Hendry's, but the last one would be his own.

The meeting done, Thuler rode over to the other hill to see how the weapons technicians were getting on.

That day passed in work, and that night he slept, the churning dreams absent for now.

Late afternoon on Saturday Thania called the arms lab to remind him of the concert. Dutifully, he rode back to the hotel. While he cleaned himself up, clothes arrived for him. He dressed in the familiar silks and leathers, and made his way down to join his staff in the bar. They were all dressed up in their best, and were waiting with shot glasses of cocaf and liquors. Thuler drank sparingly, not sure what effect would please him. Bel, Sif and Thania were in buoyant mood.

Soon they were hailed by a loud horn outside, and they walked out to see a big old limousine parked at the kerb, open doors showing off its lush interior. They piled in for the drive to the concert hall, just round the corner.

The big hall was the same one they'd used for Thursday's meeting, but this was a party crowd. Crookes gave a brief introduction to the programme and the orchestra struck up some rousing popular tunes. The crowd roared their approval at every opportunity and danced in the aisles.

Then there was a break, and the serious part began. When everyone was back in their seats, the talking soon hushed as the yearning opening chords of Barber's Adagio began, that centuries-old soundtrack to loss.

Thania watched as the players and the audience were swept up in their feelings. Down the row from her, she saw an old man weeping openly, whether with joy or loss she couldn't say. Then she looked round to see Thuler beside her, grey-faced and sweating freely. She leaned forward and whispered, 'You OK?'

He nodded, sweat beading his upper lip. 'Fine. Just got to hold out here.'

When the music had finished, he let them lead him out to the limo, where he hunched over in the seat.

Thania said, 'You've got a fever. Come to the hospital.'

Thuler shook his head violently. 'I'm OK, just get me to my bed.'

They helped him to his room, and Thania went and got a medical kit and announced she was staying. Bel and Sif left them to it.

In the night, the fever broke, and the churning madness with it. He was simply Thuler again, and would be for as long as it took. He slept a few hours.

Sunday's breakfast was a working one, over maps in the conference room. Everyone ate as much as possible while orders got given and carried out.

Thania came up, hugged him and said. 'I'm glad you're better. Maybe see you some time.' She forced a smile.

This seemed to Sif like the best moment she could find to announce she was staying on in Sheffield. 'You don't need me, Thuler, and I need a change. I've never known anything but being a bandit. You'll win, and there won't be much of a future in banditry in a year's time. When the war here's over, I'm going to study philosophy.' She smiled at the blank incomprehension on Thuler's face.

Sif hugged him close, then held him at arms' length and said, 'I'll get on with my new life then. See you sometime,' and the two women left.

Thuler and his Wolves gathered outside. A large group of Goathland horsemen had joined with them, Dirk staying on with the rest in Sheffield. They were now a force of around seventy horse, plus the Birmingham militia who rode in a fleet of trucks along with the catapults and bombs. The Brummies were nervous about riding with a ton of explosives so, by way of a safety demonstration Bel picked a blob of thread-stuff out of one of the cans and hurled it against the side of the truck. They flinched as it splattered harmlessly down the paintwork.

As Bel walked away he turned and said, 'Oh, not all of it's that safe, y'know. Some of it could blow you to bits.' He grinned and got on his horse.

Thuler watched the road ahead, where it went over the horizon. One moment, he saw a fat, pale-skinned child stomping along with a shapeless kitbag on his back. A moment later, there was just a flight of birds above that place. Then the boy again, cresting the hill and disappearing into the distance.

Chapter 29: The Deal

The convoy rode over the Derbyshire hills, the wind high, the sky bright and changeable. At Sowerby's suggestion, they headed over the tail of the Pennines to Leek, where a few militia troops joined them, then on to Stoke, where they gathered more volunteers and trucks. From here, there was an easy crossing over the Stafford Levels, elsewhere a treacherous band of swamp preyed on by bandit gangs. Local scouts leading the way, they crossed the stone causeway and started the climb up Cannock Chase.

From the top of Cannock, they could see down over Birmingham. It looked peaceful down there. Thuler asked the local commander the best way to cross the city and reach the PL compound with daylight to spare.

Captain Walker's eyebrows stayed raised while he swept his arm round to the right. 'Round the city to the east, down to Redditch, then west. And ride fast.'

The afternoon light was fading as they reached the walled stronghold of Redditch. They made a final stop to pick up more volunteers and headed across the low hills towards the setting sun.

The PL compound stood on a long lip of land projecting into the marshes below. It was a modern, circular enclosure of steel fencing, with open fields and low buildings inside. Thuler scanned with binoculars and saw no aircraft, and almost no people. He saw a glint of metal, and caught sight of a sniper behind a parapet on a roof. A few white-uniformed guards were making their way along a road that led to a gate on the near side of the outer fence.

Thuler passed the glasses to Bel. 'What do you make of it?'

Bel scanned and shook his head. 'Either they're up to something, or they're a bit understaffed, I'd say,' as he handed the binoculars back.

Thuler looked over the compound again, estimating how many troops would be garrisoned and supplied from here: Five hundred? A thousand? More? This must be the main PL base for the Midlands, was probably supplying the positions in the Chilterns where Wessex fought so often. As a major PL base, it had to go, however many or however few troops remained inside it.

His reverie was interrupted by Bel. 'We could take the place, use it. We don't have to flatten it this time.' It was as if his lieutenant had read his thoughts and deflected their course. He nodded. 'We bomb our way through to the central buildings. Then we take them out if necessary.'

'Sounds good,' said Bel. Anything short of mass slaughter sounded good.

They moved cautiously down the hill. Sniper fire rang out, and they lobbed the first series of grenades. As the smoke cleared, Thuler saw a few craters inside the enclosure, and a building with the roof blasted off. Another rifle shot rang out, and they repeated their attack. The catapult team had their range now, and they hit two more buildings. The sniping ceased.

The cavalry were on the main road in front of the gate when it burst open and a knot of maybe seven white-uniformed guards broke out. Rifle fire from the attackers' side brought down three, but didn't stop them exploding. When the smoke blew away the road was a mess of bloody rags, horses and men screaming and rolling in agony.

Thuler walked forward, across the bloody road, until he was between the open gates.

Bel came up with a megaphone, but Thuler shook his head. 'No bargaining with these people. Airburst over the central building.'

The balloon team moved round the perimeter to catch a good wind direction, then let the balloon float above the central block, its deadly cargo hanging underneath.

The Birmingham troops had never seen a major thread charge go off, and they stood shocked as the centre of the compound disappeared in a fireball, leaving behind an iridescent crater.

As soon as they could see that no-one was left alive inside the walls, Thuler turned his back on the spectacle and said, 'Our job's finished here. Any of you still with me, it's Wessex next.'

Most of the Brummies, especially the ones who were throwing up by the side of the road, elected to stay and rejoin their militias. A few local scouts joined them. The Wolves and the Goathland horsemen, hardened to this new kind of war, all stayed.

Thuler led them back up the slope, then east, then south towards the Stratford crossing. Only then did he become aware of the pain in his side. He looked down and through a hole in the bloody shirt, he saw a bite-size chunk of flesh missing, and fresh blood dripping into his waistband. He called for a paramedic, who ran over and goggled at the wound, then washed and dressed it.

The crossing was filthy and ill-maintained, dangerous in the gathering dusk. As they struggled up the hillside Thuler was very aware that they didn't know who owned this bit of land. He called one of the local scouts up and asked. The skinny, scar-faced lad said, 'Last few days, it's been quiet here. Don't know anything about ten miles down the road, but I'd reckon we can chance it here or down by Chipping Campden for a night, if that's what you're thinking.'

'It is. We stop at Chipping Campden.'

At a first glance, the little town seemed deserted. The tired fighters did a desultory check through each of the buildings, and found no-one, so they made their camp in and around the main street. They made stews out of the tinned food they'd brought from Sheffield and drank wine they found in a cellar. The wound in Thuler's side was starting to itch.

The next morning started dull, and Thuler sent scouts out in the drizzle to reconnoitre the roads to the south. They came back with no reports of any people at all, and the convoy set off in the miserable weather on a road that wound south around the swell of the Cotswolds.

At Andoversford they stopped to shelter in the abandoned town. They were eating a soggy lunch when Bel pointed and said, 'Look!' Across the little square Thuler saw a child walking, in a bubble of dry air. The rain ran off the force-field he carried with him as he walked. 'Becters,' whispered Thuler, just as the child noticed them watching him and ran off, scattering rain around him. Thuler stood up, curious about that force field. He stepped out into the rain, willing a dome to form over him. Sure enough, the rain retreated, above a shimmering volume of dry space. Bel applauded.

They set off again, and on the advice of one of the scouts they crossed over the ridge of the hill to the next village. The weather was clearing as they reached another tiny settlement of stone houses. This too was empty, deserted, and Thuler was wondering where the PL had retreated to, and whether they were marching into a trap of some kind. Then, as the clouds parted, the sun picked out a fleet of helicopters rising over the hillcrest to the south. Everyone on the ground dived for cover and started shooting.

All but one of the copters hovered well out of range, and that one approached slowly. It stopped and hovered as the trail of a rocket shot from its underside and a cottage in the road behind them blew apart. A great voice roared, shattered and jerky, out of the helicopter. '*THULER, THIS IS HENDRY. YOU CANNOT HARM US, AND WE WON'T HARM YOU. YOU NEED TO TALK WITH ME.*'

Thuler realised his force was helpless here, so he stood up, hands held high. He heard Bel's shout, the words lost in the noise as he stepped towards the copter, which was just touching down. Hendry's wiry shape clothed in khaki jumped down onto the street and ran forward, holding his hand over his head against the wind from the blades.

Thuler had an odd sensation when Hendry stood in front of him, looking ruffled, almost human for a moment. He remembered what Maira had said about Hendry and him, all that time ago, how they were 'kingpins of the world,' and for the first time, he stared into the eyes of an equal, someone who'd come to make him an offer. 'What's the bait this time, Hendry?' he said. 'Guided missile systems? Copters?'

Hendry looked at him with more respect than he used to. 'You need my help, Thuler. The PL are supplied from America, their own theocratic state with heavy industry and nuclear power, right there on the Eastern seaboard. Can you reach them from Wessex? I think not.'

'Go on,' said Thuler.

'With my resources, you could mount an attack on their home base. That's the only way you'll ever be rid of them. They're growing in military strength all the time.'

'And you're prepared to betray your old buddies, H?'

Hendry stared at him, then smirked and said, 'I told you, I always bet on the winning side. The PL were useful to get some heavy industry started again, now we're all standing round waiting for the winning power source to come along.

And you've got it.'

'Yes, I've got it, and it's staying right here with me until I choose to pass it on. But,' Thuler stared Hendry in the eyes, 'I'll supply you with ready-made weapons as long as you help us against the PL. That's my offer.'

Hendry gazed back for a long moment, then nodded curtly. 'I've started helping you already. I guarantee your troops safe passage to Wessex via the Swindon crossing. Then when you've done what you need to do in Wessex, I'll meet you back where I left you.' He turned to go. 'Oh, and give my regards to the lovely Queen Hettie.'

The copter was taking off when Hendry leaned out to deliver a final message.

'By the way, Thuler. The business at Asgard Hall – that was White Cross people, but they were out of control, fanatics. It's the price I have to pay. I wouldn't have done it that way myself.'

The copter took off before Thuler could reply. Momentarily, he considered chucking a grenade after it, but the logic of war prevailed and he turned away to his troops. He ordered them to move out, in the direction shown by the flock of white fliers, now silhouetted black against the afternoon sun. He scratched the dressing over his wound, and it came away. The wide cut had closed up, tight puckered skin around the scab, and was almost healed. He didn't know what Hendry had meant about Asgard Hall, but he had a bad feeling about it.

Chapter 30: The War in Wessex

At the border of Wessex, there was a rather ill-equipped garrison on the Swindon road. Private Pitts had returned with his winnings after a successful poker school at the Chisledon post, and he'd shared a couple of beers with Private Wylie. His townie girl Shellie was always saying how boring country life was, and he was inclined to agree, especially now she'd long since gone home.

The two soldiers dozed at their post, then suddenly realized that they were faced with a group of mounted men, the leader dressed in a blue cloak and bright red trousers. In the tricky twilight of dawn, it looked as if he had a red halo round his head. The guards looked one to the other and shook their heads, as if to banish a spectre of sleep.

The man rode up to them and declared, 'I am the Thuler. I come with arms and war-knowledge for my Queen, Hettie of Wessex.'

Pitts and Wylie felt they should be doing something, such as calling for backup, but they just stood there while Thuler continued. 'Speak up, man – I take it Queen Hettie is still loyal to Wessex and would appreciate some arms and military assistance?'

'Yes, of course she is, long live the Queen!' blurted Pitts. Wylie followed up with 'Long live the Queen!' and then stood staring dumbly at Thuler's band.

Clearly, these youngsters had not seen action yet. Pitts recovered himself somewhat, said, 'I'll get the Sarge,' and ran off.

Sergeant Massey agreed the Queen needed to meet Thuler as soon as possible, and sent for an escort from Marlborough. Thuler decided to go through this painstaking protocol, since he was still technically an exile, and didn't want to be shooting at Wessex troops.

Drinking dandelion coffee in the guardhouse, two young boys spying through the window, Thuler's Wolves enjoyed the hospitality of the garrison, although worse-equipped than they were. It was good to have somewhere to rest for a while.

In just over an hour, the escort Captain Best turned up and Thuler and the Wolves rode over the downs with him. Their story flew ahead of them, and when they stopped for refreshments at the Old Cock in Ogbourne St George, the landlord had already heard vague stories about a new electrical generating system. 'It's good to hear of your new thing, sir, good to see some hope in this country. Without your magic we could be burning down sacred groves and putting crosses up by next Yule.'

Captain Best took tired, good-natured exception to this. 'Wessex Guards not up to putting down a few Christian scumbags, then?'

'Oh, no offence meant, sir! I only meant how they say they're getting more powerful every year, and if we don't do something about it soon, it'll be the bad old days all over again.'

'No offense taken, innkeeper. We need all the help we can get. Two more pints of your fine beer.'

They rode on into the busy streets of Marlborough, then up to the Palace. There, Thuler and Best had to wait in a long room with wooden walls, like a Norse feasting-hall. It was mid-afternoon, but the walls were in shadow. The room had a timeless feel to it, as if they were not waiting at all, but had arrived, somewhere perfect and unchanging.

Then a magnificent woman stepped before them. Her elaborately-coiled blonde plaits emphasized her height; a necklace of golden runes flared at her elegant throat, sending a volley of patterned light around the hall as she turned to greet them. She was wrapped in a cloud of earthy, resinous perfume, as befits a witch. The sensuality in the curves of her breasts and hips and belly pushing against the red silk of her gown vied with the shadows in her eyes, of death and of secrets way beyond her years. It took them a shocked second to realize that this beautiful apparition was the Queen. They both drew a breath, and gasped 'Majesty,' and meant it.

Queen Hettie smiled serenely. Captive in her zone of still power, the two men could hear their raised breath over the silken rustle of her dress. She had their attention.

'Thuler, we greet you. And you, Captain Best.' She turned back to Thuler. 'We have reviewed the sentence of our court and have decided to repeal Alex Tyler's exile. You are no longer legally under the arrest of our good Captain here. Tell us what you have to say about the defence of Wessex.'

'I shall show you first, Your Majesty. To light this room –' Thuler produced a fat braid of power thread, twisted it on and proffered it to the Queen. 'It is completely harmless. Configured differently, however, a piece that size could blow that wall out.'

Thuler pulled out a forearm-size block of thread. 'This will power a truck. Or... have you got a building you'd like demolishing?' Hettie turned the light-thread over in her long-fingered hands, frowning pensively. She looked up and smiled. 'I have indeed. Follow me, gentlemen.'

The Queen swept out. Thuler and the captain followed. Outside, she summoned an aide. She spoke swiftly and the man ran off. They heard the roar of an old engine, and an antique car swung round the corner of the building, gushing heavy biodiesel fumes, and pulled up beside the Queen. The aide ran back and opened the door, and Hettie climbed into the driving seat. The aide ushered Thuler and Captain Best respectfully into the back, then hopped in himself.

Hettie turned round and grinned at them. The formality had dropped away. 'Hold on tight, men. I like to drive fast.'

The old car was obviously well-maintained, and the Queen drove it like a maniac. They tore out of the Palace compound, careered along an empty, potholed road in the fading light, pursued the broken track for a while, swerved through an ornate stone gate and skidded onto a long drive. She pulled the car up in front of a derelict house that must once have been beautiful. The Queen turned to Thuler and said, 'It's called The Gables, and it's depressing, the state it's in. We'll never fix it up. I want you to level it completely.'

Thuler looked around. 'I'll set the charge to produce a very quick surge of heat. We'll need to be a bit further away than this, for your safety.'

Hettie snorted. 'Bugger safety. I want to see the fireworks. What's the closest we can get and survive?'

It was a spectacular double blast. The power surged outwards in an egg of rippled air, like a heat-haze, then collapsed back in on itself. The second explosion was a roaring sphere of light that seemed to glow through the stones of the house for a moment before it ripped them apart. In seconds, the derelict mansion had become a smoking heap of rubble. They crouched behind the bonnet of the antique diesel, as chunks of masonry smashed into the road a few yards away.

When the rain of fragments ceased, Thuler took Hettie to see the eerie rainbows that flickered briefly in the hollows of the rubble. Pensive again, the Queen drove them back. In the High Hall, she called for beer and food. They sat at table before she spoke again. After they'd refreshed themselves, Best was excused to return to his unit.

Queen Hettie sat back. 'Tell me all, Thuler.'

'The threads will produce energy anywhere, and in almost any form you want. There's a load of spare energy in the universe, it seems, locked up in the spatial relationships between things at very small scales. All you have to do is extend these von Neumann nanites, like a polymer, through any space, and it'll pick some up. How much it picks up, and what form it comes out in, are functions of the pre-forming stage of preparing the threads.'

Hettie gave him a lofty stare. 'Typical man, you tell me lots of things I don't need to know and leave out all the important questions. Save all that technical stuff for the dinner tonight, I want to know about the power behind the threads. What happened to make you into the Thuler?'

For a moment, he went blank. How could he talk about the rape of his selfhood? He didn't want to tell Hettie or anyone else that he held himself together, day by dangerous day, by an effort of sheer will. Bluntly, he recounted the misfortunes he could bear to tell.

'I wandered North. The Pure Light took Sheffield. I kept moving. Friends were killed in the war. I was captured. Raven of Thule gave me the elekilpo threads and... I took on the PL.'

He paused, stretched and rubbed his face. This time, though, his mind hadn't fallen apart when he thought about those two selves coexisting in his skull. A servant topped up his glass. Thuler asked the question that had been bothering him since yesterday's abortive meeting with Hendry.

'What happened at Asgard Hall?'

Hettie's expression was solemn as she spoke. 'Two White Cross helicopters blew open the east gate, landed and attempted to kidnap Ambrose.'

She blinked twice. 'He had a heart attack. Uncle Ambrose is dead, Thuler. The funeral was last Saturday.'

A wave of cold emptiness passed through him. For a few moments, he remembered Ambrose's big voice, and vowed to do something to contribute to the immortality of

Ambrose Swords.

He took a deep breath. 'What about the rest of the people there?'

'A student called Jerry went to hospital, but he's out now. Susanna got a fractured foot and a few bruises.' Hettie smiled wryly. 'Trying to hurl rocks at the copter, I hear.' She looked at him. 'What is the relationship between you and Hendry?'

Thuler was asking for as well as offering a lot, so trust was vital. Still, there were imponderables about the deal with Hendry he wanted to keep to himself for now.

'Hendry is actually on our side, for the moment, and as long as it suits him. That in itself is a bet from an expert gambler. As long as he offers support, and doesn't threaten us, I say we use him.'

He didn't elaborate, and Hettie nodded, thoughtful.

Thuler changed the subject. 'Perhaps I and some of my troops could billet at Asgard Hall for now, help defend the place and not take up Wessex Guard bunks.'

Hettie said, 'See to it tomorrow. Tonight, feasting and meetings. Alenor will show you your quarters.' She stood up and added, 'How long will it take to build electrical generators and weapons from the thread-stuff?'

'If you've got the parts, three days.'

Hettie smiled and left, trailing her bittersweet perfume.

Thuler got himself and his Wolves installed, and got ready for dinner. It seemed as if he was spending half his nights with the rich and powerful these days.

The dining hall reminded Thuler of Darnham's, but on a bigger scale. All the Wolves and cavalry were seated around the lower table, and he was introduced painstakingly to various high table dignitaries including a brace of admirals, a field marshal and some representatives of religious communities. Most of their names he immediately forgot, but he remembered a few old faces, from Asgard

Hall days, none of whom he'd been close to.

A surprise was the only ambassador at the table, who turned up just as they were sitting down. Zakia Khan had ridden down with her party that day to take up her post. She'd grown into a commanding young woman, scarred but unbeaten by the war, and happily filled Thuler's ear with news of how Bradford had successfully resisted the PL incursions until their presence in the region had finally collapsed.

The meal was as sumptuous as one might have expected at a royal court, not even allowing for how hard-pressed Wessex was, and it took some time before sweets, liquors and coffees went round.

Hettie stood up to make the first speech.

'Our talk at table tonight is reddened and darkened by this council of war. However, it is a war whose tides have turned, and now it is the turn of Wessex to set a course to its end. In our land, we live to celebrate all that is great and good in life, and Ambrose Swords reminds us of true greatness. Midsummer Festival will go ahead, as it has before, and this year it will be even more radiant, with new lights, powered by the fires of the thread-stuff of Thule, the stuff that will also be powering our victory in this war.'

She gestured elegantly. 'I call on Thuler to address us.'

Thuler stood and gave a brief explanation of the power of the threads, performing what he was beginning to think of as a couple of his party tricks with short lengths of the stuff. He added, 'Some of you might have heard about what happened this afternoon to an old house called The Gables. The charge I used was the size of this tankard' He hefted the drink, drained it and sat down. He was getting good at this, he thought, as he fielded questions, mostly about how long it would take them to win the war. Fortunately, no-one asked about Hendry. Wessex wasn't ready to know that yet, not after the Asgard Hall incident.

The evening passed pleasantly enough, though Thuler was impatient to start work on the weapons. Tomorrow, he'd get back to the war.

Things died down a bit, and he got up to leave. Hettie caught his eye, with a minimal scrutiny and the ghost of a smile that gave nothing away. He held her gaze with a polite nod, then went to his room. As she turned back, she wondered how much was left of the beautiful, confused young man she'd spent a Beltane night with last year.

Night was nothing, and the morning all, as wet as it was. The Wolves and cavalry were in the dining hall, breakfasting with rain streaming down the high windows. He called Alenor on the house-com and asked to meet weapons technicians, power engineers and some well-informed officer from the Wessex Guards. He told his Wolves they had the day off while he worked with the arms factories and power stations, then they'd be in fresh billets that night.

The meeting with the engineers and technicians went much as the one in Sheffield had, with the important difference that Wessex was substantially poorer in skills and materials. Anything much more sophisticated than what he and his Wolves had started out with would be beyond their reach, let alone anything remotely hi-tech. Thuler resigned himself to building up what weapon stocks they could. Eventually, they would have to call in the deal with Hendry, but only when they ran out of armed superiority.

They drew up plans for supplying the whole of the Wessex Guards regiment with grenades and bombs over the next week, then Thuler turned to the power engineers. It seemed Wessex had plenty of diesel generators, in various states of repair, up to the big ones that supplied the businesses in the centre of town. They just needed converting to thread power, and Thuler added another item to the list of thread-types he needed to make.

The meeting ended with Thuler giving them lists of materials and equipment to commandeer. As soon as those were in place, he'd come and make the threads. They all left and he went and got his horse and set off over the downs. The rain had stopped, but the day was dull and overcast as he skirted Avebury and joined the road to Asgard Hall.

The main entrance was in a sorry state, the great wooden doors blown to matchwood, the fire-scarred timber beams of the portico pushed rudely to each side. The flag was gone.

Thuler dismounted and called, 'Hullo!'

For a while no-one came, then Susannah stood in the broken doorway, tall in a blue trouser suit, supporting herself on two crutches.

She waved her arm. 'Only a poor old cripple woman to let you in. It's Thuler now, isn't it?'

He dismounted and tethered his horse, then accepted Susannah's embrace, made difficult by the crutches.

She swung ahead of him. 'We sent all the students home after the attack.' Her face looked lined and old, he thought. 'Only me and the family left now. You want to stay?'

Thuler said, 'Yes, and I'd like to billet some of my troops here, good security and maybe they can help around the place.' He added, 'We've plenty of gold for food.'

Susannah smiled. 'We could use the company, frankly. Bring 'em all.'

Thuler stayed for a sparse lunch in the kitchen then set out back to Marlborough to fetch his equipment and the Wolves. As he was leaving, he remembered his promise of money for the household. All he could find in his saddlebag was a krugerrand, so he gave it to Susannah, who shook her head and smiled.

'I'm looking forward to seeing the expression on the butcher's face when we pay him.'

They arrived in time for dinner, giving the staff a few hours to get ready for a crowd. They'd done well – someone had gone out and bought a pig, and Susannah had raided Ambrose's cellar for some fine wine. She was pleased to see the old dining hall full again.

After a few drinks Thuler asked Susannah where he was staying.

'You know where it is, your old room. Sleep well, Thuler.'

The room was dark, and through the window he could see the clock tower, battered by the attack, the eternal clock stopped. He would get it wound up tomorrow. It was too much to think about how things had changed in the last year.

He lay on the bed, but he wasn't ready to sleep. He got up and looked out of the window. A shower of rain pattered against it, and he thought of that child in the Cotswolds, the BT who'd held the rain off.

Something bothered him about that incident, and the fact that BTs seemed to be on the move all over. Suddenly, it felt terribly important that he try to replicate the child's achievement again. Swiftly, he took the back stairs and door to the central herb garden. He stood there, the rain falling, and willed a dome to form over him. Nothing happened. He stepped back into the house, tried to make the dome happen in there, then stepped out again. Nothing.

He tried a couple more times, then gave up. Someone, and it could only be one person, was manipulating becter powers, globally.

The next day he dressed in comfortable work fatigues and savoured the pleasure of an early breakfast in the big kitchen before setting out to Marlborough and his work in the weapons factories and generating plants. He rode over the North Downs road under an overcast sky wondering about Hendry's warning. How long did he need to fight on from Wessex before he took up that deadly offer?

Work took up the rest of his attention that day, and at the end of it he fell gratefully into the arms of the Asgard House organization, revitalized by its new guests. At the great house, some of the Wolves were clearing away the rubble around the doorway. He dismounted and stood for a moment, his foot turning something over in the grass. He looked down to see a small piece of titanium steel, enameled white on one side. He hailed the Wolves as they worked and went inside to clean up.

That evening, through dinner and underneath the chatter and in bed that night, images of white copters streamed in his mind's eye. If the PL were anywhere near as well-equipped as Hendry claimed, surely they would have to strike against Wessex soon. But the only way to find out for sure was to fly the Atlantic on the word of a man he had no reason to trust. Not yet, anyway. He had to make a move, and he would find a way to hold Hendry to his side of the bargain.

As he fell asleep, the copters faded and Hettie's face appeared.

Chapter 31: The Build-up

The first job of the day took him to the other side of Marlborough, to convert a gigantic old turbine generator to thread power. That occupied the morning, and after lunch he rode over to the workshops at the Palace. He stopped off at the porter's lodge by the main courtyard and left a message requesting an audience with the Queen.

It was getting dark at the workshop and he was washing off the muck of thread-slime and engine soot when a messenger found him. The green-liveried footman with the Wodening crest on his cap delivered a letter into his freshly-washed hands.

'From Her Majesty, sir. I'll wait for your reply.'

Thuler opened the sheet of notepaper and read, in the strong, neat handwriting, 'After dinner in my rooms.' It was signed off with an elaborate H, the upper part of which formed a crown.

He turned to the footman. 'Tell Her Majesty that Thuler thanks her and will see her at dinner.' He picked up the towel and continued drying his hands. He used the engineers' shower and another footman fetched him clean navy trousers and a shirt and showed him to the Queen's private chambers.

The footman knocked, a voice said, 'Come,' and Thuler let himself in. The room was cosy, twin chesterfields in front of a wide fireplace, a writing desk by the window, a servant putting the finishing touches to dinner on a side table, then leaving.

Hettie stood and approached him, sheathed in a silvery-grey two-piece. She swept her hand towards the table, smiled and said, 'Let's eat.'

She stuck pointedly to almost-small talk during the meal, her perfect facsimile of an open gaze fixed upon him.

Eventually she sat back and raised a questioning eyebrow.

Thuler drew a deep breath and said, 'We've often wondered where the PL get their resources from. Hendry told me they're funded and supplied from a home base in one of the new States, a nuclear economy. This puts their HQ out of our reach, and leaves us at their mercy.' He paused. 'Hendry offered me a deal: his continued support against the PL, in exchange for a supply of thread weapons. I decide when I'm meeting him, and we mount an attack on the PL headquarters, using his aircraft.'

He sat back and watched her face. In her proud eyes was a question: Why do you come to me now, after you doubted me? In a low voice she said, 'What changed, then?'

He had no answer to that, but she hadn't expected one. She stood up and faced him, then she clasped his hand in hers and led him over to a settee. She placed a long hand against his cheek, half-framing him for her intense gaze. With her other hand, she unpinned her hair, and it fell, thick and tangled, around her shoulders. She brought both hands to his face, and moved forwards, drawing him out into a kiss.

The mullioned windows were open to the night, to the smells of summer herbs and the calls of foxes. Her skin cooling from the heat of sex, she pulled a shirt around her shoulders as she stepped over to look out at the darkness of the palace gardens. There was a mist of soft light over everything, the moon a waning crescent. All she could see of the town was a faint glow around the horizon, and some lights down by the Kennet Channel, where a foghorn sounded. She expanded into a sublime aloneness, just breathing and watching, her eyes slitted.

Then the holiday from herself came to an end, and she turned her back on the night. Across the bed, half-covered by a thin quilt, lay the man. The body that had contained someone called Alex, whom she'd liked, and who had ceased to exist. This – new being – is not the same, not that confused beautiful boy at all.

She blinked, her breathing fast. This man is broken inside, and deadly. But he calls to something equally dark in me… never met anyone who is strong like me in that terrible way. I think we need each other.

She woke him early, for more sex, then the working day began over breakfast in her sitting room. Sipping tea, Hettie asked, 'How long will it take to supply all Wessex's war-needs?'

'I've already made enough precursors to leave it in the hands of the techs. The rest will take a couple of days, but it doesn't need me.'

'How are we going to hold that snake Hendry to his word?'

He smiled at her use of the word 'we,' and not in the royal sense. He said, 'The prize is the knowledge of how to form and set the thread-types. As long as I keep it to myself, it's my insurance – no-one will kill the golden goose.'

'I wouldn't bet on it,' said Hettie. 'I bet the PL homeland see the threads as the devil's work. Doubly so, their being a nuclear power.'

She gave an involuntary shudder, then continued. 'Anyway, couldn't anyone else work out how to do it, given time?'

'Maybe, but I think Raven implanted something, some instructions or tiny transmitter that helps me do it, because I don't even consciously know how most of the time.'

'Could you teach it to someone else, by example?' asked Hettie.

'I don't know. Raven must have learned how to do it by hand at some stage, so someone else should be able to.'

They were both silent for a while, then Thuler told her he was taking Bel and a few other Wolves to visit a few Wessex Guards units and supervise training in thread-weapons.

Hettie declared she was coming along. 'Guaranteed morale raiser, their Queen turning up. I'm a sort of royal pin-up to some of them, I think.' She dressed in a smart khaki jacket, riding britches and high boots, and Thuler saw what she meant.

Downstairs in the Palace, Thuler checked with Colonel Roll, his army contact, that the thread-shells and grenades had indeed gone out to their border forces.

'No point turning up with the Queen, to demonstrate some weapon that's still in a box at HQ, is there Colonel?'

The reference to his royal employer deepened Roll's nervousness, his mind racing in its quest for credible data. 'All but Cornwall, sir. Roads are buggered, and we haven't converted enough Duck engines yet.'

Thuler appreciated the man's honesty, and told him so. 'How long to get the whole of the Wessex Guards mobilized and supplied?'

'Three days for most of 'em, a week for the rest, sir.'

Thuler and Hettie, escorted by the Wolves in their barbarian finery, rode up to the Swindon base, which Roll had assured them was well-supplied. Out on the practice range, a slope somewhere between moorland and brownfield, the Wolves oversaw their khaki-clad cousins zealously and clumsily loading the thread charges into various weapons. The soldiers picked it up fast, obviously hand-picked for the training. Soon, the ground of the range was full of smoking craters and a crumbling building had been brought down.

The royal party, as the base commander had referred to them in an aside to his aide, had lunch in the officers' mess. Thuler asked about incursions, and heard that no PL had been sighted at the Swindon crossing for over a month.

Next they set off west around the border to visit the Wessex Specials base at Streatley, just across a swamp from the Chilterns and their PL positions.

Thuler remembered Thania telling him about her brief time at Streatley. The memory of that old self didn't bother him this time. If the wild intimacy with Hettie last night hadn't opened that wound again, nothing would. Alex was dead, a curiosity from his past, orbiting his new sense of certainty.

They went through the same demonstrations at Streatley, these youngsters even more acute. Thuler felt good about the troops that were defending Wessex, but their efforts wouldn't make much difference to an airborne attack force. The Streatley scouts had declared the Chilterns completely empty of PL. It was beginning to look odd – what had happened to all those troops and equipment? The more Thuler thought about it, the less easy he felt.

They did the third and final demonstration on a field outside Marlborough, a burned and wretched bit of land, chosen for its nearness to home.

Back to the Palace, a footman ran up with a message. 'Bruno's back, ma'am!'

They went and got ready. Hettie came down to dinner with little Siward in her arms. The boy ran to Bruno and let the tall man lift him off his feet.

'Where's your hat?' asked the boy.

Bruno's craggy, ageless face cracked into the same warmth and playfulness everyone remembered. He fixed wide eyes on the boy's and said, 'I gave it to a pirate chief in the North Sea, whose life I'd just saved, because he hadn't got one.' Knowing Bruno, the story could be more than half-true, and Siward gazed wide-eyed at him. Bruno produced a pocket compass and gave it to the boy, who gasped and stroked it in wonder.

'That's what the pirate chief gave me,' said Bruno, 'and now it's yours.'

Siward caressed the compass throughout the meal, and after dinner Hettie had to promise he'd see Bruno again tomorrow in order to get him up to bed. When she returned to the still-lively dining room, Bruno took them all aside.

He gazed at Thuler, and nodded. 'One day, tell me about Thule. I sought it for years, as you know. Looks as if I was lucky to escape with my life. Lucky, and with the sense not to go too near Spitsbergen.'

He paused reflectively, then continued. 'But what I have to tell you: Iceland, Thuler. I joined a fleet of dragon-ships out of Trondheim – don't ask, it's a long story. The Icelanders have been resisting PL invasion for six months now. Those independent farmers weren't about to give up without a big fight, and they got one: they cleared the PL off the island, with some loss of life on their side. But the PL came back, and this time the Icelanders asked for help. We were their support effort, supplying, harrying and raiding. We drove the PL off again. That was a month ago. I got back to Whitby yesterday, with the news that a new Norwegian expedition got blown out of the water last week by two helicopter gunships, full PL insignia, guided rockets.'

Bruno looked to one side, as if unconcerned. 'Whatever cards you've got up your sleeve Thuler, now's the time to play them.'

Thuler looked at Hettie, and she nodded. He outlined the Hendry deal to Bruno, who was quick to pick up on its dangers.

Thuler took a breath and said, 'This is what we needed, Bruno, real news. Tomorrow I'm going to contact Hendry.'

‘I’m coming with you,’ said Hettie.

There was no point in arguing, and Thuler gave up, after citing her roles as Head of State and mother to no avail. It dawned on him how much he wanted, and maybe needed her with him on this final stage of the war. That night, their sex was silent and thoughtless, like a fierce dream.

Hettie spent the morning playing with Siward in the big field down from the Palace, while Thuler met Bruno in the comms room.

Bruno suggested, ‘Why not just get Radio Wessex to switch on their old transmitter one more time, and put out the message on the frequencies copters use. Gives us time for some plotting.’

They decided on a simple message, and Bruno phoned through to Radio Wessex. The defeated tones of the unemployed newsreader brightened at being given a job involving the security of Wessex, and recorded Thuler identifying himself then saying, ‘Swindon Crossing, tomorrow, noon, repeat, midday.’

Bruno said, ‘What next?’

‘OK: just the three of us to Birmingham with Hendry. I make him some bombs and charges for rockets, that’s two-three days. He supplies us with a long-range transporter or two and maybe seaplanes. We return to Wessex for our troops and crew – Wolves and Guards as far as possible and we go take a look at Iceland as a base. What about Greenland?’

‘Totally PL, as far as the North Atlantic people know.’

‘I wonder,’ said Thuler, ‘if it’s worth setting up a base at all. We lose the element of surprise, and we still have to attack a stronghold from the sea. Maybe we should just do it in one hop.’

Just before the gong went for lunch, Colonel Roll came by with reports from the border units. The PL were nowhere in evidence, as if they’d been spirited away.

They got back to the comms room to a phone call from Radio Wessex. 'Sir, it's Mr Hendry for you.' The announcer played a rec of Hendry's voice. 'This is Hendry. Will see you tomorrow. Repeat: will see you tomorrow.'

Thuler and Bruno were making lists of resources when Alenor dropped in the comms room to announce dinner would be early, in Hettie's rooms.

Over the meal, Thuler and Bruno told Hettie about the reply.

Afterwards, Hettie let Siward go and find some toys to play with. She asked, 'Thuler, have you considered what will happen to knowledge of the threads if we don't make it back from America?'

He nodded. 'Of course, I could teach it to you or Bruno, but the same applies. I haven't come up with anyone I trust, who I don't also want with me.'

'It's simple,' said Hettie. 'Children are the custodians of the future. Teach it to Siward.'

'But… he's not a BT. Is he?'

'My family haven't shown those genes so far. Apparently, Edwin had an RK test, in his old age. He'd try anything. He got very ill, came out as an RK0, radically intolerant. But that mightn't matter. You don't know for sure that only BT's can work the threads.'

'You're right. No-one's ever tried, I suppose.' Thuler went and fetched a jar of thread-mix, while Hettie went and found Siward.

They made a game of it, Thuler explaining how you had to feel for little tingles in your fingers, then turn the thread-stuff, just so.

At first Siward couldn't make the gel do anything. He giggled and said, 'It's all slimy,' but the stuff wouldn't set. Then Thuler took his hand and physically guided his little fingers, feeling the gel in detail, feeling with the fingertip nerves for nodes of energy… There, there it is! Draw it out... Once Siward knew what to do, he got the hang of it quickly. After an hour, there were tiny blobs of light and heat stuck all over Hettie's dining table.

Thuler said, 'He's learning it faster than I did.'

'But notice,' said Hettie, 'how much difference it made when you touched his hand. You entrained him, didn't you?' She took Siward's hands and wiped them gently with a cloth. 'Now, you have to keep those tricks with the gel very secret. You mustn't tell anyone, not unless,' she swallowed, 'not unless Alenor tells you that you can. It's very important, Siward. Do you understand?'

Eyes looking down, Siward nodded, then said, 'You're going away, aren't you?'

'I'm going to work away for two or three days, then I'll be back, then I have to go away again and fight the bad men, the men who killed your dad, who Uncle Jervis worked for. I'm going to help beat them, to make the world right again. Be strong for your mum, my lovely boy. I'll be home before Lammas.'

They hugged and cried a little, then Hettie took him to bed and read him a story.

That night felt like a farewell, to what she wasn't sure. The fierce sex banished the flimsy stuff of her personality and opened her to vision. Underneath the echoes of her day, rolled the machinery of the deals she'd made, making roads that branched into the future. Plenty of these roads led to tragedies, and then there were obscure tracks, dark futures yet to be worked out.

They breakfasted in the dining hall, with Bruno, Siward, the Wolves and the cavalry. Hettie said her goodbyes, Siward looking stricken but brave, and they rode out into a bright morning. They'd sent word ahead to the army camp at Swindon to give intruding aircraft plenty of chances before starting to shoot.

They stabled their horses at the army base and drank root coffee on the verandah outside the mess hall. To keep their minds occupied while they waited, they went through their options for the transatlantic attack, concluding once more that it all depended on current intelligence.

Then an adjutant ran out of the comms unit across the square, waving a sheet of paper. He announced breathlessly that they'd hailed an approaching copter and it was Hendry.

They spotted the single aircraft, flaring white in the high sun, descending towards the parade ground. It touched down and the three of them got up and walked under the downdraft to the open side-hatch. Hendry, in smart fatigues, motioned them inside, and the copter rose, turned and sped North.

No sooner were they in the air than Hendry turned to Thuler and said, 'No time to lose. You heard about Iceland? Well, the PL went back three days ago and laid siege with a fleet of copters and seaplane support. I'm waiting to hear about the outcome.'

They were flying over the spine of the Cotswolds, and looking down at abandoned villages. Thuler said, 'Where did all the PL go?'

'I airlifted them out,' said Hendry, 'and before you get onto me about that, it was a part of my deal with them. I have to keep them sweet. And that's how I know what they're doing. I took over two thousand troops to Tyrone. The PL have carved out an enclave northeast of where Omagh used to be.'

Thuler said, 'You're very tight with my enemies, Hendry.'

'In the words of the saying, I keep my friends close but my enemies closer.'

'You don't have any friends, Hendry. You never bothered with the skill of acquiring them.'

Hendry pursed his lips and said, 'In the words of another

ancient wag, if you want a friend, get a dog.' He took a deep breath and looked calculatingly at Thuler. 'I'm telling you, it can only be a matter of days before the PL strike at Britain.'

Chapter 32: Tools

They flew across the Evesham marshes and over to the west of Birmingham, to a big field outside the city. Hendry's compound was an old civilian airport ringed with the giant steel sheds of factories. Low clouds showed ruddy underbellies, reflections of industrial flame.

The pilot responded to a routine challenge from a control tower, and touched down on a strip of tarmac outside an enormous hangar.

Hendry jumped down and ushered them all inside the gigantic shed. At first, all they could see were the flashes of welding torches working up and down the great space. Then they realised they were looking at a row of dark grey planes, engines mounted on top of dramatically-upswept wings, floats protruding beneath the wingtips.

Hendry gestured proudly at the planes. 'Heavily-armoured derivative of the Beriev A-40 with improved speed and range – eight thousand miles. We copied the shielding off the Russians too – it blocks a good deal of electromagnetic pulse, and the electronics are all valve-based. Follow me.'

The agile old man led them through a maze of gantries to the base of a scaffolding tower, then waved upwards at the source of a shower of sparks. 'That fitting that's going on – extra missile launchers to carry thread warheads.'

He gazed intently at Thuler. 'Good enough for a transatlantic attack force?'

Thuler nodded slowly. 'Eight thousand mile range… we could do it in one hop, maximum advantage of surprise. What's their base like?'

'Never seen it,' said Hendry. 'Supposed to be a deep

bunker, nuclear-proof. The map shows a dip between high hills. Could a thread bomb deliver more heat than a nuke?'

Thuler thought of the runaway fireball that had melted the top of a hill in Sheffield and said, 'Probably, but I wouldn't like to see it get out of control. With a lot less heat, we could melt the ground and seal them in.'

Bruno said, 'Do we want to wipe out everyone in that base?'

'We might have no choice, as in them or us.' Thuler gave an icy grin. 'At least if we seal them in, they'll die in relative comfort.'

'If I was them,' said Bruno, 'I'd also have remote control launch silos for nukes, well away from the home base.'

Hendry said, 'Yes, we can't discount them launching from remote silos, seaplanes, even submarines and aircraft carriers. I did consider a cruise missile delivery system, but the satellites for guidance are long-dead. I checked years ago. But there is another option.'

Hendry jumped down off the steel plate and led them across the oily concrete floor. They left the building by a door at the back and crossed a stretch of tarmac to another giant hangar.

In here it was darker and quieter. The bulk of the dark plane filled the centre of the enormous space, long-bodied, deep-bellied with underslung launch units, and wings you could have sat another plane on. Hendry led them round to the front of the craft, where giant observation windows stared out from a cluster of rocket launchers.

'High flyer, will stay aloft for a day or more, even on fossil fuel. On thread power, who knows. Russian-style EMP armouring.'

He turned to Thuler. 'This is half the solution to the problem of rocket attack. Now the other half.'

He showed them back out onto the tarmac, fished a

whistle out from under his shirt and gave it three quick, shrill blasts. A dog barked somewhere then a car swung round from behind the facing hangar and pulled up.

Hendry tucked away his whistle and told the driver, 'Weapons division,' as they got in.

The factory was new, low-ceilinged and well-lit with fluorescent strips. Hettie gazed in wonder at the steel lathes spitting stinking oil, the showers of sparks from grinding wheels, the thick coils of wires and pipes, the hissing of steam, the flames of oil and gas: a world of industry unguessed at and almost forgotten.

Hendry hustled them through into a quieter, cleaner area beyond the lathe shop. Workers sat on high stools, joining tiny components together under fierce lights, passing their completed tasks on to the next worker in the line. 'Rockets,' said Hendry.

He walked up to a bench and picked a printed circuit board out of a tray full of them. 'Guts of the guidance system for a missile. We've got them working as missile interceptors. That's the other half of the solution.'

Thuler turned the board over in his hand. 'Where did you get all this circuitry?'

'The PL, where else? They're the best arms dealers in town. These are components for their own missile systems.' Thuler stared at Hendry. 'How come they trust you enough to arm you?'

Hendry gazed back. 'The PL isn't a one-man band, you know. There are factions. We're safe from the faction I deal with, because they want the secret of the threads. They're in charge at the moment. There's another faction who damn the threads as the devil's work, and wouldn't hesitate to rub you out.'

'You're walking a tightrope, Hendry.'

'Aren't we all?'

Thuler curled his lip and nodded. 'OK: we take the high-flyer, find the PL base and get it in line of sight, then target it with a cluster of hot bombs. We get the hell out, shooting down all the missiles they fire at us. You'll be in the command plane with me.'

'I wouldn't be anywhere else. You're my investment and my security'

Thuler said, 'How do you rate our chances of surviving?'

'High' said Hendry, 'given an almost-inexhaustible supply of missiles deployed by the high flyer and a backup armada of seaplanes.'

'That'll do as a starting point,' said Thuler. 'Now, thread-stuff production.'

Hendry led them out of the workshop, across a yard where forklift trucks were moving piles of steel tubes around and through a wide-open door into another factory.

Ventilation was obviously important here. The space reeked, a cooked animal stink like glue and urine. Benches in straight rows held production lines which started from vats of thick, stinking liquid. Nothing was happening yet.

'I decided to get a bit of a head start. All the piss from my workers,' boasted Hendry. 'Toilets run straight into a urea fermentation system. Good feedstuff for the threads, eh?'

Thuler looked at Hendry. 'How'd you know about the feedstuffs?'

'I've been trailing you since you left Wessex. I met bandits in Caledon who'd seen it all. The PL may well have a factory like this somewhere, just waiting for you to start it up.'

Thuler shook his head, gazing at the efficient factory space. 'You've certainly given us a head start, Hendry. With this lot, I can make enough thread-stuff to melt a country in a couple of days.'

'That's what I was counting on,' said Hendry. 'I've got

the rocket production lines ready to complete over the next forty-eight hours.'

'Call your production line in, in an hour,' said Thuler, slinging his jacket over a bench. 'The sooner I get started the sooner we can get going.'

'I'll have your lunch sent in,' said Hendry. 'When you're ready to join us again, ask any of the workers, they'll call a car for you.'

Everyone else was feeling hungry as Hendry whistled up another car. They drove to the building underneath the control tower, where he took them to his bare, bookless office. He called for sandwiches and coffee, spread two maps out on the big central desk and motioned them round.

'The Atlantic. Stuff that the pilots need to know.'

He pulled the other map on top. 'The eastern seaboard of what used to be the USA. Our target's just inland from New York City. You can still see Manhattan sticking up. The greatest city of the old world. Apparently, people were still living there fifty years ago. Now I suppose the buildings will be used by the PL.'

'Or pirates,' said Bruno.

'So where exactly is the base?' asked Hettie.

Hendry reeled off the latitude and longitude to three decimal places as he turned the map round. 'Across the Delaware River and up onto a hilly plateau, no cities nearby.' He pointed. Where someone had marked a cross at the map reference was simply a depression in the contour lines.

'That'll be where they built the entrance to the shaft.'

The food arrived, and they ate in silence, studying the land they planned to attack. Hettie thought of the breakaway Christian faction from the old British Army, the men her grandfather had fought. They must have crossed the Atlantic, presumably in the last of their planes and joined with other fanatics to start this war.

Thuler took the thread gels through the delicate first stages, to where they could be handled by anyone, then the production team arrived and got busy. Two hours after dark, they had a pile of canisters of the thread charge that would form warheads for the rockets. As the night shift arrived, Thuler washed off and one of the workers got him a car.

They met up back at the control tower. Hendry invited them into his private quarters, low-ceilinged and with little décor. An employee brought them lobster and champagne.

'A supper for champions,' said Hendry, toasting Thuler.

They were given rooms in the same block, small and featureless like those in a big hotel. Hettie sat on the hard bed, tired and thoughtful.

'Those factories we saw… the changes that the power of the threads will bring… When we have all the energy we want, it'll be a new world. The glue that holds us together will melt. I think we'll all just split apart, stop holding together with people we don't want to be with. Maybe that's the future, and maybe it's what people want – for society to disintegrate. As if it was never real at all.'

Thuler had no answer to that. He couldn't let himself think about anything except the battle they were planning.

Another day of work dawned. The first guided rockets with thread warheads had been put together by the night shift, and Thuler took a car down to a runway strip that served as a testing range.

The site was derelict, crumbled tarmac shading into flat brownfield dotted with concrete blocks and scattered chunks of masonry.

They tested line-of-sight targeting, blowing up a heap of the blocks. They set drums of burning oil a few yards apart, to test the overlays of targeted and heat-seeking navigation. Thuler was satisfied, and returned to the stinking thread factory to set off some more batches of precursor.

At the end of the morning, he tallied up all the weapons and explosives they'd produced so far, then went to meet Hettie and Bruno for lunch in Hendry's office.

Thuler reported on the weapons. 'At the present rate of production, we could be stocked up in twelve to eighteen hours. We could be getting crews on board before first light tomorrow.'

Bruno said, 'Hendry, can you organize copters to pick up the air crews from Wessex this afternoon?'

Hendry nodded and picked up a phone. 'Transport and mess hall,' he said, and gave his instructions.

The white copter at the front touched down on the Palace lawn, the other thirty filling up Thor's Field, down the hill from the Palace gardens. In the warm sunlight, young Siward charged across the lawn as soon as he saw his mum step down and run under the downdraft. They hugged long and hard, then he said, his head still on her chest, 'I've got something to show you.'

Bruno glanced over and signaled that he was in control, and she let Siward tug her up the stairs to his bedroom.

Someone had brought him a dining table in and it was covered in squared paper, taped down carefully. Drawn on it were waves, coastal outlines, cities and islands. 'It's the Battle of the Atlantic, mum.' He picked up one of a row of antique toy aeroplanes, chipped paint over aluminum fuselages and wings. 'And these are our planes,' he said, swooping it down over the map. 'And these,' he said, picking up a battered old plastic model, 'are the PL's planes.'

He looked at her with such a serious expression she could see that he understood more than she'd given him credit for. He said, 'While you're away, I'll help by praying to the gods that you'll win and come home while I'm flying my planes about.'

Hettie burst into tears and hugged her brave son.

Colonel Roll had organized the air crews as a Top Secret mission. Remarkably, the efficient officer had managed to plug the leaky Palace security and no-one seemed to know about it. The crews were hand-picked from the Wessex Specials, some oldsters with air experience from the Wessex Guard and the Navy. They all assembled at the rear of the palace, and Bruno assigned them to copters.

He was at the back door when Hettie came down the stairs with Siward. They hugged, Siward somber and serious, and said their goodbyes. Watching the last of the troops moving down to Thor's Field, Hettie mused to Bruno, 'Can we win? And then come home?'

They were silent for a while, then Bruno said, 'I'm a pirate by nature, strictly personal combat. I don't like leading men to their deaths. But we've no other options here. We've got to win.'

They'd started walking down towards the copters, Siward still waving from the doorway, when a horse and rider appeared round the side of the Palace and headed for them.

The tall, red-haired man in travel-stained combat jacket and riding trousers pulled his horse up and dismounted. He bowed to Hettie. 'Your Majesty, Riagáin ó Flannagáin brings you greetings from the clans of the Kingdom of Leinster. I have a message that I think you might want to hear.'

'We thank you and return your gracious greetings, Riagáin ó Flannagáin. Tell us.'

The formalities over, Riagáin looked from the Queen to Bruno and began his tale. 'You heard about Iceland? The PL had helicopter gunships, support planes, long-range transporters. They were going for a decisive invasion, using massacre. They moved before dawn on one of the highest-up farmsteads and just blasted it flat, killed everybody. The noise and light must have got to half the households in the land. As the light came up, they took position over another high farmstead.

'That's when the other fellow turned up. My friend, a Norwegian called Thorvaldsson watched it through a telescope. The way he put it, the sky turned all colours, like a storm from another world, and this great big aircraft appeared from the north, pushing waves of colour in front of it. Then what he described as grey elf-arrows came out of the craft and touched the PL copters. They glowed white-hot and disappeared in puffs of smoke.'

Hettie said, 'Sounds like a powerful ally.'

'There's more', said Riagáin. 'Thorvaldsson said the front copter had PL high command in it. Rumoured to be someone called Knight. This was a big mission for them, and they took a beating.'

'Thank you for getting that news to us,' said Hettie. 'It just might make all the difference.'

Riagáin gave a small bow, shook hands with Bruno and got back on his horse. 'See you after the war!' he called, and rode off.

The airlift went smoothly. They flew into Hendry's base with the red sun sinking behind the hills to the west, and made their way through the bustle of trucks and taxiing aircraft to the control tower. In a clear area in front of the red brick tower, the air crews gathered round while Thuler addressed them. 'We board at 0400 hours. Bel and Bruno will allocate aircraft.'

He felt as if he should say something significant at this point, but all he could think of was a few encouraging words. 'You're the best of Wessex, and we have the best tools. We're the world's best hope, and tomorrow we'll prove it!'

The troops had been ready for some encouragement, and they cheered.

Bruno stepped forward and said, 'Briefing in the mess hall, ask the staff for directions. Then dinner. Eat well, and get some sleep.'

At dinner, it turned out there'd been a bit of a problem at the briefing. There weren't enough experienced Wessex pilots to go round the fifty planes, and none of the Wessexers trusted the ex-PL White Cross people that Hendry had used before. Half the planes ended up flown by a White Cross pilot who had to put up with a half-trained Wessex copilot sitting next to him with his gun holster open.

Hettie didn't get Thuler to herself until after dinner. She'd held off telling anyone about the Iceland situation, because she didn't want him to hear it from someone else. She had a bad feeling. She sat on the bed, combing out her thick, pale hair and relayed the news from ó Flannagáin. She finished with the image of the aerial destroyer that had vapourized the cream of the PL airforce and looked round to catch Thuler's eye.

He was gazing through her, seeing some other world. In those eyes, she saw a hatred so absolute that it dwarfed the hates that drove this man's crusading zeal. This hatred, of the father who'd spurned and then broken him overwhelmed everything else. For the first time since she'd known the Thuler, she felt fear of what he might do.

After a while, he got up and showered. The moment passed, in the heat of their need for each other, and Hettie swallowed him, filled herself with him, drank the smell and the feel of him until she couldn't move. She drifted off into light sleep, woke to find him gone. She got up and went to the window. The world was streaked with rain, and Thuler stood in the downpour, his arms raised, his fists shaking as if in anger. She watched him, tense as a bow, drawn against the world of the rain, then he dropped his arms and came back inside.

He stood and dropped his soaking clothes on the floor. He looked over at her. 'In the Cotswolds, I saw a child, presumably a BT, holding off the rain with a force-field. I followed suit. It was easy. Later, I tried it again. I couldn't do it. Someone is adjusting becters. It can only be one person.'

She turned to the wall. Eventually, she fell asleep to the thrum of engines, the clatter and shriek of steel, the roar of flames, out there in the night.

Chapter 33: The West

The planes taxied out onto the black runways, the faintest grey glow of dawn lost against the airstrip lights. Hettie and Thuler did a morale-raising round of the troops as Bruno gathered them together and got them on their planes.

Because of their slower speed, the seaplanes took off first. The soft grey light behind them, the dramatic Berievs rose up like a flock of dark albatrosses.

The high-flyer had a minimal crew – Wessex pilot Captain Saxton in his smart green Specials uniform and two gunners at the rear, plus Thuler, Hettie and Hendry. They sat in low seats against the side of the fuselage. After half an hour, they took off into the rising light, turning and banking to the south then west. Just as they took up their western course, they rose clear of the land, and the sun flared yellow in the rear windows. Hettie saw Saxton sign himself with the inverted T of a Thor's hammer as the glorious light stabbed through the plane.

Then the light was behind them, and the hills of Cymru beneath them, then the sea, and the coast of Leinster, patched green and brown, shining with inland waters. Beyond were the great lakes and channels of central Ireland, then the hills of Slieve Aughty and the Burren, then the white rim of the ocean, grey taking blue from the bright sky and the unnameable colours of haze to the western horizon, the rim of the world.

The plane kept climbing and the sea was soon a featureless sheet of metal. They rose through thin wisps of cloud, into the bright blue of the upper air, so high that the world beneath them almost stopped changing.

When Saxton announced when they were at fifty

thousand feet and cruising speed, Hendry started talking to Thuler in a low voice.

'Sofie was the love of my young life. When she went missing I went crazy. I recruited Maira to find her. Maira recruited Bruno. You were surrounded by people looking for her, but not wanting to upset you.'

Thuler said softly, 'And Raven got her back, and killed her, and turned her into a ring he wears on his finger.'

They went silent for a while, then Hendry asked, 'Does anyone else know how to make the threads yet?'

Thuler looked aside. 'Are you worried, Hendry?'

He certainly looked it. 'Knight, my contact in PL, is dead. Killed by Raven, over Iceland.'

'I know.'

'We're not as safe from the PL as I thought.'

Hours later, they began their controlled dive straight to the target, Newfoundland just visible to the north as they broke through thin cloud. They saw the coast of what had been New England, and the landscape behind it took on texture, then details, the range of hills, the target on their map screen. Through the telescopic viewer, Thuler could see a dip in the ground, at its centre a grey disk of concrete, ringed with other disks with roads joining them. The hot bombs were ready to launch.

Then he saw the flock of seaplanes, dark silhouettes against the bright sea thousands of feet below, two of them blooming into flame. Just too late, they saw the squadron release a flock of tiny interceptor rockets, then they saw the trails of the attacking missiles before the next two went up. The radio crackled into life.

'This is Commander Revere of Pure Light Reborn. The nuclear submarine 'City of God' has taken out four of your planes and has targeted the remainder.'

Hendry grabbed a mike. 'You don't want to kill us, we've got the man who makes the power threads.'

‘Ah, the tool of the Antichrist, who struck down my misguided brother Commander Knight. We don’t need Thuler, Hendry. He can die, and you at his side.’

While Hendry was talking Thuler launched their hot bombs. ‘Listen to them, ‘City of God,’ ‘Pure Light Reborn.’ These people have such one-track minds.’

‘That’s the problem,’ said Saxton, as Thuler hit the switches.

The missiles dived through the air, down past the seaplanes that had survived the first onslaught and that were now flying over the concrete circle of the base, releasing their own bombs.

The high-flyer levelled out and joined the seaplanes moving inland. Behind them, they could see the blooms of thread-fire over the PL base, and when the smoke cleared Bruno looked down at a shining bowl of molten rock.

Things seemed to be going their way, then the sky bristled with the white trails of rockets fired from unseen launchers. The high-flyer shot out a swarm of the tiny interceptors, and they saw a constellation of white flares thousands of feet below. Two more seaplanes went down. They kept on westward, away from the attack, then out of the west a row of rocket plumes striped the sky.

Someone on the radio barked, ‘Those are nukes!’ as they let off another swarm of interceptors. Puffs of thread-light burst in front of them, but one of the missiles kept coming, its snub-nose visible for a moment before a grey bar of something like light slanted out of the sky and caught it. The plane’s radio howled.

Brilliantly visible for a moment, the rocket withered and sparked like burning magnesium, finally disappearing entirely in the pitiless light, the rod of grey vanishing back into the sky.

The plane’s audio was screaming in overload. The rainbow bow-wave announced the arrival of Raven’s impossible craft, and suddenly the next wave of missiles had disappeared, and the one that followed that.

It went quiet for a moment, as if the defenders had exhausted their resources. Then the rainbows winked out, the radio stopped screaming and a sharp, high voice came through, a voice only Thuler recognized.

'...can speak to you, shields are down, come down lower, it's safe now. The sub's gone too.'

Saxton moved away from the controls as Thuler, possessed, pushed past him and stared through the windscreen. Hettie saw his hands running over the firing system.

They followed cautiously, over the higher hills and then saw the launch silos in a dip. Raven's craft hovered above the valley and a stream of white flecks poured out of its underside, splashing against the silos like a milky tide. A net of iridescent fire grew over the ground, covering the base of the valley. Moments passed, then bumps appeared in the net. The next wave of rockets, trapped in their silos, strained against the unearthly fabric, then their warheads exploded. The net lifted in the centre and a hemisphere of unbearable light swelled under glittering black lacework. A round hole opened at the top and fierce solar fire leaped at the sky for a few seconds, then the net collapsed and re-sealed itself.

'One way to get rid of the energy,' said Raven's voice as the crackling died down.

There was silence on the radio for what seemed like minutes, then Thuler said, 'Turn and circle.' The planes banked round and flew back, circling over the valley with its sealed bunkers.

Thuler was leaning over the instrument panel. It looked to Hettie as if he was setting up firing sequences. As they banked, they saw the faceted crystal prow of Raven's ship catch the beams of the sun and become a vast pink diamond.

Thuler, his hand shaking, reached forward for the fire control and switched on the comm. In a soft voice he said, 'Raven, tell me about Sofie.'

There was a pause, then Raven's voice began speaking. 'I don't…'

Thuler's hands moved on the controls of the big thread bombs. Hettie knew this was the moment she'd been fearing, when it was all up to her. She saw it all in an extended déjà vu, as she drew her gun and said in a quiet voice, 'Thuler.'

Everything happened at once. Saxton dived to the floor. Thuler flicked the switches to release the big thread missiles, then turned towards her. His eyes went down to the gun she held. She shot him twice in the chest. His body wrenched round and fell. She heard another shot ring out and spun round to see Hendry pointing a gun at her. Without pause for thought, she fired.

Hendry turned, surprise on his face. He shook his head, as if disagreeing with the judgment of the god that had condemned him, and pitched forward at Thuler's feet.

Hettie sank down to her knees and the gun slipped from her grasp. She was unaware of Saxton correcting their course, gritting his teeth against the pain of his shattered wrist. He came over to help her up, cradling his bloody right hand.

She sat and watched through the glass. The thread bombs detonated before they reached Raven's craft, spending themselves against its shielding, rainbow fire leaping out then collapsing back to nothing. The shield held, then tendrils of white lightning shot out from the impact zone and spread over the whole of the shield.

For a moment, it looked as though the shield was going to blow apart, then it stabilized, became invisible again.

Thuler's assault on his father had failed.

The plane was circling above the melted valley. Raven's ship came to rest. Near the edge of the brown, fused land a large silo was opening, and the great tubular craft was spraying the glistening net-stuff onto it.

Again, something in the pit tried to launch, and again the net blew out into a bulge. This time though, the hole that opened in the black lattice was ragged at the edges and started to split open. The white fire that emerged branched like lightning and one of the branches hit Raven's ship. The radios screamed as Raven's rainbow shields went up, then they saw the white trail of another missile tearing in from the west. They released another swarm of interceptors, but it was too late.

Something was overloading in Raven's craft. The nuke disappeared inside the aura of rainbows which winked off then on again, and the long fuselage seemed to bend and flex. Cracks appeared where the missile fired by Thuler had hit, then spread all over its surface, cracks through which poured scintillating black light, as if pure darkness were bursting out from its insides.

The cracks kept on spreading, an exquisitely detailed fractal of death that ate up the craft, until it collapsed to a ball of dark, muddy colour and disappeared.

All that was left, was a rain of fine white dust drifting through the air.

Everyone stared in awe. Saxton spoke in a low voice. 'I saw what happened, ma'am. Hendry killed him. You and Thuler were heroes, and you tried to save him.'

He looked at her directly, as subjects seldom do their queen and she noticed his eyes were different colours, the left green and the right, hazel. 'Thank you, Saxton,' she said softly.

Chapter 34: The Road to Thule

They were still circling the burned valley. The radio had stopped screaming, and Bruno's voice came through, over a subdued roar. 'We have wounded! And we have contact with the Free American Airforce. We need to touch down with them.'

Hettie took the mike. 'We have one wounded. Two dead. I – I – we need to go back to Wessex…'

She looked back at Saxton. He could barely sit upright, his face pale, sweat drenching him. The laudanol wasn't controlling it. He must have taken another bullet, not just the one in the wrist.

'Stop here, Hettie. Let the FAA guide you down. There's no time to be lost. Something was triggered by Raven's death. Can you feel it?'

Hettie looked up, at the white glare of the sky. It was as if its dome was caught in a net, diamonds winking in the high, thin air. 'Yes. We'll come down.'

Gunner Davies stepped up and took Saxton's abandoned comms helmet. The patch to FAA came through. 'Josh Herz, Free American Airforce here. We'll get you to safety just as soon as. Listen you people: Hail the conquering heroes!'

Davies took control and set a westward course, into the vast, unfamiliar interior of America. The plane banked gently and vistas of fields, burned-black at first, then green and lush, swung into view. Hettie stayed in the copilot's seat. Somebody reached round and put a belt round her. She looked down at the controls, splashed with her lover's blood. She let her thick hair down, and wiped it over the streaks of red, too numb to cry.

A tiny airfield under a vast sky, netted with shivering diamonds. A circle of rocket emplacements. Concrete bunkers. Corn waving in the distance. Davies took Hettie's arm and led her down the steps, onto the dusty ground. The light shifted moment to moment, like speeded-up cloud-shadows. A tall man ran forward and helped Saxton. 'Everyone off the plane?'

'Yes,' said Davies. They were moving fast, scrambling towards one of the low, blocky buildings. A broad, blonde-haired woman opened a heavy door, some kind of sanctuary.

It was a big room, an operations centre for war, and it was full. Maybe thirty people were moving through it, some on stretchers, heading for a door at the rear. Bruno stood by a giant, blacked-out vidscreen, facing the room.

The tall, dark man spoke to Hettie and those around her. 'Joshua Herz, welcome to Kansas, and to the New Irminsul Tribe. Bruno here is going to bring us up to speed.'

The last stretcher took the last of the wounded through to a care room somewhere. The big ops room settled down; people stood quietly and faced Bruno. 'We don't have much time. You've seen the net of lights out there. It's started, and in the next few hours we'll see Thule's greatest project come to its conclusion. I think they're trying to re-freeze the ice caps.' The crowd went silent, then erupted with expressions of shock.

'Yes,' continued Bruno, 'it'll be the greatest climatic convulsion this planet has ever seen, short of asteroid strike. Which brings me to why we're here. I am a BT, a becter-tolerant, a subbit. Some days ago, the range of effects I am able to produce started fluctuating. Wildly. Someone, clearly Thule, was adjusting what BTs can do.' Bruno paused. 'Which leads to the conclusion that Thule has been controlling at least some aspects of what we call 'BT powers' for longer than we BTs care to think. That the extraordinary abilities that BTs acquire are not quirky personal possessions, but a few control buttons in a sea of energy. And that the power that BTs exert in their lives swims in an ocean of power, that emanates from Thule. And Thule are calling it all in, are using their own tame BTs, the Crows, for what they were originally set up: as transducers of Thule's energy economy.

'Thule has already used the Crows to seed the whole atmosphere with the nano-scale energy-conduits that make these manipulations possible. The conduits work by transferring energy from one place to another. Thule is using that web of corridors to suck energy out of the polar regions and pump it into the equatorial, or out into space. Whatever it takes to re-balance the energy system and bring about the Thule phase of the glaciation cycle.'

He went to the thick porthole window. The sky was fiercely bright. 'Pumping, pumping, as we speak.'

'But Raven wasn't the monster some think. Whilst some would say the human race would benefit from a massive culling, he built into the system the safeguard that would save most people: the BTs, the subbits. He's already finished with them. What happens now is that the BTs, including the Crows, form domes of force over wherever we are. The Crows and the other BTs have been migrating into position for weeks now. In each population centre, however small, there are probably enough of us to save most of the world's population.

'The answer to your next question: Me. I shall entrain you all, necessarily. Your energy, also, is being dragooned into the survival of our species. The worlds you've had to leave behind will be safeguarded by other BTs. If you wish to see what is happening elsewhere, you need simply to open yourself to the field we shall all be embedded in. It extends into past and future too, so be careful what you believe, during the time you are in it.'

Bruno closed his eyes and stood, silent. The situation went from a meeting, such as used to happen in the old world, to an apocalypse. As the light through the windows glared and spiraled and flashed, their minds took flight, expanded into the becter-vision entrained by Bruno. They saw a dome of force flower around and above the giant room. Hettie recalled an image of Thuler, trying to put up such a dome against the rain.

Then came overload. First, a scream, like a million things being torn apart, then a shattering, cracking noise, like the death of glaciers. There was no refuge in their bodies; their minds erupted into space, beyond words.

Hettie flung out an urgent prayer to whatever this force was, to know how Siward was doing.

She is a falcon, stooping to the lower world, eyes that could pick out the twitch of undergrowth a thousand feet below; she sees that Wessex has a protective shield over it, a trail of bubbles, everything outside it a rage of elemental chaos.

Her vision dives down to Marlborough, to the Palace. Alenor sits in a room high in the Palace. Her own room. Holding little Siward's hand. His governess is there too, in nightclothes. Impossible colours convulse outside the window. Siward's deep eyes turn towards her, as if registering her presence. Her heart leaps, she swallows, tears prick her eyes and gush down her cheeks.

The vision continues, beyond the cusp of her relief. Below Alenor and Siward, in the main dining room, the Palace staff sit, or stand, or pace, safe inside the dome of force channeled by Alenor.

Then the scene wrenches away, into other images. In Sheffield, the surface is nobbly, multiple bubbles of force abutting, overlapping. Her vision plunges in to one of the domes. A man peers out from behind a pile of rubble, just downhill from the ruins of a restored Castle, the devastation of the Battle of Sheffield. The scene is soundtracked by the vast orchestration of Wagner's apocalypse, blasted out of subbit-energy into the thick air of the hideout.

The man is skinny, prematurely aged, and honks on a gas canister. A rain of bricks and water bounces and splashes off the dome above him. Six or seven children huddle underneath his bender of fantastic force. Flashes of red light arc against the dark grey of the air.

The man looks up and sees Hettie. 'Good day, yer Majesty! Glad t'see you survived the war! Scargill Twigg at your service!' A *Götterdämmerung* climax drowns out the smash of falling masonry. The man keeps spooling his music, sheltering his little charges in a capsule of organized sound, as the world around him tears itself to pieces.

Her vision somersaults into North Yorkshire, into Goathland, dives into a wooden building. A strong, blonde woman of no more than eighteen years stands in the dining hall, her family around her, weapons on the walls. Men, swords raised, form an outer ring of steel, catching the rainbow light of the Ragnarok. The women seem to float above them, a swirling double-circle, energy pulsing between them.

With shock, she realises that some of the people in the circle are laughing, that they know what is happening, have planned and schemed for it, and are using it as a gateway to a collective, magical ecstasy.

Then she is borne, tumbling head over heels through heatless air, across the shattering fractal of the North Sea, ice rearing out of the mangled steel of its surface. She dives into the force-dome enclosing a fjord in flickering auroral light, streaming laser-green smashing off the snow-bright hillsides.

In a stone hut, War-Fox (she knows his name, without doubt) and two women sit with their arms round each other. Their combined aura is two hundred miles across, light and hail and atmospheric stresses bounce off it, sending shocks of iridescence through the air of the dome.

She spun out of herself again, and this time, beyond the world, so that she saw all those places at the same time. They were all tiny pictures. The old word *icons* came to her. Icons, scattered around a gently-turning globe of the world. Blossoms of translucent grey light flowered everywhere, domes of force, as the terrible cataclysm grabbed the planet and shook it.

Then her point of view shot back another level, into chilly space, but watching a speeded-up picture; the becter-net was showing her time travel. She saw the rise of Wessex, King Edwin looting the Bank of England, his coronation at Avebury, the first great defeat under Marcus at Berkhamstead, then Gwendoline and Peredur, and finally, herself. As if she was the end of the line; her royalty, as Queen of Wessex, what did it amount to? The heathen civilization that was Wessex, was that now ending, like the dark voice, that Beltane, had told her, or could the dream live again in newly-risen lands? This moment, outside of time, was where the sharp and terrible questioning of that night had come from, that night when she'd left her old life. She had seen the future fall of her Wessex, and already it was breaking her heart.

And now was another time; another age was being born. That prayer she'd been so reluctant to pray that night, that her people be vigilant, now that time was coming, now it was warrior virtues that they would need.

Knowledge flooded her; the power of Thule had arisen to bring about another age, and it had succeeded. This was the post-Thulean Age, when the ice encroaches from the Poles, and people of the Northern lands have to migrate south, bearing with them the memory of the high civilization they'd had to leave in the far North, the terraces of Thule shrouded in deep ice. Those who moved south would find new lands, opened up by the drop in sea-level, the draining of the flooded zones of the southern latitudes.

People would need a new courage, to carry the heathen gnosis forward into that age. New migrations, new struggles, new takes on ancient traditions. Did humans ever change? Was it ever worth trying to change them? Fervently, Hettie hoped not.

She opened her eyes. Storm sounds crested and receded. Bruno's eyes looked into hers. He was near her, sitting at a little table. People huddled in small groups, some cuddling and crying, some curled up in defensive sleep. Maybe she was the person in the room who had the most to lose. Was she? As long as Siward was safe, the future was secure.

He picked up a harp. 'Here is a song that my friend Maira loved. She is here. I feel her presence as vividly as when she was alive. It may be that death is different in the becter-net.' He swallowed. 'The song was unfinished, when I taught her it. She said it was a story waiting to happen.' People stirred, sat upright. Bruno plucked the strings, and sang softly, almost in whispering speech.

Knowing nothing in their youth ,
Like bare-boughed trees awaiting spring
Few learn they're more than what they dreamed;
Most cobble lives from others' truth

But some who sense they're on their own
And common ways they cannot tread
They dream their own and deadly path
And find the strength to walk alone

Mother, lover, home and friends
When all he loves is torn away,

What can man stripped down like that
Do with his life? On him it depends

From far above the world's dumb mystery
Beyond the clamour of the war
Comes a sound of different struggle
Minds unfettered by their history

Way beyond the mountains bare
Far off in the land of Thule
Lives a strength that few can fathom
The northern road that few may dare

In the days of history's turning,
Old stories take on sudden power
You aren't the phantom that you feared
Your myth arises from the burning

So Alex Tyler became Thuler,
Warrior, leader, mover of worlds
Songs will last a thousand years
Visionary, sacrifice, war-ruler

Beyond the world we think we know
Far off in the land of Thule
Lives a strength that few can fathom
The northern road that few may go

Her mind took flight again, into the becter-space they now all lived within, for this day at the end of the old world. She soared, past earth and air and death, watched from above, while the sunlight cracked, light spilled everywhere, over hills and valleys of unclaimed earth, bare rock washed clean by cataclysm, earth recreated by disaster, history rebooted into another cycle of tragedy and bliss, of immanent ecstasy, of life forever, forever worth the struggle.

If you enjoyed this book, please plug it on Twitter, or review it on Amazon or on your blog

Thank you!

The Author

I'm a breathwork coach and chaos magician, and my writing is fired by my explorations of miraculous healing and extraordinary synchronicities. What is too big and weird to fit into my ***non-fiction books on magic and breathwork*** gets used to create the other realities I write about in my ***short stories and novels.*** You will find a selection of my writings on my website at www.chaotopia.co.uk.

I was an early editor of the seminal journal Chaos International, and have been active for many years in the I.O.T. (Illuminates of Thanateros) and the Rune-Gild. I teach at Arcanorium online college of magic, at www.arcanoriumcollege.com.

For regular links, excerpts and updates, follow me on Twitter at @dleeahp. For blog entries on all sorts of stuff, from cosmology through to paganism via chaos magic and the Northern mythos, follow my blog at http://chaotopia-dave.blogspot.com/.

COMING SOON: *The prequel to 'The Road to Thule'...*

DAVID R. LEE'S FICTION IN ANTHOLOGIES

Sheffield SFFWG anthology 'SET IT IN SPACE AND STICK A ROBOT IN IT'

Buy from: http://www.amazon.co.uk/Set-Space-Stick-Robot-Collection/dp/0953063518

Sheffield SFFWG anthology SET IT IN SPACE AND SHOVEL COAL INTO IT

Buy from: http://www.amazon.co.uk/Space-Shovel-Coal-into-ebook/dp/B00DY3LOO6

BOOKS BY DAVE LEE

Chaotopia!

CONTENTS

Chaotopia!

Once one is fairly competent at practical sorcery, there is little of importance that remains to be said or read about the subject; the magician at this point tends to emphasize inner development in his work. It seems to me that Chaos Magic itself has reached this point; the basic ideas needed for anyone to construct his or her own system of sorcery and to hone their skills are already covered by the available books. What has been lacking so far is a Chaos magical approach to the investigation of the ecstatic states that underlie magical gnosis. This book, rather than trying to provide yet another slightly different flavour of Chaos technique, takes as its starting point the relationship between ecstasy and magic; between Chaos Magic and Chaos Mysticism, if you like.

Bright From the Well consists of five stories plus essays and a rune-poem. The stories revolve around themes from Norse myth - the marriage of Frey and Gerd, the story of how Gullveig-Heidh reveals her powers to the gods, a modern take on the social-origins myth Rig's Tale, Loki attending a pagan pub moot and the Ragnarok seen through the eyes of an ancient shaman.
The essays include examination of the Norse creation or origins story, of the magician in or against the world and a chaoist's magical experiences looked at from the standpoint of Northern magic.

Buy it as a paperback from: www.chaotopia.co.uk

The aim of this book is to provide the basic know how required to start making high quality magical incenses for ritual, celebration and meditation. Over 100 ingredients are discussed, and over 70 recipes are given. For those who wish to formulate their own recipes, comprehensive Tables of Correspondences are included.

The most comprehensive and complete book on the subject available anywhere.

Buy Magical Incense from:
www.chaotopia.co.uk/aromatics

Connect Your Breath!

24 page saddle-stitched A5 booklet with 60 minute audio CD.

In order to master Connected Breathwork (such as Rebirthing or Holotropic Breathwork), you will need a coach. After a few hours of coached sessions, you should have enough experience to do a full session on your own. Coaches aim to equip the student with enough experience to be able to work alone indefinitely if desired. The aim of this book is to support the student of breathwork in between coached sessions. The accompanying CD can be used as a 'virtual coach' for solitary sessions.

Buy from: www.chaotopia.co.uk/cyb

NOW AVAILABLE! NEW (6TH !) EDITION OF DAVE LEE'S FAMOUS
Wealth Magic Workbook

A Chaos Magician teaches the practice and theory of wealth and money magics.
Wealth is the art and science of having sufficient money and resources to work your will in the world. The Wealth Magic Workbook is a compendium of tried and tested techniques to help you do just that.

BUY THE 5TH EDITION AT DISCOUNT – **ONLY £7 + £1.80 p+p** (UK) FROM:
http://www.chaotopia.co.uk/wmwb.html